BEATTIE CAVENDISH AND THE WHITE PEARL CLUB

BEATTIE CAVENDISH AND THE WHITE PEARL CLUB

MARY-JANE RILEY

Allison & Busby Limited
11 Wardour Mews
London W1F 8AN
allisonandbusby.com

First published in Great Britain by Allison & Busby in 2025.

A CIP catalogue record for this book is available from
the British Library.

First Edition

ISBN 978-0-7490-3219-7

Typeset in 11/16 pt Sabon LT Pro by
Allison & Busby Ltd.

By choosing this product, you help take care of the world's forests.
Learn more: www.fsc.org.

FSC
www.fsc.org
MIX
Paper | Supporting
responsible forestry
FSC® C018072

Printed and bound in Great Britain by Clays Ltd. Elcograf S.p.A

EU GPSR Authorised Representative
LOGOS EUROPE, 9 rue Nicolas Poussin, 17000,
LA ROCHELLE, France
E-mail: Contact@logoseurope.eu

To Seb and Raf

CHAPTER ONE

November 1948

The evening had begun well, with Ashley Bowen whisking her away in style in his Bristol convertible to the theatre in the West End. Ever since she'd homed in on him as instructed at Alicia Gainborne's engagement party three weeks earlier, she'd been waiting for his call. Finally, it had come. She'd worked damned hard at that party to ensure he was attracted to her, fluttering her eyelashes and flattering him until she thought she might die of boredom. He was a thin man in a well-cut dinner jacket, with blond, wavy hair brushed back off his forehead. His nose was pointed and his chin weak, and she decided he was appropriately named as his looks and manner reminded her of Ashley Wilkes in *Gone with the Wind*. But she knew she would have made an impression because after all, she, Beattie Cavendish, was good at her job.

The Terence Rattigan play had been excellent, and Beattie left the Phoenix Theatre feeling moderately cheered, despite the cold and the drizzle that greeted them outside. She pulled the fur jacket her mother had given her closer around herself, while Ashley offered her his arm.

'Bit dull, I thought,' he said, as they walked down

Charing Cross Road towards his car. 'All that soul-searching at the end. Too much of that really isn't good for you, don't you think? Mind you,' he laughed, 'my classics teacher was exactly like that – stern and boring. No fun.'

Beattie smiled to humour him. 'Really?' she said. This job could become tedious.

'Yes. Hated the subject at school. Preferred history and English.'

At last. Something in common. She tried again. 'Me too. Have you read Graham Greene's latest, *The Heart of the Matter*? It's such a . . .' She trailed off. Perhaps a novel about adultery and moral crises wasn't quite the sort of light conversation she was striving for. 'And then there's Ernest Hemingway,' she said instead. 'I love his writing, don't you?' She sighed inwardly. She sounded so banal.

'Er, yes?' He looked uncomfortable, so Beattie cast around for other subjects to talk about.

He cleared his throat. 'So, Cambridge?'

She nodded.

'What did you read?'

'Languages. As I told you, my mother is French and I seem to have an ear for languages. That's why I . . .' Beattie trailed off. Ashley looked more interested in the small round woman in an ancient coat singing 'Danny Boy' loudly but tunelessly to passers-by accompanied by a sorrowful man in a harlequin suit swaying mournfully to the woman's song. Ashley put a couple of pennies in the dancing man's proffered hat.

'Bit unusual, isn't it?' he said, nodding at the singing woman. 'For a girl to go to Cambridge?'

He had been listening. 'A little.' She would not tell him

how important it was for her to be independent, to be able to earn her own money. That was the other Beattie, not the one who was supposed to hang on to Ashley's every word.

'Clever old you. It wasn't for me, though.'

'No?' She knew this, but Beattie was glad to leave the subject of herself and get back to the subject Ashley was most interested in, namely himself.

'No. Wanted to contribute to the war effort, so I joined up but didn't see the fighting. The work I was doing was, you know, a bit hush-hush.' He gave a little laugh.

'Intriguing,' said Beattie, knowing full well Ashley Bowen had been posted to a safe place and an ordinary desk job thanks to his family's contacts.

'I can't really . . .' Another self-deprecating laugh. 'You know, talk about it.'

'Of course you can't.' Beattie injected ounces of sincerity into her voice. 'And now? Banking, I think you said?'

Ashley grimaced. 'Yes. A bit of a bore, quite frankly, but a man's got to do something to keep the wolf from the door in these times of austerity.'

'Of course,' agreed Beattie, also knowing he only worked two days a week at a bank owned by a friend of the family. 'And we all thought everything would be as it was before the war, and instead three years later we still have rationing and even more deprivation than before.' What was she doing? She needed to be light and positive and as if those things didn't matter at all. 'But never mind about all that. Tell me again about your summer holidays in Deauville before the war – my mother knows the town well.'

As she tuned out Ashley's voice, having heard about holidays in Deauville at the party where they met, she felt a kind of despair wash over her. Really, the conversation was as colourless as the London streets. She looked around and felt she couldn't wait for the 'dim-out' that had been in place since the beginning of the war to end. There had been a little hope, a lifting of spirits when the Olympic Games had been held in London in the summer, but now she longed for neon lights and brash colours advertising Craven cigarettes, Bovril and Schweppes, and for people to be hurrying and bustling and enjoying life. The shadows of war still hung over them all, together with the scent of decay and despair.

Oh, but she was being too maudlin. *Pull yourself together, Beattie Cavendish. You can do this. You've done worse.*

She stumbled, slipping on the wet, uneven pavement, cracked from years of neglect. Ashley caught her elbow.

'Pardon me, miss.' A skinny man darted around her, tipping his hat before jumping aboard a passing bus.

'Are you all right, Beattie?' asked Ashley, solicitous, not letting go of her.

'I'm fine, thank you. No harm done.' She smiled as she smoothed down her jacket with one hand, the fur comforting on her skin. Her feet were hurting in the new shoes she had bought for the occasion, a blister on each of her heels.

There was a shout from behind. 'Ash. Ash.'

She and Ashley turned and there was a young woman, waving. She had a sharp pixie haircut and was wearing an old greatcoat that swamped her figure. There was a glimpse of daffodil-yellow underneath the coat. With her was a tall man with a neat moustache and goatee beard. He was dressed in a suit and open coat, made less formal by the jaunty addition of a scarlet scarf around his neck. He was at least ten or fifteen years older than the young woman.

'Felicia,' said Ashley warmly, kissing the woman on her cheek.

Beattie noticed Felicia giving her a sharp look up and down.

Felicia. Ashley Bowen's sister. Twenty-five. Lives in a flat in Soho. Single, no job. Dabbles in art. Beattie remembered the words in the manila folder presented to her when she was first given the job of getting closer to the Bowen family.

Ashley turned and shook the hand of the man with the goatee beard. 'Gerald. How the devil are you?'

Gerald Silver, forty, sometime artist and playboy with a fondness for cocaine. Fought in North Africa. Single. Parents own a crumbling pile in the Cotswolds of which they can't afford the upkeep. The family are old friends of the Bowens. Gerald is possibly homosexual. She'd laughed when she'd read that line, written by men in suits and an observation that quite probably sprang from the fact Gerald was an artist.

'And who have we here?' Gerald eyed Beattie up and down. It took all of Beattie's self-control not to roll her eyes. The man was so obvious. However, she smiled as demurely as she could and held out her hand. 'Beattie Cavendish.'

Gerald bent and placed his lips on the top of her hand.

'Ah, the young lady Ashley has barely stopped talking about. Delighted to meet you, Beattie Cavendish.'

'Gerald,' said Ashley, his face colouring.

'I think,' said Gerald, straightening up, 'this calls for a drink.' He peered up at the sky. 'And we can get out of this wretched rain. Your place, Ash? What do you say?'

'I thought we were going dancing,' said Felicia, pouting.

'Come on, Fee,' said Gerald. 'Have a thought for this old man's health.' He put a hand theatrically over his heart.

Felicia sighed, tapping her foot. 'All right, then.'

'Beattie?' asked Ashley. 'Will you join us?'

'We are your chaperones,' said Gerald, giving a theatrical bow.

Beattie thought longingly of a cup of cocoa, her nightie and her bed. 'Lovely,' she said, painting a smile on her face. 'That would be lovely.'

If she said so herself, she was doing a damned good job at getting to know the family and friends of Ralph Bowen, Conservative Member of Parliament and Shadow Foreign Secretary.

CHAPTER TWO

There was still a light rain in the air as the Bristol pulled up outside the Bowens' house in Chelsea. Justice Walk was a narrow road, a stone's throw from the river and lined with houses that whispered of understated elegance.

The night was dark, lit only by the weak light of the street lamps. As Beattie clambered out of the car she could smell the comforting smoke of coal fires and was aware of the occasional whiff of the Thames – a musty, dank smell of seaweed and decay – and she heard the distant hooting of the tugboats. She stood for a moment, never ceasing to appreciate the sound of peace, the silence of peace. The absence of noise from sirens, from fighter planes, from frenzied shouting. The absence of the glow of fires in the distance as more poor souls died or were made homeless. The absence of that twist of fear as she went where danger lurked. She welcomed the dark.

She looked up at the house, which was a three-storey eighteenth-century building with elaborate pargeting over the front door and a stone lion either side. Ashley Bowen had rooms on the third floor – he had, she knew, been bombed out of his own home but had not yet returned.

Beattie wondered if Ashley's father, Ralph Bowen, with all his money and privilege and standing, was really able to empathise with those who had come back broken from the war, those who had lost everything, families who scavenged amongst the remains of ruined buildings. No wonder people had voted for Attlee.

The rain came down harder. Ashley opened the door and they piled into the hallway, keen to get out of the wet.

It was beautiful inside, as Beattie had known it would be. The cream tiled floor gleamed and a staircase down the hall and to the left curved gracefully up to the floors above. A gate-legged table stood to one side, a silver salver sitting on its polished top. For letters, perhaps? Beattie imagined a butler handling the silver salver with white gloves, transporting important letters written by Ralph and his wife, Edwina, on thick, creamy notepaper.

'I do hope your father has a decent brandy, Ash,' said Gerald, droplets flying everywhere as he shook his head and brushed the rain off the shoulders of his coat.

Ashley grinned. 'I'm sure I can find you something to suit.' He led them into the drawing room, where a fire burnt brightly, and two lamps on polished tables cast long, low shadows on the walls. Beattie noted the fresh flowers and silver photograph frames on the oval table, a baby grand piano with its lid raised, and, hanging over the mantelpiece, the portrait of a young woman. Edwina Bowen, perhaps? A television set squatted on another table in a corner. There were richly coloured Persian rugs on the floor.

'Sit, sit.' Ashley waved to two heavily stuffed sofas covered in yards of red silk opposite each other near the fire, a table in between. 'Get warm, get dry.' He walked over to the drinks cabinet and busied himself with retrieving glasses and bottles and decanters. 'Martinis for you girls? And as it happens, I do have a decent brandy, Gerald.'

'Excellent, never doubted it,' said Gerald, relaxing back into one of the sofas, Felicia snuggled beside him. Beattie sat opposite, resisting the urge to perch on the edge in case she needed to make a quick exit.

Ashley put a tray of drinks on the table before dropping onto the seat next to Beattie. He handed her a Martini.

Beattie took a sip. It was delicious. Salty from the olive, sharp and dry from the alcohol.

'A fine drop,' said Gerald, holding his brandy up to the light.

Felicia sipped her drink. 'I do hope Mummy and Daddy realise you use their rooms and drink their alcohol when they're out, Ashley.' Her barbed comment found its target as Ashley flushed.

'They are happy for me to do so, yes.'

'Hmm.' Felicia put her drink on the table. 'And when exactly are you moving back to your own house?'

Ashley frowned. 'As soon as it's ready. You know how it is, it's difficult to obtain building supplies and so forth.'

'And it's far more comfortable here, eh, Ashley?' Gerald grinned as he drank his brandy. 'A cook, a housekeeper. So many people don't have staff any more since they all buggered off to the munitions factories when war broke out. Don't want to go back into servitude. But not here. Not at the Bowens'. Your father must pay them well. Marvellous, I do envy you.'

Ashley snorted. 'It's not as if your flat is exactly one of the new pre-fabs.'

'No, but sometimes the artist's life does pall.' He waved his hand. 'You Bowens wouldn't know anything about discomfort, though.'

'But your studio is so romantic, Gerald,' said Felicia, smiling with wide eyes. 'I adore the smell of oils and white spirit and creativity.' She had shed her greatcoat and was wearing a skirt – the daffodil colour Beattie had spotted earlier – together with a man's jumper, judging by its cut and the way it dwarfed her slight figure. The ends of the sleeves were frayed.

'Really, Felicia,' said Ashley. 'When have you ever been there?' It was clear from the look on his face that he didn't approve.

'Gerald has asked me to sit for him once or twice. And I can learn from him. Not that it's any business of yours, dear brother.'

'Now, look here—'

'It's all right old chap,' interrupted Gerald smoothly. 'As you know, your sister's quite safe with me.' He picked up Felicia's tiny hand in his large one and kissed her palm. Felicia giggled.

Beattie watched the exchange with interest, trying to work out the dynamics between the three of them. They had been friends for some time, though it was difficult to see where Gerald, being several years older than either Ashley or Felicia, fitted in. But there was an easy joshing between them that she would have expected, though also an undercurrent of something else too, something she couldn't fathom.

Early days.

'Remind me where you two met?' asked Gerald.

'Alicia Gainborne's engagement party,' said Beattie, slipping back into character, smiling and flashing a coquettish look at Ashley.

'I see.' Gerald picked up the decanter Ashley had thoughtfully left in front of him and poured himself and his friend a drink.

Beattie sipped her Martini. She stood up and walked over to the table of photographs. 'Quite the rogues' gallery you have here,' she said, nodding to the array of portraits.

'That,' said Ashley, joining her, gulping at his drink and pointing to one of a group of stiff and serious men and women in Victorian clothes and flamboyant hats sitting on a rug in a woodland glade, 'is my grandmother and her extended family on their annual picnic.' He grinned. 'They don't look as though they're enjoying themselves very much, do they? And here' – he waved at a sepia photograph in a second frame – 'is me and Felicia.' Beattie saw two chubby children sitting self-consciously on an ottoman. Ashley, the taller of the two, was in short trousers and long socks; Felicia was wearing an unflattering haircut and a fussy dress. There was not a smile between them.

'So serious,' said Beattie.

'I can remember being made to sit on that damn bit of furniture for what seemed like hours on end.' He shuddered.

'And your father with Winston Churchill.' She admired another photograph in a silver frame.

'Oh yes. The obligatory one with the great leader. My father's very fond of that one.'

'You don't approve?'

'Of my father's politics or Churchill? I neither approve nor disapprove, I'm afraid. It's all too dull. Of course, it's Father's lifeblood.'

'Has he always been a Conservative?'

'Is the Pope Catholic?' a voice drawled.

Beattie had almost forgotten about Gerald, who had obviously been listening to their conversation. He sat, a faint smile on his lips, one ankle resting on the thigh of his other leg, languid and louche. Yes, louche. That was the word for him.

Ashley grinned. 'Gerald's right. I think even the thought of being of any other political persuasion would give him the heebie-jeebies. What an odd question, what made you ask?'

Time to change the subject. She went over to the baby grand and stroked its polished wood. 'And this is a beautiful piano. Does anyone play?'

'The Steinway? My mother does.' He took a silver cigarette case out of his pocket and offered it to Beattie.

She took a cigarette and leant forward as he steadied her hand and lit it. She inhaled a deep breath of smoke into her lungs, closing her eyes with pleasure. The taste and the smell took her back to another time, another place, another man. A time and place full of danger and love. She could almost smell the woodsmoke, hear the *rat-a-tat-tat* of distant gunfire, feel the hunger in her stomach. When she opened her eyes she found Ashley watching her quizzically.

'I don't think I've ever known a woman to smoke Gauloises,' he said, as the pungent aroma wafted between them.

She blinked, dismissing the memories. 'A bad habit I picked up in France. During the war.' She smiled briefly. That much was true. She also knew he smoked Gauloises and saw it as an opportunity for them to have something in common.

'And what is it you did during the war?' said Felicia, her voice as sharp as her blood-red nails.

'Nothing too exciting,' Beattie answered lightly, looking down at her. 'A bit of driving here and there. Ambulances, generals, that sort of thing. And now' – she stubbed her cigarette out in the ashtray – 'I must go and powder my nose.'

'And what do you do now?' There was nothing friendly about Felicia's smile.

'I teach young girls to type and to be generally adept around the office. For the Civil Service.' It was her standard reply to questions about how she earnt her living – well, she could hardly tell people she translated signal intelligence from Russia and various other allies and did a bit of spying on the side, could she? Though it was a particularly dull cover story, and she felt duller every time she told it.

Felicia's raised eyebrow was eloquence itself.

'I'll refill our glasses,' said Ashley, cutting through the silence. 'Up the staircase and second on the left.'

Beattie shut the drawing-room door behind her and stood for a moment. This was where she would like to go snooping, use her talents, the talents for which she'd been recruited, but she had to concentrate on the matter in hand. Get to know Ashley Bowen, and his family.

'You have the connections,' Anthony Cooper had told her, his gaze severe. 'You were at Cambridge with his friend Julian Knight. That is your way in. Go to the party. But don't do anything rash.' *Leave the important jobs to the men*, had been the subtext of that particular remark.

No meddling.

She walked down the hallway, passing a door that was ajar. Something – she couldn't say what – made her hesitate.

The room inside was dark, though there was the occasional sliver of light from the street lamps outside, and there was a definite breeze blowing, making the skin on her arms come up in goosebumps. Odd. She peered in as the curtains parted with the breeze and she thought she could see jagged edges of glass. A broken windowpane?

She stepped inside, her hand finding the light switch.

Nothing. No light. Strange.

She took her small torch out of her handbag and shone it around.

It was a study, that much she could tell. There was a bookcase along one wall, and dour pictures of landscapes hung on another. A grandfather clock ticked sonorously in the corner. There was a small grate with the remains of a fire. Two wing-backed chairs sat regally either side of the fireplace, and at the end of the room was a desk.

There was something in the air, as if it had been disturbed. A strange smell too, that overlaid the aroma of cigarette smoke and leather, one she recognised, but wouldn't acknowledge what it might be. Not here. Not in Chelsea.

She made her way to where the breeze was coming from and yes, she had been right, the sash window had two broken panes, and it was partially open, but there was very little glass on the floor. Someone must have reached inside to push the latch before heaving up the window. She turned to the desk. There was a burgundy leather inlay with a sheet of well-used blotting paper, and a tortoiseshell and silver inkwell with matching stamp box. A letter opener lying by the inkwell looked as though it had been brought from India with its twisted ivory handle and sharp edge. She imagined Ralph Bowen opening important letters and signing documents at this desk. Perhaps there were stiff cards, stiff as a starched collar, with his name bossily imprinted upon them for him to make ready replies to invitations and enquiries.

Putting her handbag on the floor, she tried the top drawer. Locked. As were the other two. Damn. Should she use her picks?

Something made her stop and stand stock still. There it was again. The feeling that all was not well. A ripple in the atmosphere. And all at once a familiar smell. No, she had to be imagining things. She shook her head, directing the beam of her torch towards the side of the desk, to check, to be sure.

And there was a stockinged ankle, a sensible black shoe half on, half off a foot, and the smell was that of congealing blood.

Beattie went behind the desk and knelt down with some hope that she could help, that perhaps the woman had merely fallen and bumped her head.

The woman's throat had been cut with savagery and efficiency. Blood pooled blackly around her neck and under her shoulders. Beattie breathed through her nose, trying to rid herself of the ferrous smell coating the inside of her mouth and throat. It had been a long time since she'd seen so much blood and she'd forgotten the iron stink of it, the viscosity of it. This had been a violent death.

The legs of the dead woman were splayed at an awkward angle, and her thick tweed skirt had ridden up over her knees. Beattie itched to pull it back down, but she knew she mustn't. Strands of inky black hair had come loose from the woman's bun and her dead eyes stared at Beattie. What had she seen in her final moments?

Such a lonely death.

She could do one thing for the woman. Gently, she closed those pleading eyes, gave her some peace.

Beattie sighed. It was time to get the family involved, whatever the consequences for her, but before she could act she heard a step, felt a movement of air, smelt a sharp, sour smell and an arm was wrapped around her neck and increasing pressure was applied to her throat. She struggled, trying to wrench herself free, to find his eyes with her fingers, but he was holding her too tightly, pinning her body against his.

Air. She couldn't get air. She couldn't breathe.

CHAPTER THREE

Patrick Corrigan was cold. Wet. Tired. He hunched his shoulders as if he could burrow down further into his seen-better-days coat. The rain dripped off the brim of his hat and the cold needled through the thin soles of his shoes and up his legs. A sulphurous yellow light from the street lamps was reflected in the growing puddles around him. Jazz music filtered out from seedy bars. His empty eye socket was throbbing, and his good eye twitched with fatigue.

Soho. A dirty maze of streets where there were places catering for every taste.

He cursed as a bus passed him, splashing him with filthy water. People hurried by, huddling under their umbrellas, keen to get home out of the wet and the cold. Lucky buggers. Working girls not dressed for the November weather loitered in doorways, smoking, occasionally calling out to passers-by. They called to him; he shook his head, smiling, not wanting a few minutes of dubious pleasure in a piss-scented alleyway. Still, standing on the opposite side of the road from a club with a very dodgy reputation waiting for a man to finish whatever he was

23

doing at said club was not a great pleasure either, nor was it how he had imagined spending the rest of his life.

The club occupied a basement beneath the Dandelion Grill in Dean Street. It didn't announce itself, and no one would know it was there were it not for the furtive looks given by the well-dressed men who made their way up and down the stairs. The women were more brazen, not giving a stuff if anyone was looking. Corrigan admired that.

'Hello, handsome. Got a light?'

Corrigan patted his pockets. 'Here,' he said, sparking the lighter. A man leant into him. Corrigan registered a face with fine features, thin cheeks chalky with white powder, lips painted violet and eyes rimmed with black. His hair was neat and short, with a sharp parting, though plastered to his head by the rain. He touched Corrigan's hand lightly with his fingers as he drew on his cigarette.

'You going in?' the man said, indicating the club across the road.

'In?' Bloody hell, so much for him not being noticed.

The man grinned. 'The White Pearl. The club. I've been watching you and you seem . . . interested? If you're not a member, I could vouch for you.'

'Er, no. No thanks. I'm not . . .' Corrigan felt his face flame and was thankful for the dark. 'Interested. I'm waiting for someone.'

'Of course you are. It's just you seemed a bit lost?'

'No. I'm not—'

'Not lost?' The man smiled.

Corrigan shook his head. 'I'm not – lost. Thank you.'

'Shame. *Au revoir*, dearie.' The man walked away, darting across the road avoiding both cars and puddles.

Corrigan watched as he went down the stairs, giving a wave of his fingers.

Corrigan grinned to himself and touched his eye patch. It was a long time since he had been called handsome. A long time since he'd been propositioned.

The rain fell harder.

How much longer was he going to have to wait?

And how much longer was he going to have to do this job? Tailing people – mostly men who were adulterers or those who wanted to provide the evidence for a divorce – had not been his number one priority when setting up his own detective agency. But what had he expected? That he would be solving mysteries, bringing the criminals, the gangsters to justice? At first he was trying to find missing people, soldiers who'd returned home to less than a hero's welcome, who'd turned to drink or to drugs to help them cope, but had then simply fled their lives, leaving their families wondering what had happened to them. But after a while he wasn't asked to look for the desperate, but for the man who'd run off with the family money, or the man who'd run off with someone else's wife. Tawdry. And if anyone needed a seedy hotel in which to stay, he could point out a fair few. But then nor had he been happy with the idea of going back to Ireland and helping out his brothers on the farm. As if he had never been away. He didn't want that. Nor did he want the steady job on offer from Nell's father. The sacrifices of the long years of war before had to be for something.

Nell wanted him to have a steady job. She wanted regular money and a family. Perhaps a move to the country. Sunday lunch with her parents every week. The pictures occasionally. Corrigan had thought he wanted that too. After all, Nell had waited for him for the last two years. And he tried to be at least some of what she wanted him to be, God he tried. But he didn't know how much longer he could keep it up. What an utter bastard he was.

There. Coming up the stairs, looking up at the sky before unfurling his umbrella, was Ralph Bowen.

As Bowen crossed the road and came towards him, Corrigan moved back into the shadow of a doorway, grinding his cigarette under his shoe.

His quarry strode by, looking neither right nor left.

Corrigan let him get some fifty yards ahead before he began to follow.

Rain was dripping down his neck and his shoes and socks were soaked through as he trudged behind Bowen down the ill-lit streets still teeming with people. Bowen gave no sign he knew he was being followed. No crossing and re-crossing the road, no sudden tying of a shoelace, no looking at reflections in windows. And why should he? He wouldn't suspect that his wife to whom he'd been married for thirty years would even contemplate hiring a private detective to follow him. Particularly an Irishman who operated from a grubby little office in Clapham. Particularly as he was a respectable Conservative politician and one who was destined to be in a very powerful position if the Tories were elected once more. He would not suspect his wife believed he was up to no good. The question Corrigan kept asking himself was: why had Edwina Bowen not already confronted her husband when Corrigan had given her his reports of him visiting that particular sort of club in the back streets of Soho? Why did she want him to continue with the job of seeing what her husband was up to? If he were a lesser man he wouldn't be asking himself these questions, he would accept the money without too much thought, but he prided himself on his integrity, so he did ask them.

Bowen stopped and looked at his watch. Corrigan stopped also, melting again into a doorway. Bowen did not turn around. He carried on walking.

What was Bowen going to tell his wife tonight about where he had been? To his gentlemen's club was, Corrigan imagined, his excuse of choice. Did not all politicians and men of his class have those sort of clubs? Secret societies. And unless his wife wanted to break into that bastion of masculine solidarity, she could not contradict him. Also, his high-powered friends would protect him whatever sort of person he was.

The rain was falling fast and hard now. It was getting late and they'd been walking for nearly an hour, down Piccadilly, along to Sloane Square and into the very posh part of London. Corrigan thought almost longingly of his office with its smoky fire and second-hand furniture. It wasn't much, but it was private and somewhere he could pour himself a drop of Irish whiskey. He was almost certain Bowen was heading for home; indeed, he fervently hoped so as he didn't relish standing out in the cold and wet while Bowen entertained himself and another in a warm and fuggy room, but he needed to follow him to the bitter end to make sure.

The whole of Corrigan's left side began to ache, including his empty eye socket. It was the rain and cold really getting to him, creeping inside his body, wrapping itself around his bones. Bowen walked on, passing a bombsite with weeds growing through the rubble. Another ruddy hole in the cityscape. Even the well-to-do hadn't escaped the Blitz. Corrigan thought he could see the signs of a small fire behind one of the broken walls, doubtless some poor sod without a roof over his head. God, but it was miserable.

They tramped on.

Corrigan was shivering hard and gave a small sigh of relief as he saw his target stop at the corner of Glebe Place and climb steps into a church that had done well to escape the bombing. Interesting. This was the third time in the last month Bowen had visited St Margaret of Antioch and the third time Corrigan had followed him in. If he wasn't careful, the parish priest would begin to think he was a regular.

Corrigan slipped quietly through the door, pushing his eyepatch into his pocket. People didn't tend to notice his empty socket, not at first anyway. But the patch that made him look like an adventurer was certainly memorable. He pulled his hat further down his forehead and, out of habit, dipped his fingers into the holy water and crossed himself.

The church smelt of damp and candlewax and incense. So familiar. Comforting, even. The ceiling soared away to the heavens, murals of angels and saints gazing benevolently down upon him. A statue of the Madonna with a despairing face and beseeching arms loomed to one side of the altar, surrounded by flickering candles. St Joseph, who looked bloody cross, was on the other, also surrounded by celestial light.

There were four other people in the church – two men

in greatcoats that had seen better days and which he could smell even at a distance, a woman wearing a black veil saying her rosary, the black beads threaded through her fingers, and a third man on his own, kneeling before a statue of what Corrigan presumed, from the fact it was a woman but not the Madonna, was St Margaret of Antioch. He would take a guess the two men had come into the church to get warm and the third had a pressing problem he needed to pray about. Good luck to them.

Bowen had taken a seat near the altar rail. Corrigan thought of his long-dead father, who always sat at the back of the church during Mass, thoroughly disapproving of those who marched to the front. 'God likes a humble man,' was his mantra. Thus Corrigan slid into a pew at the back, keeping his head bowed low. He knelt, wincing as his bad knee made contact with the bare wood of the kneeler, and joined his hands as if in prayer.

He glanced up as a tall priest with an angular, ascetic face, his hands tucked into his cassock, came out of the sacristy and crossed over to Bowen. Corrigan watched as the priest sat beside the politician and began to talk earnestly. They were too far away for Corrigan to hear anything but the murmur of their voices. Was the priest only talking to Bowen about God and prayer and sin, or was there something more to it? Had Bowen had a Road to Damascus epiphany? Somehow Corrigan doubted it.

The priest laid a hand on Bowen's shoulder, then stood and made his way to one of the men in coats, who shook his hand. He moved to the next.

Bowen shuffled out of the pew and made his way up the aisle, looking neither left nor right. That was interesting.

Ralph Bowen in a Catholic church when he was not a Catholic, although Edwina Bowen was. Bowen had not converted on their marriage. That could have been difficult for Edwina Bowen. No papal blessing for them. Perhaps Bowen was finally repenting his sins. Corrigan doubted that very much. As far as he knew, Bowen had kept his head down during the Great War and the next. Asthma had been his excuse for securing a desk job in the War Office during the last lot. Lucky sod. Left it to the cannon fodder to fight for peace and freedom and all that bollocks.

Corrigan kept his head bowed and his hands together as Bowen went past him, leaving the church through the carved wooden door.

As Corrigan followed, he knew they were on the way back to Bowen's grand house, and for that Corrigan was grateful. Bowen walked with an almost jaunty air, as if a burden had been lifted off his shoulders. God must have got to him. Forgiven him his sins.

Bowen ran up the steps, opened his front door and disappeared inside. Corrigan noticed he closed it behind him very quietly.

Corrigan turned away. He was not required to stand outside the house all night, thank God. He'd done his job for the day. Time for that whiskey and whatever leftovers he could find in his cupboard, if he could be bothered. He stopped to light a cigarette and take the smoke deep into his lungs. Better.

A noise came from the Bowens' house. It sounded like a strangled scream that was cut off abruptly.

Corrigan didn't hesitate. Throwing his cigarette down onto the ground, he ran as fast as his bad leg would allow through the Bowens' gate and into the garden, crunching something underfoot. Glass. He looked around. There. A couple of panes in a downstairs window had been broken, and the curtain was half drawn. He peered in and made out two struggling figures. One, who appeared to be wearing some sort of mask, had an arm locked around a woman's neck. In the dim light there was the glint of a knife.

'Oi!' He shouted. 'What are you doing?' A rather silly question in the circumstances, he would think later, but one that was appropriate at that time. The person in the mask – and he couldn't make out whether it was a man or a woman – was moving the knife closer and closer to the woman's neck. Her eyes were wide and she was desperately grappling at an arm.

Bugger. Where was his gun when he needed it? At the office in the drawer, of course.

He saw the sash window had been pushed up a little, so he put his hands on the frame and opened it enough for him to be able to fling himself through and into the room, launching himself at the woman's attacker. At the same time, the woman stamped down hard on the attacker's foot, causing them to howl in pain. Sharp heels, he noticed, somewhat inappropriately. The woman then elbowed the attacker in the face before pulling herself free, causing the masked attacker to throw down the knife, sticky with blood, and jump through the open window. Corrigan tried to grab the attacker's coat as they passed, but failed, landing on the floor with a thud.

'And who the dickens are you?'

The woman he had rescued looked down at him, panting. He saw a strong nose, a red lipsticked mouth and raven hair in what Nell would probably call 'soft waves'. And piercing blue eyes that looked extremely angry under well-defined eyebrows. There were diamonds in her ears and at her throat, and her green dress had a tear at knee-height. Odd what details he noticed. Not a beauty, but what? Intriguing, that was it.

'Er . . .' Her anger surprised him; he had expected a little bit of gratitude at the very least.

'I almost had him.' Her voice was husky, probably due to damage to her throat.

'Him?'

She nodded. 'Him. Yes. He was strong, but I was quite capable of dealing with him on my own. Then you came along.' It hurt her to talk, he could see that. Posh voice, though.

'I was only trying to help.'

'Well you didn't.'

Corrigan raised his eyebrows.

She saw. 'What? You expect me to be grateful? Did you think of yourself as a knight in shining armour rescuing a damsel in distress?'

Corrigan put up his hands as if to ward her off. 'No. I . . .' He stopped as he saw a foot. And a body hidden by the mahogany desk. There was a scarf of black-red blood around her neck and more blood pooled about her head. 'Who's that?'

The woman's shoulders slumped. 'I don't know who she is, but I'd better go and phone the police and then tell the family there's a body in the library.'

'Like Agatha Christie,' he murmured.

'I beg your pardon?'

He shook his head. 'Ignore me. I was being facetious.' He crawled over to the body, trying to look at the woman dispassionately. Young. Slavic, he thought. Poking out from under an outstretched hand was the corner of a book of matches. He palmed the book, slipping it into his pocket, then pulled himself up, trying not to wince as his bad leg almost gave way. 'This looks like a cold-blooded execution,' he said, frowning. He looked up as he heard a noise. A car, he thought, going fast. 'Did you hear that?'

'What?'

'A car.'

The woman listened. 'No.'

'No,' said Corrigan, unaccountably disappointed. 'It's gone now anyway. And I'd better disappear.' There was no need to hang around; this rather strange woman was able to cope quite admirably with the situation.

'Really? Why?'

He gave a lopsided smile. 'To let you tell the family about all this. It's a wonder they didn't hear anything.'

'Far too absorbed in themselves.'

'I see. But Mr Bowen might have . . .' He stopped, realising he was about to reveal too much.

Too late. Her eyes narrowed. 'Might have what? And what do you know about Ralph Bowen?'

'He's a . . . friend.'

'A friend. Really.' Her voice dripped with disbelief. 'Yet you climbed through the window rather than ring the bell like any normal "friend"?'

He shrugged, went over to the window and climbed out, catching the palm of his hand on a shard of glass on the sill. Blood bloomed on his skin. Damn. He sucked at the wound. 'I heard you scream, so came in the quickest way. Do me a favour. Don't tell anyone you've seen me.'

She looked at him quizzically.

'Might muddy the waters.' He smiled. Something told him he could trust this woman. 'But you're right. I'm not a friend. I'm a private detective. I don't like policemen much. Oh, and don't touch the knife.'

He disappeared from sight.

CHAPTER FOUR

Beattie emerged from Green Park Tube station and began the short walk to her place of work in Mayfair. The sky was clearing and there was a tiny patch of blue – not enough to patch a sailor's trousers, but still enough to lift the heart, and Beattie thought back to how she came to be here, walking along Piccadilly, then to Half Moon Street and on to Chesterfield Street.

'We are in the middle of a spider's web, my dear Miss Cavendish,' the man with the bald head that was like a polished egg and who went by the name of Walter Smith had told her at the meeting in the Eagle public house. It was the Lent term of Beattie's final year at Cambridge. His eyes, like insects through the pebble glass of his thick-rimmed spectacles, were watchful.

'GCHQ – as we are soon to be known as – and in particular the Covert Operations Section, spreads that web far and wide. We play an important role in the security of the country; do you understand, Miss Cavendish?' This from a man who'd introduced himself as Anthony Cooper, a man with extraordinarily pale eyes that, combined with very pale skin, made him seem like a ghost. Which of course he was in many ways.

Beattie had nodded, a flutter of excitement in her stomach. The three years at Cambridge directly after the war had managed to excise some demons, but all the partying, the heady excesses and the restlessness that accompanied those excesses had left her wanting something different. Something solid but not dull. A job that offered her the security of being able to make her own decisions. She was determined not to give in to her mother's wishes for her to attend some ghastly finishing school with a view to finding a suitable husband. Oh, she knew that women were being pushed out of jobs when men came home from Europe and the Far East so it would prove difficult to find employment after her three years at Cambridge, but she had hoped to secure some sort of translation work, maybe. How her mother had sniffed at that idea. For Beattie, work meant money, which meant power over her own future.

And so when, whilst sipping sherry in the fusty-smelling rooms of her professor at the university, he had suggested there were a couple of people for her to meet, and maybe she would care to go to the Eagle at an appointed time in the next week or so? She had, as had been intended, been intrigued, and readily agreed.

'And the Covert Operations Section . . . ?'

'We like to call it COS,' Anthony Cooper had said. 'You will find we like our acronyms.' His thin lips had given a thin smile. 'And if you were going to ask how secret COS is, then it's very secret.' After sipping delicately and disdainfully at his pint, he went on to talk about patriotism and serving her country. How her experiences during the war and her proficiency in languages could be most useful.

'You would need a little training, Miss Cavendish, but your experiences with the French Resistance mean that you have plenty of experience in the field.'

Beattie had sat in her chair, rattled, though she'd kept her expression interested, thoughtful. How did they know about France? But then, if COS was part of this GCHQ organisation, they would know. But how much did they know?

'You will of course be unable to tell anyone, anyone at all about your work and you have already signed the Official Secrets Act.'

Beattie nodded and that had been that.

She hadn't seen the man with the watchful eyes, Walter Smith, since, although she did have a very strange phone call from him as she was undergoing her training at Mannington Hall in Norfolk. 'I want to give you a telephone number, Miss Cavendish, in case you should ever need to speak to me and me alone,' he had said to her.

'Oh?' Beattie had been confused.

'Don't think about it, don't worry about it. Merely take a note of it and use *in extremis*. Tell no one.'

He then dictated a number to her, which she tucked away and, as Walter Smith had advised, thought no more about.

When she turned up for her first day at work she was given a folder full of papers to translate, very dull papers, she was to find, and this carried on for some weeks until Anthony Cooper had called her into his office to inform her of 'a little job' he wanted done. That was when her heart had leapt with excitement as she was told to become close to the Bowen family. And she was doing as she had been asked, from the first time she had 'bumped' into Ashley Bowen at that rather ghastly party and engaged his interest, being 'surprised' to find they had friends in common – all part of the reason she had been chosen for the job.

She reached her building, which would have been grand in its day, its black railings topped with silver arrow finials – renewed after the originals were taken for the war effort – and a large, thick door, though when she first stepped inside she was brought down to earth. The vast hall was painted a utilitarian green and the grand chandelier that hung over the sweeping staircase could have done with a good clean. There was a desk to one side, at which sat Enid Laing, a formidable figure always immaculately dressed in a navy suit and carmine lipstick and who was both a secretary and receptionist, though she was affectionately known as 'the gatekeeper'. The doors off the hallway didn't lead to dining rooms or libraries, but to offices. No numbers or nameplates on the doors. Beattie's office was the third door on the right and had probably been a dining room or similar in a previous life, with its proportions ill-suited to being a place of work. The ceiling was high, adorned with elaborate cornices, and the windows were tall and draughty. She hoped it would be warmer in the summer.

Hanging her coat and scarf on the coat stand in the corner, she went to her desk, saying hello to the five other people she shared the room with. They were men, who scarcely looked at her as she crossed the room, two of them mumbling a 'good morning' into their files. Rory Clarke, an earnest young man with pimples and halitosis, was the only one to look her in the eye and greet her with a firm nod. Beattie didn't mind their lack of engagement; she knew there were many men around who simply thought that a woman should be searching for a husband, not working in a responsible job.

She looked at the piles of paper on her desk. Papers that had come from all over the country from operators in small rooms listening in to communications from allies and enemies alike. Papers in French and Polish and Russian for her to translate and send to the powers that be on one of the top floors, for them to decide which were important and which were not.

But the murder of the young woman at the Bowens' house had been at the forefront of her mind for the last two days. Her name was Sofia Huber, a housekeeper for the family. Only twenty-five years old. Not for the first time she felt the swell of anger at the way it was being swept under the carpet. She looked at the article she had torn out of the newspaper, knowing its contents by heart. It outlined the 'sudden death' of a young woman at a politician's house in Chelsea. Scotland Yard was investigating. That was about it. Her throat burnt with the injustice. Surely Sofia Huber was worth more than this? She deserved justice, and even a man as powerful as Ralph Bowen should not be allowed to behave as though such a crime was too unimportant for his attention. Even the police were in his pocket.

She had not enjoyed the interview with the police, a more probing one than she would have liked, as if they were trying to find something wrong with her story.

'Why did you go into the study?' the oleaginous Detective Inspector Dicky Morgan asked as she sat in a drab, windowless room with a table and two chairs either side of it. Morgan not only had an oily manner, but his slicked-back thinning hair gleamed with oil. His suit was sharp, as were his eyes. His fingers were nicotine-stained from the cigarette he held seemingly permanently between them. He had been called to the house in Chelsea straight away. Apart from him and the forensic photographer, no one had been allowed to examine the crime scene.

'The door was ajar and there was a draught,' she replied.

'What did you find?'

'I found a broken pane of glass in the window – two, actually – and a body. Sofia Huber's body. Her throat had been cut.'

'And then you were attacked?'

'I was.'

'Your attacker got away?'

She nodded. 'He did.' And it was at this point she should have mentioned the Irishman, but she did not. There was no need; he was irrelevant. And she did not like Detective Inspector Dicky Morgan. She knew he would do nothing about the killing, but maybe, just maybe, the Irishman might help. Best not to get him into any trouble, then.

'What was your relationship with the deceased?'

'I have never met her,' said Beattie calmly.

'What is your relationship with the Bowen family?'

'I met Ashley Bowen at a party and he asked me to accompany him to the theatre.'

'Why?'

That one stumped her for a minute. 'Because he liked me, I would assume. That's the normal reason for two people to enjoy an evening together. Perhaps it's a question for him.'

'Perhaps.'

On and on the questions went, round and round.

'Where do you work, Miss Cavendish?'

'I'm a civil servant. I teach girls to type.'

'We will check.'

'Please do,' she replied, knowing the cover would hold if anyone went looking for any anomalies.

Eventually Detective Inspector Dicky Morgan became tired of all the questions himself and let her leave after she had signed her statement.

Odious little man.

She crumpled the newspaper article in her hand and dropped it into the wastepaper bin, then took an envelope out of her handbag. Inside was a letter that had arrived for Beattie that morning – an invitation from Edwina Bowen to join her for tea at four o'clock on Thursday. *To thank you for your discretion*, it said. Beattie would reply later.

The telephone on her desk rang.

It was Jennifer, Anthony Cooper's secretary. 'Mr Cooper would like to see you upstairs. Pronto.'

Beattie pushed away her unfinished work.

Anthony Cooper's office was on the first floor and contained a desk, a small electric fire in a large fireplace and a green plant that could have done with watering. The room smelt of stale tobacco and burning dust. When Beattie entered, he was writing in a manila folder, his Waterman fountain pen scratching across the paper. He waved the pen at the hard chair in front of him. Beattie sat.

For a few minutes, the only sounds Beattie heard

were that of the pen, a ticking clock and a car backfiring. Eventually Anthony Cooper looked up with a semblance of a smile. He laid his pen down.

'Miss Cavendish. Your translation work is exemplary.'

'Thank you, Mr Cooper.'

'How is our little assignment progressing?' He cocked his head to one side.

Beattie's mouth was dry and she would have loved to have had a cup of tea, or even a glass of water from the jug on the desk, but neither were on offer.

'As you know, Beattie, we had heard a certain amount of chatter about the Bowens, which is of course why you have been asked to become friendly with the family. But most particularly we want to know about Ralph Bowen. Anything you can tell us, anything at all, could prove extremely useful.' He patted his pockets and took out his pipe. Then he rummaged in them for his pouch of tobacco. He proceeded to fill the bowl of his pipe before laying it on the table. 'I'm sure his son could be a mine of information.'

Beattie nodded. It had been GCHQ's listening station on the North Yorkshire coast near Scarborough that had first alerted the covert section about the Bowens. She had seen the translations. Beattie imagined the women – for it was mostly women – in the dank, smelly bunker sitting with their headphones on, monitoring Soviet communications and only going to the ladies' room when given permission. And then one of them actually hearing something interesting about a British politician and his family. More messages sent by the Soviets indicated Ralph Bowen was the politician being talked about. Frustratingly, there had been nothing since, but the top dogs, in their wisdom, thought it was something worth looking into. GCHQ had handed it over to Anthony's department to find out more. The fact that she had been at university with friends of Ralph Bowen's son, Ashley, made Beattie the obvious choice to infiltrate the family.

'And so?' Anthony was watching her, eyebrow raised. 'After the introductions to the party you have walked out with him?'

'I've become friends with Ashley Bowen, yes. As I'm sure you know, he lives off an allowance from his mother – she is the one with the money, not Ralph Bowen. Ashley enjoys clubs and champagne. His sister, Felicia, also doesn't have to work for a living, though she does see herself as an artist. I'm not sure how close they are. Gerald Silver is, however, close to the family, particularly to Felicia, oh, and I don't think he's homosexual, by the way.'

This earnt her a look down Anthony Cooper's sharp nose.

'So far the only time I've been invited to the Bowen house was the evening I found the body of Sofia Huber.' She hoped she was speaking calmly and concisely, not letting her irritation show. 'However, I have today been invited by Edwina Bowen for tea on Thursday.' She leant back. She'd had her say.

'I see.' Anthony took what she said in his stride, as if it were of no importance.

She had to clamp her mouth shut. Her teeth hurt. She thought about how easily she could snap his neck before he'd have any idea of her intention. Then, after a few moments when she'd managed to swallow her irritation, she spoke. 'Has there been more? From the Russians, I mean.'

Anthony smiled and picked up his pipe. 'Do you mind?'

'Not at all.'

Anthony tamped down the tobacco in the pipe and took a test draw. All was deemed fine. He lit it and leant back in the chair. 'A little. Merely adding to our suspicions. But we need to crack on. Time is not exactly of the essence, but we would be grateful if you could begin to obtain information to confirm Bowen's loyalties one way or another. It's not the most difficult job in the world, but it is important in its own way. Don't let us down.'

Beattie's jaw hurt with the effort of keeping her rising anger inside. She took a moment, then nodded. 'As I said, I am making good progress with Ashley. Gaining his trust, I believe.' Her fingers itched for a cigarette. 'I've met his father, though not in ideal circumstances. As I said, I will meet his mother properly shortly.' She thought about Ralph Bowen's shocked face at the news of Sofia Huber's death.

Anthony puffed at his pipe. 'Good. Good.' He leant forward. 'This could be important, Miss Cavendish. As yet we have no proof that Ralph Bowen is doing anything duplicitous.' He sat, deep in thought for a moment. 'No proof at all.'

'And yet?' prompted Beattie.

'And yet there are these rather odd communications we are intercepting. Thus, it is worth us seeing if we can find out more.' He gazed at her with his ghost-like eyes. 'We know there are people within the establishment who wish to do the West harm. People who feel the Soviet communist system has more to offer than our own democracy. A new war has begun, Miss Cavendish. The bombs at Hiroshima and Nagasaki were the beginning.'

'I see.' The bombs that had ended the war in the East but had opened up a new era of tension.

'The Soviets are trying to build a nuclear weapon, and we are trying to prevent them from doing so, though our best brains believe there could be a test of a bomb in five years' time. There are names, concrete names we have, and we need to know if Ralph Bowen meets any of those people.'

'Am I to know the names?'

'No. You merely tell us who he meets. That is your job.'

'I see.' This conversation was so frustrating.

'They are a danger to our way of life. They need to be weeded out and dealt with.' His voice was cold.

'Dealt with?'

'Well,' he said mildly. 'We can hardly put them on trial, can we? That would expose the work we are doing here at COS and GCHQ.'

'Oh.' Beattie had not expected that.

'So if Ralph Bowen is indeed a communist sympathiser – or worse – we need to know.'

Anthony Cooper poured himself a glass of water. He had small hands, almost female in their delicacy. Was there a Mrs Anthony Cooper? Obviously as his wife she would have no idea of the job he was engaged in. 'Merely pen-pushing,' Beattie imagined him saying to his wife as she cooked a delicious but hearty meal made out of nutritious vegetables from the market for him. Perhaps there were two or three little Coopers. Two boys and a girl.

'I'm sorry, would you like a . . .' He indicated the water jug. Beattie nodded.

That was better. The water was not cold but it lubricated her mouth.

45

'So,' said Anthony. 'Tea with Mrs Bowen.'

'It's to thank me for keeping quiet about Sofia Huber's death.'

'The Polish refugee.'

'German, but yes. I understand she fled Germany for Poland, but eventually had to leave that country too.'

Anthony Cooper appeared quite unmoved. 'You were able to give your statement to the police without saying anything that could undermine your position?' He shook his head with a smile. 'Of course you did; I would know by now if it had been otherwise. Very well, Miss Cavendish. It appears you are doing an excellent job.' He closed the manila folder in front of him with a loud slap.

No mention of the stranger who had rushed quite unnecessarily to her rescue, thank goodness, but there was no reason Anthony Cooper would know about the man with the pirate patch and the Irish accent. Jet-black hair shot through with grey. An eye that was a brilliant green. He had rough hands but a kind, scarred face. At least, she thought it could be kind if he hadn't been quite so gruff and off-hand speaking to her. As if she should have been grateful for his intervention. Really. She'd had the situation in hand. And even if in one corner of her mind she could acknowledge that maybe she had been in a tight spot, she would not admit it to herself. Then he did the disappearing act out of the window – the same way he had entered the room. A strange business. A private detective indeed, following Ralph Bowen.

Beattie stood, realising she had been dismissed and so was now looking forward to making herself a cup of tea. Her hand was on the doorknob when Anthony Cooper spoke again.

'One thing, Miss Cavendish, about this murder in the Bowen household.'

Beattie turned.

'Leave it alone. It has nothing to do with you. With us. Do not get involved.' He nodded his head. 'You may go.' For a ghost-like man, Anthony Cooper could sound menacing.

Suddenly Beattie was in need of something stronger than a cup of tea.

CHAPTER FIVE

Beattie unpinned her hat and threw it down onto a convenient chair when she arrived back at her flat in Pimlico's Stranger's Square. It had been a frustrating couple of days, her irritation growing by the hour. Ever since Anthony Cooper had warned her against becoming 'involved' with the murder of Sofia Huber, she had seethed inside. She didn't like being told to leave what seemed to her to be a blatant injustice. She peeled off her gloves with a snap. And she was tired. Too tired to change out of her dull clothes. She turned on the standard lamp in the corner, its yellowish light highlighting the faded rose-and-trellis wallpaper her uncle Howard – from whom she rented the flat – had probably thought fashionable in its time.

Ashley Bowen had been attentive, perhaps too attentive, taking her out for dinner one evening and dancing the next. He was smitten with her, that much was obvious, but his chatter was vague and vacuous, and he didn't want to talk about his father, so Beattie knew she had to try harder. And with gritty eyes and yawns hidden behind her hands she'd been translating messages received at Chesterfield Street – thankfully not having to travel to the headquarters at Eastcote in the suburbs – mainly from their supposed allies. 'We have to know what everyone is up to,' a COS operative told her. 'It is not enough to only know what our enemies are doing.' After VE Day and VJ Day, Beattie had rather hoped the war was over. She was wrong and Anthony Cooper was right, she thought gloomily more than once: a new war had begun.

'Well, what did you expect?' she asked the King, who peered down imperiously from his elaborate gold-framed portrait above the fireplace.

The King didn't answer.

She lit the fire, and the kindling caught with a satisfying crackle. Had she thought working for a secret part of GCHQ was going to be easy? She had to admit, she enjoyed the excitement. She had known there could be danger, and just because her first real job for COS seemed an easy one – get to know a prominent family – did not mean that it came without strings. And she had to work doubly hard to earn her stripes.

Kicking off her shoes, she padded over to the sideboard to make herself a gin and it. A cigarette was definitely needed. And food. Although she hadn't been shopping for days and didn't know what there was in the larder. Hopefully something edible.

Sitting by the fire, she leant her head back, lit a Gauloises, and attempted to clear her mind of thoughts of Ralph Bowen, Ashley and Felicia too. And the ghastly Gerald, whose expression was permanently set at condescending with the curve of his thin lip and the perfect arch of his eyebrow. But it proved impossible as they peopled her mind. She sipped her drink, and felt the spirits slide down her throat. Now, the Irish pirate could certainly not be described as louche. There had been an energy to him that had made her feel alive and she wanted to know more about him. Even though he had been extremely patronising thinking she couldn't take care of herself. A private detective, though. Which begged the question, who was he investigating and why? From what she'd gathered at the time, he'd been following Ralph Bowen. Now, why would he do that? What had he said before he left – 'Mr Bowen has only . . .', and he didn't finish the sentence. However, if she wanted to know more about him, she would have to find him.

Beattie was brought out of her thoughts by the ringing of the telephone. She sighed. At this time of night it was bound to be Maman.

'Beatrice, is that you?'

'Yes, Maman.' Who else would it be?

'How is that terrible job of yours?'

Her *maman* also thought she spent her time training girls for the Civil Service typing pool. She hated deceiving her family, but she had no choice.

She wound the telephone cord around her fingers. 'It's fine, Maman. Keeps me busy.'

She heard her mother give one of her derogatory sniffs down the line. 'Such a waste. After those years at Cambridge too. And your languages. *Mon Dieu!* I would have thought you, my darling girl, would be using your talents in a much more appropriate way. After you went against our wishes.'

She counted to three. 'I know, Maman. But it's a good job.'

'Is it? *Pfff*. And what would Jacques think, hmm?'

Beattie gritted her teeth. It was a conversation that went the same way every time she spoke to her mother. How she was wasting her talents. How she was letting them down after fighting them for the chance to go to Cambridge. And the low blow of mentioning Jack. As if she did not think of him every single day. However, there was nothing comforting she could say to her *maman*. Or wanted to say.

'I am wondering if you are coming home this weekend?' Maman went on.

'I wasn't thinking of it,' she answered carefully. She wasn't thinking of it because she thought she might be seeing even more of Ashley Bowen at the weekend. Not that the thought gave her any pleasure.

'Only Amelie has run away from her school again. Really, that child has no thought for us, her poor parents.'

Beattie sighed. Her sister was seventeen and a force to be reckoned with. She was, in everyone's eyes, the beauty of the family with her olive skin and black curls, and was mad about the movies. All she wanted to do was go to Hollywood and be a film star – not be at her cold and formal boarding school. This was the third time this year she had run away, and Beattie had no idea why the school let her continue to return.

'And I wish for you to talk to her.'

Beattie sighed. 'Maman, we have tried that; I don't make any difference.'

'You do, my darling. You do. She listens to you.'

What could she say? Certainly not that she was supposed to be getting to know Ashley Bowen and his family because Ralph Bowen, rising Conservative politician, might be a spy for the Soviets. She wondered what her mother's reaction would be if she did, indeed, tell her that. She would like the fact that her daughter was becoming cosy with the son of a Tory politician, of that she had no doubt.

'Please, my darling.' Her tone was wheedling.

What could she do? She tapped her foot in frustration. Perhaps if Maman talked to Amelie, treated her more as a daughter than an inconvenience that had to be sent away every week to boarding school, Amelie might not want to chafe against her teachers. Her *maman* had no idea about her youngest daughter, but Beattie could usually get through to her. However, she had no illusions that she could persuade Amelie to go back to school. Not this time.

She pinched the bridge of her nose. 'I will see you on Saturday morning, Maman. I'll let you know the time of the train.'

'Thank you. Now I must go, your father wants his drink.'

And her mother put the telephone down after having achieved her objective.

Beattie drained her own drink and went over to the sideboard to mix herself another. More gin, more of the it this time.

There was a loud knock on the door.

Beattie frowned; she wasn't expecting anyone.

She put down the gin bottle and went down the narrow hallway to the door.

'Felicia,' she said, surprised.

'May I come in? I've been tramping around the corridors for what seems like ages. That damn porter at the front desk didn't give me the right directions.' Felicia brushed past her, unwinding what appeared to be a tatty feather boa from around her neck and shrugging off her coat as she went through to the small sitting room, throwing herself in a chair and sitting on Beattie's hat. 'I'm sorry to disturb you, but I wanted to make sure you were all right. Ashley told me where you lived. I didn't realise it would be such a maze.'

'All right?' Beattie smiled, putting aside Beattie Cavendish of COS and turning on Beattie Cavendish who taught typists.

'Since you found poor Sofia.' Felicia placed her hands in her lap and gave a sympathetic smile.

'Yes, of course, I'm fine thank you. And I've had your mother's kind invitation for tea tomorrow.' As she said it, an odd expression flitted across Felicia's face. 'How are you?'

'We're all devastated, of course. Sofia was such a dear and worked very hard for us for the last few years.'

Beattie sat down. 'How long had she been with you?'

'Since the end of the war. She came from an agency, I believe, and Mummy wanted to give some work to refugees.'

'I see.'

'It must have been dreadful for you to find her like that.'

'Yes, it was.' Beattie was watchful.

'Though I do wonder, what were you doing in the study?' Felicia's expression was innocent enough, but Beattie thought she could detect something else behind her eyes – a sort of calculation, perhaps? 'I mean, I thought it was odd that you had gone in there. I know we'd all had a lot to drink, but still . . .'

'As I told the police, the door was ajar and I felt a draught and then saw the broken window. I thought it was odd.'

'I see. And there she was. Poor Sofia. It's too upsetting.'

'Yes. There she was.'

There was a silence that was very loud in Beattie's ears.

'I'm rather envious of your flat,' said Felicia, breaking the silence at last. 'All this space. You even have your own private restaurant and gardens. And all on a typist's salary. Goodness.' She gave an insincere laugh. 'Though some of the décor is, shall we say, unusual.'

Beattie looked around the sitting room, seeing it through Felicia's eyes. The ebony mask with its grinning face Uncle Howard had brought back from Africa leered down from one wall, battered paperback books with green and white covers decorated another, the portrait of the King above the ornate fireplace, whose eyes watched everyone in the room, and a vase from China that her uncle swore was from the Ming dynasty balanced on the mantelpiece next to an ormolu clock. The leopard-skin rug, complete with lolling head and amber eyes, completed the rather eclectic picture.

'It belongs to my uncle.' One thing she didn't have to lie about. 'He travels a lot but he's in Scotland at the moment and very kindly said I could live here for a while. He's single. It suits him.' As she said the words she wondered, not for the first time, what she would do when he returned.

'That explains the . . .' Felicia waved at the mask with distaste.

'Yes. He also has a collection of shrunken heads if you're interested?' Beattie smiled brightly.

Felicia shuddered. 'I don't think so.' Then she pointed to a photograph frame on the sideboard. 'But that's wonderful. Where was it taken?'

Beattie looked. It was one of her favourite photographs of the island and one of the few personal possessions she had bought to the flat. The photographer had captured the different hues of green and brown and red of the salt marsh, and the sky streaked with orange and blue and grey. There was an old boat listing in the slate-coloured mud. She and Jack used to play on that part of the marsh and she could remember the squelching feel of the mud between her toes before the tide came in.

'It's one of the salt marshes on Saltergate Island. Near to where I grew up.'

'Beautiful.' She went over to the sideboard and picked it up. Beattie gritted her teeth. 'Who's the photographer?'

Beattie swallowed. 'My brother.'

'I didn't realise you had a brother.' Felicia still had her back to her, but she turned around. 'But then why should I? I hardly know you at all.'

'Jack went to France during the war and never came back. Missing in action.' Saying the words never became any easier. 'He loved taking photographs. He was hoping to take it up professionally.' As always when talking about Jack, a sad feeling settled on her shoulders.

'Oh I say, I'm most awfully sorry.' And to her credit Felicia looked uncomfortable.

'Don't be.'

'But you don't know if he's definitely, you know . . .'

'Dead?'

'I suppose that's what I meant, yes.' Her visitor looked at her, head to one side, eyes wide. Back to the coquettish Felicia.

Beattie gave a brief smile. 'I have to accept it.'

Though there was still a small part of her – a diminishing part of her, she had to admit – that thought he could still be alive, alone, somewhere. And searching for her brother was another, hidden reason she had for working for GCHQ as she nursed the hope that somewhere amongst the chatter, the signals intelligence, there might be some sign of where she could begin to look for Jack. It was probably a fool's errand.

Felicia nodded solemnly. 'I hope you find him, Beattie, I really do.' She brightened. 'And when you do, he could meet Gerald. Two artists together. Wouldn't that be fun?'

'Wouldn't it.' Beattie smiled. Of course, there would be no such meeting. Ever.

Felicia's forehead wrinkled as she looked Beattie up and down. 'That is really the most frightful suit you are wearing. Almost military.'

Beattie looked down at herself, at her grey serge skirt and jacket designed to take any desire out of a man's bones. She smiled. 'The Civil Service doesn't go for enticing uniforms.'

Felicia grimaced. 'No, I suppose not, but I don't know how you can bear to wear something like that. But I suppose if what you do is boring, then the clothes must match. It is boring, isn't it?' She gave a mock shudder. 'I mean, typing and all that. Mummy says that's not for our sort of people. No offence, Beattie.'

'None taken.' People like Felicia didn't stop to think that what they said could be construed as offensive; they had all the entitlement in the world.

Felicia sat down.

There was another silence. Manners got the better of Beattie. 'May I offer you a drink?'

Felicia brightened. 'Please. I'll have what you're having.'

Beattie mixed two gin and its and handed one to Felicia.

'Ashley certainly seems smitten with you.' She raised her glass to her lips. 'But, as I said, I hardly know you. Perhaps we should rectify that.'

Beattie arched an eyebrow. 'Even if I'm not one of your sort of people?'

Felicia waved her hand dismissively. 'Oh, don't worry about that. After all, it's nearly 1950 and attitudes are changing, aren't they? We're all trying to emerge from that awful war, though I was sent to an aged aunt in Cornwall for part of it. And look at Christian Dior.'

'Dior?'

'All the beautiful clothes, the *haute couture*. Using all that fabric and embellishments. If that's not a sign the drabness of the war is being pushed further away, then I don't know what is. Mummy said she would buy me a dress when Daddy and the Party win the next election.'

'I see.' Beattie didn't really know what to say to this. As far as she was concerned, clothes existed only for her to wear. She was not much bothered with the fabric and the beauty of them. Of course, she wasn't stupid – she knew pretty clothes could turn a man's head, that intellectual rigour probably wasn't the way to a man's heart, but still.

The thought of spending a considerable amount of money on a dress was beyond her comprehension.

'I expect you think I'm rather shallow, don't you?' Felicia said abruptly.

'No, no, not at all,' she lied.

'You do. Still, there we are. Perhaps I am.'

'Felicia, why have you come?'

'I told you, I came to make sure that nasty business with Sofia hadn't upset you. Ashley wanted to come, but I told him no, it was better for me to do. Woman to woman.'

'I see. That's most kind of you.'

Felicia regarded Beattie over the top of her glass, and Beattie realised her eyes were sharp. There was more to Felicia than met the eye. Most probably the girl liked to give the impression she was empty-headed whereas in fact there was a keen brain behind all that fluff. Her mother had not sent her.

She would have to be careful.

'Thank you,' Felicia said, putting her almost empty glass carefully down on the side table. 'But there is another reason I wanted to see you. I'll be honest with you, Beattie . . .'

'Please do.'

'You're not the usual type of girl Ashley goes for.'

'Really? What is his type?' She smiled benignly. Now what was coming?

Felicia smiled. 'Oh, you know. A bit flighty. Girly. Not too much brain. And that's not you.'

Beattie wasn't sure whether she should be flattered or not. Probably not.

'And I'm not sure what you see in him.'

'Oh?'

'Come on.' Felicia took another sip of her drink. 'He's not exactly blessed with brains. Looks, possibly, but not brains.'

Not even looks, really.

'I think you do your brother a disservice.' Beattie got up and put some more coal from the copper bucket onto the fire. 'He's great company. He's fun.'

'Where did you say you met him?'

'I didn't. But anyway. We have mutual friends. From Cambridge.' She drank some of her gin and it, feeling she was playing a game with Felicia but she didn't know the rules.

'I see.'

Beattie had had enough. 'Felicia, stop beating about the bush; what are you really trying to say?'

Felicia leant forward, her expression deadly serious. 'I'm trying to say that if you're after Ashley because of his money, the family will see through you.' Felicia's pretty little features had hardened into something almost ugly.

Beattie laughed; she couldn't help herself. 'His money?' Now the game was beginning.

'Yes. I don't know what sort of hold you have over him—'

'Felicia, I don't have any hold over your brother. I enjoy his company, he enjoys mine—'

'But why? You're not . . .' Felicia looked her up and down and Beattie felt every inch of her gangly limbs and imperfect features.

'Pretty? No, I'm not. But although looks are often seen as a commodity, sometimes personality and brains can be enough.'

Her mouth twisted. 'Not for Ashley.'

'Perhaps you don't know your brother as well as you think you do,' Beattie said, giving no quarter. 'And if you're really looking for hangers-on after a bit of easy money, maybe you should look to Gerald.' Possibly she shouldn't have said that, but she was becoming more than a little irritated.

Felicia stood, putting her glass down with such force that Beattie thought it would break. 'That's a ridiculous thing to say and a slur on Gerald's good character. I'll leave you now.'

'Thank you for coming.'

Felicia's lip curled. 'Indeed.' She flounced to the door and paused. 'By the way, the invitation from Mummy. Don't be late. Mummy hates unpunctuality.'

The door closed behind her, and Beattie breathed a sigh of relief. She had been vetted and found wanting. The trouble was, she felt Felicia Bowen could be a formidable opponent.

CHAPTER SIX

As Beattie approached the Bowen house the next afternoon, promptly at four as instructed, she heard piano music coming from inside. She recognised it. Stirring, emotional. From a film? That gorgeous music from *Brief Encounter*, that was it. Oh, but that yearning between Celia Johnson and Trevor Howard. She had to admit, she'd had tears in her eyes by the end of it.

The door was answered by a harassed-looking woman wearing a pinny. Sofia's replacement, perhaps?

'Hello,' said Beattie, smiling with what she hoped was reassurance, 'I'm meeting Mrs Bowen for tea?'

'Yes, yes, come in. Go through to the drawing room. Mrs Bowen's expecting you.'

Beattie waited until Edwina Bowen finished her piano playing with a flourish. 'That was beautiful, Mrs Bowen. I love that music from *Brief Encounter*.'

'*Brief Encounter*?' Frowning, Edwina Bowen lowered the piano lid.

'The film? With Celia Johnson and Trevor Howard?'

'Piano Concerto No. 2. Rachmaninoff. I don't go to the pictures, Miss Cavendish.'

'I see.' Beattie considered herself admonished. 'I did enjoy your playing very much. And Ashley tells me you sing in a choir?'

'I do, at the Roman Catholic church, though it doesn't please my family very much.' Her smile was humourless. 'Do sit down.' It was more of a command than an offer.

Beattie sat in one of the sofas by the fire while Edwina Bowen drew the curtains against the damp afternoon.

'Annie will bring tea shortly.'

Edwina Bowen was a well-groomed woman, who wore her hair in a neat chignon with pearls in her ears and at her throat. Her rich teal day dress was sharply cut and she sat with her legs tucked to one side. Beattie felt rather dowdy next to her even though she had worn her best cashmere jumper – but it was proving rather too hot and sported a hole in the sleeve.

Annie bustled in with a tray of tea and put it on the table in front of Edwina Bowen.

'Thank you for coming to see me, Miss Cavendish.'

'I was glad to, Mrs Bowen.' She kept her arm tucked to her side to hide the hole.

'I wanted to say thank you for dealing with dear Sofia's death in such a dignified way. There would be many girls who would have made a complete fuss about the whole thing.'

The whole thing. That was one way of describing it.

'It's been difficult enough as it is,' Edwina Bowen continued, 'what with one thing and another. With Ralph being Shadow Foreign Secretary and hoping to secure a Conservative victory at the next election, we do have to be so careful.' She poured the tea into the china teacups. 'Milk? Sugar?'

'Milk, thank you.'

'But Detective Inspector Morgan from Scotland Yard is discreet. He has also said he will not stop until they arrest the perpetrator. I hate the idea of someone breaking into the study wanting to steal something and then killing Sofia. Dreadful.' She shook her head.

Beattie murmured in sympathy. 'She was a refugee, I understand.'

Edwina Bowen looked surprised. 'Why yes, she was. Germany originally, then Poland. I suppose Ashley told you. She came to me via an agency just after the war. It was so difficult to get any staff at that time – it still is now, to get the right sort of staff, I mean, with Ralph's position and all that.' She laughed. 'So I was grateful. And she was a godsend, doing housework and some cooking. Shopping too. Yes, a godsend. I think she was happy here. She was kind to Felicia, who can be a little . . .' Edwina Bowen broke off and smoothed her dress over her knees. 'We will miss her.'

'Did she have any relatives?'

Edwina Bowen nodded. 'A brother. Martin, I think his name is. The police have let him know, of course. There has been no news of her parents since Sofia and Martin left Poland. I would imagine they are not alive.'

'And no beau?'

'No. Nothing like that.'

Cups clinked on saucers.

'Ashley is very fond of you, I believe,' Edwina Bowen said at last.

Beattie bowed her head in acknowledgement. 'I didn't realise that until Felicia said yesterday.'

'Felicia?'

'Yes, she came to see me.'

'Did she indeed? I wonder why. What is it you do again, Miss Cavendish?' A casual question, delivered with precision.

'I work for the Civil Service, nothing special.'

Edwina Bowen's eyes were sharp. 'You seem like an intelligent girl, Beattie, too intelligent to be working in a job that is "nothing special", wouldn't you say?'

Beattie smiled. 'I train the women in the typist pool. Sometimes I have to travel to other offices, but not often.'

'You teach them to type? I thought there were schools for that?'

'Yes, there are. But I do advanced typing with them, improve their dictation speeds and accuracy, show them procedures around the office. The filing system, that sort of thing.'

'I suppose it's important for you girls to do things properly, particularly when you are working for the government. For my husband.' She pushed a strand of hair that had escaped her chignon back from her face. 'And the war?'

'The war?' This was becoming an interrogation. Edwina Bowen was making sure her son was walking out with someone suitable, rather as Felicia had done yesterday. And in Felicia's eyes, she was far from suitable. What would her mother think of her?

'Yes, Miss Cavendish. The war. Ralph was in the War Office. Naturally I stayed at home to bring up my family.'

'Naturally.' Beattie smiled. 'I was a FANY and drove ambulances and chauffeured generals around.' Not far from the truth.

'And your parents?'

'My mother is French and my father is an architect with his own business.' For a moment Beattie thought of her father's study with its untidy mess of pens and pencils and curling sandwiches and rolls of paper spread across the large table and the books that teetered on every available surface. 'They live in the country.' She wanted to steer the conversation away from her family. 'You must be very proud of your husband and his political position.'

'I am, Miss Cavendish. He has done very well for his family and his party. Now he wants to help his country by making sure we have a Conservative government after the next election. These Labour people are ruining it with their socialist policies, don't you think? Really, look at the National Health Service that has come into being. That cannot be sustainable.'

Beattie made a non-committal noise. Now was not the time to argue politics.

'Are you a Conservative, Miss Cavendish?'

Beattie looked at Edwina, but her expression was bland. 'I don't have any political views; I found the war put paid to those,' she said smoothly. She sipped her tea. A telephone rang.

A knock on the door. Annie. 'There's a call for you, Mrs Bowen.'

'Please excuse me,' said Edwina Bowen to Beattie as she stood.

'Of course.'

After her hostess had hurried out, Beattie stood and listened for a moment, then left the drawing room herself.

'Can I help you, miss?'

Annie was in the hallway. Edwina Bowen was on the phone, her back to Beattie. 'Yes,' said Beattie. 'I would like to powder my nose.'

'Of course. Up the stairs—'

'And second on the left. Yes, I know, thank you.' She smiled.

As she made her way to the stairs, she passed the study. Its door was shut. She shivered. She didn't want to venture into there again now, so could resist the lure of the locked door. But she was still determined to find out what had happened to Sofia.

Climbing the stairs, she listened out for any sounds. Nothing except for the murmur of Edwina Bowen's voice. Ashley Bowen had rooms on the third floor. Taking off her shoes, she ran quickly up the next staircase and found three doors. She opened the first and slipped in.

It was an austere room. Dark furniture, plain washstand. A particular aroma of citrus and tobacco – particular to Ashley. A pair of pyjamas was neatly folded on the end of the bed. Beattie thought she probably should feel embarrassed by entering a man's bedroom like this, but the thought was only fleeting. The fireplace had grey ash in its grate – no Sofia to lay a fire and perhaps Annie was not up to the task. Or it was not part of her duties.

There was a shelf above a desk containing two volumes of *The Shorter Oxford English Dictionary*, *Great Expectations* by Charles Dickens and *The Complete Works of Shakespeare*. All very worthy.

Beattie went over to the desk and peered at papers on the top. A bill from his gentlemen's club. A bill for a crate of champagne. A letter from a 'Jimmy' demanding he paid his money back right now. That was interesting. She was about to take a closer look when she heard the distant sound of a door slamming shut downstairs. The front door? Could it be one of the family who might just come upstairs? Damn, she'd wanted more time to snoop.

Light of foot, she left Ashley's room, running down the stairs to make her way to the bathroom, where she took her powder compact and Dior lipstick out of her handbag and freshened up her face. That would do. Closing the compact with a decisive snap, Beattie put her shoes back on and went downstairs.

Reaching the drawing-room door, she stopped as she heard voices. Edwina Bowen with her light, soft tone was not easy to hear; the other voice was, she presumed, Ralph Bowen's, and he made no effort to speak quietly.

'I told you, Ralph, I asked her here to say thank you for her help over that dreadful business with Sofia.' Edwina's voice.

'You don't know the girl.'

Beattie heard footsteps, then the clink of glass.

'She's a friend of Ashley's.'

'That doesn't mean to say she's not a gold digger.'

'Ralph, please.'

'Edwina, you never seem to appreciate my position. Things are very delicately balanced, and if we are to regain power at the next election we must have no slurs on our reputations.'

'Slurs, Ralph?'

Beattie felt a rising anger and tried to damp it down. Now Sofia Huber's death was seen as a 'slur'.

'It was bad enough having someone murdered in our

own house and all those journalists baying for a story.'

'You managed to sort that out.' His wife's voice was placatory.

'Yes, thank goodness. Wouldn't do to have the *News of the World* sticking their dirty fingers in our business. At least Leo Scott of the *Daily Dispatch* did what he was told. Had to. And Dicky stepped up to the plate.'

Dicky? Ah yes, the Scotland Yard policeman.

'That's a dreadful American phrase, Ralph.'

There was a sigh. 'You're right, Edwina. There's no reason someone like Beattie Cavendish should be after money. Does she come from a good family?'

Beattie raised her eyebrows.

'From the country. Her mother is French and her father an architect.'

'Hmm.'

'I'm sure you could find out more about her if you wished. But Ashley does seem to like her. Even if she is only a pool typist. Or a teacher of them or some such thing.'

Beattie had to put her hand over her mouth to prevent the mirth from escaping. A pool typist did not rank very highly in Edwina Bowen's estimation.

She heard the slamming of a car door, then footsteps up to the house. Beattie took several steps backward as the front door opened and Ashley walked in.

'Beattie, I didn't know you were coming.' To his credit, his smile and the warmth in his voice were genuine.

Beattie returned the smile. 'Your mother invited me.'

'Mother?'

'Yes. For tea.'

'For tea?' He was frowning now.

'Yes,' laughed Beattie. 'Do stop repeating me. Your mother invited me to tea because she wanted to talk a little about Sofia. That's all. Oh, and Felicia came to my flat yesterday to have a chat.'

Ashley's brow cleared. 'I see. And good old Felicia. That's why she wanted to know where you lived. She really likes you, you know. So does Gerald.'

'Really?' Beattie kept smiling. 'That's delightful to know. Anyway, we'd better . . .' She indicated the drawing-room door.

'Yes, yes.' He opened the door and ushered Beattie in.

Edwina Bowen was sitting in the same place on the sofa; Ralph Bowen was standing by the fire, a glass of what looked like brandy in one hand and a cigar in the other. He had a florid complexion, and his waistcoat strained over the beginnings of a paunch. His hair was a luxuriant grey, giving him a patrician air. Beattie held out her hand. 'Mr Bowen? I'm Beattie Cavendish.'

Ralph Bowen put his drink on the mantelpiece and took her hand. 'How do you do, Miss Cavendish.' His grip was firm, and he looked into her eyes, a smile wrinkling the corners of his eyes. Beattie was taken aback for a moment. He had presence.

'Come and sit, Miss Cavendish.' Edwina Bowen patted the seat next to her.

'I'm sorry, Mrs Bowen, I had to go upstairs.'

Mrs Bowen inclined her head. 'Of course.'

Ashley sat opposite her. Beattie smiled at him, thinking she'd had a narrow escape – it wouldn't have done for Ashley to catch her eavesdropping at the drawing-room door. 'You know, Ralph, Beattie was a FANY during the war.'

'Good, good. Helping your country.' Ralph Bowen puffed on his cigar.

'I hope so, sir,' said Beattie, as demurely as she was able. 'Actually, Mrs Bowen, I do apologise, but I think it's time for me to be on my way. Thank you for the tea.'

'I'll see you out, Beattie,' said Ashley.

The phone was ringing down the hallway as they left the drawing room and Sofia's replacement hurried to answer it. 'It's for Mr Bowen,' she told Ashley. 'Can you go and fetch him, please?'

Ralph Bowen came striding out of the drawing room and snatched up the receiver, barking a 'hello' into it. Then he stood quite still. Beattie thought he turned rather pale.

'Not now,' he said to the person at the other end, turning his back and hunching over the receiver. 'Please.' He nodded. 'I see.'

'I say, Beattie?' They had reached the door and Ashley was helping her into her coat.

'At once,' said Ralph.

'Would you like to come to the Gargoyle Club tonight?'

'The Gargoyle?' Beattie's concentration was on Ralph Bowen, who put down the telephone, stood straight, squared his shoulders and went upstairs.

'Yes,' said Ashley, a little impatiently. 'Gerald has invited us.'

'Gerald? Oh, right.'

'Please say you'll come?'

She made herself smile. 'Of course, I'd love to.' How wearying. 'Will you pick me up?' What had that telephone call been about? Whatever it was, it had knocked Ralph Bowen for six, of that she was sure.

Ralph Bowen came hurrying down the stairs carrying a small valise. He picked up his hat and coat and turned to Ashley. 'Tell your mother I have to go out. I'll be back later.' He opened the front door and walked quickly away from the house.

What was going on?

'Of course I'll pick you up. I'll see you this evening.'

Beattie remembered to smile at Ashley as she left the house, wondering if she should follow Ralph Bowen, who looked so deep in thought he probably wouldn't notice if an elephant charged after him.

CHAPTER SEVEN

His so-called office was, Corrigan had to admit, a little dreary. And miserable. Looking through the small window onto the outside world, he didn't know whether it was becoming dark earlier or there was a thick fog forming. One day he would get around to cleaning it. And have the chimney swept. Then he might have something better than a fire that smoked a great deal but rarely warmed. At least the clients didn't think he was spending their money on posh premises. That was one comfort.

He lit another cigarette from the tip of his last and looked again at the letter on his desk. Creamy luxurious notepaper and matching luxurious envelope and words that were not so luxurious. Edwina Bowen dispensing with his services. *No more need*, she had written. *Innocent explanation*, she had written. *Rely on your discretion*, she had written. He snorted. If the gentlemen of the press were to get hold of the information he was privy to they would have a field day with Ralph Bowen's reputation by writing about his adventures in a club for what they would call 'sexual perverts'. He sighed. Still. Live and let live was his motto. He shrugged, fashioning the letter into a paper aeroplane and directing it to the wastepaper bin.

Good shot.

The trouble was, Edwina Bowen, God damn her soul, was a good and prompt client. Had only wanted him to follow her husband and to let her know where he went on certain days. She would telephone him in the morning or send a letter on those days, so it was lucky he didn't have a book full of clients. And she paid up without fuss and on time. She said she trusted him, though in the beginning he hadn't been sure why. He was trustworthy, no doubt about that as far as he was concerned, but at first it had been interesting to speculate what made Mrs Bowen think he was so. His face? He laughed. His face with one eye and plenty of scars. Curiously, she did not seem bothered by his battle wounds. Had not stared. Plenty did. He knew his limitations – it didn't make following subjects in the daylight too easy. Thank God for Alfie, who he could employ on an ad hoc basis when he thought it would matter that his face was easily recognisable. Though not with Ralph Bowen. No one else. His wife had been very firm about that. Only he was to do the dirty business of tailing him. And he was to discuss the case with no one. As if he didn't know the meaning of discretion.

The fact he was a so-called war hero had swung it for him with Edwina Bowen. War hero. That was a joke. Anyway. That job was done. Now he had to wait for another dissatisfied wife or a husband who needed to prove himself unfaithful by being 'caught' in bed with another woman. God in heaven, it could be tawdry. But it paid the bills. Almost.

Yes, he would miss Edwina Bowen. Still, the job had ended on an interesting note. He pulled a copy of last week's *Daily Dispatch* towards him.

POLITICIAN'S STAFF MURDER MYSTERY

Mystery surrounds the death of a woman in a house in central London. Sofia Huber, aged 25, housekeeper at the house of Shadow Foreign Secretary Ralph Bowen, was found stabbed to death on Thursday. Detective Inspector Richard Morgan of Scotland Yard said: 'Our enquiries are ongoing, but we believe a petty thief was involved.'

A very thin story, short on details. Not much about Sofia Huber, poor soul. No mention of the dark-haired woman who had fought off the attacker. He had rather liked her style. And Dicky Morgan of the Yard. That was interesting. Old Dicky was very good at taking the heat off anyone prominent, and Bowen was prominent. He would bet a pound to a shilling Bowen had made sure Dicky was on the case.

He lit another cigarette.

Bowen would want the crime cleared up fast, or, failing that, squash any sort of interest in it. Being connected to a murder would not do his career much good, especially if anyone went digging around and found out about the old boy's trips to the White Pearl Club,

And he would love to know what was hidden behind Edwina Bowen's icy demeanour. Did she realise what the White Pearl Club was? A well-brought up lady like her? He'd been called off the case, but why now? Why after the murder? Seemed almost too convenient. And why had Mrs Bowen wanted him to follow her husband in the first place? Was she planning to divorce him? That would be messy. Maybe she wanted to have something on him. Blackmail. But was she duplicitous? She didn't seem the type. Whatever the type was.

He remembered when she had called into his office all those weeks ago. Normally, wronged wives – and he saw a great many of those – were nervous and apologetic and would rather be anywhere else but sitting in front of someone like him but at least they were pleased for the anonymity coming south of the river afforded them. Edwina Bowen was different. She was well-dressed in her sable coat and hat, her make-up perfect. She had peeled off her kid gloves as she sat down, crossing one elegant leg over another and in a calm voice had set out exactly what she wanted him to do – follow her husband when she asked him to and report back to her. No photographs. No records. She would pay him expenses as well as a retainer as the work would be on an ad hoc basis. Ad hoc was fine by him. And the retainer was attractive also. Why had she chosen him? he'd asked her. At that point she'd wrinkled her nose and looked around his office at the damp walls, the dirty window, the cold fire, and then she'd looked at him. 'Because of your Military Cross at Monte Cassino,' she'd said in all seriousness. Then she had stood, given him a brief smile and left. He'd never seen her in person again. All their communication had been by telephone or letter. By God, she was an interesting woman, though. He didn't tell people about his MC. He didn't use it to advertise his business, any more than he used his military title of major, and his medal lay tarnishing in a drawer as he had no wish to take advantage of it in any way. So therefore she must have done some of her own detective work before coming to him.

It was the first and probably last time earning that medal had been of any value.

Corrigan looked again at the article. Who had written the story? He looked again. Leo Scott. Probably another mate of Bowen's and writing what he was told. The ruling classes always had the institutions stitched up. Why should he worry about it? None of his business. Nothing he could do. No. Nothing he could do.

He sighed. It was none of his bloody business, was it? Yet still it niggled him. The casual dismissal of Sofia Huber's death. Didn't she deserve justice? What about her family? Friends? Did they not count for anything? Bloody toffs. Always able to clear up the shit. Or get someone to do it for them.

There were questions, though, that would not go away. The most logical answer was that the intruder really was a petty thief looking for valuables. But why would he be in a fusty study? And what was the good-looking woman doing there? In the dark, too. Searching for something? Or maybe she'd killed the housekeeper. No, it had been the intruder, he was sure of that. The woman had been a guest, the intruder not. A guest with particular talents. What was Sofia Huber doing in the study? Why was she murdered? And there was no doubt it was a murder; there was a bloody great knife to attest to that. And that wound had been brutal. More like an assassination. Could it have been that? Sofia Huber. Something from her past?

He sighed again, rubbing the scars on his face. And why, he thought, remembering how his feet had crunched on glass *before* he had climbed through the window, had the glass been broken from the inside out? And, perhaps the strangest question of all, what was a housekeeper doing with a book of matches from a shady club about her person? He frowned at the matches sitting on his desk he had picked up off the floor from under her hand, as if she had been clutching them. There was a smear of blood on the front. The logo of the White Pearl Club. The same club Ralph Bowen had been visiting. And inside, written in pencil, a phone number.

He leant back in his chair, rubbing his forehead with one hand. Was it interesting? Was it really? What was the point, after all? Why should he worry about it? He had done what he had been asked and had been paid handsomely – much of it for his discretion. Still, he wondered. And what was the role of the church Bowen visited so often, and was the priest only a confidante or something more?

He sighed. It was not as if he was going to see any of them again. Including the woman with the raven hair. Shame. There was something interesting about her, and she could certainly take care of herself. He smiled. He liked that in a woman. But he should forget all about it. Why involve himself in a rather odd death that was none of his business? It would only bring trouble down upon his head. And he didn't need any more trouble.

Corrigan opened a drawer in his desk and swept the book of matches into it.

CHAPTER EIGHT

Beattie hesitated outside the opaque half-glass door. A sign proclaimed *Corrigan and Partners. Private Detectives.* She saw a figure inside, sitting, she thought, behind a desk. Could this be him? Patrick Corrigan. The elusive private detective. Or a partner? Or maybe his secretary. Yes, that was more like it. There was surely a girl who did his typing, invoices and all the menial tasks.

It hadn't taken her long to track him down. She still didn't understand why she felt the need to find him, not really. What did it matter? He was at the Bowens' house and then he left. Through the window. And he had mentioned Ralph Bowen's name. And he'd helped her ward off the attacker. There was no question she would have been able to do so on her own, but he did, undeniably, help. Or maybe hindered. She might have been able to overpower her attacker herself – she'd dealt with bigger, heavier men before, but all this did not tell her why she wanted to find him. There was one reason, of course, in that death unites in so many ways.

One of the advantages of working for GCHQ was that he had been easy to find. A well-placed question here, a file retrieved there, and she had a list of private detectives in

London. There were certainly a few of them, mostly, she surmised, ex-services. But there wouldn't be many with one eye and an Irish accent. There was only one pure Irish name, and this was surely him. He also had an exemplary war record, including being decorated after fighting at Monte Cassino. Impressive. That had been one of the bloodiest battles in the Italian campaign.

Her search had led her to this building at the edge of Clapham Common. The common still showed the signs of the wartime allotments, and she'd had to skirt the spoil heap that was the result of digging out the deep underground shelter that provided temporary housing for the *Windrush* migrants. What must they feel, being thrust down into the bowels of a city that wasn't ready for them?

There was a family living on the ground floor of the building that housed Corrigan's office – and judging by the delicious and foreign smells that hung in the downstairs hallway, it was one of those arrivals from the Caribbean. She was proved right as the door opened and a black face peered out. Beattie smiled. 'I'm just going to see Mr Corrigan.'

The man smiled back. 'He's a good neighbour. A very good man.' He shut the door.

Beattie climbed the stairs.

Now she raised her hand and rapped on the glass before walking in.

The man behind the desk looked up at her, startled, as he put a telephone back in its cradle. It was definitely him. The pirate. Patrick Corrigan. She glanced around, taking in the one desk, two chairs, no secretary. No partners in evidence.

'Patrick Corrigan? Private Detective?'

Corrigan gazed at her with his one good green eye. There was no patch over his empty socket and the scars snaking down the side of his face stood out in their lividity. His expression was cool, appraising. He didn't stand. Beattie stood there, fighting the urge to look away or to shift from foot to foot. She'd seen many injuries in her time, many amputations, many disfigurements, and she knew how they could affect a man.

She blinked and cleared her throat. 'Patrick Corrigan?' she repeated.

'If you're looking for a private detective, then yes.'

His voice was as she remembered, a lilting Irish accent with a touch of harshness to it. A harshness born of a tough life, not of where he was from, of that she was certain. He sat there, expressionless. Beattie pointed to the chair in front of his desk. 'May I?'

He waved his arm. She sat down, bristling at his rudeness.

He stared directly at her. 'Are you here for the job?' he asked.

She started. 'The job?'

'Yes,' he said, a mite impatiently. 'Filing. Papers. Taking calls. That sort of thing.' He was holding a pencil that he tapped on the desk. He was watching her, expecting an answer.

'I—'

'What's your name?'

'Beattie Cavendish.'

'Well, Beattie Cavendish, have you the qualifications for the job? Can you type? File? You look fairly competent.'

She took a breath and drew in the smell of damp and

coal. *Fairly competent, my foot.* The bare bulb above his desk threw a harsh light into the dull room. There was no disguising that it needed more than a lick of paint, an introduction of some softness. A feminine touch, was that what she was meaning? There was a grey filing cabinet in one corner of the room, a bookcase full of files balanced higgledy-piggledy in another. She was about to tell him that he was being exceptionally rude and that they had, in fact, met before. She was going to point out the place and the circumstances, yet something stopped her. It had been dark when they had met at the Bowens' house, and he would not have seen her properly. She had also been wearing her glad rags and looking more presentable than usual in her evening dress and high heels. A dress that had gone to the seamstress for patching. She had been wearing her mother's diamonds, too, she recalled. Today she had taken time from work in order to travel to Clapham to find Corrigan and so was wearing her dreadful serge suit and flat brown shoes. Her hair was flat against her head thanks to the uninteresting hat she had jammed on her head. Her handbag was a dull brown leather with a quite ordinary gold clasp, and she wore spectacles on the end of her nose. A different person, surely? And only a woman. Besides, men have little regard for detail. Beattie was sure he hadn't recognised her, so this could be an excellent opportunity to find out what his interest was in Ralph Bowen and what he was doing at the house at that particular time. She was sure he would not tell her if she asked – he was bound to say it was confidential or some such nonsense. Yes, a good opportunity. It might be fruitful, and she would keep up the pretence only for a day or so and if necessary could then disappear out of his life.

'I can type and file. Miss Chessington's Secretarial College,' she said crisply, before she could stop herself. She prayed he wouldn't want to check as there was no such place. 'But I can only do two mornings a week. Would that suffice?' She thought Anthony Cooper would not baulk at two mornings in Corrigan's office, though she might have to now tell him the full story of where she had met Corrigan and why she wanted to get close to his work. Another man to smile sweetly at. Be submissive. Fawn at their feet. Admire their intelligence. For a moment she was weary at the prospect.

'Two mornings.' Again the tapping of the pencil, his regarding of her with his single eye. She gazed back steadily. 'Done.' He named an insufficient amount of money. Again that piercing look.

She nodded. Firm, that's what she had to be, no nonsense. An exemplary sort of person to be secretary. Another layer of Beattie Cavendish.

He looked her up and down. 'You look very trustworthy to me. Besides, beggars can't be choosers.'

It was good to feel wanted. 'No one else has replied to your advertisement?'

'No one who can type.'

Beattie allowed herself a smile. 'And what about your partners? Don't you have to ask them?'

'No.'

Beattie nodded. As she had thought. No partners.

'When can you start?'

'I can begin now, if you like?' The sooner she began, the sooner she could finish.

It was his turn to nod. 'Tea first. There might even be biscuits. In the back room.'

Gritting her teeth but smiling sweetly, Beattie made her way through to the back room and found a kettle on a small Formica table by an equally small electric cooker. There was a frying pan, cup, plate, knife and fork on the draining board by the sink. Above the sink was a cupboard in which she found more cups and plates should she need them. There was a tin of biscuits, which proved to be digestives on further inspection. She discovered a pint of milk on the windowsill.

As the kettle boiled, she looked around the room. Apart from the tiny kitchen corner there was a bookcase, a lumpy battered sofa and what appeared to be a camp bed with a sleeping bag rolled up neatly at one end. No pillow. An alarm clock on the floor. A radio next to it. Although it was cold and smelt of damp, the room was tidy and clean. Corrigan had clearly not forgotten his military roots. And it was obviously the place where he lived.

She found the teapot, tea cosy and tea caddy, though the tea had probably seen better days.

Beattie carried the drinks through to the front office, balancing the plate of biscuits on top of one mug, and managed to walk to the desk without incident. Corrigan was standing with his overcoat on, collar up and a patch over his eye. 'I have to go out,' he said. 'Meeting.'

She hadn't heard the phone ring, nor the door open, but she said, 'Fine. Anything you would like me to do while you're out?'

He looked thoughtful. 'Maybe. If anyone telephones, take their name and number and tell them I'll telephone them back later today.'

It was all she could do to keep her face straight. She nodded with some solemnity. 'And I'll write the name and number in the book on your desk?'

He glanced down at the large hard-backed notebook and shook his head. 'No need.' He picked up the notebook, tore a piece of paper from it before putting it into one of the desk drawers, locking the drawer and putting the key in his pocket. He laid the piece of paper on the desk. 'Write any messages on here.'

'I see.'

'And . . .' He looked around the office. 'You can put those files in order.' He nodded towards pile of brown files teetering on the edge of a chair. 'Alphabetical.'

'Shall I put them in the cabinet?'

'No,' he said, predictably. 'Pile them up on the chair. In the right order. I'll put them away later.'

'Right. In the right order. By the letters of the alphabet.' She couldn't help her sarcasm, but she regretted it immediately. It was not how this Beattie would behave.

She might have been mistaken, but she thought she saw his lips twitch. 'Absolutely. I'll be back soon.' And with that, he put on his hat and left.

Beattie sat down behind the desk and waited for a few minutes, in case he returned. She got up, crossed to the door, opened it and ran down the narrow stairs, through the delicious smells, and peered out of the door at the bottom. No sign of Corrigan. A mother pushing a pram, a young boy clattering a stick along the railings on the opposite side of the road, the rumble of a train. The skies were still grey and lowering.

Back in the office, she sat down at the desk again and

took her set of lock picks out of her handbag. It took her less than a minute to get into one of the locked drawers and take out the notebook, tutting at Corrigan's lack of security.

Beattie began to flick through the pages. It was a diary. What was she looking for? Anything unusual but, more importantly, any mention of Ralph Bowen. She ran her finger down the pages. Not many appointments. Business was clearly not thriving. She turned the pages again, and, sure enough, there on the date she had found Sofia Huber's body, Corrigan had written the letters *RB* in black ink. Below them, in pencil, were the words *the White Pearl Club* and *church?*, *Role of priest?*, *Religious or?*. She flipped further back in the diary and found RB's initials several times. The White Pearl Club was mentioned at least four times and the church, three. She delved further back and saw the letters *EB*. Edwina Bowen? When she first visited, perhaps? There were other names, other notes in the diary, but they were for different cases, of that she was sure, and she wasn't interested in them.

Then, on a date two months earlier, she found *Edwina Bowen 11.30 a.m.* It looked as though Edwina Bowen had met Corrigan and engaged his services on that morning. And what else could it be but to follow him? Corrigan was to follow Ralph Bowen. But why? Did she suspect him of having an affair? And why did it start then, back in September? She took her notebook out of her handbag and wrote down the name *White Pearl Club*.

She set the diary aside and looked through the previously locked drawer for anything else of interest. A book of matches with *White Pearl Club* stamped on it. A smear of what looked like dried blood on the cover. She opened up the book and found a number scrawled on the flap. Why had Corrigan put the matches in a locked drawer? What was the significance of them? And the number? Was it only that Bowen had visited the club? What sort of club was it?

A further fumbling and she felt something hard and metallic at the back of the drawer. She raised her eyebrows. If she was not much mistaken, it was a handgun.

Suddenly, the office door swung open. Corrigan. Beattie tried to slide the drawer shut without him noticing. Of course, there was the small matter of the diary lying open on his desk. But he didn't see that – not at first. He was staring at her.

'You're from the Bowens' house. That night.'

Direct. A point in his favour. She nodded.

'Then what the devil are you doing here?' His one good eye flashed with anger and his scars were like taut wires down his face.

'You engaged me as your secretary.'

His eye narrowed. 'Do not mistake me for an idiot, Miss Cavendish. I knew there was something familiar about you, I just didn't know what. That's why I had to walk outside, to give myself the space to breathe. I knew it would come to me then. And it did. So, I'll ask you again, what are you doing here, Miss Cavendish?' He looked to her right. Beattie knew she had not shut the drawer completely. 'And what are you doing going through my drawers?' He frowned. 'How did you open them? I'm sure I locked them before I left.'

Beattie shook her head. 'No, they were open, Mr Corrigan. I was looking for a pen. To write down any numbers when people called.' She smiled and nodded in what she hoped looked like a vague sort of way.

'Hmm.' He did not appear convinced. 'You haven't answered my original question. What are you really doing here?'

She sighed. 'Very well. I wanted to thank you, I suppose.'

'For what?'

She cleared her throat. 'For saving my life back at the Bowens' house.' Nothing like a bit of flattery to get a man to lower his guard.

He inclined his head. 'The pleasure was mine, Miss Cavendish. Now, for the third and final time, what are you doing in my office and, more to the point perhaps, what are you doing snooping through my things? Especially as I do know I locked those drawers before I went out.' He sank down into the chair opposite her, wincing as he stretched his leg. He put his hand in his pocket and took out the key to the desk drawers, placing it very deliberately on the desk.

Beattie opened her mouth to say she most definitely was not snooping when she realised he wasn't a stupid man and she really ought to tell him the truth. A version of it anyway.

'I was intrigued, if I'm honest.' Which she was. 'You appeared through the window like a . . .' She paused to think.

'A good fairy?' Corrigan supplied. There was a faint smile around his mouth.

She raised her eyebrows. 'I'm not sure you have the qualifications to be a good fairy. But you did appear from nowhere and told me you were a private detective.'

'And you wanted to find me.'

'Yes, as I said, to thank you and also to talk to you about Sofia Huber.'

'First things first. You were angry that I saved you, I think. In fact, I didn't have to intervene at all. You were quite capable of handling whoever that was in the Bowens' library. Especially with your heels.'

She smiled. 'Yes.'

'The war, I presume?'

'I beg your pardon?'

'The war,' he said, a tad impatiently. 'You obviously had a role that honed your fighting skills.'

She raised an eyebrow. '"Honed my fighting skills". Something like that, yes. But as you say, the heels helped.'

'And you want to talk about the dead woman.' He leant back in the small chair until it teetered on two legs, hands clasped behind his head. Beattie hoped the spindly wood would take such treatment.

'I do.'

'So why pretend you want the job I was offering and why snoop?' His tone was bland, but his eye glittered.

'As I'm involved with the Bowen family – with Ashley Bowen, particularly' – she cast her gaze down, as if self-conscious – 'I obviously wished to know what your interest was in his father.'

'Obviously.'

'And you were desperate for someone to be your secretary.'

'Do you not have a job already?' He looked her up and down, at her dreary suit and utilitarian shoes. 'I don't think it's family money that enables you to move in the Bowen circles. Civil Service at a guess.'

'You're right. Typist. Well, I teach typists. And teach them how to type and file properly.' She smiled. She quite wanted to slap him.

'Useful but dull. And you wanted some excitement.'

'Maybe. And I have a few days' holiday at the moment. I think I panicked. Yes, that's it. I panicked.' Once more she found herself smiling as sweetly as she was able. Which was not saying a great deal as she didn't do sweet very well. 'I said I would work for you because you looked as though you needed help.'

He snorted.

'And I thought I could find out about you and Ralph Bowen.'

He raised an eyebrow. 'Me and Ralph Bowen.'

'As I said, why is a private detective interested in the father of a friend of mine?'

'Hmm. And how did you find me?' he asked.

That was the tricky question. But she'd had time to think.

'I have a friend who is Irish. He goes to places where a lot of Irish people socialise and he asked around. And you are not' – she gestured at his face – 'unmissable.'

He rubbed his hand down the wounded side of his head and she regretted being so direct. She shifted uncomfortably on her seat.

There was a silence for a minute or two. She tried to sit perfectly still. Then said, making her voice bright, 'Would you like me to make you another cuppa?'

He stood, kicking the flimsy chair. 'I'll do it. You're not my secretary any more. You're my guest.'

She followed him through to the back room. 'You live

here, too, don't you?' She pointed at the camp bed and the sleeping bag.

'Very observant,' he said, filling the kettle and lighting the gas.

'It's difficult to find accommodation these days, isn't it? What with the bombed-out houses and the housing shortage . . .' She stopped, realising what a ghastly, idiotic mistake she'd made. She should have bitten off her tongue.

'Yes indeed,' Corrigan said calmly, swirling hot water around the pot. 'And all those notices proclaiming "No dogs, no Irish" play a part too.' He tipped the water out of the teapot and put three spoons of tea into it. 'John downstairs has the same problem. "No blacks" added to the list. Fortunately we have a landlord who loves money more than he hates dogs, the Irish and blacks.' The kettle was boiling again. He took it off the heat and poured the water into the teapot. 'There,' he said with satisfaction. 'Warm the pot, pour just-boiled water over the leaves. Let it steep for five minutes. That's how Ma taught me, and her ma before her.' He put the knitted tea cosy over the pot with a flourish.

'I'm awfully sorry,' Beattie blurted out. 'I didn't think.'

He shrugged. 'It doesn't matter.'

She stared at him. She wanted to tell him that it did matter. That he had fought for freedom, had fought with the English and he deserved to be respected, that he'd been decorated, fought in bloody war battles and she did not understand why people could not see this. Why there was such prejudice. Did these stupid people not realise they owed their freedom in part to people like Corrigan? That he had given his youth for them to be able to not allow

Irish people in their houses? She was angry for him. Her shoulders tensed; her stomach knotted.

'It matters,' she said quietly.

'Maybe. But there's nothing we can do about it.' He poured the tea. 'And besides, as you can see, I have everything I need here.' He took the tea through to the office. 'So. Sofia Huber. Let's start there. Why does her death bother you? You know she was only twenty-five?' He sat down behind his desk. Beattie perched on the hard chair opposite.

He wanted to change the subject. But she couldn't let it go. 'It's like you not being able to get somewhere decent to live because you're Irish; that matters. Because Sofia Huber's was a lonely death. No one seems to care, apart from her brother, I suppose. She came over here, a refugee seeking safety and she gets murdered. And Ralph Bowen is doing his damnedest to not only cover it up, but to bury it as though her life never mattered. And although she wasn't any older than me I suspect she'd had a hard life.' She blew on the tea in her mug. 'And that's not right. It must have been so hard for her and her brother to leave everything she knew. Away from her own country. Escaping the Nazis.'

'Hmm.' He looked thoughtful. 'You're right. Her death seems to have been swept under the carpet and I do wonder why. Of course, Bowen wouldn't like the publicity, but even so. And he brought in Dicky Morgan from Scotland Yard, who is adept at covering up inconvenient deaths.' He took a sip of his tea and swallowed it with satisfaction. 'That's better than the dishwater you served up. Now, tell me what you know.'

Beattie let the comment about her tea-making abilities

go. 'She was the Bowens' housekeeper. As I said, she has a brother. And she appears not to have had any romantic interest in her life.'

'Right. So we talk to the brother. Find out more about her.' He took a digestive biscuit left over from the last tea-making round and bit into it. He pulled a face. 'Soft.'

'What about Ralph Bowen?'

'What about him?' Corrigan sniffed the biscuit.

'You haven't yet told me of your interest in him. Why were you following him?'

'Because his wife asked me to. But I don't know why she wanted me to do that and I don't know why she asked me at that particular time. Back in September.' He looked uneasy. 'But I've only told you that because you obviously know already.' He nodded at the book on his desk. 'From my diary.'

Beattie ignored the comment. 'She must have given you some reason? Or do you always do as you're asked without question?'

For a brief moment, Corrigan looked as though he was far away in another time and another place. Then he blinked. 'I try not to. Not these days,' he said quietly.

She realised she had revived an old memory, quite possibly a memory he had long since buried.

'But,' he continued, 'if the money is good, then I don't ask too many questions. And I thought it was most likely the old cliché of man having affair, woman wants evidence. It can even happen to politicians.' He smiled wryly.

'There's more to it than that, though, isn't there?' Beattie leant across the desk and opened the drawer, taking out the book of matches again. 'What's the White Pearl Club – that's in your diary too – and where did you get these matches from? And look at this.' She pointed to the brown stain. 'It looks like blood on the cover.' She opened up the book. 'And there's a number.'

'What's a nice girl like you doing with Ashley Bowen?'

The abrupt change of subject made her sit up, metaphorically. She hoped Corrigan had not seen any change in her demeanour. 'He's fun,' she replied, as casually as she could. 'I haven't had a lot of fun these last few years. He's taken me out to shows. Dancing. Meals.' She shrugged. 'Why not?'

'How did you meet?'

'Mutual acquaintances. From Cambridge.'

'Ah.' Corrigan smiled. 'I understand. Bluestocking.'

'Bluestocking? That's a very old-fashioned view. No. Maybe. Taking an opportunity. Does it matter?' It made her cross to think Corrigan disapproved of her choice of man to walk out with. Not that she was walking out with Ashley Bowen. Or even wanted to, not in her real life.

'No. Though I still wonder what you are doing with Ashley Bowen and his sister.'

'Felicia?' She was surprised. 'You know her?'

'I make it my business to know a little about my clients' families. It can help. She's interesting. And there is the odious friend.'

'Gerald Silver.'

'That's right. Gerald. Who has his finger in many unsavoury pies.'

Beattie wanted to know more about Gerald and Felicia, but she sensed he was leading her away from her original question. She would not be so easily led. She tapped her finger on the book of matches. 'The White Pearl Club,' she said. 'That's in your diary. I imagine Ralph Bowen went there once or twice?'

Corrigan nodded slowly, as though he had expected her to return to the subject. He cleared his throat. 'I have to admit I took the matches off Sofia's body. The book was under her hand.'

She hadn't expected that. 'Oh. What was Sofia doing with a book of matches that had come from a club Ralph Bowen was in the habit of visiting?'

Corrigan gazed at her for a long moment. 'Beattie Cavendish, there is something about you that makes me trust you. I hope I'm not wrong.'

Beattie was not sure she reciprocated the sentiment. 'Tell me about the White Pearl Club.'

'Ah. Well. It's a sort of gentlemen's club.'

'In what way is it a "sort of" club?'

'Hmm. It caters for, shall we say, exotic tastes.' He took a tobacco tin and cigarette papers out of his pocket and rolled two cigarettes. He offered one to Beattie.

She took it and leant forward as he lit it. He then lit the second one for himself, taking his time. Delaying tactics. It amused her.

'Exotic tastes?' She blew a couple of perfect smoke circles. 'Like homosexuality? Sado-masochism? Spanking? Prostitutes?'

She enjoyed watching him squirm as the colour rose in his cheeks. He was probably not used to women talking about such things.

'All of that, Miss Cavendish. Yes. Indeed. Possibly.' He coughed.

94

'Someone and something for everyone, then. I think you may call me Beattie now. The number on the book of matches, have you rung it?'

'Not yet,' Corrigan said. 'No time like the present.' He picked up the telephone and dialled. Beattie could hear it ringing. And ringing. And ringing.

Eventually Corrigan put the phone down. 'I'll try again later.'

Beattie nodded. 'Right. The next thing we need to do is to visit the club, because Sofia obviously had some connection to it, but first I think we should pay our condolences to her brother, Martin.'

'We?'

'Have you anything better to do? No. I thought not.' Beattie stubbed out her cigarette and put on her hat and coat. 'Are you coming?'

The day, thought Corrigan, was proving interesting.

CHAPTER NINE

'How did you find out Sofia Huber's address?' Corrigan asked, lighting a cigarette as they emerged from the Tube at Aldgate East and began walking along Whitechapel Road, passing limbless army veterans selling matches and razor blades and girls offering posies of flowers for a few pennies.

'I asked Felicia Bowen.'

'Didn't she think it was strange?' He turned left suddenly. 'This way, it's a bit quicker.'

Corrigan led her through gates and onto one of the many building sites in the East End. New houses – many of them prefabricated – were being built to try and take care of the acute housing shortage. The city skyline was a scribble of the long arms of cranes. Under slate-grey skies, workmen shovelled sand and grit from towering piles, while others carried hods of bricks on their shoulders. Underfoot, the cold, mean November rain had turned the ground claggy with mud. For once Beattie was glad of her sensible shoes, though she hoped her one pair of good lisle stockings would not become muddy and wet as she skirted scaffolding and girders. Corrigan was wearing workman-like boots.

'A fit country for heroes to live in,' muttered Corrigan. 'Damn Lloyd George. Didn't happen then. Won't happen now. Anyway, as I said, didn't the Bowen girl think it odd you wanted Sofia Huber's address?'

'Possibly,' Beattie said. 'But I said I wanted to meet Martin and tell him how sorry I was about his sister.' Another lie. A good job she had no moral compass sometimes. Again, it had been easy enough to find the Hubers' address with the resources of COS and GCHQ at her fingertips, so there had been no need to alert any of the Bowen family about what she wanted to do.

As they walked through the building site, Beattie tried to surreptitiously rub some of the mud off her shoes.

'Remind me why we are going to see Martin Huber?' asked Corrigan.

'It's too early to go to the White Pearl.'

'And?'

Beattie sighed. 'I found Sofia's body.' Did she really have to explain all this again? She was feeling a slight twinge of guilt as it was for veering off her COS brief, though she justified it by telling herself Sofia had been working for the Bowens and she might find out more about the family.

'I know that.'

'I know you know,' she retorted crossly. 'I want to know why she died. I want to know who killed her. There is no point in leaving it to Scotland Yard.'

'And certainly not to Dicky Morgan.'

Beattie hopped over a puddle. 'Evidently not. She was a refugee. But she has family. And no one is investigating.'

Corrigan stopped. 'Except us. When you came into the office earlier, I had just been speaking to Edwina Bowen.'

'And?' She stamped her feet, hoping he would hurry up as they were freezing.

'She said I had probably heard about the unfortunate death of her housekeeper but on no account was I to go to the police about following Mr Bowen, and I was to forget all about her and the family, that it would all be wrapped up very shortly. That, she said, was what she had paid me so handsomely for. And if I disobeyed her there would be consequences. And then she put the phone down.'

Beattie stared at the Irishman. 'Golly.'

'I don't like being told what I can or cannot do, however "handsomely" I've been remunerated. And I particularly don't like being threatened.'

Corrigan spoke normally, but Beattie caught the steel in his voice.

'I thought you came with me a bit too easily,' she said.

He gave a rare smile. 'There's always method in my madness.'

'You see what this means, though?' She carried on walking.

'What?'

'There is more to this than meets the eye.'

She stopped again. Corrigan sighed and stopped too. 'We'll never get there if we keep stopping like this.'

'We could have taken a cab.'

'I don't think so. I wasn't that handsomely rewarded.'

'I . . .' Beattie clamped her mouth shut. She was going to say she could have paid, but thought someone prickly like Corrigan might not appreciate it and it could lead to awkward questions. Instead she said, 'I haven't told you when I was seeing Edwina Bowen the other day, Ralph

Bowen went out in rather a hurry after a phone call.'

'So?'

'He looked . . . worried at the very least.'

'Did you follow him?'

'I did,' she said. 'He walked for quite a long way up and down streets until we finally stopped at the Chelsea Embankment Gardens, where he sat down.'

'And then?'

'And then nothing. He sat with his little case on his lap for quite some time. It was dark by then, though I could see him by the light of the street lamps.

'Did anyone, for instance, sit down next to him, give him anything?'

Careful. She knew what he was thinking, and it wouldn't do to give herself away.

'What do you mean?'

'As if he was meeting someone, perhaps?'

She pretended to think, then shook her head. 'No, not at all.' She almost smiled to herself as that was exactly what she had been waiting for, someone to surreptitiously exchange valises, or for him to do a dead drop somewhere along the river, but there was nothing of the sort, nothing to say he was a spy. He had looked so sad.

'And then what did he do?'

'He went home.'

She had followed him all the way home, then had to hail a black cab to get back to her flat in order to get ready for what turned out to be a tedious evening with Ashley. It had followed the usual pattern of drinks and dancing and more drinks and more dancing until Ashley had dropped her off outside the large arch that marked the riverside entrance to Stranger's Square. She'd managed to escape after enduring a drunken kiss from him.

'I do wonder, though, what he told Edwina,' she said. 'About where he'd been.'

'Going to the House. Going to see a friend. Any number of excuses. A great number of men prevaricate about their movements. Not everybody wants their wife to know what is going on.'

He said it with such solemnity that a bubble of laughter rose in Beattie's throat.

'What?' asked Corrigan. 'What is it?'

'Nothing.' She took a piece of paper out of her pocket and studied it, then looked up. 'Here we are.'

They were standing outside a row of solid brick houses that had escaped Hitler's bombs, though there were signs that all was not well: peeling paint, rotten window frames, smashed tiles on the pavement.

'He might not be in,' said Corrigan.

'He might not. But he might.'

Beattie pressed the bell and heard it chime indoors.

There was no reply.

'A wasted journey, then,' said Corrigan.

Beattie pushed on the door, which swung open. 'Come on,' she said.

They stepped into a small, dim hallway.

CHAPTER TEN

Beattie wasn't sure what she'd expected as she opened the door to the front room – something simple, maybe. Plain, solid utility furniture. A serviceable electric fire. A table, a couple of chairs, perhaps. But this was altogether very different. She found herself in a room that was crowded with furniture. An uncomfortable-looking chaise longue, a lumpy velvet two-seater sofa. Two stuffed birds – a faded peacock and a fat, evil-looking pigeon – perched on a table, beady eyes staring at her. A bamboo plant holder complete with some sort of fern trailing out of it. Another holder with what she fancied was an aspidistra in dire need of some water. A glass-fronted cupboard with a collection of highly decorated plates on its shelves. A smell of violets. A fine layer of dust over everything. A silence.

Corrigan strode around, as much as he was able with all the clutter. 'Hello? Hello? Martin?'

There was no reply.

'He isn't here.'

Beattie glared at Corrigan. 'Well, that's obvious, isn't it?' Nerves had made her fractious. She did not want to find another dead body, especially that of Sofia's brother.

'I'll go upstairs,' said Corrigan. 'You have a look in the kitchen.'

'Stand right there. Hands up.'

An accented voice came from behind them. A young man's voice with a tremor he was trying hard to disguise.

'Turn around. Very slowly indeed if you please.'

Beattie and Corrigan turned around very slowly indeed and were faced with a young man, wide-eyed and grasping a German Luger with a shaking hand.

'We don't mean you any harm,' said Beattie, as gently as she could. 'We're looking for Martin Huber.'

'Why?' the young man demanded, staring at Corrigan, at his one eye, at his scars.

'I want to talk to him about his sister, Sofia.'

'Sofia is dead.' His hand shook even more. Beattie was frightened he might fire the gun unintentionally. 'My sister is dead.'

'My name is Beattie Cavendish and I found your sister's body.' She spoke carefully and slowly.

'The friend of the Bowens?'

'Sort of. No, not a friend,' she amended as she saw anger bloom in his face. 'I know the family.'

'Do you? Do you really?' His laugh was bitter.

'Martin? It is Martin, isn't it?' Corrigan's voice was soft, unthreatening. He held out his hand and took a small step forward. The air pulsed with tension. 'Hand me the gun.'

Martin Huber waved the weapon. Beattie flinched. 'Why should I?'

'We're not going to hurt you.'

He jutted out his chin. 'I don't know that.'

'Please,' said Corrigan again. 'You don't want to hurt

either of us. I'm a private detective and I can help you. So can Beattie.'

'I'd like to know more about Sofia,' said Beattie. 'She sounds as though she was brave and fearless.'

'She was.' Then Martin began to sob. Noisy sobs that made his shoulders heave. He lowered the gun and Corrigan quietly took it from his hand and put it down on the table. He led Martin to the over-stuffed sofa.

Beattie sat next to him and put her arm around his thin shoulders. 'I'm so sorry,' she said, gently. She looked at Corrigan. 'We're so sorry.'

Martin dashed away the tears. 'They told me a family friend found Sofia. But you say you're not a friend. I haven't been allowed to see her, not even to identify her. As if I'm some child. She is – was – my only family.'

'I was at the house when I found her,' said Beattie. 'Did you know the Bowens well?'

Martin shook his head. 'No. I saw them a few times, but mostly they were not really friendly. Mrs Bowen was – a little. She tried, anyway. But people treat us refugees like their good works, to put salve on their rotten souls. Do you understand? They are doing us a favour while at the same time making sure they look good.' His fists were clenched. 'They have no idea, no idea at all what we have been through merely to arrive in this country. The cold. The lack of food. The fear.'

Beattie gently took one of his fists in her hand. 'Can I get you something to drink?' she asked. 'A cup of tea, perhaps?'

This brought a sad smile to Martin's face. 'Tea. You English think that tea cures everything. Even my uncle thought that. He liked to think he had become very English, you see.'

Beattie squeezed his shoulders. 'You're right. We always think anything can be cured with a cup of tea. Apart from my mother, who's French. She likes a glass of red wine.'

Martin dashed a tear away from his cheek. 'That sounds better.'

'Your uncle?' Corrigan looked around the room. 'This is his house?'

'It was. He died. Just before the war ended. This is where our parents sent us to escape the Nazis. We were lucky,' Martin continued. 'At first, anyway. I was ten and Sofia was fifteen and we had Uncle Stanislaw and somewhere to live. Though we struggled with your sheets and blankets.' He gave a small smile. 'We were not used to them and didn't know where to put ourselves in the bed. So. We managed during the war, even though Uncle Stanislaw wanted to send us away, but we refused. We managed. Times became difficult, so Sofia joined an agency to find more work. That's how she came to be working for the Bowens.'

'And was she happy?'

Martin nodded. 'At first, yes, though the work was hard and she said nobody took any notice of her as a person or asked her about herself and her history, about how she came to this country. She was invisible, but she never complained.'

Martin's fingers twisted in his lap. 'Then one day Uncle Stanislaw went into hospital and never came home so Sofia looked after me. She cooked and she cleaned and she washed the clothes when she came home at night.

Sometimes she was so tired she could not eat. But when she was free we would walk and talk and she was so good. So good. Uncle Stanislaw had been a tailor, and he was teaching me. He said I had a flair for it. But after he died, well.' He shrugged. 'I managed to get some work in a tailor's shop with one of Uncle's friends. And we had a roof over our heads. And now she's dead.' He looked straight at Beattie. 'Who would want to murder my sister?'

'That's what we want to know,' she replied.

'Do you? They told me her throat had been cut. Ralph Bowen came here, you know.'

'To tell you about Sofia?'

'No, no, I already said, that was Mrs Bowen. Mr Bowen came here to offer me money.' He almost spat out the words. 'I said no. I told him I didn't want his blood money. I say to him I want Sofia's killer to be caught. He said that was not possible because it was a petty criminal who had broken in looking for jewellery and the police wouldn't catch him. He asked if I wanted to talk to the police. Of course I said no. I don't like the police. Even after all these years in this country, I still don't like the police.'

'No.' Beattie squeezed his hand. He was not so much younger than she was, but she felt protective towards him.

Martin sat up straight and glared at Corrigan. 'You're a private detective? What is a private detective doing about the murder of my sister?'

'I want to help find her killer.'

'So the police really are doing nothing.' He was desolate.

'Let's just say, as I don't have to answer to anybody but myself—'

Beattie coughed.

105

'I can go places the police can't. Talk to people.'

Martin nodded. His hand was cold in Beattie's. She felt him trembling. He opened his mouth to speak and there were tears in his eyes. 'She has been buried, you know. In the Jewish cemetery. The Bowens arranged it, they said it was for the best and that Jews like to be buried quickly. They were telling me that.' He laughed harshly. 'I was there and it was raining. But she is under a lovely tree. How did they know that was what Sofia wanted? They didn't. They just assumed that I would do as they said, and I did, I did.'

Beattie didn't know what to say, so she said nothing, squeezing his hand again to let him know she was there. 'You did the best you could,' she said, eventually. 'And Sofia knew you loved her, and she loved you. Remember that.'

The young man nodded, dashing away the tears that trickled down his face. 'She did love me. You know, she carried me along the railway tracks into Poland? She wasn't much bigger than me, but she carried me so far. There were people dying all around us. The Germans had rounded up the Jews, whether they could walk or not. Ill people. Old people. Children without their parents. We were lucky; we still had Mutti. Then.'

'Martin, your door was open when we arrived,' said Beattie when Martin looked more composed. She kept her voice soft; it was like coaxing a reluctant puppy.

'I saw you outside the door. I had been shopping. You looked like the authorities.' He gave a sad smile. 'I don't like the authorities. I thought you might have come for me.'

'And the gun?'

Beattie saw Martin's shoulders tense up. 'You might have wanted to harm me.'

'Harm you?'

Martin looked from one to the other. 'I have been followed.'

'Followed?' Beattie echoed again.

'Yes. And the telephone rings and there is no one talking at the other end. The other night I wasn't able to sleep and I was sitting here in the dark and someone tried the front door. Then I heard them at the back door, but they were both locked so whoever it was couldn't get in, so they went away again.'

'Did you look out of the window?'

'I tried,' said Martin. 'But it was dark and raining. Whoever it was hurried away into the shadows. He was wearing a thick coat and a hat.'

'What sort of hat?' Corrigan had taken a notebook and pencil out of his pocket and was making notes.

Martin pursed his lips. 'I don't know. A large hat, that is all. A man's hat.' He turned to Beattie, gripping her hand hard. 'What are you going to do?'

'Everything we can,' she replied. 'I have connections.'

'What connections?' Corrigan looked at her, frowning.

Damn. She had spoken without thinking. 'Obviously the Bowen family,' she said, ignoring Corrigan.

'Indeed,' said Corrigan drily.

Now Beattie shot him a look. 'We'll get there, Martin. I promise you.'

'Also I am afraid because someone has already been in here.'

'What do you mean?' said Corrigan, busily writing in his notebook.

'Exactly that. I got home one day and the house felt odd, smelt differently. I saw that things – things like Olaf – had been moved. And upstairs, in Sofia's bedroom, a drawer had been left open. Not much, just a little, but it was enough.'

'Hang on.' Corrigan was pinching the bridge of his nose. 'Who's Olaf?'

'The peacock, of course.'

'Of course,' murmured Beattie.

'But nothing had been taken?'

Martin shook his head. 'Not as far as I could tell.'

'You came from Poland, is that right?' Corrigan wrote some more.

'Yes, Germany, then Poland. The Germans didn't want us.'

'Weren't you listening, Corrigan?' said Beattie.

'I want to get it straight.' There was no rancour in his voice. 'Martin, did you come on the Kindertransport?' he asked, referring to the rescue effort that took place just before the war when thousands of Jewish children from Nazi-occupied Europe came on trains and aeroplanes to Britain to be placed in foster homes around the country.

Martin nodded. 'Yes. It was hard. I was young, though, and it was like a great adventure to me at first.' He looked into the far distance, memories obviously swirling around in his mind. 'You have to know that Sofia was a good sister, as I told you; she looked after me well. Since I can remember, she looked after me, made sure I didn't get into too much trouble. She sang to me, played the piano for me when I was out of sorts. She loved the piano.' He smiled sadly. 'We were happy. Leaving was hard. But we have made a life in your country. Sofia had been writing a diary about it all, quite recently.'

Beattie looked at Martin. 'A diary?'

'Yes, she told me she was trying to write about her life in this country. She'd become very sad and worried. I kept asking her what the matter was, but she wouldn't say, but in the evenings she would sit and write in her diary.'

Beattie hesitated, then said, 'May I see it, Martin? I don't want to pry, but it might help.'

He nodded. 'I understand. But it is in Polish. She liked to read and speak in our language when she could, to keep it alive for us, she said. Uncle wasn't so happy; he said we should embrace English and learn to love it. She did that too.'

Corrigan frowned. 'Then you'll have to translate it for us, Martin.'

'No,' said Beattie, smiling. 'The Slavic languages were . . .' She stopped, realising she might be giving too much of herself away. What the hell. 'I studied the Slavic languages at Cambridge.'

'Languages?' Corrigan whistled. 'Fancy.'

Beattie ignored him and looked around the room. She saw a framed photograph of a young woman on a pebble beach with long hair blowing around her face, vibrant and laughing; her mouth was full and her eyes danced. Sofia Huber. She was wearing a skirt and blouse and the sea was behind her. Different to the person drained of her life and her soul she had found on the floor of the Bowens' house. She nodded towards the photograph. 'What a lovely picture of your sister, Martin. Did you take it?'

Martin shook his head. 'No.'

'Do you know who did?'

'No, I didn't ask. She didn't like me asking about her private life.'

'It's a very happy photograph. Do you know when it was taken?'

Martin frowned. 'A few months ago, perhaps?'

'She seems happy.'

'She was, then. It was only recently she withdrew from me. Wouldn't tell me what was happening in her life. She said it was not my business.'

'Did she have a lover?'

'Corrigan,' said Beattie, looking at him, eyes wide and angry.

'Well . . .' He shrugged. 'It's got to be asked.'

Martin sat up straight, his back and shoulders stiff. 'If she did, she didn't tell me. Perhaps because she knew I wouldn't have approved.'

He'd had his suspicions, then. 'Martin, may I take that photograph? Only for now?'

'The one of Sofia? Why?'

'I might want to talk to some people about her, show them a photograph to maybe jog their memory.'

Martin thought for a moment, then nodded. He took it out of its cheap frame and handed it to Beattie, who put it away in her handbag. 'Please try and find out what happened to Sofia. And quickly,' he said. 'I'm so frightened.'

She thought for a minute as an idea came into her head. She frowned. But what would her parents think and would they object? Surely not, her mother did like helping people in trouble, even if she didn't have a lot of time for her daughters. However, it would be blurring the boundaries. Her boundaries. She would be mixing work and home and that could lead to difficulties. She would have to be very careful how she handled it. It could work, though. She spoke before she had time to change her mind.

'You must come with me.'

Corrigan turned to look at her, astonishment plain on his face. 'What do you mean?'

'Exactly that.' Beattie was firm, certain she was doing the right thing. 'I've got to go home to my parents' this weekend so Martin can come with me. He'll be safe there. He can come back to my flat tonight and we'll go tomorrow.'

'Beattie.'

'Don't be silly, Corrigan. It'll be fine. My parents live on an island – Saltergate Island – there's only one way onto it and one way off it.'

He frowned.

Beattie laughed. 'Are you worried about my reputation?'

'Well, no.' He looked uncomfortable.

'Good. You shouldn't. It's nothing to do with you and I'm not bothered about my reputation anyway.'

She let go of Martin's hand, who had been looking from one to the other during the exchange. 'Collect your things and we'll leave.'

Martin scurried into the bedroom.

Corrigan leant forward and spoke in a whisper. 'Are you sure about this, Beattie? I mean, we don't know the lad. He could be a maniac, a murderer. He could be making it all up, the whole thing about him being followed; the mysterious phone calls could all be a story. Anything. Beattie? Are you listening?'

Beattie put her finger to her lips. 'Shh.' She'd heard a scrabbling noise at the front door and had crept quietly to the door of the sitting room.

Corrigan raised his eyebrows. Beattie cupped her ear. 'Listen,' she mouthed.

There it was again. A faint noise, as if someone were suppressing a cough. Then a scratching noise. Someone was outside the door. Trying to get in? Listening to their conversation?

Corrigan nodded. 'I hear it,' he whispered.

Beattie tiptoed down the hallway to the door, then, as she reached it, tripped over an umbrella stand in the shape of an elephant's foot.

'Right,' she said, whipping open the door.

A figure in a black coat and a trilby was hurrying down the road. Beattie set off in pursuit, but the person jumped into a car idling by the kerb, which then took off down the road.

'Damnation,' said Beattie, as the car raced away.

'Did you see who it was?' asked Corrigan when Beattie returned to the house, giving the elephant's foot a good kick on the way in.

'No,' she said. 'Only someone in a coat and hat.'

'You would never have caught them,' said Corrigan sympathetically.

Beattie looked at him. 'Nor would you,' she retorted.

'I wasn't saying—look, I'm sorry if I've offended you.'

'No. Sorry. That was unnecessary.' It was. Totally unnecessary. She was just cross with herself for not being faster. And for tripping over the damn umbrella stand.

'What's wrong?' asked Martin when he saw Beattie and Corrigan standing by the window.

'Nothing,' they both said in unison.

'I can't find Sofia's diary. I don't know whether it's been stolen or if she's hidden it too well for me to find. I don't know, I'm sorry. But it's not here.'

CHAPTER ELEVEN

Doors slammed, the guard blew his whistle and steam curled past the outside of the window as the train pulled out of Colchester station, gathering speed.

Beattie peered out of the window, watching and studying the people on the platform who might be taking too much of an interest in a country train on a branch line heading for the Essex coast. She sat back in her seat, as sure as she could be that she hadn't been followed so far. She had been on alert at Liverpool Street too, looking for anyone acting suspiciously, anyone taking more than a casual interest in her and Martin.

A man walked past their compartment, peered in, moved on.

She yawned. She had been up late the night before writing a report for Anthony Cooper. Not that there was much to say, other than she still wanted to find out more about the death of Sofia Huber, that there was a missing diary and it could be important to the whole operation. (*Let him dismiss that*, she'd thought grimly as she wrote). She said Bowen possibly thought she was a gold digger, that Ashley enjoyed her company and she'd had to fend him off more than once and she wasn't sure how far she should go. *Answer that one, Mr Cooper.* She'd sealed the envelope and put it in his tray before she changed her mind.

The journey from Liverpool Street station to Colchester had been uneventful. Beattie had attempted to read the newspaper but could scarcely concentrate for all the thoughts whirling around in her brain. Martin had stared moodily out of the window.

Now, as the train made its way to Saltergate Halt, Beattie looked over to the young man, who had fallen asleep as soon as the train had begun to move. His head lolled against the window, his face child-like in repose. He looked so young, surely younger than the twenty years to which he confessed? And now what was he going to do without his sister? He had a reasonable job, but what of his future?

Martin gave a little snort, then settled back against the cold window.

He looked so defenceless, and it had nearly broken her heart when he told her the evening before over a bowl of tomato soup and a fatty lamb chop that the first words of English he knew were 'I'm hungry, please may I have a piece of bread?' He remembered very little of his and his sister's flight to England, only that Sofia carried him through woods, and along a railway line, where she stumbled often, and the cold. Oh, the cold! He tried to learn not to think about how cold it was, but to think of warm fires and mugs of hot chocolate. Sofia used to tell him that if he thought of warm, happy things he would be warm and happy. It didn't work, he had told her, sadly.

Beattie had asked him if he knew whether his parents were still alive. He had shaken his head. He had no idea, he'd said. But he hadn't heard from them in all these years and he and Sofia – his voice had tripped over her name – presumed they had been sent to a concentration camp. If they weren't dead, he was sure they would have tried to find him and his sister.

The train pulled into Saltergate Halt with a hiss, a belch of steam and a squeal of brakes. Beattie woke up Martin and they gathered their bags from the luggage rack before stepping down onto the platform. She glanced around to see if anyone else had alighted from the train, but saw no one, though the hairs on the back of her neck stood up. She stopped for a moment, listening and looking. But could only hear the sound of the train pulling away, leaving a silence in its wake. She shook her head; she was being paranoid.

The wind was cold, but the clouds parted, and rays of sunshine lit up the outside of the blue-painted waiting room and the three red fire buckets hanging on its outside wall. They crossed the track to where Wilf from Dungers Farm was waiting with his grey Fergie and a trailer of straw bales arranged as seating.

'Hop up, Miss Beattie,' he said, giving her a helping hand as she scrambled into the trailer. 'You too, Mr . . .'

'Martin. I'm Martin.'

'Mr Martin. Find yerself a space.'

Beattie gave Martin a reassuring smile as he scrambled onto the trailer.

The tractor puffed contentedly along narrow country lanes and past ploughed fields. The hedgerows were bare, but Beattie knew in the springtime they came to life with hawthorn blossom and nesting birds and the scent of elderflowers filled the air. She pulled her coat tightly around herself, trying to keep warm. Martin's shoulders were hunched inside his thick jacket.

They crossed the Strood – the ancient causeway across to Saltergate Island. The clouds had gathered again, and the light was slowly leaching away. Neither of them spoke. Beattie tried not to think of the Roman centurion who was supposed to haunt the crossing at this time of year.

Soon, Wilf turned off the main road and down the narrow lane that led through the village proper. They passed the Dog and Partridge and the old Baptist church, then the cottages, smoke curling from their chimneys, gardens put to bed for the winter.

The ribbon of houses came to an end, and there, set back, was her childhood home. Salter House, the Arts and Crafts building with its distinctive butterfly-plan shape, its red brick with pebbles and flints and barley-twist chimneys and large French windows so beloved by her father. As Beattie felt that old regret clutching at her heart she wished, not for the first time, that she could feel pleasure visiting. On the surface, there was no reason not to – her childhood had been happy, she'd had a brother who adored her and was her constant companion and a little sister who had arrived, somewhat unexpectedly, some years after her own birth. A welcome surprise for Maman and Father. Her father's job as an architect meant that they had wanted for nothing. And they were part of the fabric of the village. Often when she looked back, she saw endless sunshine, playing in the rivers and the streams, scrumping apples from their neighbour's orchard. The years before the war were filtered through a rosy hue.

But that was all window-dressing.

There were memories she had buried deep, memories of feeling there was no way she was ever going to match up to her brother, Jack, that he was the most deserving of her parents' time and attention. And money. That he was the one destined for Cambridge, not her. That he was the one destined for medals and great acts of valour, not her. So when he disappeared over France during the war, her parents crumpled and withdrew into themselves, each nursing their pain separately. She knew her *maman* worried about her, but only worried that she would make a good match and be cared for by someone else and settle down to the life of a wife and mother. A prospect that made Beattie weak with dismay.

Wilf stopped the tractor near the front door.

'Come on, Martin,' said Beattie. 'We've arrived.'

Martin had been sitting with his eyes closed. 'I was thinking about Sofia,' he said. 'We were playing in our garden at our house. Before the war. Before everything.' He sat up straight. 'Are you sure your parents won't mind me coming to stay?'

'Positive. There's plenty of room.' Her mother had initially been frosty on the telephone, but had softened when Beattie told her Martin's story. Part of it at least. Her father, who these days usually stayed working in his study from dawn to dusk if he wasn't away overseeing his latest project, probably wouldn't even notice. 'Come on.'

She stepped down from the trailer. 'Thanks, Wilf,' she said, waving at him.

'Pleasure, Miss Beattie.'

The Fergie puffed away.

The arched solid wooden front door was flung open and light flooded out, illuminating the wooden floor of the hallway beyond.

'Beattie, you're here.' Amelie came running over and flung herself into her sister's arms. 'I've missed you so much.'

Beattie dropped her case and hugged her sister, breathing in her particular smell of Pears soap and lemon shampoo, noticing how much she had grown in the few weeks since she had seen her last. 'You shouldn't be here, my lovely Amelie.'

Amelie drew away from her. 'I know.' She smiled. 'But I am and so are you.'

Not only had Amelie grown in height, but a beautiful young woman with her chestnut curls and blue, almost violet eyes was emerging from the young girl Beattie had in her mind. She wore a simple cream dress with a rosebud pattern. 'How sophisticated you look, my darling,' she said.

'Better than my horrible school uniform,' said Amelie, 'I quite want to be like Elizabeth Taylor. She's been in London, you know, but Maman wouldn't let me go up to see her.' She then noticed Martin hovering uncertainly behind Beattie and frowned. 'Who's this?'

Martin stepped forward, holding out his hand. 'I am Martin Huber and I am charmed to meet you.'

Amelie looked at Martin's hand, then a smile spread

across her face. She took it. 'Lovely to meet you, Martin. Are you Beattie's new beau? No, you can't be, you're too young.'

'Amelie.' That was so typical of her sister. Opened her mouth without thinking.

Martin smiled. 'I am a friend. I mean, Beattie is my friend; she has rescued me.'

'Like a puppy?'

Martin nodded solemnly. 'A little like a puppy, yes.'

'Martin needs somewhere to stay,' said Beattie briskly. 'Maman said she didn't mind.'

'Beatrice.' Her mother stood in the doorway, the light from inside creating a halo around her. Beattie suppressed a smile. 'I trust your journey was satisfactory. I apologise for not meeting you, but with petrol rationing we have to be careful what journeys we make.'

Beattie picked up her case and walked towards her. 'Maman.' She kissed her on both cheeks. 'We had a lovely journey with Wilf.' She couldn't ever remember a time either of her parents had greeted her at the station.

'Thank you for coming,' her *maman* whispered in her ear, her voice breaking slightly.

'Oh, Maman.' Beattie was saddened. Poor Maman. 'This is Martin, Maman; he's the friend I told you about who needs somewhere to stay for a few days.'

Maman stared at Martin as a strange expression flitted across her face. Beattie recognised it as loss, but then her *maman* smiled and spread out her arms. 'Of course, of course. There is no problem. We have plenty of spare rooms. And it will be nice to have more young people around. Come in, all of you.'

'You don't say that to me, Maman,' said Amelie, pouting.

'You are a problem, my lovely daughter.' She stroked her younger daughter's hair, then ushered them all in.

Later, after a supper of roast chicken (poor Evangeline's egg-laying life had come to an end, Maman said carelessly) and potatoes, Beattie and her mother were sitting in the drawing room, the radio murmuring in the background and the wooden shutters closed against the island's cold and damp. A fire burnt in the grate, casting a dancing light on the faded leaves and flowers of the wallpaper. Her father had returned to his study to work. An important project in Norwich, he'd told them over supper. A chance to design something other than standard post-war housing. He didn't wish to be disturbed. Her mother had looked resigned to his absence. Amelie had gone up to her room – she had homework to do, she said, resentful that despite her escape from school they had sent her work to complete. Martin had retired to bed, scrupulously polite in his thanks for her mother's hospitality. Beattie tried to relax, but it was difficult. Even here, at home, she was playing a role; she couldn't let her guard down.

Maman was sitting under the Benson lamp-stand, embroidering yet another intricate sampler, silver thread glinting in the dim light of the room. Her glasses were on the end of her nose and she was frowning. Beattie saw new lines on her mother's face, more streaks of grey in her hair, and that she was squinting to see the stitches. Behind her, amongst the photographs of aunts and uncles and long-forgotten cousins that dotted the walls, was a framed photograph of Jack – he was standing in the orchard, laughing, looking over his shoulder. Above him the sky would have been blue with a few wisps of cloud. Taken before the war, it was Beattie's favourite picture of her brother and she wished she could remember what he was laughing at, who he was looking at. That was the trouble: she hadn't held on to the component pieces of the memory.

It was always when she was at home that she missed her brother the most. He had been so vital, so alive, and her parents had been alive, too. Now she felt as though the vibrancy had been sucked out of Maman and Father, that when Jack went missing, a glowing light went out of their lives. Out of her life too. It was what had spurred her on to be brave, take more chances. Until that terrible day when she'd had to be so brave it nearly destroyed her. However, sometimes she wondered why she and Amelie weren't enough for their parents.

'Tell me about the young man you brought home.' Her *maman* cut a piece of thread, before beginning to sew again. 'His sister died, you said.'

'Thank you for taking him in, Maman.' What she really meant was: thank you for not making a fuss when she'd turned up with Martin. Somehow Maman had sensed the boy was fragile. Sometimes her *maman* surprised her.

Soft cello music came from the wireless.

'Yes. Actually . . .' She hesitated. 'She was murdered.'

Her *maman* gave a sharp intake of breath. 'I see. And you brought him here because . . . ?'

Beattie sighed inwardly. How much should she say? But she should at least tell her *maman* what was going on. Some of it, anyway.

'His sister was murdered in the house of a friend of mine. I thought he needed somewhere where he could recover. Out of London. The countryside.' All at once she wondered if she was putting her family in danger by bringing him here. But no, she had been very careful and she owed it to Sofia to keep her brother safe. She hadn't been able to save other women, she hadn't been quick enough to save Sofia, but she could save Sofia's brother.

Her mother held out her work in front of her, examining it first one way, then another. She obviously judged it perfect, as she continued with her stitching.

'He has no other family?'

'No. None. They fled from persecution in Germany and then Poland before the war, and were living with their uncle until he died. Sofia was looking after Martin.'

'And their parents?'

Beattie shook her head. 'They don't know what happened to them, but I can only guess they died in one of the concentration camps.'

'I see.' Her mother selected another thread colour. 'It's good of you to help, Beattie, but you always had a strong sense of right and wrong.' Beattie felt a pang of guilt at her *maman*'s words. 'And this friend you talk about, anyone we know?'

Anyone interesting is what she meant.

'He's the son of a politician. A Conservative politician.'

'I see.' Her *maman* snipped a length of thread.

'It's nothing, Maman. A friend, that's all.'

'How disappointing.' The cello music swelled, then died down. 'I miss Jacques.' She threaded her needle.

'I know you do,' Beattie replied softly.

'Your father and I, we think of him every day.'

'So do I.' *Do you think of me every day?* She wanted to ask but dared not.

'You were inseparable as children. You used to get him into such scrapes.'

'I think he was the one getting me into scrapes,' Beattie laughed.

'Maybe.' Her mother smiled softly. 'Like the time he dared you to swing on a rope over the river and you fell in and he rescued you but neither of you said a word.'

'I didn't know you knew,' said Beattie.

Who had he been rescuing in France?

A small smile hovered on Maman's face. 'You think we didn't know what went on? What naughtiness you were getting up to? Naturally we did.'

'I should have realised.' A rare moment of intimacy with her *maman*.

'Maybe you will one day, when you have children of your own.'

'Maman,' said Beattie, a warning note in her voice.

'I know you don't like me to talk about it, my darling, but you are getting so old and will soon be left on the rocks.'

'On the shelf.'

'Pardon?'

'I'll be left on the shelf.'

'Precisely,' said her mother triumphantly.

Beattie sighed. Her mother was incorrigible.

'And it is not as though your job is anything, is it? All that typing.' Her *maman* was stabbing at her embroidery now. The subject of her daughter's inability to find a suitable suitor always made her angry. Beattie saw a tiny bubble of blood on the end of her *maman*'s finger.

'I'm teaching people to type better. To be good secretaries,' Beattie replied. She didn't want to be talking about her job, lying to her *maman*, not now, not at this time.

'Those years at Cambridge. At least you had something in your favour. Then.'

'I have brains but not looks, is that what you mean?' Beattie spoke mildly; she was long used to her *maman*'s disappointment that in looks she took after her paternal grandfather. At least, her *maman* had told her, an education would stand her in good stead and perhaps she could marry a learned professor. Jack had always told her she was strong. She enjoyed being strong.

'All that education and you waste it.'

'I don't think I'm wasting it, Maman.'

Her mother didn't reply.

The chimes of Big Ben came from the radio. Nine o'clock.

'You should get a television,' said Beattie. 'It would be nice for you in the evenings, when you're on your own.' She said it gently, not wanting Maman to take offence. But she saw her mother's shoulders stiffen.

'I am not lonely.'

'No, but Father—'

'Your father has his work to do.'

'I know, but—'

'Leave it, Beatrice.' Her mother's voice held a warning note, but Beattie couldn't keep quiet.

'He neglects you, Maman.' She thought about supper, and how her father had been reading as he ate, how he barely said a word to any of them.

'Don't you dare say that, Beatrice. Don't you dare. Your father is worth ten of his brother Howard, the man you seem to idolise.' Her mother almost hissed her brother-in-law's name. Her father's younger brother had helped fund her three years at Cambridge. Her *maman* always referred to him as '*le mouton noir de famille*'. Always with a moue of disapproval.

'I don't idolise him, Maman. I don't understand why you don't like him.'

Her *maman* sniffed. 'It doesn't matter. But your father, he is driven. He wants to help people.'

Beattie knew from the set of her *maman*'s mouth that she wasn't going to get anything out of her mother on that particular subject. Beattie suspected it had something to do with the fact her uncle was a womaniser and an adventurer – so different to her father.

They sat in silence for several minutes.

'Tell me about Amelie.' Beattie wished she had something to do with her hands.

Her *maman* put the embroidery on her lap. 'Ah, Amelie. Yes. I don't know what to do with that child. She is so wilful.'

'What has she done now?'

There followed a story about Amelie and chickens and a fox, all of which sounded both amusing and irresponsible but didn't get away from the fact that Amelie had been sent home from her third school in three years. 'But,' said her *maman*, 'they have given her schoolwork to do so there is hope they will have her back. She has too much spirit.'

'But this is a good thing, surely?'

126

'Is it?'

It is, Maman, it is. But Beattie only thought this; she didn't say it. 'I'll come back more often,' she said, as the soothing tones of Alistair Cooke and his *Letter From America* began on the radio.

Her mother picked up her embroidery again. 'There's no need.'

Tiredness washed over Beattie. If she wasn't careful, she would crumble. After all the emotions of the last few days she had hoped to gain some solace and comfort from coming home. It wasn't to be.

Her *maman* carried on stitching, her face wearing her habitual frown.

'I'm sorry I'm a disappointment to you, but I can't be Jack. And I have a job and a life to lead and so has Amelie. Maybe she has some idea of what she would like to do when she leaves school.'

'You're a bad influence on her.'

'You wanted me to talk to her.' Beattie despaired; could she never do anything right?

'I want her to be a lady. To marry well. That's what I want you to say to her. But perhaps it was too much to hope. She doesn't care about me and your father.' She threaded her needle, squinting in the bad light.

'Maman—'

'And I know you aren't Jacques.' This was said quietly. And if Beattie hadn't known better, she would have said there were tears in her *maman*'s eyes.

As Beattie passed Amelie's room on her way to bed, she saw a sliver of light under the door. She knocked and went in.

It never took Amelie long to stamp her presence in her bedroom. Clothes littered the floor, and her dressing table was a jumble of bracelets and brooches and lipsticks and nail polish. Beattie was glad her father would never venture into Amelie's room – she couldn't even contemplate the extent of his temper if he saw the make-up and jewellery Amelie owned. She remembered her last major argument with him had been when she had come down to breakfast wearing crimson nail polish. He'd told her to remove it, telling her only tarts wore polish that colour. She'd refused. The encounter had left her shaking. But perhaps he wasn't so harsh with his younger daughter. Beattie hoped that was the case.

Amelie was sitting cross-legged on her bed reading a magazine. *Picturegoer*, with Robert Mitchum on the cover.

Amelie scrambled to hide it under her quilt, pulling her schoolbooks towards her. Beattie smiled.

'It's all right, Amelie, I won't tell.'

'It's just . . .' Amelie pointed at her books.

'I know, schoolwork is boring. But important.' How dreary she sounded.

'Why?'

Beattie sighed. She had thought, like millions of other women, that the war had made a difference, that they could be seen as equals with men. It hadn't worked out that way, though. The thing was, she wanted to encourage Amelie to be independent, to follow her dreams, not to be hobbled by a backward-looking society, by the dreariness of the aftermath of war. If only she could tell Amelie about what she really did, that there was excitement to be had.

'So you can make a living, stand on your own two

feet. Whatever Maman and Father say, you don't have to depend on a man to get by. It's good to have money to buy yourself freedom and education.'

'Do you think you'll ever marry?'

'One day, maybe. But it has to be the right man.'

'And it has to be for love.' Amelie was decisive.

Beattie looked at her sister, so grown up in some ways, but still a child. And yet she herself had only been a year or so older when she had become a FANY. She had grown up very fast then. She sighed inwardly. 'It would be helpful.' That was the best she could do.

'I'm pleased you're home, Beattie, even though I know Maman begged you to come and sort me out.'

Beattie laughed. 'I don't think there's any "sorting you out" that either I or anyone could do. You are a strong young woman, Amelie, and I am very proud of you.'

'Then why isn't Maman?' For a moment she looked like the child she was. 'She says I will never be as successful as Jack if I don't work hard. Beattie?'

'Yes?'

'I don't remember Jack very well.' Her voice was quiet, and Beattie detected a tremble in it. 'If it wasn't for the photographs in the house, I'm frightened I wouldn't remember his face.'

'I find it hard sometimes,' Beattie admitted. 'And I try to hear his voice in my head and fail miserably.' She smiled.

'Maman and Father loved him the best, didn't they? That's why they're always so sad.'

Beattie's heart contracted. 'No, sweetheart. It's just that when someone you love dies you keep them in a special place in your heart. And of course, they can never do anything to upset or hurt you so they become immortal in their goodness, do you understand?'

Beattie wasn't sure she had explained properly, particularly as Amelie was, in fact, right. Jack had always been, and still was, the favourite of the family. Not only because he was male, but because he was strong and kind and funny. He'd been able to defuse arguments, particularly when their mother was impatient or imperious towards their father. He was the golden boy. Destined for Cambridge and then to follow Father into architecture. He could paint, take photographs and write beautifully. He was excellent at sports. When he was lost somewhere in France her parents had been devastated. And that's when the house on the island, which had once been filled with laughter and light, became dark and unhappy.

'He laughed a lot,' said Beattie. 'He had one of those laughs that made you want to laugh with him.'

'I think I remember that.'

'And he loved animals and birds – all sorts of wildlife. We used to go down to the mudflats and dig up ragworms and look for beetles.'

'Eww,' said Amelie.

'He loved you when you were born. And when you could walk he wanted to bring you along on our adventures. I'm afraid I was the one who wanted to leave you behind.'

'Oh, Beattie.'

Beattie grimaced. 'I know, a rather horrid older sister.'

'Hmm.' There was a silence. Amelie bit her lip, ran her finger over the cover of one of her schoolbooks listlessly. 'I do get lonely, you know. I have friends at school but sometimes I want Maman and Father to notice me.'

'Is that why you do the things you do at school? To get noticed?'

Amelie nodded. 'It's like being an only child in some ways. And Maman's thoughts are always with Jack.' Her sister said this in not a self-pitying way, but matter-of-factly, which made it worse. Beattie hugged her close.

'You can be whatever you want to be.'

'A movie star?'

'You can be anything you want to be,' said Beattie again with even more fervour, hoping it would be true for Amelie, despite the setbacks she was bound to encounter. 'If you want to be a movie star, show Maman and Father that you can work hard and then maybe you could go to drama school.'

'Drama school.' Amelie glowed. 'Is that possible, Beattie?'

'Anything is possible for you, darling girl.'

'When I'm a movie star,' said Amelie, retrieving her magazine from under the quilt, 'I shall come and see you in your miserable little flat in London. I shall arrive in my Rolls-Royce, encased in furs and dripping with diamonds. And I shall have two, no, three, handsome young men at my beck and call – one of them might even be Ronald Reagan – and I will take you out for tea at The Savoy, or The Ritz.'

'Claridge's?'

Amelie clapped her hands, laughing. 'Or Claridge's.'

Beattie kissed Amelie on her forehead. 'I look forward to that day, my darling. Especially being taken out for tea by my sister. And now, I'll leave you to your schoolwork. Or your magazine.'

Amelie smiled. 'Thank you, Beattie.'

Beattie closed the door behind her, wondering if she had helped Amelie at all, and was suddenly assailed by a memory of loud and violent voices. Jack and her father arguing. She remembered she had been walking up the stairs when she'd heard them from her father's study, and had seen Jack emerging from the room, pausing to shout one more thing at his father before slamming the door behind him. He had rushed out of the house. Sometime, during that night, Jack had returned, collected his things, and left to fight the war. Beattie never saw him again.

She still hated him for leaving in that way.

And she could still remember his exact words to their father, and the hatred on his face. 'You have ruined my life, Father. There is no point any more. But rest assured, I shall ruin yours.'

What had he meant by that?

CHAPTER TWELVE

Corrigan sat in the corner of the pub nursing his pint of Guinness and listening to the rebel songs sung by his countrymen to the sound of the fiddle and drum. He hoped no policemen would walk by and hear the songs, or, if they did, they wouldn't realise what they were hearing. He liked this pub; he felt safe here, amongst people he knew, amongst fellow Irishmen. It was nothing fancy. Smoke hung in drifts beneath a ceiling painted brown by the tar of thousands, millions of cigarettes. The walls were lined with rusty-red button-backed banquettes, many of which were worn shiny with use. Rickety chairs clustered around tables marked with tacky rings and sporting ancient beer mats. The landlord, Danny Mulligan, ran a tight ship, not allowing too much drunkenness and brawling, which was a tall order when dealing with these men, some of whom were far away from loved ones and had put in a hard day's work on the building sites. Homesick men working in what was often a bloody environment. For some, the Wagon and Horses was a home from home when they were working on the lump.

He took a deep draught of his pint, wiping away the

creamy foam moustache from his top lip. God, that was good. He took his tobacco tin out of his pocket and began to roll himself a cigarette. That Beattie Cavendish was an odd one. All frumpy clothes and shoes and lip, yet he had felt there was much more to her than that. That she was hiding her true self. The image did not ring true. Cambridge. Bloody hell, Cambridge. That was a thing. And he thought about the way she had handled herself – evening gown and all – at the Bowens' house when she was attacked by that murdering scum. Now that was what he called classy.

But she didn't half talk a lot of shit.

He moistened the cigarette paper with his tongue, picking a stray shred of tobacco off his lip, then lit it. What was he to make of her? And her gallivanting around with that dim pretty boy, Ashley Bowen. Sure, but he had looked into the whole Bowen family before he took the job. Even had a word with a policeman friend of his and learnt that Edwina and Ralph Bowen had been married for some thirty years, that he was a bright politician with a great future. There were no untoward incidences in any of the family's lives. The only sour note he had found was the refusal of Ralph Bowen to convert to Catholicism when they married. That must have been difficult for Mrs Bowen. Probably Ralph Bowen thought it might harm his career. Selfish prig.

It still rankled as to why Edwina Bowen had not given Corrigan a reason for engaging him to follow her husband. Often the wives who came to ask him to do that very thing were weepy or angry. Not cool and detached as Mrs Bowen had been. And all those letters, each of which he'd been told to destroy as soon as he'd read it. It was a crying shame to see that expensive paper go up in flames. He'd told her of the White Pearl Club and his visits to the church. When he had relayed information to her on the telephone, her voice had also been calm and controlled. Corrigan had reached the conclusion Edwina Bowen was a woman wound as tight as a spring and perfectly capable of handling herself. He imagined the household to be unloving, but he could be wrong.

Perhaps he was being unfair and just couldn't understand it because he came from a large boisterous family with six brothers and one sister who were brought up by a strict ma and a loving pa in a small stone house on the Atlantic coast of Ireland, where a fine mist was the norm and dolphins could be seen playing amongst the waves. He could not conceive of rattling around in a large, cold London house with nannies and housekeepers and servants.

He drew smoke deep into his lungs. That was good. What was Beattie Cavendish's story? She was right, of course, he knew she was right, that Sofia Huber's death should not be treated as insignificant. There had been too many of those – insignificant deaths. He sighed. And she had not been shocked when he told her about the White Pearl Club and who were its clients. Ladies of the night and homosexuals. She had raised an eyebrow and said, 'Someone for everyone, then?'

And who had Ralph Bowen been visiting? A whore or homosexual?

He had to admit he didn't know. That had not been in his remit.

He stretched out his legs, feeling the ache deep in his bones.

Draining his glass, he elbowed his way to the bar for another. When he sat down, he took the book of matches he had found under Sofia Huber's hand out of his pocket and looked at it again. He was glad he had not left it with her body – he was sure that Dicky from the Yard would have managed to lose it as a piece of evidence. He turned it over and over in his hands. The number. He should telephone that number again to see who it belonged to and perhaps someone would answer it this time. The question was, why did Sofia Huber have such a book of matches? The other question was, had she telephoned that number? And yet another question – his head was beginning to hurt, though that was more likely due to the two whiskies he had drunk before the Guinness – had Sofia Huber ever visited the White Pearl?

The singing was becoming raucous, with a lot of friendly joshing going on. Beer slopped from glasses to make the floor even more sticky. The cigarette smoke was thicker, almost choking. Corrigan rolled and lit another of his own. He knew how quickly tempers could flare and the good humour turn into fighting.

He finished his pint, picked up his coat and put on his hat. No time like the present.

'Hey, Corrigan.'

He looked in the direction of the voice. His leg was stiff, aching. He needed to walk, to exercise it. He kept his face still. Finn McNulty was raising his pint. Known as one of the toughest Irish lads in London. Always up for a brawl.

'Come on, boy. Share a pint with us.'

McNulty's friends flanked him. Like McNulty, their noses showed at least one break apiece, and each of the three of them had a jagged scar from a broken glass or bottle somewhere on his face. The hands that held pints were meaty, calloused, working men's hands.

'What's stoppin' you?' There was an edge to McNulty's voice.

Corrigan held his hands up. 'I would if I could, Finn. You know that. But I've got to be somewhere.' It made him smile to think what the man would do if he told him he was visiting a club catering for men and women who had very different tastes to McNulty's. At least, he presumed so. Though if there was one thing he'd learnt over the last ten years it was not to make assumptions about fellow human beings.

'Sure you have. You can spare five minutes for a drink with friends, can't you?'

Corrigan walked over to the bar where McNulty and his friends were standing, putting his hand in his pocket. He fished out two florins and slapped them down on the bar. 'I have to go, but here, buy yourselves a drink.' He tried not to wince as he thought of what he'd have to go without the next week.

McNulty scooped up the money. 'Now, there's generous of ya.' He turned to his friends. 'Wouldn't you say so, lads?'

'Aye,' came the chorus.

Corrigan touched the brim of his hat as he left the bar, wondering if the Irishman was in a protection racket with the gangsters that prowled London since the end of the war, and concluding he probably was in one way or another.

The night was cold and the sky clear for once. Corrigan pulled up the collar of his coat as he walked. The streets were crowded, men spilling out of pubs. Women too. A couple of women whistled to him. He laughed and carried on his way. The stench of decay mixed with the night air filled his nostrils and vast swathes of land were still rubble from the bombing this part of London had received.

He reached Clapham South Tube and bought his ticket for Tottenham Court Road before heading to the platform.

Corrigan arrived at Dean Street, which was teeming with life, and stood across the road, watching people go in and come out of the White Pearl Club just as he had many times before when waiting for Ralph Bowen. He rolled and lit a cigarette. His plan was to try and get in, be a visitor for the evening. See for himself what went on inside and perhaps ask about Sofia Huber.

He threw his cigarette down and ground it under the heel of his shoe. He should take more time to smoke a whole one sometime, not waste it.

He crossed the road.

As he stepped onto the opposite pavement, he was grabbed by his elbow.

'You don't want to hang around here,' said a voice in his ear. 'Come with me. Now.'

Corrigan was so surprised that he fell into step with the man beside him. 'Who are you?'

'It doesn't matter, but you don't want to be here, trust me. Walk quickly. Don't run. Don't look. Don't draw attention to us.' The man's face was covered by a navy-blue scarf.

Suddenly there was a screech of brakes, and Corrigan looked back over his shoulder. Four policemen tumbled out of a black Wolseley, then there were ear-piercing whistles as more bobbies rushed across the road, feet pounding, hands on helmets, truncheons at the ready. They all piled down the steps into the basement housing the White Pearl Club.

'I told you,' the man hissed, 'don't look round. Keep going.'

Corrigan and the man carried on walking quickly down the road. Then a whistle sounded behind them.

'Oi! You. Stop.' The whistle again. Heavy footsteps coming closer.

'Bugger,' murmured the man. He gripped Corrigan harder. 'We've got to run. Now.'

Corrigan responded to the urgency in the man's tone, and to the sound of footsteps pounding the pavement behind him and began to run.

'This way. Quick.'

The man led him down a side alley that smelt of piss and rotting vegetables.

They darted around rubbish bins and old cardboard boxes that reared up out of the dark until they emerged at the other end and rounded a corner, only to be faced with a padlocked gate into private gardens.

'Quick, shimmy over the gate.'

Corrigan heard the sound of metal falling on concrete and some loud swearing – the copper hadn't managed to avoid one of the bins.

The man pulled himself up and over the locked gate effortlessly, then ran into a dark patch of shrub.

Shimmy? Bloody hell. With his dodgy leg and hip? Negotiating the bins and boxes had been hard enough. Still, no other way round it if the stranger was to be believed. Corrigan threw himself at the gate, managing to grab the metal at the top with one hand, then scrabbled over in a less than gainly fashion. He dropped to the other side and raced towards the shrubs.

The man put his fingers to his lips and pointed. Corrigan saw the copper rattling the gate of the gardens, but he was panting hard and showed no inclination to try and climb the railings to continue the chase. The copper looked hard through the bars. Corrigan and his rescuer stayed perfectly still, although Corrigan's leg was sending shooting pains up his body and into his skull. Eventually the copper turned away.

They waited for five more minutes, before the man led Corrigan across a well-manicured lawn that was so perfect it must have escaped becoming an allotment during the war. The flower beds were clear of weeds and the shrubs had been pruned.

'I know,' said the man, seeing Corrigan looking around. 'A garden for the toffs.'

It was certainly a cut above most of the gardens he saw, which struggled against weeds and neglect – a bit like so many of the houses and flats that hadn't been blown apart by bombs or builders. Skeletons of houses. Houses that had families trying to get by. Families where the widows had aged prematurely, or the husbands had come home damaged. More than three years since VE Day and the city was still ravaged by poverty. Austerity, that was its given name.

They reached the other side, and the man made short work of the gate in the railings there. Corrigan sighed, then hauled himself up and over the gate for the second time, his arms, shoulders and legs all protesting.

'Come on,' said the man. For a moment Corrigan considered telling the man to go to hell, but he wanted to know who he was and how he had known there was going to be a raid on the club. Corrigan hurried to catch him up until they came to a café with steamy windows, making it impossible to see inside properly. The man steered him inside.

The café was warm and damp with the smell of people who had little to lose. The tables were covered in paper cloths and the aroma of fried food and burnt toast hung in the air. Several patrons littered the room; most had the haunted look of people who had nowhere else to go to get a warm drink and something cheap to put in their stomachs. The man led him to a table and Corrigan sat.

'I'll go and get a couple of teas, shall I?' said the man, unwinding the scarf that had covered much of his face.

'It's you.' Corrigan sat disbelieving as the man revealed himself to be the one who had spoken to him outside the club the last time he had followed Ralph Bowen.

The man grinned. His cheeks were rouged this time, and he was wearing red lipstick. He held out his hand to Corrigan. 'Kit,' he said.

Corrigan took his hand and shook it. A firm – but not too firm – grip.

'Patrick Corrigan. How do you do.'

Kit grinned again. Corrigan could see what a strikingly beautiful man he was with his high cheekbones and wide brown eyes. His blond, slicked-back hair was slightly too long. Rakish, Corrigan thought. Was that the right word for a man like him?

'So, shall I?' Kit said.

'What?'

'Get you a tea?'

'Er – yes please.'

'And egg and chips? Flo does a wonderful plate of egg and chips.'

'Fine.' Corrigan felt as though he was in a film, or on the stage. Five minutes earlier he'd been standing on the pavement getting ready to go into the White Pearl Club, and now he was in this café talking to Kit. Whoever he was. 'Though . . .' He patted his pockets and brought out some coins. 'Perhaps I should buy it for you, being as you saved me from a prison cell.'

Kit stayed his arm. 'Nah. You're all right. This way you'll owe me even more.' He winked at Corrigan before going over to the counter.

He came back with two strong mugs of tea and set them down on the table.

'So, Patrick Corrigan, you seem neither gay nor in need of a woman, so what have you been doing lurking outside the White Pearl Club?' Kit grinned as he stirred three spoons of sugar into his drink.

Corrigan was curious. 'How did you know there was going to be a raid on the club?'

Kit laughed. 'Coppers were hiding in the empty offices opposite. They'd been there for a few days. I'd clocked them and knew it was a matter of time. And they like to raid the club every so often anyway. They reckon there's too much sex and stimulants going on in there.'

'And is there?'

Kit raised an eyebrow. 'Maybe. But you haven't answered my original question.'

The café door opened, letting in a cold blast of air. Corrigan looked up nervously. A cowardly part of him didn't want to be caught here, in this odd little café, with Kit. But it was only a bedraggled man, wanting a hot drink.

Another laugh from Kit. 'Don't get yourself in a pickle. No one's going to come in here and nab you. Coppers leave this place well alone. I think they're terrified of Flo.' He nodded towards the woman behind the counter who was serving the bedraggled man. She was large, her apron stretched tight across her bosom and stomach. Her face was unsmiling. Her bare arms looked strong – she would beat McNulty in an arm-wrestling competition, thought Corrigan.

'I see what you mean,' he said. He drank some of his tea. Strong and hot.

'She looks after me, though, does Flo. Makes sure I'm fed and watered.' Kit gave Flo a little flutter of his fingers. 'I like it here. It's safe.'

The bedraggled man took a seat in the corner, Flo went back to cooking and the smell of frying filled the air. Corrigan's mouth watered.

'And?'

Corrigan sighed. 'I'm a private detective.'

'Thought as much.' Kit leant back, satisfied.

'A client asked me to follow her husband. So I did.'

'And he led you to the club.'

Corrigan nodded.

'Who is this man? We have all sorts at the club. Lords, ladies, politicians, boxers, poets, writers. A real rich variety.' He chuckled.

Corrigan took his tobacco pouch out of his pocket,

together with the cigarette papers. 'Would you . . . ?'

Kit nodded. 'I have many vices, and smoking is but one of them.'

Corrigan nodded and rolled them each a cigarette. 'I can't tell you that. Confidentiality, I'm afraid. But . . .' He considered his companion.

Kit leant forward, eyes glittering as if waiting for some juicy gossip. 'Yes?'

At that moment, Flo stamped over with their plates of food. Corrigan put the cigarettes down and kept quiet until after the woman had gone.

'Has anyone called Sofia Huber been to the club?'

Kit frowned as he put his unlit cigarette by the side of his plate, drowning his chips with tomato ketchup before tucking in. 'With that sort of name she must be foreign?'

'That's right. A German Jew. About twenty-five years old. Came over here before the war.' Corrigan took a more modest amount of ketchup. The chips were, surprisingly, not greasy and the fried egg cooked as he liked it. He dipped a chip in the yolk.

Kit shook his head. 'I don't recall anyone with that name. But then, contrary to what you might think, I don't often go to the White Pearl, only when I need a bit of, uh, sustenance, I suppose you would call it.' He winked at Corrigan. 'Why do you want to know about this lady?'

'It's to do with a case I'm looking into. It's of little consequence, just an avenue I'm exploring.' Corrigan shrugged dismissively. He did not want Kit to become too interested.

Kit's eyes glittered. 'How exciting. And don't give me that flannel; there must be a reason.' He slurped his tea and put his knife and fork together, patting his stomach. 'Flo does wonderful chips.'

Corrigan nodded, draining the last of his mug of tea. 'I would say so.'

'Anyway.' Kit pouted. 'I can see you're going to keep schtum.'

'There's nothing to tell.' Corrigan wiped his mouth with the paper serviette, then screwed it up and left it by the side of his plate. He picked up his cigarette and lit it, also offering a light to Kit. 'She may or may not have something to do with the club, but it was an avenue I wanted to explore.' Corrigan was careful to keep the talk about Sofia in the present tense. He stood, taking some coins out of his pocket that he put on the table. 'Please, I insist you take some money.' Then he handed Kit a rather dog-eared business card. 'If you do remember anything, please write to me. Or telephone me if you can.'

'I will, Patrick. It was nice to meet you.' His sudden, wide smile lit up his face, making him look years younger. Underneath the lipstick and the rouge he probably was no more than twenty. The same age as many of Corrigan's friends who died on the slopes of Monte Cassino. 'And maybe next time you could tell me how you got those scars on your face and the empty eye socket. And the limp.'

Usually Corrigan felt a mixture of anger and embarrassment when someone asked about his scars, but Kit had asked him as if it were the most natural thing in the world.

'Maybe I will. But there's nothing to tell, only the usual.'

Kit nodded. 'The war. I thought as much.'

'Take care, won't you,' said Patrick, all at once feeling

responsible for the boy's welfare. He blinked. He had a strange feeling, almost a vision, and he had learnt over the years to take notice of the feelings or visions. Something to do with being the seventh son of a seventh son, his ma used to tell him. For years he had laughed off any suggestions of mystical powers, saying he was using his instinct or had a lucky guess, until the vision that had predicted the death of several of his comrades in battle.

'Don't worry about me,' said Kit. 'I'm like a cat. I've got at least nine lives. You don't mind if I stay and have a bun do you? No point in going to the club tonight.'

'Or for a few nights, judging by the number of policemen who piled in.'

'True. Flo'll look after me, won't you, Flo?' He waggled his fingers in a sort of wave.

Flo glared at them both.

'She's a pussycat,' said Kit. 'And has got a heart of gold underneath that austere appearance.'

'I hope so. And remember—'

Kit held up Corrigan's card between two fingers. 'I'll telephone you if I think of anything. Maybe I'll telephone you anyway.' He winked again, knowingly.

Corrigan laughed, but as he headed for the door, he couldn't shake off the feeling, *the vision*, that something bad was going to happen.

CHAPTER THIRTEEN

Sunday dawned cold and clear, the sky was a paintbox blue, and Beattie could smell the crisp air that brought with it the faint tang of brine.

She rose early and, leaving the house by the flight of steps descending from the terrace to the sunken garden, found Martin wandering around the gravel paths.

'Did you sleep well?' she asked him.

'Perfectly, thank you. There is little noise. I think I heard a fox and a rabbit. The rabbit was squealing; that wasn't so good.'

'No, not so good. I'm going for a walk; would you like to join me?'

'I think not,' he said. 'I will take the air, admire your father's gardens and prepare for breakfast, particularly the fountain, I think.'

Beattie looked at the three circles of stone on top of one another spouting water high into the air. 'Yes, one of Father's favourites.' She patted Martin's arm. 'I'll see you later.'

She crossed the lawn, wanting to find the path that led out to the marshland when she heard her name being called. *Maman*. She turned.

Her mother, who was wearing a cornflower-blue dress that flattered her figure, was waving. Her father was standing next to her, looking at his watch. Beattie's heart sank as she made her way over to them.

'Are you coming with us to church, *ma chérie*?' There was a flicker of disapproval or perhaps disappointment in her face as she looked at Beattie, who was dressed in trousers and an old jumper with a tatty jacket thrown over the top. There was not a strand of hair on her mother's head out of place, and she had on her customary face of lipstick and powder. She smelt of Chanel. As always, Beattie felt dowdy in her presence. 'Young Martin slept well, I understand.'

'Virginie, we must go.' Her father, his shock of white hair as thick and luxurious as it had been twenty years ago, looked at Beattie down his patrician nose. He brushed an invisible speck of dirt off his coat. 'Please go and change, Beattie.'

Beattie smiled, wanting to defuse the tense atmosphere that had arrived with her parents. 'Actually, I thought I'd go for a walk,' she said carefully. 'It's a lovely day for once and I would like the fresh air. Better than London's grime.' She smiled, hoping her father was not going to argue.

Too much to hope. His anger was quick to rise, and had been so since Jack was lost.

'We always go to church on a Sunday, Beatrice,' said her father, tapping his foot. 'You know that and when you are under my roof I expect you to do as we ask. Amelie will be down shortly.'

'Father, please understand I haven't been to church for a long time.' All at once she felt weary, and any new spring of optimism was leaching out of her body. Her father knew her feelings about God – any god – ranged from indifference to anger, and had done for a number of years.

Her *maman* nodded, and suddenly to Beattie she looked tired, a little defeated perhaps. 'Thomas. Please.' Her mother's look was pleading.

A vein throbbed above her father's left eye. 'Virginie. Come. Now.' He stalked off without another word.

Beattie's temper boiled over. 'Maman, how can you endure this?'

'I don't know what you mean.' Her mother had grown pale.

'The loneliness. Father. His work comes before everything. He doesn't talk to you, and when he does he gives you orders.' She realised she had raised her voice.

The sound of the slap echoed in the air. 'Enough. Enough. You talk about "enduring". You do not know the meaning of the word. You don't understand. How can you understand? How can you understand about love?' Her *maman* was shaking as she turned away from Beattie.

Beattie, shocked, her hand to her cheek, watched as her *maman* followed her father.

'Wait, Maman,' she called. 'What did Father and Jack argue about, the night he left?' Suddenly, urgently, she wanted to know.

Her *maman* hesitated for a moment but didn't turn around. 'It is the past, Beattie,' she said, then walked on.

She gritted her teeth. She would not give in to the rawness at the back of her throat. No, she didn't understand, that was the problem. Perhaps she didn't want to. But what she had said was true. Father, who had always worked so hard, who had always been a distant figure with a somewhat cold demeanour, had become more so since the war, since Jack had been lost.

She mentally shook herself, then began to follow the lane from the house down to the slatted boardwalk that led to the edge of the estuary, the air now briny and smelling distinctly of mud. Waders picked their way through the water, oblivious to the cold. She watched as a spoonbill lifted its beak into the air over and over again, gulping down the shrimps it had found stranded in a pool. An egret, its snow-white plumage standing out like a cloud, took off into the sky. Nature rooted her. Coming home was always a mixed experience, but to come here, to the edge of the estuary, was soothing to her soul. It was here where her memories were some of the happiest. Her memories of Jack some of the happiest.

Walking on, she found an old wooden bench, its slats worn and cracked. She sat down, breathed deeply, closed her eyes and let the gentle sounds of the birds and the water wash over her. She would not think of Maman and Father and the argument with Jack. One day she would find out what it had been about. One day, she would understand. Perhaps her mother was right about one thing, that she didn't understand about love.

She pushed those thoughts away and thought instead about Ashley Bowen. There was the sort of man she would not normally become involved with. He was too weak, too entitled; he thought the world owed him a living. But then he did not want for anything, having been indulged by both of his parents, particularly his mother, for too long. He was also vague about his father, seeming to know very little about his work when she had gently probed him. Trying to prise information out of him was like trying to get a flea off a dog. Perhaps that was because there was nothing to say. Maybe the Russians were talking about someone else, or something else. Perhaps Bowen's position as Shadow Foreign Secretary was enough to cause interest from the Soviets without there being any other sinister reason.

She sighed. There was a reason she had been asked to do the job – the surveillance – so she would continue doing it to her utmost ability.

Then there was Sofia. What had she done, or what had she seen to merit such violence towards her? And Anthony Cooper had told her categorically to stay away from the whole 'mess'. She couldn't do that. And wasn't it strange that Sofia had a book of matches from the White Pearl Club, the very same place her employer had visited more than once?

It was all a conundrum.

She wasn't sure how long she'd been sitting there when she felt she was being watched. It was like a trickle of water down her back, the awareness. She sat quite still before standing up and walking on. Slowly, she turned, and saw someone in a dark coat and hat hurrying away along the boardwalk and back towards the lane. She went after the figure, but they picked up their pace steadily, not stopping, not turning around.

'Stop!' she shouted, without any great hope that whoever it was would.

The figure broke into a run, and soon reached a car that was parked by the hedgerow. They jumped in and roared away.

Beattie stood, hands on hips, watching the car disappear down the lane. A dark coat and hat. A car. They seemed to turn up everywhere. She frowned. But who was it? Why were they following her? How had whoever it was known she was here, on Saltergate Island? She had not been followed to Liverpool Street; she had made sure of that, with her and Martin taking a taxi to Sloane Square, getting off at Great Portland Street and heading to Oxford Street to change lines. On the way, they'd hurried through a small grocer's shop, leaving through a back entrance – much to the bemusement of the shopkeeper. Eventually they had ended up at Liverpool Street station. She surely would have noticed if she'd had a tail by then, but still she had been alert and watchful at Liverpool Street and Colchester. So her follower today had to be someone who knew she was coming here. But who? Only Corrigan knew she was coming to the island.

Unsettled, she made her way home.

Her parents and Amelie were still at church when she arrived back at the house, though wonderful smells were coming from the kitchen thanks to Mrs Barnaby, who came and cooked for them on Sundays. She found Martin sitting in the drawing room by the fire, staring into its depths.

'Did you have a good breakfast, Martin?' she said.

He looked up. 'I did, thank you. And now I am smelling lunch. Your family enjoys food, I think.'

'They were lucky during the war living in the country.'

'Sofia would have loved it here.'

'She was a good sister.'

'Yes. She was. I wish I knew . . .' He shook his head. 'Maybe we'll never find out who murdered her. She thought she was safe, you know that? After Leipzig, after Danzig, she thought she was safe.'

Both Beattie and Martin continued gazing into the fire. Beattie picked up the poker, thrusting it into the middle to move the coals so it burnt more brightly.

'Martin, did Sofia ever go to a club called the White Pearl Club?'

'No.'

His answer came too fast, too hard.

Beattie looked him. His lips were pressed tightly together and his knee was shaking. He was also twisting the fingers of one hand with the other. Again. 'Martin,' she pressed, 'are you sure?'

The flames of the fire leapt and turned, making dancing shapes above the coals. 'Why don't you go to church?' Martin asked, without warning.

'I lost my faith in a god a long time ago. It would be hypocritical of me to go.'

'I see. You're a good person, Beattie.' He sighed from the bottom of his soul. 'I go to the synagogue but I think we have been abandoned. I think Sofia was abandoned, otherwise how could she have died in such a terrible way and the person who did it has got away with it?'

'They haven't got away with it,' said Beattie with determination. 'Corrigan and I are doing our utmost to bring her killer to justice.' Oh, that sounded so grand, she hoped she could live up to it.

Martin nodded. He looked at the floor. 'Yes,' he said finally. 'Sofia worked at the White Pearl Club, as a waitress.

Only occasionally, to, how do I say it? Make ends meet. And to save a little money to go back to Germany to find out what happened to our parents.' He looked directly at her. 'But I think she met someone there.' He took a deep breath and worried his bottom lip. 'Someone she liked.'

Connections.

CHAPTER FOURTEEN

Corrigan spent a restless night on his camp bed. He was haunted by a strange dream of men with no faces and who entered his bedroom and leant over him. In his dream he could smell sweat and blood. He watched as his office door opened and faceless men entered carrying—

He awoke with a start, the dream in his head and the conviction he had dreamt of the future. Something bad was going to happen. He knew he should take notice of it. When he was younger, he had dismissed his ma's stories about the seventh son of a seventh son. How they had second sight, how some were healers. He liked to think of himself as a pragmatist. That was until he dreamt he was playing poker with seven comrades just before the Battle of Monte Cassino and he saw five of their faces dissolve into nothingness. He forgot the dream until after the battle, when those same five comrades didn't come home. Since then, Corrigan had tried to listen to what his second sight might be telling him. Sometimes he had dreams, sometimes visions, sometimes a feeling accompanied by heightened senses.

Faceless men. He would watch out for them, he thought

as he opened his eyes to the day, though in reality the vision was probably brought about by the copious amount of whiskey and Guinness he had drunk the night before.

He shivered. Damn, he was cold. His hot water bottle had long since lost any warmth, and his leg and scars ached. Even putting his heavy greatcoat on top of the sleeping bag had hardly kept him warm. His nose felt like ice, and he could see his breath in the air. Eventually he slid his body out and shivered again as his feet touched the cold lino. Frost had feathered the window overnight and cold air seeped through the cracks between glass and frame, despite old newspaper plugging the gaps. He hobbled over to light the gas fire and then went to the sink to wash and shave.

He stared into the mirror as he scraped the undamaged parts of his face with the razor. What must Beattie Cavendish have thought of him, this one-eyed man with the scars snaking their way down his skin and who walked with a limp, drank too much and lived in the room behind his office? He splashed his face clear of soap, then wiped it with the towel slung around his neck. And what was he doing wondering what Beattie Cavendish thought anyway? Except of course for some reason that he couldn't fathom but would eventually work out during one of his sleepless nights, she had somehow convinced him to put in time, unpaid time at that, looking into the death of Sofia Huber. Perhaps it had been an opportunist thief and they were seeing shadows where there were none and Ralph Bowen was simply queer or needed kinky sex and his wife wanted proof. Oh, but there were so many unanswered questions, and Beattie Cavendish had somehow made him believe they were not questions he could leave because they were nothing to do with him. This time he could do something.

After he dressed in a clean shirt and his becoming-very-threadbare suit, he peered into his cupboard for breakfast. Not much. Bread and strawberry jam, the jam courtesy of a cheated-on wife for whom he'd found enough evidence to persuade the husband to do the right thing. It had a little white mould on the top that he scraped away with a spoon. That would have to do.

Then he took one of his most treasured possessions down from the top shelf, a small aluminium stove-top percolator he'd brought back from Italy at the end of the war. He put some coffee beans in a grinder (and thank goodness for Bruno at the café around the corner, who provided him with the beans) until they became a fine powder. Then he filled the coffee maker with the beans and the water and put it on the heat to wait for the hissing to begin. It soothed him, this ritual every morning. Though he didn't like to be reminded of the Italian campaign, he had loved Italy, particularly when the war had ended. He smiled to himself as he remembered the day peace in Europe was declared. He was in a small village in Northern Italy and it was the most dangerous day of the war, what with people celebrating by letting off grenades and firing machine guns into the air. He'd sought refuge in a church to light a candle for his family, and that was when he'd realised that God had deserted him. He shook his head. He remembered his ma saying that God hadn't deserted him, he had deserted God. Who knows?

He turned on the wireless as he ate his meagre breakfast

and drank his strong, black coffee. As he stood at the sink to wash up his plate and cup, he began to get a familiar buzzing in his head and could smell honey and newly mown grass. Danger. His senses became acute. The hum of the overhead fluorescent light. The smell of his carbolic soap. The scratch of his collar on his neck. The rough cotton of the tea towel. The rumble of a nearby train. The buzzing became louder, the smells stronger. Imminent danger.

A sound from his office. The door closing. Footsteps. Rustling. More footsteps. Then he heard drawers being opened, files flung onto the floor. A chair being kicked over.

Corrigan slipped quietly to the connecting door and flattened himself against the wall. Sure enough, the door handle began to turn, slowly.

The door was flung open, all pretence at stealth had disappeared, and a man stepped into the room, looking from right to left. Corrigan had time to register a bald head, a shiny suit and an iron bar before he launched himself at the intruder, one arm reaching out to wrench the iron bar away, the other landing a satisfyingly crunching punch on a nose. He had the element of surprise and the man staggered, but he was strong – and he had a companion.

Corrigan didn't have time to see the second man before he was hit on his left side and then kicked in his left knee. Pain went shooting through his body and then his head as he landed on the floor. He tasted blood in his mouth. He felt himself being kicked some more, in his kidneys, in his side, his back. He curled himself in a ball in an effort to fend off some of the blows, but pain was radiating all through his body now. More kicks.

In all this neither intruder had said a word, their only sounds being grunts from the effort they were putting in.

Then a final blow to his head he didn't see coming that made his brain rattle in his skull and his ear explode and Corrigan's world went dark.

'Welcome back.'

A smell of antiseptic. The clicking of heels. The swish of an apron. Corrigan struggled to open his eye. A vase of greenery on a table. High windows. Dark outside. His head hurt. So did his back, his stomach, his shoulders. No point in itemising his aches and pains; his whole bloody body hurt. 'Ouch,' he said, wanting to say something to Beattie, who was sitting serenely by his bedside, a magazine in her hand. Like an angel. He groaned. He must have hurt his head very badly.

She raised her eyebrows. 'Ouch indeed. You have been well and truly beaten up.'

Corrigan shook his head, and immediately regretted it. Waves of pain snaked around his skull. Beattie's voice sounded as though it came from the bottom of the sea. 'Have I? I suppose – I don't really know. I do, but . . .' His memory was faulty. He could remember looking in the mirror and thinking about Beattie. What was he thinking? No good. Couldn't remember that detail. A good job, perhaps. But – what? – yes, he'd had one of his feelings, then he'd heard noises . . .

'I heard sounds in the office,' he told her. 'I'd got out of bed and had eaten my breakfast. Then I heard the noises as if someone was searching for something.'

'I thought you had lost your faculties for a moment

there.' Beattie put the magazine on the bed. 'You're right. They were. Your office is a complete mess – papers strewn around, drawers jemmied open . . .'

'Jemmied?'

'Yes,' said Beattie, impatience evident in her voice. 'A jemmy was used. You know, a crowbar with a curved end?'

'I know,' said Corrigan, trying not to smile, mainly because it hurt. 'I'm only surprised you know.'

She waved a dismissive hand. 'Don't be so patronising. As I was saying, your office had been thoroughly worked over, and so have you.'

Corrigan put a tentative hand up to his head and felt a bandage. His other hand also wore a bandage, and he had a sudden memory of one of the men stamping down hard on his fingers. He hoped they weren't broken. He tried to move his legs, and although it hurt like bloody hell, he could move them. 'How did I get here?'

'I came back from Saltergate Island this morning and I thought I'd come and find you, see if you'd got any further.'

'Further?'

'In our investigation.'

'Of course.' God, his head really did hurt. He tried to wriggle his bandaged fingers and felt some movement. Good. Not broken, then.

'And I found the door wide open and saw the place had been ransacked. I went through to the back and found you unconscious. I couldn't wake you, so I called an ambulance. Thought that would be best.'

'Thank you.'

'A pleasure. I cleared up a little and eventually made

my way to the hospital. That was this morning. It's now seven o'clock in the evening.'

'Blimey.' He'd been unconscious for most of the day. 'Did they take anything?'

Beattie stared at him. 'I have no idea.'

'You've got a couple of right shiners there, lad,' called out an elderly man with a patchy white moustache and even patchier white hair from the next bed. He put down his newspaper. 'And a good woman there.' He did up the top button of his pyjamas. 'They beat you up good and proper, didn't they?'

Corrigan nodded, and again wished he hadn't.

'I'm Charlie, by the way.'

'Hello, Charlie,' said Beattie and Corrigan together.

'You piss— sorry, lady – you annoyed somebody right and proper, then, if they beat you up and ransacked the office. What are you? Gangster?'

Corrigan smiled, and felt a throbbing in his gums. A loose tooth. 'You're right, I did annoy someone, but I'm not a gangster, I'm a private detective.'

'Same difference. Irish, are you?'

'Yes.'

'Hmm.' He picked up his newspaper again.

Corrigan shrugged. A ward orderly came in with a trolley of tea and toast.

'It wasn't a random attack,' said Beattie. 'Except finding you there was probably a surprise.'

'Probably. I broke his nose, though.'

'Satisfying.' Beattie laughed. Then she took his unbandaged hand. 'But, Corrigan, they could have killed you.'

Blimey. Beattie looked almost upset.

'And you shouldn't have gone into the office. They could still have been there.'

'Well, they were not. What do you think they were looking for?' She let his hand go. He didn't want her to.

'The diary? I don't know. Maybe they saw me outside the White Pearl Club.'

'Outside the White Pearl Club?' She pushed the glasses up her nose in an endearing way. *Endearing? Corrigan, what the hell are you thinking?*

'Ah, yes. About that.' And he told her about his failed attempt to get inside the club and how a young man called Kit had rescued him. He watched her trying not to laugh as he recounted how he'd had to run from the cops and climbed fences. 'Anyway, you and I are quits now.'

The orderly put a cup of tea on Corrigan's bedside table. 'You want one, love?' she asked Beattie.

Beattie shook her head. 'That's very kind of you, but no thank you. What do you mean, we're quits?'

'I saved your life. At the Bowens' house. You saved mine. Probably. That's it.'

'That's it?'

'Yes. I—'

'Patrick T Corrigan!'

Beattie and Corrigan, and all the other seven heads in the ward, turned towards the doors.

There stood a petite woman in a smart emerald-green woollen coat and a felt cloche hat on top of bouncing brown curls.

'Gosh,' said Beattie.

Corrigan gave a very quiet groan. 'Nell.'

The woman walked over to Corrigan and put her handbag on the end of the bed. 'What have you been doing? Was it a husband? Someone's lover?' She burst into tears. 'I've been so worried, imagining all sorts of things in the taxi over here.' She picked up her handbag again and took out a handkerchief.

'How did you know I was here?'

Nell dabbed her eyes. 'When I got to your office I saw that someone had forced the door open. That nice Jamaican family who live underneath came and told me – well, the father did. John, he said his name was. He said men with iron bars had beaten you up and that an ambulance had come for you and was bringing you here. We were supposed to go out for dinner. Do you remember?'

Corrigan groaned. 'I'm sorry, Nell.'

'It's hardly his fault that he couldn't meet you, is it?' said Beattie.

'I don't need defending,' said Corrigan testily, foreseeing trouble ahead.

'I didn't say it was – who are you?' she said, noticing Beattie for the first time.

Beattie held out her hand. 'Beattie Cavendish. And I apologise for being so rude.'

Nell took her hand with some reluctance. 'How do you do. That's quite all right. I'm Nell Gardener, Patrick's fiancée. And what are you doing here?'

'I called the ambulance.'

Nell studied her for a moment, frowning. Then her face cleared. 'Oh, are you a . . .' Nell stopped and nodded at her.

'A what?' said Beattie.

163

Nell looked around the ward. 'A client,' she whispered.

Beattie laughed. 'No, I'm not a client. I'm a—'

'Colleague,' said Corrigan. And now he didn't know if his headache was from the attack or from the meeting of the two women.

'That's right.' Beattie smiled. 'We are working on a case together.'

'And is this case why he got beaten to within an inch of his life?' Nell made it sound as though they were dealing with rats coming up from a sewer.

'No.'

'Possibly.'

They both spoke together.

'Well, which is it?' She looked at Corrigan, then Beattie.

Corrigan sighed, feeling uncomfortable, and not just from his injuries. 'They were looking for something, the men who came in. I don't think they expected me to be there.'

'I knew no good would come of you camping out in that back room, Patrick.'

'Nell.' There was a warning note in his voice. 'We've talked about this before.'

'I know, but—'

Corrigan leant his head back on his pillow. He was drained; his whole body throbbed. He really didn't want an argument with Nell. Not here, not in the hospital. Not with Beattie Cavendish on hand.

He felt a cool hand on his brow. 'I'm sorry, darling. Of course, you're right. We have to focus on your recovery.' Nell turned to Beattie. 'I'm sorry, Miss Cavendish. It doesn't do to argue in public.'

Beattie touched her arm. 'You're upset, of course you are.'

'Yes.' She caught her bottom lip between her teeth. 'Thank you.' She turned to Corrigan. 'Please, Patrick, you promised me this job wouldn't put you in danger. You said it was all about finding missing people or helping disgruntled spouses or people who owed money to other people. That's unsavoury enough. You didn't say anything about men with iron bars.'

Her eyes glistened with tears and Corrigan felt like a heel. He took her hand. 'It's what I do, Nell.'

'Not any more,' said Nell fiercely. 'Please. You know Father will give you a job.'

Corrigan closed his eyes. He did not want a steady job in an electrical firm, however successful a firm it was. It would kill his soul. Perhaps he should accept it, for Nell's sake. But then he would be beholden to someone else, at their beck and call all day. With his detective work he was his own master.

He opened his eyes to see Beattie disappearing out of the ward. 'I'll think about it, Nell.'

Nell kissed him softly. 'Thank you, darling. You won't regret it. Now, you rest. I'll sit here and read to you.'

'Not just one but two women around your bed,' said Charlie, slurping his tea. 'If that's not the luck of the Irish, I don't know what is.'

CHAPTER FIFTEEN

'Are you sure you should be here?' Beattie put a cup of tea on Corrigan's desk before sitting across from him. 'You look awful.' She couldn't help but stare at his puffy eyes and the bruises on his face that were a glorious artist's palette of greens and yellows, reds and purples. The bandage around his head was beginning to fray, and the one round his hand was looking decidedly grubby. She had also noticed him biting back pain as he had sat down to look through his appointment book. But, oddly, Beattie was glad to see him back on his – albeit shaky – feet.

'Thank you.' Corrigan looked melancholy.

'And I made the tea just how you like it.'

'Thank you again.'

She pushed the sugar bowl over to him. 'Seriously, though, Corrigan, I think you should have stayed in hospital. It's a lot more comfortable than the camp bed in that back room. And I'll bet a pound to a penny it's damp back there too.'

'I couldn't stand any more of Charlie,' he said, wincing as he ladled the sugar into his tea. 'And I've slept in a lot worse places, believe you me.'

Beattie did. She knew exactly what he meant.

'I was bored, too, and I want to get back to work.'

'I get the feeling,' said Beattie, choosing her words carefully, 'that your fiancée – Nell – doesn't want you to do this type of work.' The pretty, doll-like Nell, who made her feel too tall, too gangly. Not that it mattered.

Corrigan didn't answer for a minute, then he sighed. 'You're right, she doesn't. She would like me to work for her father at his electrical firm. Somewhere near Waterloo. In the back room, of course, so I won't scare the horses. His firm's been very successful and will be even more so, what with the number of homes we're supposed to be building for the returning heroes.'

Beattie nodded. 'My father says that about his company. He's an architect. Everyone needs an architect, he says.' She tucked her hair behind one ear. 'Martin seems happy, by the way.'

'Oh?'

'I rang my *maman* this morning.'

Corrigan eyed her. 'You look guilty, Beattie.'

'Do I? I suppose I feel a little guilty expecting Maman to look after Martin, someone she doesn't know at all.' She brightened. 'But I spoke to Martin as well as Maman and all seems well.'

'There. You don't have to worry.' Corrigan drank his tea, took out his tobacco tin and began to roll a cigarette. He offered it to Beattie, who took it.

'Maman and I, we, well, we don't get on.' She inhaled the smoke from her cigarette.

'I see,' said Corrigan, lighting his own roll-up.

'I don't expect you do, not really. I'm not the person she wants me to be.'

'Beattie,' said Corrigan, his tone gentle, 'you don't have to tell me anything.'

'No, I don't, do I?'

'So, Beattie Cavendish, what are you doing here at my office?'

The telephone on his desk began to ring.

They both looked at it.

Corrigan didn't pick it up.

The ringing stopped.

'It could have been someone wanting your services,' Beattie pointed out.

'It could have been.'

Neither spoke for a moment.

'What do you mean?' she said eventually. 'Why shouldn't I be here?'

Corrigan leant back in his chair. 'I've got to admit, you're a bit of a mystery, Beattie. You say you're a typist. A teacher of typists, but you don't say for whom.' Beattie opened her mouth. Corrigan waved his hand. 'Oh, I know you say the Civil Service but somehow I don't believe you. You say you are walking out with Ashley Bowen, but I don't see you as that sort of woman.'

She snorted. 'What on earth do you mean, "that sort of woman"?' She looked around for an ashtray. Corrigan pushed a saucer towards her.

'So. A typist. Walking out with Ashley Bowen, who frankly is what could be called a bounder, a cad or merely a drip in certain circles.' He grinned. 'What wonderful English words. Perhaps they're not fair, and rather "wet and stupid" fits him better. Then there's you. A typist who can pick locks. You're not easily shocked.' He stood and limped through into the back room. Beattie tried to stop her heart from beating too hard. She wasn't enjoying Corrigan's analysis of her. 'Why are you seeing Ralph Bowen's son?' he shouted through the open door.

'I like him,' she said, a little too defiantly. She had to be careful.

'Really? And the awful Felicia and Gerald?' he said loudly enough for her to hear him.

She had the sense he was disappointed in her, and for a reason she couldn't explain, she didn't like that feeling. 'I agree, Felicia is rather awful. But I'm not interested in her, and Gerald is far too interested in himself.'

'Gerald is a formidable character. Don't underestimate him.'

Beattie rolled her eyes.

Corrigan came back with the Huntley & Palmers biscuit tin. 'I thought we could do with a treat.' He took the lid off and his face fell. 'Ah.'

Beattie peered inside. All the digestive biscuits were now green with mould. 'I'm not sure I fancy one of those, but thank you,' she said with a faint smile.

'Indeed.' Corrigan returned her smile and put the lid back on. 'They'll keep for a rainy day, I suppose. And Ralph Bowen?'

'Ralph Bowen?'

'Yes, what do you think of him?' His expression appeared guileless, but she could see the interest in his face.

'I don't know him, not yet.'

He nodded.

'But you know him,' she said, leaning forward, wanting to make her point. 'You've been following him, so what is it

169

that drives him, do you think?'

'I'm not sure.' He looked at her, his eyebrows raised in faux innocence. 'I don't know if he goes to the White Pearl Club for . . .'

'Pleasure?'

'Pleasure.' He grinned. 'Or something else.'

'Martin told me that Sofia used to work at the White Pearl Club as a waitress.'

'What?'

'I said that Martin told me—'

'Yes, I heard you. What do you think this means?'

'I'm not sure yet,' said Beattie. 'But I think it's even more urgent we get to the White Pearl Club as soon as possible. Preferably when there isn't going to be a raid.'

'Ouch,' said Corrigan. 'I'm working on it.'

'And that's going well, isn't it?'

'Give me a chance.'

'But you nearly messed it up last time and you could have been arrested. Nell wouldn't have liked that, would she?' That, acknowledged Beattie to herself, was below the belt. 'And talking of your fiancée, you haven't said whether you're going to take a job with her father.' She should keep quiet but it was like worrying a sore tooth.

Corrigan shifted around in the chair, obviously trying to make himself comfortable, and nodded and Beattie's heart sank. 'I'll have to. It's only fair. She's been waiting for me to agree on a date for our wedding and after that settle down to a steady job. You've seen her; she's pretty and clever. A school teacher. Music. She's too good for me.' His face was gloomy.

'How did you meet her?' Beattie had almost come to the end of her cigarette.

Corrigan tapped the ash off his cigarette into the ashtray. 'One day I'd just finished a stake-out – I was watching someone – and it started to rain. I didn't have my umbrella with me, so I took refuge in the National Gallery. I could have stayed in the entrance porch but something made me go in, my sixth sense, my—'

'Sixth sense?'

'I'm the seventh son of a seventh son.' He waggled his eyebrows and tried to sound solemn and mysterious but came over as slightly mad. Beattie laughed.

'You'll be telling me you fraternise with leprechauns and see the Virgin Mary in visions at Knock.'

He raised an eyebrow. 'Don't have such a closed mind, Beattie Cavendish. You'd be surprised. For some reason—'

'That'll be your sixth sense.'

'Maybe. Are you making fun of me?'

Beattie kept her expression neutral.

'I sought out the Caravaggio,' he went on. 'Nell was there and we began talking. Later she said that I'd looked so sad she had to talk to me. She was kind. She didn't seem to notice all this.' He gestured to his missing eye and the scars that ran down his face. 'She was one of the first people to look at me without pity in their eyes.' He shrugged. 'It was important at the time.'

'And now?'

Corrigan seemed to shake himself. He put his hands, palms flat, on the table. 'And now, Miss Cavendish, we need to get on with our case.'

'And Nell's wishes?'

'I'll deal with those all in good time,' he said, firmly. 'She understands me.'

Beattie breathed a silent sigh of relief. She had thought he might be going to say that he was not interested in Sofia Huber, that he wanted to do as Nell asked and she would be left on her own. She refused to acknowledge a thought sitting in the back of her mind – that she would miss him.

'Tell me more about what Martin said to you,' he said.

Beattie frowned. 'It obviously pained him to tell me about the job at the club in case I thought any the less of his sister. Then I asked him why she took the job there when she had a perfectly good one with the Bowens. He said that Sofia wanted them to have more money. Apparently she had a plan for the two of them to go back to Germany.'

'And what about the diary?'

'The diary, yes. He was upset. He said he had never read any of it, Sofia kept it pretty secret, but he had the feeling there was probably a lot of personal stuff in it. And he asked the question, who would steal the diary and why?'

'Precisely. Or perhaps it's just well-hidden.'

'Maybe. Or perhaps there's something in the diary, something Sofia wrote, that someone, somewhere didn't want seeing the light of day. All we need to do is find out what. And to do that we need to find the diary. Especially if that's what the men who attacked you were looking for.'

'It all comes back,' said Corrigan, rolling another two cigarettes, 'to why Sofia was murdered and by who.'

'Obviously. And no thank you,' she said when Corrigan offered her a cigarette. 'Martin said their father was a scientist who Sofia thought held secret meetings in their house but he had no idea what they were about. He said he was a young boy climbing trees and collecting tadpoles; he wouldn't have bothered about what his father was doing. Sofia was older, inquisitive.'

Corrigan nodded. 'Secret meetings. Very cloak-and-dagger. Could be something or nothing.'

Beattie opened her mouth to tell Corrigan she thought she and Martin had been followed to Saltergate Island. She closed it again. He would only fuss and ask awkward questions. 'And where does Ralph Bowen fit into all this?' she asked instead. 'Or is it a coincidence?'

'What? That Sofia Huber who works for the Bowens gets a job at a club her employer frequents. More than a coincidence, I would say.'

'But . . .' She stopped. What she wanted to know was did this whole sorry mess have anything to do with Ralph Bowen and the suspicion that he might be some sort of spy? A Russian spy, she corrected herself. Or was she becoming so involved in the Sofia Huber murder that she was not doing her job properly? Perhaps Anthony Cooper was right and she should put Sofia's murder to one side.

'What? What is it, Beattie?'

She shook her head. 'Nothing. Why did Edwina want you to stop tailing Ralph Bowen?'

'She gave no reason.'

'It's a bit of a coincidence too, don't you think, that Sofia gets murdered at the same time Edwina gives you your marching orders?'

'Maybe she got what she wanted.'

'And what was that?'

'The places he went and the people he saw, which, apart from the Houses of Parliament, were the White Pearl Club and the church. The Holy Trinity, I would say.'

'Right. The church. Are those visits significant?' Beattie drummed her fingers on the desk. 'And we still come back to why she wanted her husband tailed.'

Another raised eyebrow. 'I would have thought that was obvious, given the reputation of the White Pearl Club.'

'The White Pearl Club,' said Beattie. 'It's come up again and again and is the one thing that links Sofia and the Bowens. Shall we ring the number that was on the book of matches again?'

He nodded.

The telephone was picked up at the other end. Beattie leant into Corrigan so she could hear the conversation.

'Ralph Bowen's office,' a woman with a cut-glass accent said.

'Sorry, wrong number,' said Corrigan, putting the phone down as if it burnt him. 'That was unexpected,' he said. 'Another conundrum. Why does a housekeeper have the number of the Shadow Foreign Secretary?'

'Written on a book of matches that came from a questionable club?'

The phone rang.

'I think you should answer that,' said Beattie. 'After all, you need the work.'

Corrigan sighed and picked up it up.

Beattie heard a voice speaking quickly. She caught a few words. '. . . thinking . . . Huber . . . club . . .'

Corrigan put the phone down and stood, taking his coat from the coat rack. 'I'm off.'

'Where are we going?' Beattie shrugged on her coat.

'That was Kit, the chap I met the other day. He wants

to see me. Says he has some information about Sofia. I'm to meet him in Kensington Gardens.'

'Righty-o,' said Beattie. 'What are we waiting for?' She jammed her hat onto her head and picked up her handbag.

'You're not coming,' said Corrigan. 'Kit said I was to be alone. He sounded . . .'

'What?'

He frowned. 'Frightened, I think. And if he's got something to say, then I don't want him to run off if he sees you.'

'Oh.' Beattie was disappointed. 'I see. But if I'm with you, surely—'

'Besides,' interrupted Corrigan, 'haven't you got a job to go to?'

She blinked, snapped back into her role. 'Er, yes, that.'

'Yes, that. The typing. The job that earns you a living. A job you're lucky to have.'

'As I said, I have a few days off.' Beattie clamped her mouth shut. Bloody typical man, patronising and annoying, and also trying to do all the heroics. Beaten half to death and now he wanted to meet some man who said he had information about Sofia. 'What if it's a trap?'

'A trap?'

'Yes, a trap.' Lord, he was irritating. 'He – this Kit – could be working for them, anything. There could be people there ready to use their crowbars on you again.'

He laughed. Infuriating.

'In Kensington Gardens? In broad daylight? I don't think so.'

'So there's nothing to stop me coming, is there?'

'No, Beattie, you are not coming. And that's an end to it.'

Paternalistic claptrap. 'Look, I found Sofia Huber; I have talked to her brother. I'm getting to know what sort of person she was. I want to know what happened to her, now more than ever.'

'Then you'll let me go and see what I can find out.' He reached behind his head and began to unwind the bandage. Beattie saw him wince as he had to tug it free where the blood had dried on his skin.

She folded her arms. 'You're not in any condition—'

'I've had worse. And,' Corrigan continued, 'don't try to follow me because I will know.'

No you won't. You certainly would not if I choose it.

Oh, but his indifference to danger irritated her, made her cross. 'Very well. Go.'

'I'll let you know what he says.'

'Here,' said Beattie, scribbling on a page of Corrigan's notebook before tearing it off and handing it to him, 'this is my telephone number and address. And my name. In case you forget whose it is.'

He took the piece of paper. 'I will let you know, I promise.'

Beattie turned to leave. 'By the way, Corrigan, what does the "T" stand for?'

'The "T"?'

'Yes. When your fiancée found you in the hospital, she called you Patrick T Corrigan.'

'Did she, so?'

'Yes.'

He tapped the side of his nose. ''Tis a secret, Beattie Cavendish,' he said in the most Irish of accents. 'Only the leprechauns know.'

CHAPTER SIXTEEN

The trees were bare, and the sky threatened above, but Corrigan enjoyed walking in the park that was an oasis of green in the city. A piece of countryside. He had even seen sheep grazing earlier in the year. It had surprised him – this green – when he'd first arrived in London. He'd imagined the place as one of chimneys belching out thick black smoke, factories with smells to catch at the back of the throat, too many trams and cars and cabs, and piles of rubble that were playgrounds by day and reminders of war by night, and it had all of that, but it also had the magnificence of St Paul's, of the Tower of London, of its elegant bridges and the stoic people. It had energised him and, despite the casual ignorance he had found day after day because of his accent, he had found himself falling in love with it. If he stopped and breathed, here in the gardens, he could almost imagine the air was fresh with the tang of the sea. Almost. Truth to tell, his imagination didn't quite stretch that far.

Kit had sounded panicked on the telephone, and Corrigan couldn't deny it, but the main reason he didn't want Beattie Cavendish with him was that he did think something untoward could happen. He intended to be very careful.

Kensington Gardens. Near the Peter Pan statue, Kit had said. Between that and the river.

Corrigan stepped out along the footpath by the Serpentine. It was doing his legs good to stretch out the muscles, and the fresh air was helping heal his wounds. Although it was a cold and gloomy day, there was still a mother and a well-wrapped child taking the air, a man with a tiny dog, a uniformed nanny with her charges in a large posh pram. He relished the ordinariness of it all, something a few years ago he didn't think he would live to see.

As he drew near to the statue of Peter Pan surrounded by its bronze squirrels, rabbits, mice and fairies, he saw a man looking out over the water. Kit. He recognised that scarf and the way he stood. Next to him was a woman who was throwing bread to the ducks. The woman, who had unremarkable features and wore a headscarf knotted under her chin, turned to Kit to speak to him, urgently and rapidly. He watched as Kit nodded slowly.

Kit turned and looked at Corrigan and mouthed a word. *Sorry*.

Then the woman tucked her arm into his and they both walked quickly away.

'Kit, Kit, hold on a minute!' Corrigan shouted.

'Excuse me, sir?' Two police constables stood either side of him. 'Could you come with us, please.'

'What for?' Corrigan wanted to run after Kit, ask he what he meant, but, more importantly, what he had to say about Sofia Huber.

'Please. Just come with us. It will be easier all round.'

As Corrigan was hurried away between the two coppers, he saw a tall man with glasses, a trilby and a black coat watching him expressionlessly. As soon as Corrigan caught his eye, the man turned and walked away.

The room was square and windowless, lit only by a flickering fluorescent tube. It smelt of despair and sweat and was cold, so cold that Corrigan could see his breath in the air. He had been in this godforsaken place for what felt like hours and he was tired and desperately wanted to wash his hands. His head had begun to ache again, and his bruises throbbed. He felt a bit dizzy, too. He needed a cigarette. He could hear distant voices, the slamming of doors, muted laughter. There was a table scored with mostly indecipherable graffiti.

On one side of the table sat Corrigan. On the other a thin man with a long, sharp nose, cold eyes and a pencil-thin moustache, aged in his fifties, Corrigan reckoned. Probably a bit disillusioned with his lot. Unhappy at home too. Corrigan enjoyed speculating about people. He'd introduced himself as Detective Sergeant Rogers. Rogers was smartly dressed, with a well-pressed – if shiny – jacket and neatly knotted tie. He had taken a packet of cigarettes out of his pocket and put it on the table, lining it up with the thin folder he had brought in with him.

Corrigan looked at the cigarettes with longing.

'So, Mr Corrigan, you were meeting Mr' – he looked down at the file on his desk – 'Pearson in Kensington Gardens?' Rogers avoided looking at him. Probably didn't like the sight of his scars and empty eye socket, he thought.

'I was, yes. I told you all this.' He tried to keep the impatience out of his voice as he knew there was no point in riling the policeman.

Again DS Rogers looked down at the file in front of him. 'So you said. You said you, ahh, were going for a walk in Kensington Gardens with the express purpose of meeting Mr Pearson.'

'Yes,' said Corrigan, even more wary now than he was at the outset of the interview and he wondered why the word 'express' seemed laden with menace. He did, however, have some inkling of where it might be leading.

'Mr Pearson is well-known to the police.' DS Rogers sniffed with disapproval.

'Oh?' Not a surprise.

'How do you know him, this Mr Pearson?' The name was said with distaste.

'As I said, I met him outside a club.'

'Indeed. Outside a club.' Another sniff from Rogers, another glance down at the file in front of him. 'The White Pearl, I believe?' Rogers looked as though saying the words physically pained him. 'A club of ill repute.'

'And, as I said earlier, I had been following someone for a client of mine. The client had gone into the club. I was waiting for the client to leave. Mr Pearson offered me a light for my cigarette.'

'Indeed.'

DS Rogers's 'indeeds' were beginning to get on Corrigan's nerves.

'Indeed, yes,' Corrigan said, his attempt at being patient deserting him.

It was the wrong thing to say, the wrong way to say it.

'Yet you won't tell me who your client is? Or was?' Aggressive now.

'No, Detective Sergeant. As I have already explained, it's a matter of client confidentiality.'

'Even though you're in more than a spot of bother?'

Corrigan shook his head. 'I'm not entirely sure what "spot of bother" I'm supposed to be in. And I've been here for rather a long time. May I have a drink of water?'

'This is not The Ritz, Mr Corrigan. Now—'

'What exactly am I being accused of?'

A huge sigh. 'Nothing. You are being accused of nothing. Yet. I only want to establish the facts.'

'I've told you the facts. And if I'm not being accused of anything, then I am free to go.' Corrigan stood.

'Please sit down, Mr Corrigan. The sooner we get this sorted out, the sooner you can leave, otherwise things could go badly for you. Now, then.' Rogers shuffled a couple of sheets of paper. 'Mr Pearson says you approached him. You wanted to meet him. You wanted to . . .' DS Rogers's lips became even thinner. 'Need I go on? It's not right what goes on between queers.'

Corrigan laughed. It was as he'd thought. 'That's ridiculous. And I think you know it.'

'Indeed not. We only have your word. Or Mr Pearson.' He looked up at Corrigan.

'I was meeting him because he asked me to. He had some information for me,' Corrigan explained as patiently as he was able. 'He was talking to a lady before I saw him; perhaps you could have a chat to her. Or' – he leant forward, having had quite enough of the interrogation – 'you could even talk to the police constables who collared me in the park and they will say to you that I hadn't even spoken to Kit – Mr Pearson – before they nabbed me.'

'You said you spoke to him earlier. Made an assignation.'

'I did. For information. He had information about a case I'm looking into. How did you know I was going to meet him?'

Rogers sniffed. 'We received a telephone call. Anonymous. Warning us there could be trouble. In broad daylight. We were given clear descriptions of the two of you.'

Corrigan frowned. What was going on here? Kit must have told someone about this meeting. But who? And why? Or – and the thought made him go cold – could his phone be tapped?

Rogers cleared the phlegm from his throat. 'You're Irish, is that correct?' A swerve.

'Yes. I don't see what that's got to do with the price of fish.'

Rogers sucked on his teeth and laced his fingers together. 'We've had a lot of trouble with the Irish over the years. With you Irish. How do I know you're not over here, taking advantage of our hospitality while all the time you're plotting against us, making bombs and suchlike?'

'Ye gods!' Corrigan rolled his eyes. 'Make your mind up. Either I'm a queer or a terrorist.'

'Perhaps both?'

This was becoming tedious. 'DS Rogers, I am known to the police as I am a private detective. I have friends in the police force; just ask around. Please. I've been patient as you have questioned me on a quite frankly flimsy premise. Let's get this done and dusted.'

The door of the interview room opened, and Detective Inspector Dicky Morgan strolled in, carrying the smell of misguided superiority and an undertone of sweat with him. Corrigan was almost pleased to see the odious little man.

'Patrick, how's it going?'

Dicky Morgan's nasal voice set Corrigan's teeth on edge, but he knew he had to make an attempt to be pleasant. He smiled thinly. 'I'd like to know what I'm doing here.'

Dicky Morgan jerked his head towards Rogers. 'You can go now, Jim.'

Rogers huffed and puffed as he collected his meagre file together and stalked out of the room.

Dicky Morgan smiled. 'He didn't like that, did he. Probably thought he was on to a winner with you.'

Corrigan made himself smile. 'Whereas you and I both know that there was no substance to the allegations.'

Dicky Morgan smiled briefly. 'Allegations? This is a friendly chat, that's all.' He pulled out the chair, its legs scraping across the floor. 'You've been in the wars,' he said, nodding towards Corrigan's face.

'An altercation with a couple of men carrying crowbars.'

'I heard.'

'And are you investigating?'

'Of course. Unlikely to get anywhere, though. Nothing to go on, you see. Especially as your office was nice and tidy by the time we got there. Still.'

And they bloody well didn't want to. Corrigan knew this.

'OK. Let's cut the bollocks. What am I doing here really?'

Dicky Morgan chuckled. 'Well, looks like you've really pissed off some important people.'

'Like who?'

'All this looking into the White Pearl Club. Not healthy, you see?' Dicky Morgan ignored his question.

Corrigan's mind was racing, though he kept his face still. 'What do you mean?'

'Why are you investigating it anyway? It's a place for whores and homos. I didn't think you were that way inclined. See.' He leant forward and Corrigan could see his open pores and smell his meaty breath. 'Just stop. Right? Not too much to ask.' He smiled.

'I was working for a client. That's all.'

'And, er, Beattie Cavendish.'

'Miss Cavendish? What about her?' Corrigan sat up. Now what was going on?

'Stay away from her, that's my advice.'

'Why?'

Dicky Morgan sighed. 'Take my advice, will you? You wouldn't want anything happening to her or you. You specifically. After all, who's to mourn the loss of one more Paddy? One more terrorist? Because we could do that, you know. Make you' – he snapped his fingers – 'disappear. Stop, that's what I say, otherwise you will find yourself on the wrong side of the law. Your war record will only take you so far.' Dicky Morgan stood. 'You can go. For now.'

Outside, Corrigan lit up a cigarette and breathed in smoke and London air. His shoulders came down from by his ears. It was all he could do in there to keep his temper. Morgan had been goading him. But he now knew what it had all been about; it was an elaborate warning.

Someone didn't want him to look into the activities of the White Pearl Club. And Beattie. Why would he be warned not to have anything to do with Beattie? Whoever was making the threats – and he knew there was someone behind Dicky Morgan pulling his strings – whoever it was didn't realise that he didn't respond well to threats, not well at all.

CHAPTER SEVENTEEN

As Beattie pushed open the door of Mes Amis, the busy sounds of chatter, the clatter of cutlery on plates and the soft strains of Debussy greeted her and her heart lifted. This restaurant in Marylebone Lane was one of her favourite places in London, where in the past she had met Uncle Howard when she was down from Cambridge. He would bring her here and they would sit on the bentwood chairs amongst the diners who wore an assortment of dress from moth-eaten cardigans and workmen's trousers to silk dresses and peacock-feathered hats and many of whom were foreigners, refugees, émigrés. There would always be a cloud of cigarette smoke, a warm welcome and delicious food ranging from buttery fish to silky soup to a delicious French cheese. She hadn't been since she left the university and Uncle Howard had moved to Scotland 'for the clean air', he'd told her, something Beattie had found odd as he was always complaining of the cold and she couldn't see that Scotland would suit him. Still, it had been his choice but she missed him. And she would always be grateful for the chance he had afforded her.

It had been hard to watch the expressions that crossed

her *maman*'s face when she'd told her and Father she was taking up Uncle Howard's offer of paying for her place at Cambridge. Maman had drawn herself up to her quite formidable height and breathed hard through her nose. Always a bad sign. Jack and she always knew to make themselves scarce when their mother's lips thinned and nostrils flared.

'*Quelle est cette absurdité?*'

Maman always spoke in French when she was roused.

'You didn't mind when Jack said he was looking forward to taking up his place,' Beattie protested hotly.

'*Exactement*. His place, Beatrice, not yours. His.' Her mother's eyes clouded with pain. 'And he is not here.'

'No. But I am. And I have gained a place to study modern languages and—'

'As Jacques was to do.' Her *maman* crossed her arms over her bosom.

Beattie was determined to stand her ground. '*Oui, Maman*. As Jacques was to do.' She would not flinch under her mother's glare.

'So, you have your mind made up?'

'Yes, Maman.'

'And Howard is paying for you.'

'Yes.'

Her mother had said no more, just let her disapproval be known by long silences and heavy sighs. Once again Beattie had disappointed her *maman*.

'*Mademoiselle?*' A man with a handlebar moustache and a jacket three times too small for him greeted her with a small bow.

She smiled, thrusting all thoughts about Uncle Howard

and Maman and the question of why Maman disliked him so much to the back of her mind. 'I have a table booked for two for lunch. My name is Beattie Cavendish.'

The man bowed again, and if he was surprised that a woman should come on her own into a restaurant he didn't show it. 'Of course. This way.'

They wound a path through the tables to one by the window, and Beattie heard Polish, French, Italian and even a Russian voice, and that's what so delighted her about the place. It truly was an adventure of discovery.

With great ceremony, the man pulled out the wooden chair and bade her sit while putting the piece of paper that served as the day's menu down on the table with a flourish. She faced the room, as she had been taught to do.

He gathered up her coat, hat and gloves while she settled back to wait, rolling her shoulders in an effort to dispel any tension in them.

After Corrigan had left for the park, Beattie decided against following him and thought she should return to work. No sooner had she sat down at her desk than her telephone had rung.

'Anthony Cooper here. I wish to talk to you. Over lunch, perhaps. Is there somewhere you would wish to go?'

Startled, she had named the first restaurant that came to mind – Mes Amis.

'I know it,' said Anthony Cooper. 'I will see you there in an hour.' His voice was clipped and dismissive, which made her feel as though cold tapioca pudding was sitting, undigested, in her stomach.

'A penny for them, Miss Cavendish?' Anthony Cooper in his grey flannel suit with his black Civil Service coat over his arm and hat in hand stood in front of her. He smiled. The smile didn't reach his eyes.

Beattie blinked. 'I was thinking of my mother. Do join me, Mr Cooper.' As if she had invited him for lunch.

The man in the tight jacket whisked Anthony Cooper's coat away.

'Thank you, Miss Cavendish.' He indicated to a waitress who was hovering near their table. 'A glass of water for me, please. And you, Miss Cavendish?'

Beattie's heart sank. Water.

Anthony Cooper seemed to take pity on her. 'Perhaps a glass of wine?'

Beattie smiled with relief. 'Thank you.'

'Of course, sir.' The waitress hurried away.

Anthony Cooper sat, placing his hat on a spare chair and looked around the café. 'I remember coming here as a young man before the war, the day before the coronation,' he said. 'I was with my aunt, and we were lucky enough to know people with a balcony overlooking the route. We were up early, keen to see the great event. It rained that day. Grey skies. But no one minded. The crowds were happy, pleased for the new King and Queen. Especially after all that nasty business that went before. We didn't know what was to come, of course. We sat there with our Thermos flasks of tea and our egg and salad cream sandwiches and rejoiced together. It was a different world then.' He made a noise, which could have been a little laugh.

Beattie didn't know what her reaction should be, so she kept quiet.

The waitress came back to the table with their drinks.

'Are you ready to order?' she said.

Beattie's stomach grumbled. 'I'll have the sole, please, with a *salade romaine*.'

'Plat du jour, please.' He looked at his watch. 'I haven't got long.'

'Oh,' said Beattie, 'I—'

'No, you have what you wish, Miss Cavendish, please. You're obviously hungry.'

It did sound rather like a censure, but she was hungry. She had a sudden thought of Jack, who always used to tease her about her appetite, telling her she ate like a docker. That was before the war, of course. Deprivation and rationing – which had only just begun to be lifted earlier in the year – had taken that pleasure away and now she restricted herself to small bites of anything pleasurable to make it last longer. A delicate piece of fish beautifully cooked with perhaps a little melted butter would be a particularly delicious treat and she was determined to savour every mouthful, however monk-like Anthony Cooper was being.

Anthony Cooper took another sip of his water.

She picked up her wine and was about to drink when he spoke again.

'It has come to my attention that you have been in the company of a certain private detective, one Patrick Corrigan. Irish.' His lip curled as he said the last word.

Ah.

'He's a friend.' *Careful*, she told herself.

'Really? And how did you meet him?' He had another sip of water, his eyes watching her over the rim of the glass.

'I met him at Ralph Bowen's house.' That much was true.

'I see. It has also come to my notice that he has been following Ralph Bowen, so isn't it a little odd you met him *in* the house?'

Beattie was silent. *Careful, be very careful.* 'I met him *at* the house, not *in*. Outside in fact. He was not as careful as he thought he was being.'

'I see.'

Beattie breathed a silent breath of relief.

'And,' Anthony Cooper continued, 'do you know why this Corrigan chap was following a politician in whom we have a great interest?' He blinked. Slowly.

She waited a moment. 'His wife asked him to.'

'I see. And you visited Corrigan in hospital when he got in the way of men carrying iron bars.'

Beattie twisted in her seat. 'How did you . . . ?'

'Come now, don't be naïve.' For the first time, Anthony Cooper sounded less than mild.

Beattie pressed her lips together. She decided she really didn't like Anthony Cooper very much.

'I also know you visited Sofia Huber's house and spirited Martin Huber away. Where is he?' Anthony Cooper's long fingers played with the cutlery on the table.

Spirited. Really. 'Safe. At my mother's.' So the watcher on the island wasn't anyone from COS.

Anthony sighed and crossed his legs. 'Your job is to find out information about Ralph Bowen. Please stick to that. There is no need for heroics; all we want to know is if he says anything out of the ordinary, or mentions any names, or if his son says anything of interest about his father. That's as far as you need to go.' He pursed his lips. 'It's a simple enough job. Please do as I say or your time in COS could be very short. There are others who can carry out simple orders such as those that have been given to you. And I think I've already asked you to drop any interest in pursuing reasons why Sofia Huber might have been killed and I will say again, it is none of your business.'

The waiter placed their food in front of them. Beattie's mouth watered at the sight and smell of her delicate fish that was, indeed, running with butter. Anthony Cooper's ham in Madeira sauce with green beans and boiled potatoes looked less appetising. They both began to eat in silence, Beattie conscious of every mouthful and praying that butter was not dribbling down her chin.

Anthony Cooper pushed away his half-finished lunch. 'I have to get back. I will pay the bill before I leave.' He looked around, and signalled to a waiter, indicating he wanted his coat. 'I hope to see you at your desk this afternoon. Please appreciate I had this chat with you away from the office as I didn't want to make it official in any way.' He nodded to her glass of wine. 'And you should be careful with the drink, Miss Cavendish.'

The man in the tight jacket handed Anthony Cooper his coat and Beattie watched as he threaded his way through the tables, settled the bill and left.

She leant back in her chair and took a large gulp of wine.

What was happening here? She was being warned off, that was clear. But something didn't add up. He said he wanted to talk to her away from the office. Why? He wasn't only being nice and kind; that wasn't in his nature. Which meant there was something going on beneath the surface and she would have to scratch around to find it.

Maybe ruffle some feathers as she went. Could she afford to do that? She enjoyed her job, it was beginning to give her an element of satisfaction, but there was something off about Anthony Cooper and she would find out what that was, of that she was determined.

She asked for another glass of wine and carried on enjoying her meal, this time not caring if butter was dribbling down her chin.

CHAPTER EIGHTEEN

Beattie looked in the bathroom mirror as she applied her lipstick, rubbing her lips together then blotting them with a tissue. There. A last dab of powder and she was ready. An evening with Ashley Bowen beckoned, which was a good thing in light of her 'talk' with Anthony earlier in the day. She didn't like being treated as though she was a silly young girl with no idea about the world. She'd had more experience in her life than many, and she had been lucky to come out alive. She wondered what Anthony had done in the war. She shut her purse with a vicious *snap*. And what had all that cloak-and-dagger business at the restaurant been about, for goodness' sake? Why was he following her? Knowing her every movement? Why had he wanted to know where Martin was? The thought of it was making the rage rise in her chest. At least she knew Martin was all right – Maman had sounded quite chipper on the telephone this evening, saying she was enjoying having a young man around the house, though Amelie appeared a little 'struck' by him. Beattie had smiled at that. She really should telephone Corrigan soon, too. She had to be careful there, though, not to expose herself for what she was. The trouble was, she had almost forgotten who she really was.

She took a sip of the gin she'd poured to give her a little bit of Dutch courage.

Then there was the call she and Corrigan had made to the number written on the book of matches. Straight through to Ralph Bowen's private office. What was Sofia Huber doing with that number? It indicated that there was more to her relationship with Ralph Bowen than that of employer and employee.

And where was her diary?

She sighed.

That was all for tomorrow. She adjusted her hat. Tonight she was going to a concert with Ashley, a concert and choir in a church. Handel's *Messiah* by candlelight featuring Edwina Bowen in the choir. Not exactly what she would have chosen, as though she enjoyed classical music and even church music, churches themselves were anathema to her. How could she believe in a god who had let her down time after time? It was no use spouting all that free will nonsense; that cut no ice with her. Still. It was a chance to do her job. Try harder, perhaps. It was all very well, she mused, but she couldn't exactly chase after Ashley, could she? Times might be different now, but some things never changed. And she didn't want to be perceived as 'fast' by Ashley, otherwise he would drop her very quickly. No, she had to play this one straight and wait for him to make the advances. Something Anthony didn't seem to understand.

Wretched man. He had no idea what the world was like for women. He seemed to think she could wander up to Ashley and immediately be asked back to his house, where she would meet all the family and get chummy with Ralph Bowen. Shadow Foreign Secretary Ralph Bowen. The trouble was, she couldn't complain about it because he would be all 'I told you so' and 'this is why we shouldn't employ women'. *Well. Here's mud in your eye, Anthony.* She finished her gin and reapplied her lipstick.

There was a knock on the door.

Time to enter the fray.

Though Beattie had no truck with church, religion and all that it represented, she had to admit the building where the concert was being held was beautiful. Banks of candles lit all areas of the church, casting a soft light on the judgemental faces of the Virgin Mary, Jesus on the cross and assorted saints. Reflections of the colours of the stained-glass windows danced on the stone floor. There were tributes to various good people of the parish in the form of plaques on the walls – a couple of former priests, a bishop. The audience sat restlessly in the hard pews, the choir and their open books facing them – with Edwina Bowen in the back row – and the small orchestra in front.

She leant into Ashley. 'What's the name of this church again?'

'St Margaret of Antioch,' he whispered back.

Beattie sat back in the pew. The name rang a bell, but it wouldn't quite come to her why.

Felicia was sitting the other side of Ashley, gazing around the church, a bored expression on her face. She was inevitably accompanied by Gerald, who was stifling a yawn. Ralph Bowen was ramrod straight, his lips in a thin, unsmiling line.

She leant towards Ashley again. 'Doesn't your father like this sort of thing?'

Ashley gave a twisted little smile. 'Not really. He calls religion the opiate of the people. A rather Marxist comment for a Tory, don't you think? And he doesn't like to set foot in a church, says it gives him hives.'

'I see,' said Beattie. And now she was surprised, because she had just remembered where she had heard the name of the church before – it was the very one that Corrigan had followed Ralph Bowen to on more than one occasion. 'Yet here he is, supporting your mother.'

'It wouldn't look good if he didn't. He isn't keen on Mother singing in the choir, says it's not what our sort of people do. But Mother told him she was trying to fit in with his constituents, to show them she was one of them. He couldn't argue with that.' Ashley grinned.

The conductor came in from the side. A funny little man with long, unkempt hair and a rather shiny dress suit. He bowed to the audience, turned to the orchestra and choir and held up his hands.

For a moment there was complete quiet and stillness in the church.

The overture began.

Soon Beattie found to her surprise that she was lost in the music, the comforting biblical words sung with smooth, mellow tones or soaring high sopranos. It was all leaving a suspiciously unmovable lump in her throat. And when it came to the *Hallelujah* chorus, she was undone.

And then it was over, and the audience was clapping politely.

'Mother was good, wasn't she?' said Ashley.

'Extremely good,' she said, though of course, Edwina Bowen, having no solo part, was merely one of the choir. She glanced across at Ralph Bowen and saw that his face had relaxed; he was almost smiling. And was there a suggestion of tears in his eyes? Could the beauty and majesty have got to him too?

Standing right at the back of the church, having slipped inside, was Corrigan. He too had been moved by the music and thought how much Nell would have loved it – there was so much music in her soul – but it had surprised him to find an event going on in the church that evening. He'd come to talk to the parish priest about Ralph Bowen's visits, and had not banked on there being hundreds of people around. But then, his ma would be proud of him for being inside a church at all. And so many times recently.

Once the concert was over, and the musicians had packed their instruments away and the choir had dispersed, Corrigan went to find the priest. Father Kevin, according to the notices on the board at the back of the church, which Corrigan had read and almost learnt by heart during the two-hour concert. There were some parish noblewomen who were sweeping the church, snuffing out the candles and generally making it ship-shape for God. Corrigan wondered which one was the housekeeper – Roman Catholic priests always had a housekeeper.

'Did you enjoy the concert?'

Corrigan almost swore. Father Kevin had appeared by his side without him noticing.

'I did, Father, thank you.'

Father Kevin smiled. 'It's a fine thing, isn't it? An oratorio composed by a Lutheran – devout by all accounts – with libretto compiled from the King James Bible by a devout Anglican. A fine thing in a Catholic church.' He tucked his hands into the sleeves of his cassock. 'Thomas Aquinas argued that something is beautiful when it has three things – wholeness, harmony, radiance. The *Messiah*, I believe, has all three.' He gave a gentle smile. 'And now having regaled you with my thoughts, perhaps you could tell me how I can help you. I have seen you in the church before, have I not?'

Even if he had wanted to, there was no way Corrigan was going to lie to Father Kevin. He might not go to church any more, but he didn't want fire and brimstone to rain down upon his head.

'I have, Father.'

'I recognised your—'

The priest didn't have to say any more.

'The lack of an eye? My scars?' Corrigan's tone was impatient, he knew, and he regretted it immediately. He could hear his ma tutting in his ear.

Father Kevin frowned and put a hand on his shoulder. 'I'm sorry, my son, I didn't mean to offend you.'

Corrigan sighed. 'You didn't, Father. Sometimes I'm a little touchier than I should be. And you can help me, I think.' He took a deep breath. He might as well come straight out with it. 'Is Ralph Bowen a regular visitor to your church?'

'Mr Bowen?' Father Kevin laughed. 'I should say not. Mrs Bowen, however, does attend Holy Mass every week and sings in our choir. And plays the organ gloriously on occasions. She is a talented lady. But why do you ask?'

Corrigan took another deep breath. 'I know I can rely on your discretion, Father.'

The priest bowed his head. 'Of course.'

'I am a private detective and Mrs Bowen—' He stopped. This was proving difficult. He looked around to make sure there was no one in earshot. 'Mrs Bowen asked me to follow her husband on one or two occasions.'

Father Kevin's face fell. 'Oh dear, that doesn't sound good. Not good at all.'

'I'll collect up the missals, shall I, Father? Before we go back for a late supper?' An overweight woman in a tweed coat came bustling around them, watching Corrigan with sharp eyes.

'Thank you, Patricia, that would be grand. So which part of Ireland did you say you were from?'

'Near Cork,' Corrigan replied. 'And I recognise the trace of an accent in you, Father. Dublin?'

Patricia bustled away. Father Kevin laughed. 'I should say so. But I've been here more than forty years, so I'm surprised you could still tell.'

'Ah, I'm good at that.'

'I'm sorry . . .' He waved a hand towards Patricia, who was now piling up hymn books on a table. 'My housekeeper. She does like to keep an eye on me. Now, where were we? Ah, yes, Ralph Bowen.' He frowned. 'I talk to many people—'

'But not many Shadow Foreign Ministers?'

'We are all the same in the sight of God. But let me think.' He looked up, as if for divine inspiration. 'I know he came in one evening quite late to say Edwina wouldn't be able to get to choir that week. Then there was another time he was asking some advice about one of his constituents.' Father Kevin gave another of his gentle smiles. 'And you know I am not able to tell you about that. But that's all I can think of at the moment. Now, I really should be going or Patricia will be throwing my supper into the bin.'

'Before you go, Father.' Patrick laid a hand on his arm. 'Have you ever heard of a lady called Sofia Huber?'

'Sofia Huber?' The priest thought for a moment, his head on one side. 'I can't say I have. Now I really must go. But if you want to stay and have a peaceful minute or two, then you're very welcome. Maybe I'll see you at Mass one day?'

'Maybe,' said Corrigan, thinking it would have to be a cold day in hell first and trying not to see Ma's face in his mind's eye.

However, he did accept the priest's invitation to sit down in one of the pews. There was no doubt that it was peaceful in the church now everyone had left, even though the wood was hard on his backside. And there was still a residual warmth in the air. He closed his eyes.

He thought about how the police had hauled him in and warned him off the White Pearl Club. Someone had got to Kit, and through Kit to him. It smacked of dark forces at work, of someone, somewhere trying to manipulate him. Why? Was it to do with Sofia Huber's death? Or something to do with Ralph Bowen? And Beattie Cavendish, who was she really? Then he thought of the sneer on Dicky Morgan's face and how he had wanted to land a punch on his ugly mug there and then.

He was getting nowhere.

Corrigan stood and made his way out of the pew,

resisting the urge to genuflect. He knew where he was going right now. The White Pearl Club. It was time for answers because there was something going on that was very wrong, very wrong indeed. He wanted to find out why Sofia Huber had her hand on a White Pearl Club book of matches when she died. And why she had a direct line to Ralph Bowen. There was something more to Sofia Huber than met the eye, and he was determined to find out what. Particularly as he could have sworn when he'd asked the priest about Sofia Huber there had been a shift in his expression indicating he had heard the name before, and particularly in light of information Corrigan had received earlier in the evening from an old contact in the police force – Sofia Huber had been pregnant when she died.

CHAPTER NINETEEN

Beattie hurried away from the church along the dimly lit streets to the King's Road, where she could easily find a taxi, grateful for when the moon peeked out from behind the clouds. She had managed to extricate herself from the Bowens, only feeling slightly guilty about not going back to their grand house for a 'snifter', as Ralph Bowen put it. Slightly guilty because it would have been another opportunity to do her job as demanded by Anthony Cooper, but she consoled herself with the knowledge she had been invited to a cocktail party at the house the very next evening. There had been an awkward moment when Ashley had caught her hands and looked into her eyes and said, 'Do you have to rush off?'

'Yes,' she'd said, injecting a note of regret into her voice. 'I have to be at work early in the morning.'

'Surely the typists can wait. Only, I'm becoming rather fond of you and would like to see more of you. Please come back to the house?'

'Ashley, I can't,' she said, pulling her hands gently away from his. 'I do have to be up early. My job is important to me.'

There was disappointment in his eyes. He leant into her and kissed her lips.

She had been so startled that she didn't react. Ashley smiled and told her he would look forward to seeing her the next evening.

Beattie sighed now as she carried on walking. Still, at least she was fulfilling her remit. She was getting to know Ashley Bowen.

Reaching King's Road, she put two fingers in her mouth and whistled, enjoying the loud and piercing noise, which immediately found her a taxi. Her parents had been annoyed with Jack for teaching her something so unbecoming for a lady. She, of course, loved it, and always whistled for a taxi when she was on her own.

Despite the cold and gloomy night, the streets of Soho were thronging with people on their way to and from the cafés and bars that lined the streets. Working girls eyed her suspiciously as she walked past and Beattie wished she didn't feel quite so prim and proper. Jazz music – so modern and so *different* – vibrated on the air, out of the lighted windows of bars and nightclubs. There were Italian voices mingling with English all around her.

And there it was, the Dandelion Grill, and beneath it, the White Pearl Club. Of course, there was nothing to indicate it was a club of some repute, but if she observed the faces of the men who went up and down the dark steps in their smart coats and with furled umbrellas, they mostly wore furtive expressions or refused to look anywhere but at their feet. There was the odd one who looked defiant, almost pleased with themselves. There were women too, faces heavily made up, wearing gaudy clothes and high-heeled shoes Beattie could only dream of being able to walk in.

No point in wasting time.

She made her way down the steps.

She had no compunction about entering what many would call a den of iniquity; she'd done worse things in her life and the sight of naked men or women or women dancing with women or men with men was not going to trouble her. She had one thing on her mind, and that was to find out about Sofia Huber and the White Pearl Club.

She pushed open the door at the bottom of the stairs and found herself in a poky entrance hall painted purple and black with a small desk blocking her way through to the club. Music filtered out. There was a stench of cheap perfume and sweat and cigarettes. Behind the desk was the dim interior of the club. Scantily clad young women. A tiny dance floor. A small stage. On the stage was a voluptuous woman with a smoky, sexy voice singing a Marlene Dietrich song. Behind the desk sat someone in a blonde wig and lashings of mascara and rouge. The person could have been a man or a woman, Beattie wasn't certain which.

'Are you a member, ducky?'

'No,' said Beattie.

'Then you can't come in, gorgeous as you are.'

Beattie smiled. 'What do I have to do to become a member?'

'Pay me the joining fee.'

She delved in her handbag for her purse. 'How much?'

'Depends.' He, for Beattie was sure the person was a he

by the timbre of his voice, leant forward into the light and smiled, his pink lipsticked mouth stretching wide. There was lipstick on his teeth, but Beattie said nothing.

She took some coins out of her purse and proffered them up.

'That'll do,' the doorkeeper said, snatching the money out of her hand and lifting a wooden flap fixed to the end of the desk. 'As long as you ain't a copper or a copper's nark.'

'I'm not,' laughed Beattie. 'As far as I know anyway.'

The doorkeeper grinned, looking her up and down. 'Not sure you're in the right clothes for here.' He waved two men, hair brilliantined so it shone and wearing suits and wary expressions, through without comment. Obviously regulars. They looked at Beattie with curiosity.

Beattie had taken her coat off to expose her sensible skirt and jumper – sensible for a cold church, perhaps not so appropriate for the White Pearl Club. She shrugged, seeing the look the doorkeeper gave her. 'It's what I dressed in earlier.'

'You can always take some of it off, if you know what I mean.' The doorkeeper winked. Lasciviously.

Beattie laughed. 'I think I know what you mean. What's your name?'

The doorkeeper pursed his lips. 'Depends who's asking.' He licked his lips. 'I'm Morris some days, Marlene others.'

'Like Marlene Dietrich.'

'My heroine.'

There was clapping from within the club as the singer finished her Dietrich song.

'And today?'

'Marlene. At the moment, anyway.'

'Marlene,' said Beattie. 'My name is Beattie Cavendish.'

'Charmed, I'm sure,' said Marlene, shaking her hand.

'Marlene, do you know a lady by the name of Sofia Huber?'

Beattie showed him the photograph Martin had given her.

'Why are you showing me this?' Marlene asked.

'Do you know her?'

'Course I do. And I know she's dead.' Marlene's lip trembled. 'She was one of the good ones. Always passed the time of day with you, asked after the family. Customers loved her too. But she never lost sight of herself.'

Beattie wanted to hug this person who looked so sad.

Marlene straightened up. 'Why are you asking these questions, Miss Cavendish?'

'I want to find out who killed her.'

'I heard it was a petty thief, robbery gone wrong.'

Beattie narrowed her eyes. 'Can I trust you?'

Marlene nodded.

'I think it was more than that. Look.' She took out the newspaper clipping from her handbag she had brought with the photograph of Ralph and Edwina Bowen at a charity function. The photograph was a little blurry, but Ralph Bowen's features were clear. She showed it to Marlene.

Marlene's face closed up.

'You know who this is, don't you?' said Beattie.

Marlene stared at her. 'Rose,' he shouted. 'Rose, can you come here, I need a break.'

A woman with heavy make-up, false eyelashes and

dressed in a corset and tail feathers sashayed through a door at the side of the desk. 'You called?'

'I did. I need to talk to this young lady for a few minutes. About someone.'

Rose clasped her hands together. 'Someone?' She narrowed her eyes. 'Who?'

'It doesn't matter,' said Marlene. 'Stay here.' Marlene grabbed Beattie's wrist and led her into the room next door.

It was a mean little room smelling of powder and smoke and sweat. There were mirrors and hooks for clothes. A couple of chairs and a sink and a kettle. Marlene – or maybe Morris now as he'd taken his wig off to reveal black slicked-back hair – sighed.

'Marlene—'

'It's all right, I'll be Morris now,' said Morris wearily. 'It'll be easier. Wig's too hot anyway. Since the war I haven't been able to get any decent ones. Do sit.'

'What do you do when there's a police raid?' Beattie took out her cigarette case and offered one to him. She liked Marlene and Morris.

He shook his head. 'Not for me, ducky. They're dangerous.' He smiled to acknowledge the irony of his words. He pointed to a door she hadn't noticed because it was covered with hanging clothes. 'That leads to a back alley and we run. Simple. But then the police raids are mainly for show.'

'Oh?'

'Come on, ducky. You know the score. Gangs, protection rackets. Dirty coppers. London's full of 'em. Has been since the end of the war. During it too. Some of 'em even come here.' He sighed. 'Crime thrives in times like these, when the good stuff is in short supply and when we're all looking over our shoulders wondering who the enemy is now. Nobody trusts anybody any more. And people like me, well, you know. That's why I've found a home here.' Morris picked up a bottle of brandy and two lipstick-stained glasses. 'Fancy a snifter? You can buy champers in the club but it's pricey.'

'A snifter would be lovely, thank you, Morris.' More enjoyable than being with the Bowens.

After they were settled, Morris with his drink and Beattie with hers and a cigarette, Morris sighed deeply. 'You need to be careful, ducky, who you ask questions about. Some people don't like to be recognised, if you know what I mean.'

'I know you recognised Ralph Bowen in the newspaper clipping I showed you.'

He held up his hand to tell her to stop. 'People don't tend to use their real names when they come here, and privacy is assured. If it wasn't, then they wouldn't come. And I don't know you from Adam – or Eve – so why should I talk to you? Even though you seem like a very nice lady,' he added.

Beattie opened her mouth to answer, but Morris jumped in first. 'You see, it's also dangerous to start flashing names and photographs around willy-nilly. You have to be careful, do you see?'

'I do see, Morris. But Sofia died before her time and I want to find out why.'

'And he . . .' Morris pointed to the news clipping. 'He has something to do with her dying?'

'Well, she worked for Ralph Bowen, yes – what?'

Morris was looking at her hard. 'Sofia worked for him?'

'Yes,' Beattie answered eagerly. So he had seen both Sofia and Ralph, together, of that she was certain.

Her certainties were soon called into question.

'Sofia worked here.' Morris sniffed. 'She always had a good word to say about everybody.'

Beattie nodded. 'She was trying to earn extra money. Did you ever see them together?'

Morris shook his head. 'Not *together* together, if that's what you mean. I have definitely seen him' – he jabbed the paper – 'two or three times. Of course, I'm not on duty every day, so there could have been other occasions—'

He was interrupted by much shouting and the sound of a fist pounding on a table.

Morris jumped up and raced out into the dingy hallway, Beattie following on his heels.

She was met with the sight of Corrigan, bouncing on his feet, an angry but determined look on his face, squaring up to two bearded and black-haired men, one large with too many muscles, the other small and lean with a ferrety face.

'I have paid my money and now you bastards won't let me in.'

'*Nyet,*' said Ferrety-Face, his hand on Corrigan's chest.

Russian, thought Beattie. One of the new enemies. And then she noticed that Corrigan was flanked by a man, also hefty, but with flaming red hair and pale skin. His fists were bunched in readiness.

'*Nyet,*' Ferrety-Face said again, glaring at Corrigan and his companion. 'Not for you, you leetle sheet. You one-eyed piece of sheet. You never come into my club. *Never.*'

'I'm only asking—' began Corrigan, before he had to duck as a fist threatened to connect with his chin. Corrigan's companion tried to climb onto the desk, readying himself to hit back, but Corrigan hauled him back to the ground. Good job too, as Beattie thought neither Corrigan nor his companion were a match for the two Russians.

Sheet? Ah, of course.

'What's happening here, can't you see you're scaring the girls?' said Morris.

Beattie saw Rose in the corner, shaking. She thought Morris looked a bit pale too.

'You lazy queer,' said the large Russian, looking over his shoulder at Morris. 'You go fuck yourself.'

Morris held up his hands defensively. 'Now, Igor . . .'

'Mr Kuznetsov to you,' he snarled. 'This is my club.' He squared up to Corrigan.

'Our club, my brother,' said Ferrety-Face aggressively.

'Mr Kuznetsov,' Morris addressed Igor tentatively. 'May I help to resolve this disagreement?'

'No. And why weren't you here at the desk? You were drinking at the bar?'

Beattie thought that was rather rich, coming from a man who was wreathed in alcohol fumes.

'You can go and find another job.' Igor Kuznetsov glowered underneath his eyebrows. He leant over the desk and grabbed Corrigan's coat lapels. 'And you. Don't ever come here again.'

Beattie stepped forward. 'Mr Kuznetsov?' She smiled her most dazzling smile.

Igor Kuznetsov looked her up and down. 'Who are you?'

'My name is Beattie Cavendish.' She thrust out her hand and waited for Kuznetsov to take it. There were a tense few moments, then Kuznetsov did indeed take Beattie's hand in his big paw, letting Corrigan go at the same time.

Beattie shook his hand. 'Delighted to meet you, Mr Kuznetsov. I'm afraid it was me who has been taking up Morris's time; please don't blame him. And I'll leave now and take these two gentlemen with me.' She kept smiling.

'You know them?' He still glowered.

'I'm afraid I do.'

Her smiles and deference were working; the Russian visibly relaxed.

'Rose,' bellowed Kuznetsov. 'Get back here. You.' He pointed to the cowering Morris. 'You behave. Nice to have met you, Miss Cavendish. I do not wish to see those men again.' He turned to his brother, who was clenching and unclenching his fists, balancing on the balls of his feet, spoiling for a fight. 'Viktor.' So that was his name. 'Back to business.'

Morris scuttled into the side room, while Beattie took hold of Corrigan's arm and tugged him towards the stairs. She felt his resistance so tugged harder. 'And you,' she said to the flame-haired man, pushing him in front of her.

They emerged into the busy night-time London street where Beattie breathed a sigh of relief to feel the cold air on her face. She turned to Corrigan. 'What on earth were you doing? If that's the way you go about your detective work, I'm surprised you have any clients at all.'

'Oh, but she's a feisty one, Corrigan, and no mistake,' said the flame-haired man.

Beattie glared at him. 'And who, exactly, are you?'

'Finn McNulty at your service,' he said with a small bow. 'Corrigan's right-hand man.'

'Really?' Her voice was cold. What had happened in the club was so stupid.

'No, not really,' said Corrigan. 'I took him with me for support because I knew the Kuznetsovs wouldn't let me in on my own. Finn here told me he had a good relationship with the brothers.'

Beattie wondered what that meant. A protection racket?

'But it seems he hasn't. No more than you, Corrigan,' said Beattie, still cross with them both.

'No problem at all,' said Finn, slapping Corrigan on the back. 'No problem at all.'

'So what was your plan? To shoulder your way in and then what?'

Corrigan had the grace to look sheepish. 'I suppose I hadn't got much further than thinking I needed to get inside the club. Then I was going to see who I could talk to.'

Beattie raised her eyes to heaven. 'Really? That was it?'

'Now, what I think yous both need is a little drink,' said Finn. Then his face clouded over. 'Though I'm not sure about the little lady.'

'A drink would be fine for this *little lady*,' said Beattie. 'I need to talk to Corrigan here. Which way, Mr McNulty?'

'Um . . .'

'It's all right, Finn, Beattie will be fine, I can tell you that much.'

'Excellent,' said Beattie, feeling like a schoolmistress shepherding unruly boys. 'Then let's find a taxi and get out of here. Before there's a police raid or somebody takes our picture.' She began to march down the street, wanting to put some distance between herself and the club.

All at once, out of a side-street, ran Morris. 'Miss Cavendish,' he said, clearly out of breath.

'Morris.' Beattie stopped, surprised.

Morris stopped, panting, bent down, hands on the top of his knees. 'Miss Cavendish, Beattie, thank you for saving my bacon in there.'

'That's fine, Morris, please don't worry about it. If it hadn't been for those two great lummoxes' – she pointed to Finn and Corrigan – 'that wouldn't have happened.'

'Could you show me that newspaper clipping again?'

She dug it out of her handbag.

Morris peered at it. 'That's it. Thought so. Like I said, I've seen 'im a few times. And then I thought, hang on a minute, and that's when I knew I had to come and find you. Thing is, I've seen her as well.'

'Her?'

'Yes, her.' He pointed. 'She came to the club just before Sofia was killed.'

Morris was pointing to Edwina Bowen.

'Well, well,' said Corrigan.

'Who the devil are they?' asked Finn.

'That puts a different complexion on things, doesn't it?' said Beattie, her face grim.

CHAPTER TWENTY

'Like the shebeens of the old days, eh, Corrigan?' said Finn, dragging the back of his hand across his mouth and putting his half-drunk pint down on the bar with relish.

'Aye, something like that. You all right there, Beattie?'

'Sure she is,' said Finn – shouted Finn – clapping Beattie on her back. 'She's one of us.'

Beattie smiled as she drank down the hoppy beer, the malt smooth on her tongue. 'But I'm not sure, Mr McNulty . . .'

'Call me Finn, please, Miss Cavendish.'

'And I'm Beattie. As I was saying, wasn't it illicit spirit they used to make in shebeens?'

'Illicit spirit, illicit anything. Good health.' He raised his glass. 'Now, I'm thinking you twos want a chat without me around, is that right? Why don't you go and sit over in the corner by the fire? It's cosy an' all over there, and a bit more fitting for a young lady.'

Beattie smiled. 'Don't worry about me, Finn, I've been to all sorts of places in my time.' She looked around the Wagon and Horses – Corrigan's local in Clapham – at the old and the young men supping or swilling back their drinks, pretending they weren't looking at her with some curiosity. The place smelt of alcohol and cigarettes and sweat, the floor was covered in sawdust and sticky mess, yet Beattie felt safe. She thought no one would dare to cross Finn McNulty.

'I'm sure you have. I'm sure you have.'

But Finn was right, Beattie wanted very much to talk to Corrigan, and not just about the photograph of Edwina Bowen.

'So,' said Corrigan, as they sat down by the fire that was flaming and spitting. 'Edwina Bowen. Well, well, well.'

'What did you think you were doing?' The words burst out of Beattie.

Corrigan put down his pint. 'What do you mean?'

'What do I mean? *What do I mean*?' She closed her eyes to steady herself. 'You could have got yourself killed back at that club. You should know better than to cross the Russians. What were you thinking?'

'I didn't realise Kuznetsov was going to be there.'

'What? You *know* him?' She gulped down the beer, hoping to quell the anger fizzing inside her.

'I've come across him, yes.' He looked down into his pint. Avoiding looking at her, Beattie thought.

'Right. How?'

Corrigan shifted in his chair. No, he *squirmed* in his chair, Beattie was pleased to see.

'I, um, helped his wife. Well, she was his wife. Not any more. I helped in a business capacity, you understand.'

Beattie raised her eyes to heaven. 'No wonder he looked as though he wanted to kill you.'

'No wonder,' muttered Corrigan.

'And Finn?'

'What about him?'

'Why was he with you?'

Corrigan laughed. 'Why do you think? Look at the size of him. Almost a match for Kuznetsov.'

'Almost,' said Beattie, her lips twitching. 'He was your protection, was he?'

'Something like that. Look, Beattie, you may think I'm stupid . . .'

'I don't, actually, Corrigan.'

'But I knew I was going into the devil's den. And people like that only know one language.'

'Maybe.'

'Believe me, they do. Another?' Corrigan pointed at her empty glass.

'Why not? Though are you sure we're safe from the law in here? After all, it's the middle of the night.'

'I'm surprised you're worried, after your performance at the White Pearl.' He smiled. 'We're safe. Coppers know better than to tangle with Finn. And I'll get you home safely.' Corrigan stood.

'That's good of you.'

He looked at her. She looked at him, her gaze steady.

She watched as he went to the bar, trying to disguise his limp. She would not feel sorry for him.

'Right,' Corrigan said as he put another pint in front of her. 'What do you think about Edwina Bowen visiting the White Pearl?'

'She could have been going to see what her husband got up to, you know, after your reports? But then, did he get up to anything?'

'What do you mean?'

'Exactly that. Was he cavorting with queers? With prostitutes? Or with Sofia?'

'What did your man Morris say?'

'Before we get to that, what did your man Kit say about Sofia?' She stifled a yawn. It was late and it had been a very strange day what with the meeting with Anthony and then the *Messiah*. Not to mention the Russians at the White Pearl Club. She was ready for her bed. The drink had begun to make her sleepy, and she needed to keep her wits about her for this double life she was leading.

'Ah.' Corrigan stretched out his leg. 'Kit.'

'What about him?' She was curious to see a look of sadness, or perhaps disappointment on Corrigan's face. 'What did he tell you?'

'Precisely nothing.' And Corrigan went on to tell her about how Kit had run away, how he had been hauled into the police station and effectively warned off looking into Sofia's death.

'Hmm,' Beattie said at the end of his tale.

'You don't seem unduly surprised,' Corrigan remarked, watching her closely.

Beattie thought quickly, trying to match his gaze. Obviously she couldn't tell Corrigan about her meeting with Anthony Cooper and the fact she had been warned off too; that was something that had happened to COS Beattie, not to the Beattie whom Corrigan knew. She sipped rather than gulped her beer this time. But how serious was this all becoming? 'Do you think that when he called you, Kit really meant to tell you something?' She was trying to direct the conversation in a different direction.

'I do. He sounded truly frightened on the phone, but desperate to talk as well, if you know what I mean.'

Beattie nodded.

'I'm sure he had something to say,' Corrigan continued. 'But the woman in the park obviously put the fear of God into him. He left me for the wolves to devour.'

Beattie smiled. 'That sounds drastic.'

'It was jolly uncomfortable, I can tell you that,' he said with feeling. 'That bastard – pardon me – Dicky Morgan told me in no uncertain terms to back off. Warned of hell and damnation and charges if I didn't.' For a second he wondered whether to tell Beattie of his suspicion about his phone being tapped but decided against it. It was only a suspicion after all.

'So are you?'

Corrigan looked at her, a smile on his face. 'What do you think? It takes more than a scurvy eejit to frighten me. And one more thing – Sofia was with child.'

'With child?'

'Having a baby,' said Corrigan, somewhat awkwardly.

Beattie sat back in her seat. 'Well, that's a new one. How do you know?'

'I have friends everywhere,' said Corrigan.

'I'm sure you do.' She grinned, then grew sober again. 'Sofia, expecting a baby. I wonder whose it was.'

'We could be looking at a simple crime of passion? Discarded lover?'

'More like a lover who couldn't afford for his mistress to get pregnant because of the scandal,' said Beattie.

'Could be. I take it you're talking about Ralph Bowen? I mean, that would make some sort of sense, wouldn't it?

Especially as the number on the book of matches went through to Bowen's office.'

'Yes,' said Beattie slowly. 'But didn't you say that Sofia's death looked more like a cold-blooded execution?'

Corrigan drained his pint. 'I did. But still . . .'

'Maybe the father wasn't Ralph Bowen. Maybe there was someone else on the scene?'

'Martin had his suspicions about a gentleman friend, didn't he? But he didn't know for sure. The only man we know about is Ralph Bowen. We don't know if there was anyone else close to her.'

'And then there's the church,' said Beattie thoughtfully. 'Perhaps Ralph was going to the church to pray for forgiveness? Confess to the priest? Perhaps some of Edwina's Catholicism had rubbed off on him.'

'Apparently Bowen wanted to ask advice about one of his constituents. Another time he went to the church to tell Father Kevin that Edwina would be late for choir or organ practice or something.'

Beattie looked sceptical.

'I know,' said Corrigan. 'I didn't believe Father Kevin either.'

The fire had burnt low. Beattie couldn't stop herself from yawning. All the thinking and the wondering was giving her a headache. And she knew she had to go to the office in Mayfair in the morning to catch up with her translation work. Then there was the cocktail party. The thought of that made her groan inwardly.

She stood up, gathering her coat and gloves before picking up her hat and handbag. 'I have to be up in the morning to go to work. And I have a cocktail party to attend in the evening. At the Bowens'.'

Corrigan perked up. 'I could come with you. We could case the joint.'

Beattie laughed. 'Now you're sounding like someone from a Hollywood gangster movie. Besides, I'll be there with Ashley. I can hardly take you, can I?'

He sniffed. 'You have a point. And it's not as if I'd go unnoticed.' He stood. 'I'll see you home.'

'There's no need, Corrigan. I'll be all right.'

'I'm sure you will, but I'll see you home, nonetheless. My ma would never forgive me if I let a lady walk home in the dark on her own.'

They left the warmth of the pub and Beattie managed to hail a taxi almost immediately, her whistle impressing Corrigan, who gave her an admiring look.

'Now I can't do my duty and see you home,' said Corrigan.

'You didn't think I was going to walk all that way, did you?' Though her spending on taxis was exorbitant. Thank goodness she had something of an expense account from COS. 'My mother,' she said. 'Gives me a small allowance for taxis. She doesn't like to think of me walking or catching the Tube late at night.' *Stop talking. Too much. Keep the lies minimal.*

Corrigan shook his head and opened the taxi door.

'Let me know how the cocktail party goes, won't you?' said Corrigan.

'It's just a cocktail party.'

'But you could, you know, do a bit of spying for us?'

'Spy on the Bowens?' She pretended to consider it. 'It's a thought, Corrigan. I'll keep my eyes and ears open. Goodnight.'

For a moment Corrigan seemed to hesitate and lean towards her and Beattie had an odd feeling deep in her stomach, a flutter, a feeling she'd not had for many years. Then she climbed into the taxi and Corrigan turned away and the distinctly odd moment dissolved.

After paying the taxi driver, Beattie hurried to Stranger's Square and was about to push open the front door when she heard a noise behind her. She whirled round.

'Miss Cavendish? Beattie?'

'Hello?' she said, her body tense, ready for flight.

'It's Nell. Patrick's fiancée. May I come in? I've been sitting here waiting for you. It's a little cold.'

If she looked closely, she could see that Nell had her arms wrapped around herself and was shivering despite her good woollen coat. 'Come in, come in,' she said.

Nell wiped her face with her hand and followed Beattie into the brightly lit grand entrance hall with its high ceiling and marble floor, where Beattie nodded to the porter before getting into the small lift. They travelled to the third floor in silence.

'Here we are,' said Beattie, putting her key into the lock.

Beattie put a match to the fire and made Nell sit close to it. The woman looked pale, almost ill. 'I'll make us a cup of tea and put a drop of brandy in it; that should warm us both up.'

Soon they were both settled in front of the fire and the room was slowly heating up. Nell's teeth had ceased chattering.

Beattie sipped her tea, feeling the warmth of the brandy

slide down her throat, joining the brandy she'd had with Morris and the beer she had already drunk. She had to keep her wits about her. 'What is it, Nell?' Though she had a fair idea of what Nell was going to say.

'It's Patrick,' she said. 'I'm so worried about him. He's quite fragile, you know, what with his war wounds and what happened at the end of the war.'

'What did happen?'

Nell was quiet for a moment. She shook her head. 'He must tell you that; it's something he's ashamed of and it's his story, not mine.'

Beattie understood; she felt the same way about what had happened to her and Luc. 'I see,' she said.

'No, you don't see, not really. He shouldn't be doing this running around, getting beaten up, talking to the wrong people – who knows where he might end up?'

Beattie wondered what Nell would say when Corrigan told her about being held in a prison cell for much of the afternoon. And that he had gone to a disreputable club this evening. Or perhaps he wouldn't tell her. Either way, it was none of her business.

'But he loves doing it, Nell,' she said gently.

'Does he?' Nell looked at her, lips trembling, doe eyes glistening with tears, and Beattie could understand why Corrigan wouldn't want to hurt her.

She nodded.

Nell sighed. 'It would be much better if he had a steady job with my father with a steady wage. We could move to the country. Have a family. He could heal.' Nell's hands shook as she drank her tea.

Beattie bit her lip. She could understand what Nell was

saying. Why, after all these uncertain years, she wanted some certainty. A normal life. A house. Children. Evenings by the fire. Sewing. Reading. Not too much excitement. Life. Isn't that what she yearned for sometimes, even though she knew it would never be for her? But she sensed in Corrigan a restlessness similar to her own, that he wasn't the sort of person to settle down and play happy families. She could be wrong, of course.

'I expect you think I'm weak and silly, only wanting a home and family.'

'Not at all.'

'You're doing something with your life. I should be jealous.'

Beattie reached out a hand. 'No, don't think that. Never think that. We choose different paths. Besides, you're a teacher; you help form the minds of children. That's worthwhile. What I do is very dull.'

Nell waved a hand. 'Maybe, but you know your own mind. I sense you're someone not easily swayed by what people think you should do. You seem to have a plan. After the war I was expected to marry, settle down, have a family.'

'And there's nothing wrong with that, if that's what you want.'

'Easy to say,' she said, her voice bitter. 'Sometimes we're not given a choice. Anyway.' She seemed to shake herself. 'Were you with Patrick tonight?' Nell asked.

Beattie nodded. 'We went to a club we thought Sofia Huber – the girl who was murdered – might have had some connection with. We didn't go together; I'd been at a concert and I went after that. Corrigan obviously thought

along the same lines. So we were there, but not together.'
You're doing it again. Babbling. Stop it.

'I see.'

Please don't ask.

'What sort of club?'

Oh dear. Beattie sighed. 'Not a very reputable club, I'm afraid.'

She nodded. 'Did he put you in danger? I couldn't bear that.'

'No. There was no danger.' Not really.

Nell nodded. 'The thing is, I know he told me he was going to give up the detective work, but I'm not sure I believe him, but you, Beattie, you could persuade him. Will you help me?' Her voice was pleading.

'I don't see how—'

'He trusts you, I think. If you said to him to make this his last case, or even to give up now, then he might listen. Please. Before things go horribly wrong for him.'

Instinctively, Beattie took her hand. 'I'll do my best,' she said, trying to forget that rather odd moment she had shared with Corrigan as she got into the taxi. 'Though ultimately it is up to him.'

'Soon, Beattie, please. Very soon.'

Beattie nodded.

Later that night, when sleep eluded her despite her exhaustion, Beattie knew she had to at least try to get Corrigan to do what Nell wanted, even though she felt sad at the prospect of never seeing him again. Then she told herself not to be so silly. Someone like her couldn't afford to become attached to people. To anybody.

CHAPTER TWENTY-ONE

Corrigan was on his first pot of tea of the morning when Nell turned up at his office.

His phone had rung twice; both were wives, one terrified with the possibility of her husband having an affair, the other worried about her husband's gambling. He had made appointments to see both of them and then he wondered why he'd done that. Hadn't he said to Nell he would give it all up? Yes, but not at this moment. Just another couple of jobs. After he and Beattie had found out who had killed Sofia Huber and why. If the coppers and whoever else thought that threats against him would stop him looking into Sofia's death – murder – they didn't know him at all. And he wanted to know who he'd, as Dicky Morgan put it, 'pissed off'. Someone important, he'd said. Who was more important than Scotland Yard? MI5 or MI6 at a guess. Very likely MI5 if they really thought he was some sort of Irish terrorist. He thought of his brothers back on the farm near Cork. Liam was a hothead; could he be involved in something? But no, it wasn't about that. It was about Sofia Huber and Ralph Bowen.

He poured himself another cup of tea and ladled the

sugar in. Where did Beattie fit in? He didn't totally believe that guff about her typist job and she was certainly a strange one, with her no-nonsense attitude and terrible taste in clothes. Yet there was something . . . He shook his head. A definite something on her doorstep last night. He had felt it and he knew she had too. What had stopped him from following the feeling through? A sense of decency? Now that thought made him laugh.

'You seem happy today.'

Corrigan looked up to see Nell standing in front of him. He had been so wrapped up in his thoughts that he hadn't heard her enter. He leapt up. 'Nell.' And came round the desk to kiss her. She tasted sweet and familiar. She kissed him back and he put her arms around her, feeling her fragility. For a moment, a fleeting moment, he wondered how Beattie Cavendish would feel in his arms.

'What is it, Patrick?' Nell stepped back, a puzzled look on her face.

'What do you mean?'

'You went away from me for a second there.'

'Did I? I'm sorry, I wasn't aware of it.' He pulled her closer and kissed her on her lips.

She smiled. 'Never mind,' she said, sitting down in one of the chairs by the desk. 'Have you seen Beattie this morning?'

A stab of guilt. Did Nell know he was thinking about Beattie? How could she?

'No,' he said. 'Should I have done?'

He saw Nell swallow. 'I think I made a bit of a fool of myself.' Her finger traced a pattern in the dust on the desk. 'I went to see her. Last night.'

'Last night?'

'She said you'd been to a club.'

'Yes, but not together. It appears we both had the same idea. It was to find out a bit more about—'

'Sofia Huber, yes, Beattie told me. But then do you know what I did?'

'Tell me.' For some reason his heart was beating faster than he could reasonably expect it to.

'I begged her, Patrick. I begged her to persuade you to let go, not to keep on with this Sofia Huber thing. Or at least to make it your last case.' Tears ran down her cheeks.

'Oh.' He could only imagine how humiliating that must have been for her.

'When I got home I realised how much I had demeaned myself.' She stood up. 'I can't do this any more, Patrick. I love you very much, but I can't do this.' She took a hankie out of her pocket and wiped her eyes.

'I love you too, Nell,' Corrigan said hoarsely.

'Maybe you do. I don't know. But not, I think, in the way that I love you. And at the moment we want different things.'

'I'll work for your father, Nell.' He was desperate now. He grabbed her hands. 'We can buy a house. One of the new houses they're building. I can do it, Nell. I can. We'll have a garden for me and a piano for you and two boys and two girls and—'

Nell shook her head, pulling her hands from his. 'I don't think you can, Patrick. I think the pull of finding out, of righting wrongs, of trying to atone is too strong.'

'I'll see a head doctor.' Really desperate.

'Do that. But not for me, for you.' Very carefully and deliberately she twisted off her engagement ring – a simple gold band with a tiny diamond – and put it on his desk.

She turned to go, giving him a sorrowful look. 'By the way, you were supposed to have lunch with me yesterday. You didn't turn up. Again.'

The sound of the door closing behind her felt final.

Corrigan shook his head. She would come round, of course she would. She was his Nell. She loved him. He opened a drawer and put Nell's ring inside.

He rolled a cigarette and sat for a long time, smoking and thinking.

The *Daily Dispatch* office was noisy with the jangling of telephones and the loud chatter of men in waistcoats and shirts with their sleeves rolled up. Most were typing furiously or smoking furiously. Some had mastered the art of doing both. Every available surface was covered with paper – newspaper, typewritten paper, paper covered with scribbled handwriting. There was an air of urgency and expectancy.

'He's over there,' the woman from reception told him. 'With the pencil behind his ear.'

The man with the pencil behind his ear was sitting typing like a madman, looked about thirty and had slicked-back hair and glasses. He had a cigarette smouldering in an ashtray beside him and he wore red braces. The braces put Corrigan on edge.

'Leo Scott?'

'Who's asking?' Scott didn't look up, didn't pause in his typing.

'My name's Patrick Corrigan and I'm a private detective.'

'Yep.' *Clack clack clack* went the typewriter. *Ding* went the bell as he hit the return lever.

'Can I have a word? Please? About the murder of Sofia Huber.'

Did he imagine it, or was there a slight hesitation in the flight of Scott's fingers over the typewriter keys?

'Sofia Huber?' *Clack clack clack. Ding.*

'Yes.' He stood right in front of the journalist, trying to force him to look at him.

Scott sighed, ripped the paper out of the typewriter, put it on top of a pile on his desk. He looked up and did a double take at the sight of Corrigan's face. 'Take a seat.' He picked up his cigarette, held it between his thumb and first finger.

The man wore braces like a toff and smoked like a navvy.

Scott moved a pile of newspapers and books to one side. 'Sorry. Had to get that done. Now, Sofia Huber, you say?' He stubbed out the cigarette.

'That's right.' Corrigan sat.

'I wrote a story about her death, yes.' He slicked back his already slicked-back hair. 'There wasn't much in it, though. I believe the police think it was a petty thief.'

Corrigan stretched out his legs and frowned. 'What sort of journalist are you?'

Scott shrugged. 'I don't know what you mean?'

'I thought journalists liked to get to the truth. That they left no stone unturned and all that.'

Scott blushed. Good. He was getting to him.

'We do. I do.'

'So, Sofia Huber?'

Scott looked around the newsroom. Everybody was concentrating on their own work; no one was listening in. He lowered his voice. 'What's your interest? A private detective, you say?'

Corrigan handed over one of his battered cards. 'I know the woman who found Sofia Huber's body. Let's just say she is not convinced that her death was the result of a "petty thief".' He drew quotation marks in the air.

Scott studied Corrigan, peered at the card, turned it over in his hands. Hesitated. Then spoke. 'I wrote a story.'

'A story?'

'It wasn't . . .' He looked around again. 'It wasn't . . .' He shook his head. 'What was published in the paper wasn't what I had written originally.'

Corrigan stared at him.

'I'd written the killing had been quite brutal, without going into details. Readers can be squeamish about that if you're not careful. Could inspire letters to the editor and all that. I'd said some stuff about Sofia Huber and her position in the household. A bit more about Ralph Bowen. I questioned the police investigation.'

'In what way?'

'I thought Scotland Yard jumped to conclusions too readily.' He offered a cigarette to Corrigan. They both lit up. 'You see, I got to the house pretty quickly after it happened, I was one of the first. Well, you would, wouldn't you? A prominent member of the opposition, a swish part of London and a murder? That's a story.'

Corrigan could see the enthusiasm in Scott's eyes.

'But I really wasn't welcome.'

Corrigan laughed; Scott looked hurt.

'All right, all right,' Scott said with a wry smile. 'I was more unwelcome than normal. Everybody had been told not to talk to me. But I found out a few juicy bits. Asked a few questions in the story I wrote that I thought the police should have a look at. It was a good piece. Not prize-winning, I know, but a solid story.'

'And then?'

'And then.' He shrugged. 'And then Webster – that's the news editor – said I had to pare it down to the bare essentials. Not ask questions, not embellish it – I ask you, as if I embellish my stories – and just report the facts. I was reporting the facts. When I asked why he'd torn it to shreds he dissembled until I pressed him. He admitted he'd been leant on.'

'By Bowen?'

'That was my question.' Scott sighed, and tapped his cigarette on the edge of a cup. 'And his answer was "partly". I mean, nobody wants to be associated with a grisly murder in their own home, especially if they've got their eyes on high office, but normally old Webster doesn't bother about that. He likes to upset the gentry, he says. Especially the Tories. Bit of a closet Labour supporter is our news editor and he's not easily intimidated.' He frowned. 'In fact, he's not intimidated at all. By anything. Or anyone, which makes it even more mysterious. No, he didn't say it outright, but he hinted it came from higher up the food chain.'

'Higher up?'

Scott leant forward and whispered, 'MI5.'

'MI5?'

'Shh.' Scott looked around. 'Keep your voice down. I'm putting my job on the line even hinting at it. But that's my guess.'

'Your guess?'

'Yep.'

'And why are you telling me?'

'Don't know, really. I think it's because I'm bloody angry. And you're listening.'

'Well, if you're right, then you should keep your mouth shut.' Corrigan meant it.

'I know, I know, the walls have ears and all that. But if you're looking into Sofia Huber's death, take care, won't you? And for now I've been relegated to robbery and suicides.' He picked up a photograph and flicked it with his thumb. 'This poor chap. Fished out of the Thames last night. He's a known homosexual so I suppose that's why he drowned himself.'

Corrigan couldn't help but glance at the photograph. He did a double take and looked again.

'He hadn't been in there long; he was found by a tramp on the waterline. A friend at police headquarters sent this photograph to me.' Scott shook his head sorrowfully. 'We can't print it, though. Too much for our readers.'

There was no bloating of the body, nor much discolouration though his full lips were dark and there was purple bruising around his eyes, but the face was relaxed and child-like. It was Kit.

Scott was watching him. 'You know who this is.' The journalist stated this as a fact.

Corrigan nodded slowly. 'I do. His name was Kit Pearson. Suicide, you say?'

Scott looked at Corrigan carefully. 'What do you know that I don't?' He tapped the picture with his finger.

'Nothing. But you could do a little digging.'

'Not suicide?'

'I didn't say that. It could be worth a few questions.'

'How well did you know him?'

'A little.'

Scott narrowed his eyes. 'Tell me more.'

'I can't, not yet. Look. Do some asking around, see what you come up with. Maybe find the tramp who found his body. I promise you, if I can, you'll be the first to have the story. If there is a story.'

Scott shook his head. 'You're talking in riddles.'

'Look. Like you, I have to protect my sources.'

'I understand that.' Scott looked down at Kit. 'Poor bugger.'

'Yes,' said Corrigan. 'Poor bugger.'

'But why should I listen to you? I've already had a dressing-down from Webster; I don't want or need another one.'

'I'll give you something.' Corrigan paused. Then, 'Sofia Huber was expecting a baby when she died.'

Scott raised his eyebrows and whistled. 'Not old man Bowen? Exercising his *droit du seigneur*, the old rogue?'

'We don't know.'

'We?' He frowned. 'Does that include the lady who found Miss Huber? A Miss' – he picked up a notebook from his desk and flicked through it – 'Beatrice Cavendish. They wouldn't let me speak to her, either.'

'Maybe.' The man was sharp.

'There's a lot you're not telling me, Corrigan, but

you've told me enough to make me curious. I'll have a dig around.'

'Let me know what you find out.'

Scott narrowed his eyes again. 'I might.'

'As I said, I'll help you when I can.'

The newspaper man nodded. Took a swig from a cup on his desk then made a face. 'Yeuch. Cold tea.'

Suddenly Corrigan felt he was asking too much, that he was leading the young man into danger. 'Scott, be careful, won't you?'

Scott nodded. 'I will.'

CHAPTER TWENTY-TWO

Light spilt out from the windows onto the pavement, and Beattie took a deep breath as she made her way to the front door of the Bowens' house. For some unaccountable reason, she was nervous. Perhaps, she reasoned, she was worried that she was not wearing the right clothes? Though she had made an effort and was wearing a dress of midnight-blue silk, with a slight flare in the skirt and a shawl collar that showed off rather too much of her décolletage. She was also wearing her last precious pair of nylons. She took a deep breath. She knew she could do this. Tonight she was Beattie Cavendish who was the girlfriend of the son of the Shadow Foreign Secretary.

The door opened as she was poised to use the knocker. Ashley stood there, glass in hand, looking passably handsome in black tie and tails. Golly, this really was a swish do.

'Beattie, I saw you coming; I've been waiting for you.'

He was, Beattie could see, slightly drunk. There was a sway to his body and his eyes were too bright.

'Come in, come in. It's lovely to see you.'

Annie took her coat and Ashley led her through to the drawing room.

The room pulsed with light and conversation. The scent of expensive floral perfumes and sharp male cologne hung in the air, joining forces with smoke from cigarettes, pipes and cigars. Flowers covered every surface – impressive for November – and maids in starched aprons scurried amongst guests dispensing champagne and canapés.

'My dear Beattie, how are you?' Gerald Silver loomed in front of her, managing to look both smart and bohemian in his velvet jacket and cravat. He bent to kiss her cheek.

Beattie did not recoil.

'Felicia is here somewhere,' said Gerald. 'I'm sure she'll be pleased to see you.'

'I'm sure,' murmured Beattie, taking a glass of champagne from Ashley as Gerald moved away. 'This is very impressive, Ashley, I must say.'

Ashley beamed. 'Isn't it? Mother likes to put on these soirées after one of her spectacular concerts. A sort of "thank you". She knows so many people.'

'And there are fellow politicians here, too?'

'Yes, there are. Oh look, here's Charles, one of my old school chums. He went to Cambridge; you might know him.' He began to lead her towards a slim man with a large forehead. 'Charles.' He waved. Beattie resigned herself to a long and possibly dull conversation with Charles.

'It's nice to see you here, Miss Cavendish.' Edwina Bowen appeared on her shoulder. 'You go and talk to Charles, dear,' she said to her son. 'I'll have a word with your lovely friend.'

Beattie took a salmon canapé that was offered.

'So you enjoyed our little concert, then, Miss Cavendish?'

asked Edwina Bowen, her gaze darting all around the room as if she were waiting for someone more interesting to come along. Or was it more that she was anxious and tense?

'Please, do call me Beattie. And I did. Very much. The music was magnificent and the choir, of course, excellent. I understand from Ashley that this party is to thank people who came?'

'It is, yes. And many of the singers.'

'And Mr Bowen must be proud of you.'

'Ralph? Yes, I suppose so. Tell me again, Beattie, how did you meet Ashley?'

'At Alicia Gainborne's party. We have some friends in common, from Cambridge University.'

'Ashley didn't go to university.'

'No, I know.'

'It's not that he couldn't have gone, just that he . . .'

Was lazy, thought Beattie, immediately disliking herself for being uncharitable.

'Well, let's say it wasn't for him,' Edwina Bowen finished.

'It isn't for everybody,' Beattie said kindly.

'No. But it makes me wonder what a clever girl like yourself sees in Ashley.'

'I'm not that clever.'

For a moment the party seemed to stop as Edwina Bowen looked at her with shrewd eyes. 'Oh, I think you are, Beattie. Cleverer than a girl working in a typing pool should be. Why is that, do you think?'

'I'm not just working in a typing pool, Mrs Bowen; I teach girls to type and to take dictation, do exacting office work. As you know, a good secretary is worth her weight in gold.' She gave a deferential smile.

'If you say so. Now, if you'll excuse me, I must see if Ralph has arrived. He's been at the House, you see.'

Beattie nodded.

After Edwina Bowen left her, Beattie let out a breath and made her way over to the piano, on top of which lay music books. Beethoven. Chopin. Bach. Edwina was obviously an accomplished pianist. There were sheets of manuscript paper, some blank, some already notated. Others had musical notes written on them in pencil. Did Edwina compose music as well?

'You look thirsty.'

Gerald Silver appeared over her shoulder and handed her another glass of champagne. Beattie accepted it, although she was beginning to feel a little tipsy.

'And you have been abandoned.'

She smiled. 'Thank you. And I've only been abandoned temporarily while Ashley talks to some old friends.'

'Nonetheless, he shouldn't leave a beautiful woman such as yourself on her own.'

Beattie laughed. 'You do talk tosh, Gerald.'

Gerald smiled, not in the least abashed. He looked her up and down. 'Hmm. You look delectable tonight. Are you enjoying yourself?'

Beattie bit back her annoyance. 'Cocktail parties are not quite my thing,' she said. 'But Ashley wanted me to come.'

'No,' said Gerald. 'I can't imagine they would be. Still. There are some interesting people here tonight. The odd artist, sculptor even. See, Barbara Hepworth is over there –

she is becoming rather famous.' Beattie saw a middle-aged woman with dark wavy hair looking mildly uncomfortable as two women talked at her. 'They're always glad to have some patronage from the great and the good. Tories or not.'

'Is that what they do for you? The Bowens? Give you patronage?'

Gerald laughed. 'I could be insulted by the way you put that, Beattie, but I do, in fact, find your forthrightness charming. However, I have to say, you are quite correct in your supposition. They introduce me to the right people.'

'The right people?'

'Those who have enough money to buy my work.'

'I see.'

'You're surprised? Did you think I was some sort of dilettante who enjoys daubing pictures and bedding models in my garret room?'

Beattie laughed. 'I didn't think anything, Gerald, though Felicia certainly has the eye for you. She sees you as a sort of romantic hero, I think, even though you are far too old for her.'

At this he sighed, and Beattie felt the beginning of a liking for Gerald Silver.

'I am too old for her and she is not my type.'

'What is your type?' Beattie was beginning to enjoy herself at last.

'Older. Experienced. That way, women are not any trouble; they don't expect so much.'

At this, Beattie shook her head. How insufferably egotistical the man was. 'You can't have had so much experience with women if you think they don't expect much.'

He raised his eyebrows. 'Then it's a shame you are taken, Miss Cavendish.'

'You're flirting with me, Mr Silver. I am not old enough for you. And sadly, I'm not entirely sure that Mr and Mrs Bowen think I am a suitable person for Ashley to be walking out with.'

'I don't know why. You're very personable.' He gave her a look that made her feel like a pinned butterfly.

She arched an eyebrow at him. 'I'm not sure "personable" is the best compliment.'

He tilted his head to one side. 'You really are quite the mystery.'

He was laughing at her, Beattie realised.

'Who is quite the mystery?'

Felicia appeared by Beattie's side, drink in hand.

'I was saying that Beattie is quite the mystery,' said Gerald, not looking at Felicia but holding Beattie's gaze.

'Isn't she just.' Felicia looked her up and down with a sneer on her face. 'Still here, then.'

Beattie looked sharply at Felicia. The young woman's eyes glittered with drink or anger, Beattie couldn't be sure. Was her animosity because she was friendly with Ashley or was it something more?

'Here?'

'With Ashley.' She hiccupped. 'Whoops,' she said, covering her mouth with a delicate hand. 'I would have thought he'd have found you out by now.'

'I admire your mother's prowess in music,' said Beattie evenly, determined not to be cowed or irritated by Felicia.

Felicia finished her glass, beckoning to a waitress for more. 'Yes, she is talented.'

'And writes her own music. Perhaps I could hear some one day.'

'That will be up to Mother. And I doubt you'll be around for long enough. Now, Gerald, I would like to talk to you.' And with that she took Gerald's hand. He gave her a rueful look and a shrug, as if to say, *What can I do?* Beattie didn't give two hoots, apart from the fact she thought Felicia Bowen could do with learning some manners. Nonetheless, despite not giving those two hoots, she watched as Felicia led the suave Gerald away.

Ashley made his way over to her. 'Enjoying yourself, my darling?'

She noted the use of the word 'darling' and supposed she was making progress. She had to concentrate on her job. She looked up at him and smiled. 'Yes, thank you.'

'Gerald keeping you company, I see.' He took out his silver cigarette case and offered her one. She took it, and enjoyed inhaling the rich, sharp stink of Gauloises again.

'Not really. Talking, passing the time.'

'You have to be careful with him, Beattie. Not give him any encouragement. He has, shall we say, a reputation.'

He sounded so pompous Beattie wanted to laugh, but she also felt a large stab of irritation. Was he jealous? 'I'm perfectly able to parry Gerald's advances, I can assure you, Ashley.'

'Very well,' he said stiffly.

Beattie caught his arm. 'I'm sorry, that was waspish of me. Look. Why don't we go dancing? Or have a late supper somewhere. Just you and me.' Lord, but it was the last thing she wanted, but she made herself smile. Prettily.

'I'd like that.' He kissed the top of her head. 'Very

much.' He looked around. 'I do wonder where Father is, though. It's unlike him to miss this party; Mother would never forgive him. And where is Mother? She seems to have disappeared too. Perhaps there's been a crisis in the kitchen.'

This gave Beattie an idea. 'Go and see if you can find him. Perhaps your mother will have heard something about him by now. I'll wait for you here. And I promise I won't let Gerald lure me away.'

She watched as Ashley left the drawing room, then followed him out, as nonchalantly as possible. She saw him walking quickly down the hall on his way to the kitchen. Good.

Making sure no one was watching, she slipped across the hallway to the study. The door had been left half open, but she pushed it to behind her. The room was dimly lit by the standard lamp in the corner. Thankfully it didn't smell of blood any more, but of polish and lemon. The heavy curtains were pulled shut over the long windows and the books posed blankly on the bookshelves.

She ran over to the desk, her heart in her mouth, thankful for the thick rug that muffled her footsteps. There would not be a dead body this time. At least she hoped very much there wouldn't be one. But she hadn't finished her snoop around the desk and some instinct, some intuition, told her she should look in the drawers while she had the chance.

The desk was tidier than it had been before. The inkwell and matching stamp box sat neatly on the top. The blotter on top of the burgundy leather inlay was creamy and free of any scribbles or splodges of ink. There was a neat pile of correspondence on one side, letters written on thick, headed notepaper. Glancing at it, she saw Edwina Bowen's name at the top. Her correspondence, not his. Beattie filed that thought away. On the other side of the desk was a pile of paper. Music paper, some notated, some not. Was this perhaps Edwina's desk?

She tried the top drawer, remembering last time it had been locked. It slid open easily. Ration coupons, ledgers, bills – household bills, she thought as she cast her eye over them quickly – and a book. George Orwell's *Animal Farm*. Interesting.

The middle drawer contained various items of stationery. A fountain pen with a bottle of blue ink and one of black. Some rubber bands. A few paperclips. A pair of scissors that looked very sharp. Envelopes, large and small.

The bottom drawer was locked.

She took her picks out of her pocket. It only took a few seconds and she was sliding it open.

It was empty apart from four pieces of notated sheet music.

She stared. Why would anyone put four pieces of sheet music in a locked drawer? She looked at the top one. 'In the Bleak Midwinter'. The second: 'O Come All Ye Faithful'. She frowned. Christmas carols. In a locked drawer.

Voices. Outside the door. She paused, senses on high alert.

The door handle began to turn.

For an agonising moment, Beattie froze. Stupid. The standard lamp had been on and the door left ajar, which probably meant someone had been in the study only recently. Her training kicked in and she pushed the drawer shut, looking for somewhere to hide at the same time.

Where?

Behind the desk. She could just about squeeze herself in the space between the desk and the wall and hoped she was hidden by the three under-desk drawers.

The door opened and she heard the murmur of the party, the strains of music. Then it closed, blocking out the noise.

Footsteps.

She willed her breathing to be silent, though she could hear the blood pounding in her ears.

'We'll be private in here, Ashley.' Edwina Bowen's voice.

'What do you want, Mother? Where is Father, do you know?' Impatience from Ashley.

'Oh, I know where he is, all right; he telephoned a few moments ago to apologise for missing the cocktail party.' There was a definite anger in Edwina's voice.

'And?'

'He's in Brighton.'

'Brighton?' said Ashley, his voice echoing Beattie's silent surprise. 'What's he there for? Is it something to do with parliamentary business? Something hush-hush?'

'It's where he used to take his little tart.' Beattie felt Edwina spitting the words out.

'His little tart? Mother, that's very strong, you know.' She heard the strike of a lighter, then smelt the familiar smell as Ashley lit and breathed in the smoke from a Gauloises. 'You can't surely mean that Father had a mistress?' His voice was cool, unhurried.

'Very strong to call her a tart? It may be very strong but that's exactly what she was. And he took her there for—'

'I know what for, Mother.' He sounded almost bored, as if it wasn't a shock to him to find out his father had a mistress. 'Don't they all, these men of power, don't they all have what you might call "a little tart"?'

'You seem remarkably sanguine about it, Ashley.' There was a steely note to her voice. 'And I do wish you wouldn't smoke those revolting cigarettes.'

'Mother. It's not that difficult to imagine, you know. And do you know who this tart is, this mistress?'

Beattie imagined his lip curling.

'Mistress, that's a fine word for her.' Disdain in Edwina's voice. 'Sofia Huber, of course.'

'Sofia?' This did surprise him. 'Our Sofia?'

Edwina snorted. 'His Sofia, more like.'

'And why is he there now? Sofia's dead, so, why would he go down there?'

'God knows; I don't. But he needs to come home before anyone realises what the old fool has done.'

'Mother, did you know about Sofia?'

'Of course I did. I'm not stupid.'

Beattie wasn't surprised. Things were beginning to make some sort of sense. The photograph she had of Sofia, could that have been Brighton?

One of her legs was beginning to get pins and needles. Her neck was hurting and one of her arms was at an awkward angle. She was desperate to move her body, and it was becoming harder to keep still, to keep her breathing quiet and even. What she wouldn't give for a cigarette to take her mind off her contorted body.

'I want you to go and find him and bring him back.'

'Now?'

'Yes, now. Before he does something silly.'

'What do you mean?'

'Oh, I don't know. Throw himself in the sea, though I sometimes think that would be a blessing for all of us. But there would also be such a lot of fuss about it. I couldn't bear it.'

'But it's eleven o'clock at night. Can't I go first thing?'

Beattie wanted to laugh. Ralph Bowen had a devoted son there. The pins and needles were beginning in her other leg. She tried to rub them away. The crick in her neck was getting worse.

The sound of Edwina sighing, a lengthy sigh. 'No. I want you to go now.'

'That's most annoying, Mother. Do you know where he's staying?'

There was a bark of laughter from Edwina. 'Of course I do. The Old Ship. He probably thinks it's more discreet than the Grand. Stupid man.'

A small silence. 'Very well. I'll go and tell Beattie I'll take her home.'

'Won't she think it strange?'

'She has to go to work tomorrow, so she'll probably be quite glad.'

'For God's sake, don't tell her why, will you?'

Beattie could imagine the horror on Edwina's face. She wanted to laugh and had to stuff her fist into her mouth.

'She wouldn't say anything to anyone.'

Thank you, Ashley, for your confidence.

'Say absolutely nothing,' said Edwina, a ferocity in her

voice that was difficult to miss. 'I'm telling you not to say anything to anybody. Not a thing. We can't take the chance that this could come out.'

'Very well, Mother.'

'Thank you.'

The sound of footsteps retreating.

There was silence, and Beattie hoped that Edwina wouldn't take it into her head to sit at the desk or start looking at the books. Her prayers were answered as after a minute she heard the library door close and liberation for her legs and neck was at hand. But then there was the sound of a key turning in a lock.

She was trapped.

There was absolute silence in the room, apart from the ticking of the grandfather clock. Cautiously, she peered out from beneath the desk. Definitely no one there. The relief was immense, though now she was faced with the tricky situation of getting herself out of the study. She began to unfold her body, one limb at a time, until she was on all fours, with cramp gripping the muscles in her calves, making them like iron, and she reached back to try and massage the pain away.

Beattie went to lock the bottom drawer again, but something nagged at her. She opened it and took the four pages of sheet music out and put them in her bag. She rummaged through the papers on top of the desk, found four more pieces of music, and put them in the drawer before locking it again and straightening the papers on the desk.

Stretching as she stood, the pain finally left her muscles. She flexed her arms and rolled her shoulders. She was not made for hiding under desks, she decided, as she reached the door of the study. She smoothed down her dress, hoping it didn't look as creased to other people as it did to her.

She tried the door. Sure enough, it was locked. Taking the picks out of her pocket once more, she used one on the door. If the key had been left in the other side of the lock, she could be in a bit of a jam.

Thankfully it was not.

The pins aligned, the inner chamber rotated and she was free.

She opened the door slowly, making sure there was no one lurking in the hallway. Had she time to lock the door again? She didn't think so, so she had to hope that whoever came next to the study would think someone else had unlocked it or they had forgotten to lock it in the first place. She mentally crossed her fingers.

'Ah, Beattie. Where have you been? I was looking for you.' Ashley's citrus aftershave and cigarette smoke heralded his arrival.

'I just had to . . .' She waved her hand vaguely in no particular direction.

'I see,' said Ashley. 'Look, I'm most awfully sorry but something's come up and I need to take you home.'

'Has something happened?' she asked, managing to sound suitably concerned.

'Nothing for you to worry about.' He ran his hand over his hair. I could get Gerald to—'

'No, no, please don't worry.' That was the last thing she wanted. 'Just call me a cab.'

'No, I'll—'

Beattie put a hand on his cheek, smiling. 'A taxi is fine. I have to be up early anyway. You do whatever you have to do and telephone me when you can.' It was interesting how little she felt for him, and how much she thought of him as part of a job she had to finish.

'Are you sure?'

'Of course.'

'I'm most awfully sorry.'

'I said, it's fine.' Another sweet smile.

Thank you.' He caught her hand in his and kissed her fingers.

Not five minutes later, Beattie was standing on the pavement under a light waiting for the cab, having resisted Ashley's requests that she have someone wait with her. 'I'm not a delicate little butterfly, Ashley.'

She looked around. The night was dark and cold. The street was empty. She was standing by Ashley's Bristol. She took a small penknife out of her handbag and, kneeling down out of sight, she stuck the knife into the tyre, banging it into the rubber with the heel of her hand. Pity. It was a nice car. She moved along the car and performed the same act on his rear tyre. There. That should buy her some more time.

Now for a plan.

CHAPTER TWENTY-THREE

'It's perfect, Corrigan, don't you see?' Beattie paced around his back room, making him feel more tired than ever.

'Beattie, it's nearly midnight.' He yawned to make his point. The woman was bonkers. She'd banged on his door loud enough to wake the devil himself, and certainly loud enough to wake the family down below, and he'd had to haul her in before they thought he was some sort of Lothario.

Beattie stared at him, hand on hips. 'Where's your sense of adventure?'

'I left it in Italy,' Corrigan said grumpily, pulling his dressing-gown cord tighter. 'As I said, it's nearly midnight and I need my sleep.'

'No you don't. You told me you only slept fitfully.' Her eyes were bright and she looked as though she had more than enough energy for both of them.

He yawned again to make a point. 'Why did you come here, Beattie? What made you think I would want to join in this hare-brained scheme of yours?'

'I thought you would relish the thought of talking to Ralph Bowen. Look.' Her hands painted pictures in the air. 'You said Sofia was expecting a baby. What if—'

'Oh, no, Beattie,' groaned Corrigan. 'Don't say what I think you're going to say.'

'I am going to say it. What if it's Ralph Bowen's baby?'

'I agree it looks a possible scenario. There didn't seem to be anyone in Sofia's life other than the Bowen family.' He cleared his throat. 'There could, of course, have been other reasons for her condition. Apart from love.' He looked uncomfortable.

Beattie raised her eyebrows. 'An assault?'

'Perhaps. Even taking payment for favours. She was trying to save money to return to her homeland, and the club is, well ...'

Beattie thought for a minute. 'But from everything Martin has said, she was trying to keep a good home for him. He also said she had met someone at the club. And don't forget there's the photograph we saw where she looked so happy. It seems to me she was in love with someone.'

'Perhaps you're merely a romantic?'

'Maybe. But indulge me. If that were so, who else could be the father?'

'Ashley?'

Beattie laughed. 'I could say something rude, but I'm too much of a lady. No, I find that highly unlikely. And before you say it, I can't see Gerald not taking as many precautions as possible not to become a father. Besides, Edwina Bowen is convinced that there was something between Ralph and Sofia. Apparently he has taken her to Brighton in the past. In fact she called Sofia his "little tart".'

'Nice. The town where anything goes. Ralph it is, then,' said Corrigan.

'I understand from your tone you're highly sceptical about the idea. But wouldn't it still be the thing to do to talk to Bowen? I worry that he could be in such a funk he might do something silly.'

'You mean . . . ?'

Beattie nodded. 'Exactly that. And . . .' She looked sheepish.

'And?' he encouraged.

'And I want to get there before Ashley but there are no trains at this time of night and I haven't got a car.' The words came out in a rush.

'So?'

'You said you had transport.'

'Did I?'

'Oh, for goodness' sake, Corrigan, stop asking me questions. Yes, you told me you had transport and so I thought we could go to Brighton together in your car.'

'My car?' Now he was in trouble, and he couldn't remember ever having told Beattie he was in the possession of a car.

'You're at it again. Yes, your car. Please, Corrigan. It's a chance to talk to Ralph Bowen that we might not get again.'

What was it about this woman that made him want to do as she asked? Even in the middle of the night. When he was feeling dog-tired. 'But won't Ashley get there at the same time? I presume Ashley is also hotfooting it to Brighton to find his father?'

'Yes,' she replied, impatience in her voice. 'But we'll get there first.'

'How can you be so sure?'

'I stuck a penknife in his car tyres.'

'You did what?' Corrigan couldn't help laughing. This woman was full of surprises. And he had never seen her like this – animated, excitable. Not words he'd use about Beattie Cavendish normally.

'Well, I didn't want him to get to Brighton first, did I? Come on, Corrigan. Talking to Bowen might go a long way to solving the mystery of Sofia's death.'

There was something else there, Corrigan could see it behind her eyes. More than wanting to find out about Sofia. What was it? Part of the mystery of Beattie Cavendish. Maybe this would be a good opportunity to unlock that mystery.

'It could be dangerous,' he said.

'Dangerous?'

'Come on, Beattie. I've been beaten up and threatened, and now . . .'

'Now?'

'Kit's dead.'

'Kit?' He saw the shock in her eyes. 'Kit, the man who you were going to meet by Peter Pan?'

'The very same,' he said grimly. 'I went to see Leo Scott, the *Daily Dispatch* reporter who wrote the original story about Sofia's murder – he wore terrible red braces, by the way – he said he'd been leant on by his editor, who in turn had been leant on by someone more powerful.'

'Such as?'

'MI5, he thought.'

'MI5? Golly.'

Beattie's eyes were wide with surprise – perhaps too wide? Was she really surprised?

'Exactly. Also, while I was there, Scott was in the middle

of another story, the suspected suicide of Kit. Though we –
Scott and I – don't think it was suicide.'

'What do you think it was?'

'Murder.'

'Murder?'

Now he could see she was shocked.

'Think about it, Beattie. Kit had been warned off telling
me what he knew about Sofia, therefore he obviously knew
too much, otherwise, why bother?'

'Oh, Corrigan, that poor boy.' There was a look of
sorrow on her face.

He nodded. 'I've asked Scott to do a little more digging
over Kit's death, see if there's something we're missing. So
if we go, then we have to be very careful, even though I'm
not sure what of.'

'I agree,' said Beattie, determination on her face. 'Let's
not wait any longer. Also, once we know more about
Sofia's death, then you'll be able to tell Nell you'll take
that job at her father's company. It's for the best, I think.
Though I don't think you should. But that's your business.'

'Ah. Nell.' Sadness washed over him.

'What? Has something happened?'

'I know she came to see you.'

'Yes, yes she did.'

'She came to see me also, afterwards. She thought she
had humiliated herself.'

'No, not at all,' said Beattie, shaking her head. 'I
absolutely understood what she was saying.'

'That makes no difference; it was how she felt. And
now it seems I might not have to worry about her or her
father's job.'

'Corrigan.' Beattie looked dismayed. 'It's all my fault.'

He shook his head. 'No it's not. It was coming to a head anyway. I'm not sure how I feel.' *Stop.* What was he doing, laying his feelings on the line like this? He'd never done it before and he should not be starting now. He shrugged. 'Anyway, it will resolve itself one way or another. I suggest you go and sit in my office.'

'Why?'

'So I can get dressed. Unless . . .'

'Ah. Of course.'

'And I'll make some coffee before we go, to keep me awake.'

'So you have got a car,' said Beattie triumphantly.

'I have transport, yes. Now let me go and dress.'

While she waited for Corrigan to put his clothes on and make the coffee, Beattie thought about what he'd said. Kit dead. Not suicide, possibly murder. And the mention of MI5. She put her head in her hands. The anger started to rise in her. *Stop it*, she told herself. She knew that if she let the anger take over she would not think clearly, and she needed to think clearly. But everything seemed to be about as clear as mud at the moment. Both she and Corrigan had been warned off looking into Sofia's murder, which of course had the effect of both of them wanting to do exactly that and with more vigour. But why? Why would Anthony and COS go to such lengths, for she was sure it was COS involved in all this mess and not MI5? Or maybe she was wrong and the security service did have a finger in the rotten pie? If she only knew what the pie was. But Kit. Would they have killed Kit? And why?

She was going to have to confront Anthony and soon.

She heard Corrigan moving around and the noise of the coffee grinder and then the sound of the tap as he put water in his precious stove-top pot. The delay was beginning to get on her nerves. She was trying to be adventurous Beattie, spontaneous Beattie, when what she really wanted to do was to drag him to his car and make him drive to the south coast.

And then there was Nell. Yes, she was sad about what had happened with Nell, if she had really meant what she had said to Corrigan. Perhaps after this she, Beattie, should make a supreme effort to bring the two of them back together.

She stopped. Why did she feel miserable at the thought? Was she really sad about what had happened with Nell? As she did often, she stopped to examine her feelings. She liked Corrigan and felt that he treated her as an equal. She liked that too. She also had the impression he wanted to be doing something useful and worthwhile by righting an injustice. But Beattie was fair, and she could see that working at a company that provided people with electricity in their homes was worthwhile, even if he was relegated to the back room. Beattie felt a surge of anger. Except that wasn't worthwhile; that was vicious. And she couldn't see *him* in one of those newly built houses on the outskirts of London at a nine-to-five job. Perhaps she was jealous. That was a ridiculous thought.

Corrigan came out of the back room.

'Here. Coffee.' Corrigan handed her a cup.

She drank, trying to chase away the thoughts in her head.

'So what's the plan?' asked Corrigan, sipping his coffee.

'The plan?'

'You must have a plan.'

'Not yet, but I'll think of one. Now, drink up and let's get moving.'

Some minutes later, they were walking down the dark and deserted streets on the way to Corrigan's garage. It was cold, but thankfully no rain.

'Thought of a plan yet?' asked Corrigan.

Beattie sighed. 'Get to Brighton and walk along the promenade, see if we can find him.' It seemed simple to her.

'It's a long prom.'

'Or we could go to his hotel and knock on the door.'

'You know where he's staying?'

Beattie was irritated. 'Yes.'

Corrigan laughed. 'Of course you do. Here we are,' he said, coming to a stop outside two garage doors on an ordinary street. He took a key out of his pocket and unlocked the padlock before pulling the doors open. He shone his torch inside.

She gasped as the torchlight played on a green and silver motorbike. 'A Royal Enfield Bullet,' she said, walking into the garage and running her hand over the machine, feeling its graceful lines. 'I used to ride these in the war.' She stood still, trying not to let the memories overwhelm her.

'You'll have to tell me about it some day,' he said, smiling, clearly pleased at her delight.

'Maybe.'

'Here.' He handed her an RAF flying helmet and goggles. 'You'll need these. And,' he added, looking at her doubtfully, 'this.'

It was a rather dusty ex-army greatcoat. 'I've only got one pair of gauntlets,' he said.

'Goodness, it really will be going back in time.' She took off her woollen coat and hung it up on a convenient peg on the wall, before pulling on the greatcoat. 'It's a good job I'm not a small slip of a girl, isn't it?'

'You look fine.'

'Fine. Thank you.'

'I mean you look great. Fabulous. It all really suits you. I mean . . .'

Was that a blush she saw creeping onto his cheeks? 'Oh, do shut up, Corrigan.'

'Sidecar?'

Beattie shook her head. 'I'll take the second seat, thank you.'

And she swung her leg to sit astride the motorbike.

'You're going to have to put your arms around me to hold on, you know.'

'Am I? Or shall I just hold on to the side of the seat?'

'If you want to fall off.'

The ride down to Brighton was exhilarating, with Corrigan pushing the motorbike to its limits at times, going far faster than a man with one eye and a gammy leg had a right to do, but somehow, with her arms just about managing to fit around his greatcoat, she felt perfectly safe. She was free, she was herself as the night flashed by. Only her, Corrigan and the bike. There was something elemental about it.

All too soon they were speeding through the gates of Brighton, the stone pillars marking the northern entrance to the town, and Beattie felt a beat of disappointment the ride was going to end. The sky was clearer here, the moon shining brightly, helping to light their way. They were soon riding through the built-up areas, past the great oaks of the Steine and towards the sea that glistened under the stars.

Corrigan pulled up near the Palace Pier, and they both jumped off the motorbike.

A biting wind blew off the water, but the air smelt fresh and salty to Beattie. She could see white-topped waves and hear the sea's tinny noise as it pulled and pushed along the shingle beach. She loved the town, coming to stay with her best friend, Polly, during university holidays when she couldn't bear to go home. And before that was the weekend after the end of the war with a man her *maman* would have thoroughly disapproved of. Dominic. But it had been such fun. She smiled to herself. Brighton was fun. And brash and all fur coat and no knickers with its veneer of respectability hiding a seamy side. But it was a town that welcomed everybody, whatever their proclivities. She remembered the story Polly had told her about a woman two centuries earlier who'd escaped the London slums by dressing as a man to join the army, only to be discovered when she was wounded in battle. Honourably discharged, she chose Brighton as the place for a cross-dressing female soldier to settle. Became a friend of the Prince Regent. Beattie loved that story, and often thought she might end up in the town one day and she wouldn't have to worry what anybody thought of her. Like Polly.

'Not many attractions open at this time of night,' said Corrigan, breaking into her thoughts. 'No ice cream, no fish and chips. And I am hungry.'

Beattie laughed. 'I'm sure we'll be able to find some breakfast in the morning.'

'What is the plan, if we can't eat?'

'The plan. Yes. I told you. Walk along the prom to see if he's sitting on a bench contemplating his life.'

'In this cold?' Corrigan shivered as if to make his point.

'Maybe not,' she conceded. 'Then we go to his hotel and knock on the door.'

'That's all you've got? As a plan?'

'Yes. I was going to think more about it in the car, but since your car was a motorbike, I couldn't think properly with the wind and the speed and the freedom. But come on, it's not a bad start.'

Corrigan raised his eyebrows.

Beattie looked at him, beginning to think that maybe it had been a stupid idea to come down to the coast in the middle of the night, but she'd been so focused on getting to Bowen first that she had wanted to get on the road before Ashley. Now they were here and she was forgetting who she was supposed to be. She was cross with herself.

'You're frowning, Beattie. Come on, let's go to the Old Ship and wait until it's time for breakfast.'

Beattie shook her head. 'No, I am going to walk for a short while. It's beautiful and so quiet. Look at that sky and the stars so far away.'

Corrigan snorted. 'Of course it's quiet; it's not even three o'clock in the bloody morning. What have I let myself in for?'

'Come on, live a little.' She smiled. 'I came here once for an all-night party. Ended up skinny-dipping in the sea at this time of the morning. Mind you, it was the summer.'

'I'd say that makes all the difference. There is no way I'm taking this coat or any clothes off to go naked into that sea.'

Beattie's mouth twitched. 'I'm very glad to hear it.'

Corrigan held out his arm. 'Come, Beattie Cavendish, let us parade down the prom.'

'If we go this way we'll eventually arrive at the Old Ship.'

They walked slowly along the deserted promenade, Beattie comfortable being arm in arm with Corrigan, the silence and the dark making it feel dreamlike. It was almost as if they were in another world, another time. And for once, the restlessness inside her subsided.

'There,' said Corrigan, stopping abruptly.

'Hmm?' asked Beattie, still in her otherworldliness, not thinking of the here and now, but of somewhere timeless where she felt no pressure from Maman and Father or Anthony Cooper and no guilt about Luc and France.

'I think we may have found him.' He pointed to a man slumped on a bench. He had a hat pulled low over his face and a coat pulled tight around him. A scarf covered the bottom of his face.

Beattie was instantly alert. 'Bowen?' She removed her arm from Corrigan's.

'The very same.'

All at once the cold was sharper, the stars brighter, the sea louder and Beattie stopped. 'How do you know?' she said.

'I would like to say I recognise the shape of his jaw, the way he sits, the way he holds himself. But it's more prosaic than that – I've seen the red striped scarf before.'

Beattie wanted to laugh, but knew it wasn't appropriate. 'You stay here,' she whispered.

'What, don't you trust me?'

'Trust you to do what?'

'I don't know, say the right thing, sing a song.'

'I think it's best if you stay away until I've gained his confidence.'

Corrigan nodded. 'You go and talk to him. I'll go for a walk, get out of your hair, so to speak. And Beattie?'

'Yes?'

'Don't forget to ask him about his visits to the church.'

Beattie moved forward slowly and quietly. She sat down on the bench next to Ralph Bowen. Despite his stubble and the haggard face aging him twenty years, Beattie knew it was him.

He didn't acknowledge her presence.

Beattie waited a moment or two. 'Mr Bowen,' she said. 'It's Beattie Cavendish.'

He lifted his head and turned slowly to look at her. 'Who?' His voice was dull and full of pain.

'Beattie Cavendish,' she repeated. 'Ashley's friend.'

'Beattie Cavendish.' He frowned and sat up, straightening his shoulders. 'What the hell are you doing here?' His voice was full of anger.

'I came looking for you, Mr Bowen. I think people are worried about you.'

His face twisted. 'I doubt that very much. But they needn't be. I'm perfectly fine.'

'I don't think you are,' said Beattie, putting a hand on his arm. 'Perfectly fine people don't come down to Brighton in the middle of the night and sit on a bench in the cold watching the sea.'

Bowen looked down at Beattie's hand on his arm as if

it were a particularly nasty species of slug. She removed it. 'I'll go back to my hotel in the fullness of time. I only wanted to remember. Now go. Leave.'

'Remember?'

'Yes,' he said irritably. 'Sofia.'

Beattie couldn't be sure, but she thought she saw tears glistening in Bowen's eyes. Or perhaps it was the wind.

'You were in love with her,' she said, her voice gentle.

He nodded. 'I was.' His voice was less angry. 'And I like to think she was in love with me, but perhaps that's an old man's fancy. What would she see in me? Security, perhaps. The knowledge I could help her in life.' He looked at Beattie. 'You see, you may think me a fool, but I'm not. She was warm and kind, perhaps looking for a father figure. She was kind.'

'And did you know she was expecting a baby?'

He nodded. 'I did. I had a phone call not long ago. I didn't know what to think.'

Beattie remembered the call, how Ralph Bowen had turned pale.

'And that's what made you . . .'

'Run away? Yes.' He gave a sort of smile. 'Not very distinguished behaviour by a Member of Parliament and hopeful Foreign Secretary. Though I think those hopes will shortly be as dust.'

'It may not destroy you.'

'It will if that brother of hers has any say in the matter.'

'Martin Huber?'

'Yes, him.' Ralph Bowen's face grew dark. 'He could be trouble. He needs . . .' His shoulders slumped. 'It doesn't matter.'

'It does matter,' Beattie persisted.

'No.' His expression was implacable.

Beattie thought about how Bowen had effectively shut down any investigation into Sofia's murder. 'Why didn't you want to know who killed her?'

Another twisted smile. 'I'm a pragmatist, Miss Cavendish. Surely you know that men seeking power are ultimately the most selfish? Although I knew I loved her, I can and do accept I love power and politics more. I didn't want the scandal; I want to be Foreign Secretary when the Tories win the next election. I thought I could ride it out, but the emotion – I have never known anything like it.' He bowed his head. 'I actually miss her.' He lifted his head and stared out over the sea.

The waves were unchanging, the push and pull on the shore unceasing. Beattie remained silent.

Bowen heaved a great sigh. 'I betrayed her memory by pretending she meant nothing. But what could I do? Any news of the affair could have broken me, ruined my career. Then I heard she had been carrying my child. That's when I knew real pain. But it will pass.'

'And what about your wife?'

Bowen turned and looked at her. 'Edwina? What about her?'

'She knows about Sofia.'

'She knows?' His shock was real.

Somehow Beattie wasn't surprised that Bowen was so naïve. 'Yes, she does. But not about the baby.'

'It's that ruddy priest,' Bowen spat.

'Priest?'

'The one at the church she insists on going to all the

bloody time. Mass, choir, playing the ruddy organ. She knows I don't like it.'

'You've been to the church, though, too, haven't you?'

'I go for the occasional performance to be a support. You saw me at the *Messiah*.'

'But you've been on your own too.'

His head jerked round. 'How do you know that?' The politician's look was back in his eyes – hard and calculating.

'I do, that's all.' Beattie held his gaze.

He turned back to gaze at the sea. 'I went to seek solace. Does that surprise you, Beattie Cavendish?'

It did, rather. 'You were feeling guilty?'

'I was.' Another great sigh. 'Sofia had been secretive in her last two or three months; I thought she was becoming tired of me. It made me think about what I was doing. I generally don't like introspection, but there we are. I thought, if Edwina gained a serenity from going to her church, I might too. I thought I might seek and find forgiveness. I think I was a little mad. Love can do that to a man. Even one such as me.'

'Did you find it? Solace and forgiveness, I mean?'

'No,' he hissed. 'All a load of baloney. And Father Kevin, he's a rogue. He could only tell me to pray for myself and vote Labour. He wouldn't tell me anything about what Edwina was thinking. God didn't come down and say I was forgiven. I have to deal with this on my own.'

'Do you want to know who killed Sofia?'

'Does it matter now?' His voice was hard.

'It matters for her brother. It should matter to you.'

'It did; it does.' He then seemed to sit up straighter, pull his shoulders back as if he had made a decision. 'But I'm inclined to agree with Edwina that it was a petty thief who was disturbed at the time. There's nothing to be gained from upsetting the apple cart. It was only when I found out about the, um, baby, that I wanted to be by myself, for a little while.'

Beattie's pity for the man was turning into something else, anger. 'That "apple cart", as you call it, is a young woman who died in the most dreadful of circumstances. She deserves to be remembered and her death...' *Avenged*, was what she was about to say, but perhaps that wasn't appropriate. 'The circumstances surrounding her death to be resolved.'

He blinked. 'Thank you, my dear, leave it to me now. It doesn't concern you. I shall return to London later today. I need to talk to Edwina and then I will concentrate on my work. Politics is all-consuming. I would be grateful if you would say nothing about all this to my son.' The expression in his eyes changed from sorry to calculation. 'I wouldn't want your life to be made difficult, if you take my meaning.'

Beattie breathed in and out slowly, controlling her anger. Really, this man was impossible to deal with. 'Are you threatening me?'

'Not at all. I just think that to keep your counsel would be good for all of us. Under the circumstances.'

'I see.' In minutes Bowen had gone from a man with a broken heart to shrewd, calculating politician. A chameleon. Beattie almost admired him. Almost.

'And why did you go to the White Pearl Club?'

A hint of a smile flashed across his face. 'You can be anybody you like there. I was able to see Sofia. Talk to her sometimes.'

And occupy one of their private rooms, thought Beattie.

'But mostly I went to be near her. How did you know?'

Beattie shook her head. 'I can't tell you that.'

'I would, of course, deny it.'

'Ashley will be arriving soon to take you home.'

'Really? That's a nuisance.' And with that, he stood, politely doffed his hat and began to walk away.

Corrigan appeared and sat next to her. 'Well?'

She shook her head, wanting to laugh but feeling outraged at the same time. 'I don't know what to make of him. First of all I was sorry for him as his feelings for Sofia seemed genuine. Then he began to tell me I couldn't say anything about meeting him here because it wouldn't be good for me.'

'He threatened you?' Corrigan laughed. 'Politicians are so very arrogant. They think the whole world revolves around them and we will all fall in with what they say. And what about the church? Did he have a reasonable explanation as to why he was there?'

'He said he went to gain some peace and to talk to the priest. But Father Kevin was a rogue, told him to vote Labour and wouldn't tell him Edwina's innermost thoughts.'

Corrigan raised an eyebrow. 'That's no surprise. There isn't much love for the Tories in Ireland, and Father Kevin is an Irishman.'

'Do you think it was as simple as that? That he went to ask God for forgiveness and to discover Edwina's innermost thoughts?' Beattie was convinced there was more to Ralph Bowen's story than he had told her.

'I believe so.' He took his tobacco pouch and papers out of the pocket of the greatcoat and began to roll a cigarette. 'Why, what else could it be?' He looked straight ahead, handing her the roll-up before making one for himself. Beattie stared at the cigarette in her hand. Her *maman* would be shocked at her smoking in the street; it was not 'seemly'. Beattie leant forward as Corrigan sparked his lighter, cupping the flame in his hand. She inhaled.

'Nothing,' she said, wondering if Bowen was visiting the church for another reason. It couldn't be the location for a dead drop, could it? She had heard that at Brompton Oratory behind a particular pillar was a favourite spot as a dead drop for some spies, popular given its proximity to the Russian Embassy. Perhaps one in a church was a favourite for Ralph Bowen, with St Margaret of Antioch taking the place of Brompton Oratory. Yet Bowen's dislike of the priest had seemed real. Intense. But that might not mean anything.

Corrigan stood, and leant against the railings, smoking his cigarette. 'Beattie, I know you're not telling me everything.'

'I don't know what you mean.' Suddenly she was uncomfortable under his gaze.

'I think you do. You are not who you say you are, are you?'

'Which of us is?' Beattie got up and stood beside him. 'Corrigan, I really want to get to the bottom of who killed Sofia. I don't think Ralph Bowen was behind it. He says it probably was a petty thief. But I don't believe that either.'

She wrapped her arms around herself. The cold wind had started up with a vengeance.

'You're right. People keep warning us off when we try to find out her killer; surely that wouldn't happen if it had only been a petty thief? And then there's Kit. I think he was murdered because he knew something. So, who are these people?'

She turned and looked at him. 'I don't know.' How easily the lies came even as she stared into his eyes; how easily she slipped from one role to another. It was frightening. One thing of which she was certain: Anthony Cooper, GCHQ and COS were involved somewhere.

Corrigan frowned and his mouth was tight. He looked at his watch. 'Time we were getting back.'

'To London?'

'Where else?' His tone was cold; she had angered him. He thought she was not telling him the whole truth. He was right, of course, but there was nothing she could do about his anger.

The sky was still dark; there would not be dawn for another couple of hours.

'There was one thing.'

'Yes?' He pulled on his cigarette.

'Talking to Bowen, I got the feeling that Martin might be in some danger.'

'So you're worried about him.'

'Yes. I thought we could go to a friend of mine for a wash, maybe a quick nap and some breakfast, and then go to Saltergate Island on the way back to London, make sure everything's all right. Even warn Martin to be extra careful.'

'You thought that, did you?' He threw the cigarette over the railings and gave a deep sigh. He turned to her. He looked tired, she could see. In pain, too. Which was another reason for suggesting they go to see Polly first. 'And who is your friend?'

'Her name is Polly. We were in the war together. I trust her totally.'

'And will she mind us calling on her at . . .' He squinted at his watch again. 'Almost four in the morning?'

Beattie smiled, what felt like her first proper smile for hours. 'She won't mind. She doesn't sleep much. Come on, she's only in Kemptown.'

Beattie was right – Polly, short with wild red curls and wearing a silk dressing gown emblazoned with a red dragon, welcomed them to her three-storey townhouse with open arms despite the early hour, and soon they were sitting in front of a roaring fire toasting bread and drinking sweet tea, Beattie having told her the reasons why they were in Brighton in the first place. It was a relief to talk to her friend about it all.

'It's been too long,' said Polly. 'And typical of you to turn up without notice.'

Beattie grimaced. 'I hope you don't mind?'

'Of course not. It's always lovely to see you. Marianna of course is still asleep. She sleeps the sleep of the dead but will be sorry to have missed you.' She smiled. 'And who is the Irishman?' She raised her eyebrow, still smiling.

They both looked at Corrigan, who was fast asleep, his head against the back of a chair, a piece of buttered toast dangling from his hand, legs stretched out. Beattie reached forward and took the toast out of his hand. 'I wouldn't want a greasy mark on your polished floor. And he is Corrigan. A private detective, as we told you.'

'Nothing more?'

'Nothing more,' she said firmly. 'We both have an interest in Sofia's murder and he is helping me. I don't have the time or the inclination for anything "more", as you put it.'

Polly smiled. 'It wouldn't matter, as well you know. It's so lovely to see you, but I don't quite understand what brought you this way?'

Beattie sipped her tea. 'As I told you, Polly. It's all to do with the murder of a politician's housekeeper. I couldn't let it go. It felt like when Angelique died blowing up that bridge and nobody cared.' She bit her lip. 'Because she was Luc's sister.'

Polly took Beattie's hand. 'I remember. But she was the sister of a traitor and no one trusted her.'

Beattie winced at the word 'traitor'.

'I know that, Polly. But she didn't deserve to be left lying like a broken doll by the side of the road. I've never forgiven myself for not having the backbone to go against the others and insist she at least be buried properly.' Scenes from that day swam in her mind. The silence. The fear. The adrenaline spike. The explosion and then the shooting, the bloody shooting. And the smell of death. They'd succeeded in what they had to do, but Angelique was dead. Sometimes Beattie wondered whether it really was the Germans who killed her, or an angry member of the Resistance. 'It's part of the reason I feel that Sofia should have justice, should be remembered properly. That we should know who killed her.'

Polly nodded and Beattie was grateful to her friend who had been there with her and who understood her. 'How is Freddie?'

Polly grinned. 'Still flying. Cargo planes this time, for the Berlin Airlift. He says when the weather's bad they actually have to land at Gatow and hand out parcels. And sweets for the children, and that, he says, can become a real scramble.'

'I'm glad he's safe, Polly.' Freddie was the only family member Polly had left after her parents and aunt and uncle were killed by a bomb during the Blitz.

'He'd like to see you again one day.'

'It's been too long.'

They sat in a comfortable silence.

'And you're able to get time off from your typing job to gallivant around the country?' said Polly, poking the fire.

The light was beginning to filter through the edges of the curtains. Dawn was breaking. Beattie nodded. 'Yes. I am.'

'I see. Teaching typists, isn't it?' A smile hovered at the corner of her mouth.

'Making them excellent secretaries, yes.'

They looked at one another in tacit agreement. Neither would say the truth. Beattie had not told her friend of her job in GCHQ, but Polly knew her well enough to know that Beattie would not settle for something that would tide her over until she found a suitable marriage-material man. Beattie knew Polly wondered what her real job could be, and, knowing her friend, she probably had a very good idea.

'Go and rest, now, my darling,' said Polly. 'I'll put a

cushion behind the Irishman's head and a blanket over his body. He'll be fine. You go upstairs.'

'Wake me in an hour?'

'Two,' said Polly.

CHAPTER TWENTY-FOUR

Corrigan rode his motorbike over the Strood, Beattie's arms tight around his waist and the wind scouring his cheeks. The morning weather had chosen to be kind, with a weak sun pushing the light cloud out of the way. The air felt crisp and clean, though cold. When they reached the actual island, Corrigan pulled up and tugged off his flying helmet. He looked around at the fields, some of them ploughed, some with winter barley. Others had sheep grazing.

'Reminds me of home,' said Corrigan, gazing around, smelling the grass and the air. 'It's the space. No buildings. A horizon. Dammit, I miss it, much as I like London.'

'Do you ever want to go home?' Beattie asked.

'Sometimes,' said Corrigan. 'My brothers and sister and my ma would like it, I know that. And I will, one day.' Homesickness pierced him. 'Perhaps you would like to come with me?' The words were out before he could stop them.

Beattie looked so put out he wanted to laugh. 'It's all right, I didn't mean it. Of course, you can always go by yourself. Or maybe Ashley Bowen will take you. It's God's own country.'

'Er . . . maybe.'

'After all, it's not as if you don't have plenty of holiday. Time off. A very generous employer.' He was deliberately goading her.

All at once Beattie turned to him. 'What are you trying to say, Corrigan?'

'I'm not trying to say anything.' Was it his imagination, or were Beattie's shoulders looking tight and defensive? He considered what he was about to say. 'But when I was asleep, I wasn't.'

Beattie frowned. 'What do you mean? You're talking in riddles.'

'I was, as Ma used to say, resting my eyes while you and Polly were talking.'

'You were eavesdropping.' Her eyes were glittering with anger and her body was ramrod straight.

'Hardly.' He was affronted, though he felt a little guilty. 'You were talking; I couldn't help overhearing.'

Beattie waved her hand to dismiss his words. 'Same difference.'

A silence. Beattie was obviously not going to say more.

'Polly is one of your best friends?'

'She is,' Beattie replied stiffly. 'We served together, as you probably gathered, and she always looked out for me and me for her. She helped me through some difficult times. Her brother Freddie is her only family. But she's found happiness with Marianna.'

'Her lover?'

'Yes.'

'Who was Luc?'

Beattie looked up into the sky.

Corrigan waited.

'He was someone I loved, once. French Resistance. I loved him very much; I trusted him with my life. And then I killed him.'

Corrigan was startled but didn't want to show it. 'I see.'

'No, you don't, not really. He was a traitor and I had no choice.' She seemed to shake herself. 'I thought I had no choice. But that was then. During the war. This is now and I think we should get to my parents' house, don't you?' She turned away from him and put her flying helmet back on.

Corrigan caught her arm. 'We all know what it's like to lose someone you love, but to lose them like that . . . I can hardly imagine.' His words felt inadequate. Trite.

'No.' She hesitated. 'You also heard me talking about Angelique?'

He nodded.

'And now you may understand why it's another reason I want to find Sofia's murderer.'

'I do.'

'So?'

Corrigan turned the ignition and kick-started the motorbike. 'Time to move.'

It wasn't long before they were turning into the drive of Salter House and stopping outside the door. Corrigan whistled. 'Nice place. Aesthetically pleasing.' He had never seen a building so simple and yet so beautiful. He could count at least eight chimneys. That was a lot of fires to make up.

Beattie raised her eyebrows. 'It's a money pit and frightfully cold in the winter.'

'Cosier than my office, I suspect.'

The front door was flung open to reveal a tall woman with powdered cheeks and sharp eyes. Her greying blonde hair was twisted into a French chignon, and she wore a flowery dress with a cardigan flung carelessly but beautifully over the top.

'Beatrice, my dear. How wonderful to see you. And *quelle surprise*.'

'Maman,' said Beattie, kissing her mother on each cheek. 'I'm sorry to arrive without much notice.'

'It's of no consequence. You must come inside and take off that awful coat.' Beattie's mother looked at Corrigan. He felt a little like a beetle under a microscope. 'And your friend, too, he must come in.'

Corrigan noticed the hesitation over the word 'friend'.

'Maman, this is Patrick Corrigan. A colleague.'

'How do you do, Mrs Cavendish,' said Corrigan, holding out his hand.

'How do you do, Mr Corrigan.'

'Patrick, please.'

'And you must call me Virginie.'

'Virginie,' said Corrigan. He liked Beattie's mother immediately. She didn't flinch or look away from his ruined face or seem to notice his eye patch and preponderance of scars. If she did, she was too well-mannered to comment.

'Come in, come in, I have fresh coffee. Beattie, Amelie will be pleased to see you.'

'Amelie?'

'Amelie is my sister, Corrigan,' said Beatrice. 'My younger sister. She should be in school, but school and Amelie do not make good bedfellows.'

'Beatrice, really,' said her mother.

'And Father?'

'In Norwich. On business.'

Was he imagining it, or did Beattie relax at her mother's answer?

'Beattie, is that you? Really you? How lucky we are, so many visits.' A young but beautiful girl who looked not unlike Elizabeth Taylor ran full tilt into Beattie's arms, winding her arms tight around her. 'Urgh,' she said, wrinkling her retroussé nose and leaning away from her sister, 'this coat is rather, well, it smells disgusting.'

Beattie laughed. 'I suspect it smells that way because it's been hanging in Corrigan's dilapidated old garage for weeks on end and has never been cleaned. But it kept me warm on the motorbike.'

Amelie tilted her head to one side. 'Corrigan?'

'Yes.' She pointed to him. Corrigan smiled.

'How dashing,' said Amelie. 'A flying helmet and gloves. Like Errol Flynn. And who are you, Mr Corrigan?'

'Dashing' was a good word, though Corrigan knew he wasn't a patch on Errol Flynn. Certainly not with his single eye and snaking scars. He inclined his head. 'I'm a friend—'

'Colleague,' interrupted Beattie.

Corrigan allowed himself a small smile. 'A colleague of Beattie's.'

'You're very welcome, isn't he, Maman?'

'He is indeed.' He might have imagined it, but did Beattie's mother appear a little relieved that he was merely a colleague and not a friend? He probably wouldn't be seen as someone suitable for Beattie. 'Now,' continued

Beattie's mother, 'coffee first and then you can tell me why you have come all this way on that thing' – she pointed to the motorbike – 'after a sudden telephone call.'

Corrigan had to admit that Virginie's coffee was delicious. Strong and black with plenty of sugar, just how he liked it. There was home-made shortbread, too. They were sitting in the front room, the parlour his ma would call it, with a crackling fire and a cold breeze whistling through the old window frames. A rug with a peacock pattern hung on the wall. Odd. Amelie sat on the floor by her sister's feet. He navigated his way through numerous questions from Amelie and Virginie about Ireland, of which he waxed lyrical, his war, over which he glossed, and his injuries, about which he offered little.

'I like your colleague,' said Beattie's mother, carefully pouring more coffee. 'I think he likes you.'

'We are working on a case together,' she said, without looking at Corrigan. She was still angry with him then.

'A case?' Virginie put the coffee pot down. She frowned. 'I'm confused, Beatrice. What do you mean, "a case"? What sort of "case"? And what does it have to do with teaching girls to type?'

Corrigan watched Beattie, wondering how she was going to explain that slip of the tongue.

Beattie blinked. 'What I mean, Maman, is that Corrigan is a private detective.'

'How thrilling,' said Amelie, clapping her hands. 'Like Sam Spade.'

'Amelie loves the pictures,' said Beattie. 'She hopes to go to drama school, don't you? If you work hard enough.'

Amelie pouted. 'I am working hard.'

'A private detective. I see,' said her mother, who, Corrigan could see, clearly didn't.

'A private detective who is looking into the murder of Sofia. I'm helping him.'

Virginie put her hand to her throat. '*Mon Dieu*. What are you getting yourself mixed up with now, Beatrice?'

'I'm not becoming "mixed up" in anything, it's only that sometimes two heads are better than one.'

'But what about your work?'

'I thought that wasn't important to you, Maman?'

Corrigan felt Beattie bristling; there was obviously tension about her typing job with her mother no doubt having higher hopes for Beattie than the Civil Service.

'It isn't, but . . .' Beattie's mother looked around helplessly.

'Well, then.'

Beattie was good, thought Corrigan, admiringly. She muddied the waters like a professional.

'So, may we speak to Martin? Where is he? Is he out?'

Virginie frowned. 'I thought you knew. He is gone.'

'Gone? Gone where?' said Beattie, a piece of shortbread halfway to her mouth.

'Two men from London came to the house yesterday, they were friends of his, and he went away with them.'

Beattie put the shortbread down. 'You didn't tell me when I phoned this morning.'

'Beatrice, you did not ask.' Virginie looked bewildered.

'But I've been phoning every day, wanting to know how he is; you know I'm concerned about him.' Corrigan watched as Beattie visibly reined in her temper. 'And you've waited until now to tell me?'

Her *maman* waved an arm dismissively. 'You worry too much. He is very – how do you say – self-sufficient.'

Her *maman* was infuriating. 'Maman, did he go freely?'

'Of course he went freely; why shouldn't he? He is not a prisoner here.' She laughed; Corrigan supposed the laugh would be described as 'tinkling'.

Beattie frowned. 'I know, Maman. What I meant was, did he go freely with the two men?'

'They spoke Polish to each other,' said Amelie. 'And they did seem to be friends because they did a lot of laughing and hugging. I asked him if he had to go and he said he did. He said there was more information about his sister, about Sofia.'

This worried Corrigan. He thought about being warned off looking into Sofia's death, about the fact that Beattie had been too; he thought about the body of Kit, recovered from the water. 'And he definitely went willingly?'

'Yes,' said Virginie, impatience in her voice. 'I have told you this. Why wouldn't he? He said he had been very happy with us but it was time he faced up to life; those were his very words.' Virginie leant forward. 'Why is this so important, Mr Corrigan?'

'There are some bad people about and . . .'

'Are you saying' – Virginie's voice was steely, her eyes piercing. He wanted to squirm on his seat like a naughty boy – 'that Beatrice – that you, Mr Corrigan, as you seem to know all about Martin – have put our lives in danger in some way?' Displeasure radiated from her. 'I will have to tell your father.'

'Not at all,' interrupted Beattie. 'No one knew he was here.' Tension was thick in the air.

'His friends did,' Virginie pointed out. 'They telephoned to speak to him.'

'At least he's safe,' said Corrigan. 'He's probably at his home.' He wasn't so sure.

'He was happy here,' said Amelie. 'But he said his sister was important, what had happened to her was important.'

'And he was right,' said Beattie. 'Did you ever feel there was anyone watching the house?' she asked.

'No, why?' Her mother's eyes narrowed.

A short pause that didn't go unnoticed by Corrigan. 'I only wondered if his friends had come straight from London or had been waiting to talk to him, waiting to see if the coast was clear.'

'"The coast was clear"? What does that mean?'

'It means that perhaps his friends didn't want to be seen, that they wanted to talk to Martin on his own, without you or Father around,' said Amelie helpfully.

'I see.' Though Corrigan didn't think Virginie did, not really. The poor woman looked as confused as hell.

Corrigan looked across at Beattie and saw the guilt weighing on her shoulders, guilt in the shadows on her face.

'There is no problem,' said Corrigan soothingly, in an attempt to defuse the atmosphere. 'The young man is sure to have friends who were looking out for him. Perhaps he'd had enough of the countryside and wished to go back to London. We'll go to his house and see if he's there, make sure all is well.' He slapped his hands on his thighs and stood. 'If you would excuse me, Mrs Cavendish, I must stretch my legs before we continue our journey.'

'Surely you won't be leaving us so soon?' said Beattie's mother, her face falling.

'Maman, I think we must. I'm so sorry.'

To Corrigan, Beattie looked as though she couldn't wait to leave.

'Beattie, I have something to show you. Please come. It's a new magazine.' Amelie held out her hand, then looked at Corrigan. 'Truthfully I want to talk about you, Mr Corrigan.' And it was an impish smile she gave.

'Amelie.'

'Come on, Beattie.'

The two sisters left the room. Corrigan sat back down. Virginie poured him more coffee. There was a silence.

'Is she telling the truth, Mr Corrigan?'

'I'm not sure what you mean, Virginie?' He looked at her hopefully with a wide-eyed and innocent expression on his face. She returned his look with one that said she didn't believe his innocent expression.

'Oh, I think you do, Mr Corrigan. I'm not sure that Beatrice is entirely truthful with me ever. She can be quite . . .'

'Focused?' He smiled.

'Hmm. A little like that.' Virginie returned his smile. 'I like you, Mr Corrigan – Patrick – but you see, Beatrice and I do not always see eye to eye. She took the death of her brother very badly. As did we, her parents. Sometimes I feel we let her down.'

'I see.'

'She has told you about her brother?'

Corrigan shook his head.

'He was lost in France in forty-three. His body was

never found. We have, of course, tried looking for him, writing to the relevant authorities. Thomas – Beatrice's father – even went over to France to look for him. Although he found a café and a farm where they remembered him, he found no trace. In fact, the farmer said they were sure he'd been killed by the Nazis. Beatrice found it hard to accept. She still does.'

'I see.'

'So, I'll ask again, is Beatrice telling me the truth about her involvement in this case of yours? I don't want her to be in any danger.'

'Beattie . . .' Corrigan stopped. He was going to say that Beattie could well look after herself, that she was obviously skilled in combat and had been trained well. He knew that; he felt that. But he thought if Beattie hadn't told her mother, then it was with good reason. So, pushing aside the thought of Beattie looking at him with that cool expression after he had gone to 'rescue' her, he said, 'Beattie is safe with me. I'll do everything in my power not to let any harm come to her, I promise.'

Virginie looked at him. 'That will have to do. I love my daughter – both my daughters – Mr Corrigan, but sometimes it is not easy for a mother to get on with her daughters. We – er – how do you say it?'

'Clash?' Corrigan said helpfully.

'Clash, yes, that is a good word. Beatrice is her own person but she thinks I put her dead brother's memory above what I feel for her, a living daughter. I do not. Please, Mr Corrigan. I can see you are a good man, if not the man for Beatrice, but I ask you, please look after her.'

'I will,' promised Corrigan, thinking that Beattie would

hate to think she was being 'looked after', but what else could he say to her mother?

'And now, Mr Corrigan, I suspect Beatrice will have had enough of me and Amelie's magazines and will be wanting to travel back to London.'

As the words left Beattie's mother's mouth, Beattie and Amelie came back into the drawing room. 'Time for us to go, Corrigan.' She embraced her mother stiffly. 'Thank you for the coffee, Maman. It was lovely to see you all.'

'I shall miss you. Again.' Amelie's voice was small.

Beattie left her mother's side and put her arms around her sister. 'I will see you again very soon, little sister.' She kissed the top of Amelie's head.

'Corrigan.'

Her voice was imperious. Corrigan suppressed a smile.

The wind was sharp and the air cold as Corrigan rode the motorbike towards the sea. Beattie wanted to taste the sea air, feel the sand between her fingers before returning to London. He stopped on a path next to the sandy shore, and Beattie jumped off the bike, taking deep breaths. 'Feel it, Corrigan. The air. So clean and pure.'

He nodded. 'Even better than Brighton.'

'Of course it is. Better than anywhere. When I was away all those years, first the war and then Cambridge, I would dream of this air. This sight.'

'The grey sea?'

'Yes, and even the grey skies when they're here. Sometimes the sea sparkles and the light makes it look as though it has a fine web of diamonds. I love watching the geese grazing on the nearby fields. And sometimes, in the sand, you can find old bones.' She knelt down and let the sand trickle through her fingers.

'Bones?'

'Bison, monkey, wolf, bear. Those sort of bones. Do you think Martin's safe?' She didn't look at him.

'I hope so,' said Corrigan. 'If they were genuine friends he went with.'

'We need to check, don't we?' she said.

'Beattie, is this getting out of hand?' He spoke carefully.

'What do you mean?'

'You asked your family if they had noticed anyone watching the house.'

She stayed still, her back to Corrigan, but he could see, even in the thick greatcoat, her shoulders go stiff. 'I did,' she said.

'Who was watching the house, Beattie?'

She stood up slowly and finally turned to face him. 'I don't know, Corrigan. There was someone spying on me, but they made off in a car. Somehow they had followed me from London.'

'Why haven't you told me this before?' He knew he sounded cold, but he was angry, dammit. Beattie never gave him the whole picture. She swerved and obfuscated until he couldn't see what was going on, and by doing so, she was putting them all in danger.

'I can't explain.' Her face was expressionless.

She infuriated him. 'Beattie, you never tell me the truth. Only your version of it.' He felt a rising anger. 'I trust you, and yet I don't. I would trust you with my life, I think, but in anything else?' He shook his head. 'Why are you so difficult to get to know, Beattie?'

She raised her eyebrows. 'Perhaps it's because I don't want you to know me.'

He sighed. 'Very well. But do you have any idea who could have followed you? Could it be the same people who keep warning us off looking into Sofia's death? Who may have killed Kit?'

He saw her visibly shake when he said that – he must have struck a chord. There were things she was not telling him, he knew that.

'There are a group of people in MI5 called the Watchers,' she began carefully. 'They stand on street corners with their black coats and their trilbies and their cigarettes and think they are invisible.'

'And what do these Watchers do?'

'Oh, for goodness' sake, what do you think they do? They watch.'

'Watch? Who?' What was happening here?

'Anyone of interest. The thing is, they only work during the day and no weekends. And they don't travel out of London.' She laughed with derision. 'As if spying was a nine-to-five job. I dodged them at Liverpool Street station. So if anyone did follow me here, to Saltergate Island, it wasn't one of them.'

'I'm confused. Why should you be worried by these "Watchers"?'

'Because I'm friends with Ashley Bowen, and of course the powers that be would look at everyone who was in the family orbit.' She said this so smoothly.

'How do you know this?'

She shrugged. 'I just do. So what I'm trying to say is, if there was someone watching me here, then it probably wasn't someone official.' She turned away from him once more.

'Bloody hell, Beattie.'

Corrigan looked into the sky and saw three gulls curling and screeching. There was a boat out on the water. Perhaps someone was watching them now, from there. Who exactly was warning them not to interfere? Dicky Morgan hadn't dropped any clues, but for a top Scotland Yard detective to be involved and one who was friendly with the Bowens, then it must be some government thing. Scott had mentioned MI5. Beattie talked about MI5 Watchers. Were they into something over their heads?

'Beattie,' he said. 'Events are becoming out of control. I'm not sure we should go on with this.'

Beattie whirled round, her face drained of colour. 'But we have to, Corrigan. It's not only Sofia; it's your friend Kit, too. You said there was no such thing as coincidence. It's even more important now. Look, we have to make sure Martin is safe and we have to find Sofia's diary.'

Corrigan took hold of her shoulders. 'We're in too deep. Who knows who they – whoever they are – will come after next. Amelie? Your parents?'

Her face twisted with anger. 'That's a low blow, Corrigan.'

'But you know I'm right. Even Nell could get hurt.' Nell, his stomach twisted as he thought of her. She had given him so much and he had thrown it all back at her. She deserved better. He breathed in to steady himself. 'It's becoming too dangerous, Beattie.'

'So you're going back to adulterers and fraudsters and standing outside seedy nightclubs?'

'Ouch. You know how to make a man feel good.'

'Or maybe to a safe little job and a house and a garden and children?'

He whistled softly. 'Beattie.'

'It's true, though, isn't it?'

He saw her fury spilling over.

'Maybe. And you can go back to Ashley Bowen and get on with your life of charming him and teaching girls to type.' They were cruel words, he knew.

'What do you mean, charming him?'

'You know what I mean. That's what women do, isn't it? To get a husband?'

Beattie stared at him. 'I thought you were better than that.'

'Perhaps I'm not.' Anger made him curt.

'Can we go, please, Corrigan?'

'Certainly.'

The journey back to London was fast and furious and bitter.

CHAPTER TWENTY-FIVE

Another cold and dreary day in London. Beattie emerged from the Tube station and hurried to her Mayfair office, determination in her stride and posture. Her only hesitation was at the front door of the building. She knew she had to handle it carefully; after all, she didn't want to do anything that might jeopardise her job with GCHQ.

'Ah, Beattie, there you are, I have a translation we'd like you to work on.' Enid hurried over and placed the paperwork on Beattie's desk.

Beattie smiled. 'I'll get on with it. I do need to see Anthony, though.'

Enid nodded. 'He is in today.'

Putting on her glasses, Beattie worked through the translation, a missive from the Russians about rising tensions in the West over the atom bomb, before setting it aside and rising to leave and climb the stairs to Anthony Cooper's office, her hand in her pocket, clutching the newspaper article she had found.

'Enter.'

Anthony Cooper didn't look up. He wore half-moon glasses on the end of his nose and he was writing as usual, his pen scraping across the paper. Beattie stood awkwardly, before deciding to sit down without being asked.

Eventually Anthony put down his pen, looked up and steepled his fingers.

Beattie was not going to be intimidated. She lifted her chin and returned his gaze.

'What can I do for you, Beattie? Is there anything more interesting about Ralph Bowen that you have not put in your report?'

'There is. Sofia Huber was pregnant and Ralph Bowen is the father.'

He blinked, but not another muscle on his face moved.

'I see,' he said eventually. 'The pregnancy we knew about. The other, well. That is news, but not surprising.' He tutted. 'There is nothing more stupid than an old fool. Really, what was he thinking? His career could be over.'

'I doubt it,' said Beattie. 'He's done a good job of pushing Sofia Huber's death into the shadows, as you know, and I'm the only one asking questions.'

'And you know about the baby how?'

'I went to Brighton and found Ralph Bowen after I heard Edwina Bowen talking about the matter. I also know about this.' She reached into her pocket and brought out the short newspaper story Leo Scott had written about Kit Pearson. All the story did was chronicle his name and that he had been found in the Thames. And that his death was a probable suicide.

Anthony scarcely glanced at it. He flicked the piece of paper away. Beattie held her temper by biting the inside of her cheek.

'What has this to do with me?'

'Perhaps nothing,' Beattie began carefully. 'But it does seem odd that shortly after you told me to have nothing more to do with Sofia Huber's murder or with Patrick Corrigan, and after Corrigan was prevented by the police from talking to this man, Kit Pearson' – she jabbed her finger at the newspaper cutting – 'that Kit Pearson is found dead in the bloody Thames. Supposedly by his own hand.' Beattie fought hard to keep her voice under control. 'It's a twisted tale, isn't it?'

Anthony's mouth worked as if he had swallowed a wasp. 'This Kit Pearson, whoever he might be, killed himself. That is the conclusion of Leo Scott's story.'

'I know that. I also know Leo Scott has a habit of writing stories – perhaps being made to write stories – that help prominent people out of a, shall we say, difficulty. And I do not like being threatened, Anthony. By you or anyone else. I suspect that perhaps you shouldn't have threatened me in the way you did. I suspect that's not how COS or GCHQ really works. I am a good asset to you. I can speak several languages, I fought in the war, I have a lot of experience. I don't like to be crossed. I suspect you went out on a limb for some reason when you threatened me, and I don't know why. But I will find out.' She stood up. 'Now, I have agreed to meet Ashley later today; if there is anything to report, I will let you know. Oh, and one more thing.'

Anthony stared at her with his unnervingly pale eyes.

'Are you having me watched?'

'We watch everyone.' His pale eyes didn't blink.

Anger helped her sweep out of the room.

When Beattie returned to her desk, she realised her

hands were trembling and she let out a shaky breath. She didn't know where she'd found the strength to speak to Anthony like that. Most likely she would lose her job, a job that was worthwhile and that she knew she would become better and better at doing. But she had to stand up for herself, and for others. There was something at play here that she wasn't seeing.

She sighed and snatched at her papers in front of her. The words swam on the page. Corrigan had lost faith in her because she couldn't tell him the truth, so now she was alone in her fight for justice for Sofia.

Bloody Corrigan. Who did he think he was, listening in on her private conversations, then having the temerity to say he couldn't go on looking for Sofia's murderer, or words to that effect. She'd be better off without him. She'd been alone most of her adult life; she was used to it. Bloody man. She banged her typewriter keys hard.

Maybe she should stop? Maybe she should concentrate on her work, and her work alone? At least that way she wouldn't face the wrath of her superiors. Though it could be too late for that, of course. She sighed and put her head in her hands.

Stop it, she told herself. This was a foolish way to act. She had to start thinking clearly. She had been too cruel to Corrigan. After all, he hadn't had to help her in the first place; he'd fallen into it, really. It was her job, her business. Yes, Corrigan had been obliging, found out things she wouldn't have been able to, such as the death of Kit, but she was perfectly capable of looking into things on her own.

Perhaps, though, he was right and it was becoming

too dangerous? There were dark forces at work here, she was certain of it. More than the death of a housekeeper. A housekeeper who had been loved but had not been murdered by Ralph Bowen, she was sure of that.

So back to the original question – why was she murdered? And by whom?

Not because of her involvement with Ralph Bowen, surely? Beattie tried to work it through logically. Sofia Huber was murdered, efficiently as Corrigan had pointed out. She was killed in the study at her employer's house. At night. What was she doing there? She was pregnant with Ralph Bowen's baby. Could she have been blackmailing Bowen? But Bowen seemed to genuinely have cared for her. And her brother, Martin, had said he thought there was someone Sofia cared about. If Bowen had killed her it would have been messier than it was. Passionate, even. Not a cold-blooded execution.

She kept coming back to that: execution.

Martin. She must try telephoning him again at his house, in case he'd gone back there, though she very much doubted it. But she needed to know he was safe. He'd left Saltergate with friends, so she shouldn't really be worrying about him, but there was a niggling level of anxiety in her stomach, and she needed to know that his two friends were exactly that, friends. She sighed. But she didn't know where to look.

She was at a dead end. No nearer to finding out who had killed Sofia, but knowing she had managed to annoy her boss in a major way. Probably had put her whole future in doubt. Quite possibly had put Martin in danger. And her family. And had alienated Corrigan. He'd probably gone back to Nell by now, and good luck to them both. But Corrigan knew about Luc, about Angelique. He knew what made her weak, and she didn't like that.

This was ridiculous. There was no point in sitting here feeling sorry for herself. She had to have a plan. It would come.

Sitting up straight, she pulled her translation papers closer to her and buried herself in her work.

The next time she looked up at the clock, it was lunchtime and her colleagues were pulling on coats in order to find some fresh air after the stuffiness of the office.

'Would you care to join me for lunch, Miss Cavendish?' Rory Clarke, he of the halitosis and now a deep blush, stood in front of her desk.

'Not today, thank you, Mr Clarke.' She gave him as genuine a smile as she could summon.

Rory Clarke nodded, then scuttled out of the office, clutching his hat and briefcase.

Oh dear.

She picked up the phone, dialling Martin's number but getting no answer, then she, too, left the office.

She shivered and pulled her coat more tightly around herself and strode quickly away from Chesterfield Street and towards Green Park Tube station. She hurried down the escalator, and jumped on a train to South Kensington, and from there to Temple. She kept her wits about her, making sure there was no one following her as she left the Tube and emerged into the open air. She walked for some minutes until she found what she was looking for. A red public telephone box. She picked up the handset and pushed in her pennies before dialling a number that she had memorised. She pressed the button when her call was answered.

'News desk, please. Leo Scott.'

She listened to the buzz and the clicks on the line.

'Leo Scott speaking.'

'Mr Scott, you don't know me, but my name is Beattie Cavendish. I believe you know a friend of mine, Patrick Corrigan.'

There was a silence at the other end so long that Beattie felt compelled to speak again. 'Mr Scott?'

'Miss Cavendish, I'm afraid I don't know of any Patrick Corrigan, so I can't help you.' His voice was cool and decisive. He put his phone down.

Beattie looked at the handset in frustration.

Right. Plan B.

Ten minutes later, she was outside the *Daily Dispatch* building in Shoe Lane off Fleet Street. She pushed open the door and found herself in the reception. Behind the desk was a middle-aged woman with her hair in rolls, wearing crimson lipstick and a severe expression. Beattie put on her best smile.

'Excuse me?'

The woman glared at her.

'Please could you give Leo Scott a message?'

'I'll see what I can do.'

'Could you ask him to meet me in café along the road. The Quick Brew.'

'And who shall I say wants to meet him in the café?'

Beattie smiled. 'Just tell him a lady was asking. A lady with an Irish friend. I think he might come. Thank you.'

Sure enough, not ten minutes later as Beattie was

drinking her tea and smoking a cigarette, Leo Scott arrived. She could tell it was him by the way he stood at the doorway of the café, trying to look casually around the premises. His macintosh was undone and his trilby a little askew. But it was mainly the red braces that gave him away. She smiled at him.

'Miss Cavendish?'

Beattie held out her hand. 'Mr Scott. Do sit down. I'll order some tea for you.' She nodded to the hovering waitress, who scurried away.

'I don't have long, Miss Cavendish.'

'Nor do I, Mr Scott, nor do I.'

He looked around before sitting down. 'I only came because you obviously know Patrick Corrigan. I'm sorry I was short on the phone, but I'm not sure who's listening these days.'

'I'm working with him. Sort of.'

'I see.'

'But I think you knew that,' said Beattie. 'He came to see you about Kit.'

The waitress placed a pot of tea, cup and saucer and fresh milk in front of Leo. He pushed it away.

'I don't mean to be rude, Miss Cavendish.' He looked at his watch. 'But I have deadlines to meet. Why did you want to meet me? It was obviously very pressing.'

Beattie took a breath. 'Have you found out anything else about Kit and his death? Corrigan said you were going to dig a little deeper. I wondered if you'd had any joy?'

'And why should I tell you? I don't know you. You say you know Corrigan, but I've no proof of that.'

'Corrigan, one eye, many scars, charisma. Charisma

that makes you not see the scars. Irish accent. Rude. Pushy.'

Scott laughed, and took out his cigarette case, offering one to Beattie. She took it. 'You do know him.'

'I also have his card. Here.' She pushed Corrigan's business card across the table.

Scott picked up, turning it over and over in one hand, as if he were thinking carefully about something. He put it back down on the table and Beattie took it. Finally he spoke. 'I wasn't allowed to speak to you after Sofia Huber's murder. I was warned off by Bowen and Dicky Morgan. And when I tried to write a decent story about what happened, my news editor practically threw me out of the building. He'd been leant on.'

'Corrigan said. Security services, you thought.'

'Exactly. Have you any idea why?'

'None whatsoever.'

'Hmm.' Scott looked at her through narrowed eyes. 'I get the feeling you wouldn't tell me even if I were on the right track. However, I can help you. I have found a witness who saw Kit being pushed into the Thames.' Scott blew three impressive smoke rings.

'Tell me more.'

'What's in it for me?'

'The story. The whole story.' Or as much of the story as she would be able to tell.

He studied her. 'All right,' he said eventually. 'The witness is a Stanley Dawes. I don't know what he was doing around that area, up to no good I should think because he won't go to the police, but he says a car stopped on Westminster Bridge and three men got out. Two of them were holding the third man. They then pushed that someone over the bridge. Good old Stan heard the splash. He said he left sharpish. Didn't want to be seen in case he was the next to go over. It was about half past eleven, he said. Kit's body was found half an hour later washed up not far from the same bridge.'

'How did you find Stanley Dawes?'

Scott irritatingly tapped the side of his nose. 'Sources, Miss Cavendish.'

Beattie clicked her tongue. There wasn't time for this. 'Couldn't you persuade him to go the police?'

Scott laughed – it wasn't a reassuring laugh. 'Come on, Miss Cavendish. For people like Stanley Dawes, the police don't represent safety.'

Beattie thought of Dicky Morgan and how easily he turned away from doing the right thing. 'I see. Can I meet him? Now we know Kit was definitely murdered? Perhaps I could talk to him, and then maybe, I don't know, go to someone trustworthy at Scotland Yard. I do have friends.'

'So do I.' Leo Scott pursed his lips. 'I'll see what I can do.'

Oh, for the love of God. 'Thank you, Mr Scott. I appreciate the information, and if I could meet Stanley—'

'As I said, I'll see what I can do. Though it is my story and Stanley is still thinking about whether he wants to be involved. My guess he won't, even if offered money. He was badly frightened by what he saw.'

Beattie nodded. 'I see. I would still like to meet him.' She stood, putting some coins down on the table. 'And now I must get back to the office.'

'Which office is that, Miss Cavendish?'

'Civil Service, I'm afraid. Frightfully dull.'

'Really.'

She found his stare unnerving.

'Thank you for your time.'

'It's a pleasure.'

Beattie left him blowing smoke rings across the table.

CHAPTER TWENTY-SIX

When Beattie arrived home to her flat that evening, she was unsettled. She didn't know which way to turn. Indeed, everywhere she did turn, she found herself up against dissemblance and dead ends. She couldn't see a way to crack the mystery of Sofia's murder; nobody was willing to break ranks and help her – they were either too frightened or had been muzzled by MI5. That bloody organisation. Were they poking about in COS's business? And, by default, her business? Both MI5 and MI6 had a troubled relationship with GCHQ at the best of times.

Why kill Kit? What had he done that made him dispensable? Seen something? Heard something? But what? Or perhaps she should be asking who killed Kit? The person who had killed Sofia? MI5? Who? It was a jigsaw puzzle that had many of the pieces missing.

And Martin Huber seemed to be missing. She had tried telephoning him several times during the day, but with no luck. There had to be a reason why he left Saltergate with his friends so suddenly. It must be something to do with Sofia.

She began pacing the floor, feeling the space was too

small, too confined, too masculine. The King glared at her from above the fireplace that was full of cold, grey ash. What was she missing? She flung herself into a chair, before springing up again to make herself a Martini. There, on the table where the drinks lived, were the sheets of music she had taken from the locked drawer in the Bowens' study. She looked at them again. Hand-notated Christmas carols. 'In the Bleak Midwinter', 'Hark! The Herald Angels Sing', 'O Little Town of Bethlehem' and 'Away in a Manger'. But what did it mean? She frowned, trying to make sense of the musical notes on 'In the Bleak Midwinter', then holding the paper up to the light in case she was missing something. Secret writing, hidden messages, microdots. Anything. She stared at all four pieces of music, not really seeing the notes now, just thinking. Tonight was Edwina Bowen's choir rehearsal night at the church. Edwina Bowen had been seen at the White Pearl Club. This music had been locked in a drawer in Edwina Bowen's desk.

She grabbed her coat and gloves.

Beattie stood to one side watching the men and women turning up for choir practice at St Margaret of Antioch. The night was cold, soupy, a thick fog forming.

She spied Edwina Bowen, emerging out of the fog, swathed in an emerald-green woollen coat and a stylish hat, hurrying along the pavement, a large handbag over her arm. Beattie melted into the shadows. A group of women were following, chatting noisily, so Beattie, affecting a limp and placing a black veil on her head that covered the top half of her face, slipped in behind them and entered the church.

Immediately the smells of incense and damp assailed her nostrils. Without the candles that had bathed the church in soft light for the performance of the *Messiah*, the statues loomed over her and judged her at every turn, and murals on the ancient walls told of blood and suffering. She shivered, partly through cold and partly through memory. It was a church such as this, though smaller and even colder, in which she had hidden with Luc and four other members of their cell for over a week, surviving on what little offerings the priest could bring them every day or so. Eventually they managed to escape, though not until the priest – a stocky man enveloped in his black garb – had been taken away and shot by German soldiers. His God had not come forward for him then.

The church was surprisingly busy for a weekday evening in late November, with men and women milling about near the altar. Someone was playing Christmas carols softly on the organ. Other people were sitting praying in the pews. Two women also wearing black veils stroked their rosary beads as they fell between their fingers; three men sat hunched at the back of the church in heavy coats, probably there to keep out of the cold. Beattie was not far behind Edwina Bowen but thought her disguise was good enough should she decide to turn around.

Edwina Bowen strode purposefully down the aisle towards the parish priest – what had Corrigan said his name was? Father Kevin, that was it – who was standing looking as though he was waiting for her.

Beattie followed and slipped into a pew at the front of the church, keeping her head bowed and mouthing words to look as though she was praying if anyone happened to look. She concentrated, trying to hear the voices of the priest and Edwina Bowen.

'Edwina, lovely to see you,' said Father Kevin, his voice quiet. Beattie had to strain to hear his words. The priest laid a hand on Edwina Bowen's shoulder with a smile. 'What do you have for me this evening?'

'Father, I won't be playing the organ for you today.'

Father Kevin's smile slipped, just for a moment. 'Why is that?' He cocked his head onto one side. Was it Beattie's imagination or was the priest holding Edwina Bowen's shoulder a little more firmly?

'I don't have the music.' Edwina Bowen looked straight at the priest without flinching.

There was a pause. Father Kevin took his hand away from her shoulder. 'Oh?'

'I have . . .' For the first time, Edwina Bowen seemed unsure of herself. 'I have mislaid it, Father.'

Father Kevin's eyes narrowed. 'That is most unfortunate, Edwina. Most unfortunate.' His Irish accent held a slight threat. 'You will have to bring it another time.'

'I will, Father.'

'Good.' He turned on his heel and walked away, his shoes making no sound on the flagstones.

An odd exchange, though maybe she was seeing conspiracies everywhere. The choir readied itself to sing and Edwina Bowen hurried to line up behind other women. A dapper little man with a neat moustache sat at the organ and cracked his knuckles, preparing to play.

As the opening notes of 'We Three Kings' filled the church, Beattie left the pew, retiring to one near the back of the church and bent her head once more, but keeping her eyes wide open and her senses alert.

The rehearsal went on with voice exercises, then carols were rehearsed with the notes from the organ soaring mightily to the very roof of the church. Soon there were prayers and responses from the Mass, and Beattie allowed herself to get lost in the beauty of the Latin words and the music, if not their sentiment.

A figure caught her attention. A man walking with intent down the aisle and taking a seat halfway down the church. He, too, bowed his head as if in prayer. From what Beattie could tell, the man was tall and heavy-set – though a build could easily be disguised – and his hair was black and unfashionably long, curling over his collar. She watched carefully as Father Kevin appeared and sat next to the man and whispered into his ear. The man stiffened; his face went red. Father Kevin put a hand on his arm. A restraining hand? The man shook his head angrily, said something to Father Kevin, who seemed to pale. Father Kevin stood and left.

The man shook his head once more, made the sign of the cross, then got up and strode out of the church.

Beattie heard the church door slam shut behind him.

Could her suspicions be correct?

She stood, left the pew and hurried after the man, hoping she wasn't too late.

The fog was denser than it had been earlier, swirling around, making it difficult to see too far ahead. She looked left and right, and spotted the man hurrying down the street, almost swallowed by the fog, but she picked up her pace, staying behind him. He didn't turn around, or pretend to tie his shoelace, or hop on a bus at the last minute. He didn't know he was being followed, even though Beattie was convinced he would be able to hear her footsteps echoing in the thick, damp air.

Beattie also had an idea where the man was going, and it was not long before she was proved right.

The White Pearl Club.

Edwina Bowen had been seen at the White Pearl Club.

Sofia Huber had worked there.

Sofia Huber had been expecting a baby. Ralph Bowen was the father.

Everything was connected.

The telephone was ringing as Beattie pushed open the door of her flat. Dammit. She needed to find Corrigan, but the insistent bell made her pick up the handset from its cradle.

'Where are you?'

Her heart sank. Ashley.

'We were meant to be at a party.' His voice was petulant. 'You were coming here and then we were going to the party at the Heywoods'. With Felicia and Gerald.'

Her mind was already racing with excuses. 'I'm so sorry, Ashley, but I have a terrible headache. A migraine, I think. I've been asleep.'

'A migraine? You never told me you suffered from migraines.'

'Ashley, there's a lot about me I haven't told you. That is why we are getting to know each other, slowly.' The more slowly the better. 'I think I need to stay at home, I'm so sorry. Do give Felicia and Gerald my regards.'

'I see.' His voice was doubtful. 'Perhaps I may see you tomorrow?'

'Hopefully,' she lied. 'I will telephone you.'

'I hope you're better soon.'

Lord, the Heywoods. She was glad she had managed to avoid that. Too much talk of hunting and shooting and fishing. As dull as could be.

Beattie picked up the music she had found in the drawer at the Bowens' house and left her flat and Stranger's Square.

'Corrigan? Corrigan? Are you there?' She kept banging loudly on the front door that led to the stairs to his office. 'Come on, come on,' she muttered, before banging on the door once more.

'One minute please, one minute please.' She heard the bolts being drawn back, and a key being turned before the door opened, and John from the family in the flat underneath Corrigan peered out, together with aromas of spices and onions that made Beattie's mouth water and she realised she had eaten nothing since breakfast. 'Ah, it's you, the young lady who comes to see Mr Corrigan. Miss Cavendish, isn't it?'

'Yes it is, and I'm so sorry for the noise, but it's rather urgent. I'm looking for Corrigan. Mr Corrigan.'

'I know who you mean, but he's gone out. He left earlier. I think he might have gone to the public house he favours. He likes a pint. Or three.'

'Thank you, Mr . . . ?'

'Call me John, everybody does.'

'Thank you, John.'

'But, Miss Cavendish.' He put out a hand to stay her. 'Those places are not for ladies such as yourself.'

She smiled, touched at his concern. 'I'll be fine, John. Please don't worry.'

Noise and cigarette smoke greeted Beattie as she entered the Wagon and Horses, the noise dipping as she elbowed her way through the crowds lining the bar three or four deep. She hoped against hope that Corrigan was in his usual table at the back in the corner.

'And what's a lovely lady such as yourself doing in this place?'

Beattie looked up from her pushing and elbowing to see a large man with a rampant red beard and rheumy blue eyes brandishing a pint pot of ale. Liquid sloshed over the sides.

'I'm looking for someone, thank you.' She made to move, but he blocked her way. 'Please let me pass,' she said briskly.

'Could I be that person? The one you're looking for?'

She looked him up and down with cold and stern eyes. 'I very much doubt it,' she said.

'Oh, but I think I might be.' He leered at her, leaning in towards her, his beery breath enveloping her.

He belched.

'Seamus, Seamus, leave the lady alone, you great eejit,' Finn McNulty called from the other side of the bar. 'You won't win out against her. And she's a friend.'

Beattie continued looking at Seamus. 'And I could hurt you in a moment.' Her gaze was steely and Seamus seemed to wilt under it.

Seamus's eyes opened wide, and he held up both hands, more ale sloshing onto the floor. 'Sorry, sorry.'

'You will be,' Corrigan said, as he appeared at Beattie's side. 'What are you doing here, Beattie?' He took hold of her elbow. His face was stern, and with his black eyepatch he looked even more like a craggy pirate.

'I came to see you; what else would I be doing in a public house?'

Corrigan shook his head disbelievingly. 'You really are something, Beattie Cavendish. You could have come for a drink, perhaps?'

'I don't think so. I've come all the way across the river to see you.'

He looked surprised to see her, of course he did; after all, they'd hardly parted on good terms. In fact, she didn't think she'd ever see him again, but she needed him now.

'I will get you a drink.'

When they were both settled with their glasses, Beattie couldn't wait any longer. 'Corrigan, I have to see Nell.'

'Nell?'

'Yes, Nell.'

'My Nell?'

'Yes, your Nell, for goodness' sake, Corrigan, what other Nell is there?'

'I don't understand.'

'It's perfectly simple. I need to see your erstwhile girlfriend. I don't know where she lives and I haven't the time to do a whole lot of detective work.'

'That's my department.'

Beattie raised an eyebrow at this. 'Stop interrupting. Please,' she added because she thought she had better be polite. 'I'm sorry. I know we parted on bad terms. I know that you and Nell are not happy together, but it is imperative I speak to her about music.'

Corrigan took an annoyingly long, slow slug of his beer. He put it down on the pock-marked table. Laughter and shouting came from the men at the bar. Songs were being sung – in Irish, if she wasn't much mistaken. Likely to be rebel songs. She wondered if Corrigan knew the words, if he sang them too. *Stop*. She was drifting away from the matter in hand.

She rooted around in her handbag, taking out one of the sheets of music, glancing around to make sure no one was taking any notice of the pair of them, hidden in the corner. No one was looking. She slid it across the table to Corrigan.

'It's music.' He looked baffled.

'I realise that. I need someone to look at it and I remember Nell saying she loved music.'

He scratched his head. 'Yes, she teaches it.'

'Does she have a piano?'

'She does, why?'

'I want to talk to her about this music.'

'"In the Bleak Midwinter"? The Christmas carol?'

'Corrigan.' She shuffled her chair closer to him, wanting him to sense the urgency that had gripped her. 'It's important. Please.'

'Now?'

Beattie shrugged. 'It's as good a time as any. And I think that time could be of the essence.'

'Beattie, not everybody operates late into the night and this is all very cloak-and-dagger.' He sighed. 'Nothing has been simple since I met you in the study at the Bowens' house, has it?' Corrigan drained his pint. 'Lord, but you have a lot to answer for. I'll take you to Nell's, it's not too far from here, though I don't think she'll be pleased to see either of us. At any time of the day or night. Come on.'

It took them several minutes to exit the public house, thanks to too many people slapping Corrigan on his back and offering to buy him a pint.

'You're popular,' Beattie remarked as they walked quickly down the road, the yellow of the street lamps casting a sickly glow through the fog.

He laughed. 'They're only hopeful of free advice when they end up in the nick after three pints too many and a brawl on the street. They're trying to soften me up.'

'That would be hard,' Beattie muttered.

The rest of the walk was completed in silence. Beattie had nothing to say to Corrigan. She also feared if she did begin to talk to him she might let something slip, something about her real work. Corrigan was a dangerous man to be around. Deceptive. And too easy to talk to.

'Here we are,' Corrigan said eventually.

Beattie found herself standing in front of a terraced house with a white painted front door. The garden in the front was neat. The whole place had an air of comfort and care. There was a light on in one of the downstairs rooms.

Corrigan knocked on the door.

Silence. He knocked again.

'Patrick, what are you doing here?' Nell peered around the door. 'And Beattie. This is certainly a surprise.'

'May we come in?' Corrigan, having taken off his hat,

was twirling it around and around in his hands. He was nervous, Beattie realised.

'I . . . I'm not sure. I thought . . .'

'This is my fault,' said Beattie, stepping forward. 'I needed to see you urgently.'

'I see.' Now Nell had recovered from her shock, her voice was hard, and she was very definitely unwelcoming.

'If we could come in, Nell, we would appreciate it,' said Beattie, understanding that Nell was probably feeling embarrassed about laying her heart open to Beattie a few days before.

'Really? And why should I let you into my home?'

Beattie didn't blame Nell for her reluctance, but it she was becoming extremely cold standing on the doorstep. 'Only for a minute,' she said.

Nell sighed and held the door open. 'A minute, then. I was having my cocoa before bed as some of us have to work in the morning.' She glared at Corrigan. 'And don't be too long. Mother and Father are due back at any moment and I don't want them seeing you here.'

She led them into a cosy sitting room with books along one wall and on another, several watercolours above an upright piano. There was a display cupboard with china ornaments inside, including two very fine shepherdesses. The mantelpiece over the fireplace was adorned with a carriage clock and several silver tankards. Embers glowed in the grate.

Once they were all sitting down, furnished with cups of tea reluctantly but politely provided by Nell, Beattie placed the four pieces of sheet music in front of their reluctant hostess.

'I was hoping you could look at these and see if they make sense. Please.'

Nell frowned. 'Is this to do with your case, Patrick? The murder?'

'It might be,' said Beattie, her voice gentle. She knew Nell was keeping tears inside. 'Can you help? I know you enjoy music and Corrigan says you teach it.'

Nell looked at the first piece of music. '"In the Bleak Midwinter". I love that carol.' Her voice was sad. 'I was so looking forward to Christmas. But now, I don't know.'

Corrigan took her hand. 'Nell. Please.'

Nell extricated her hand from his. 'Not now, Patrick.'

She began to hum the tune. Then she looked at the music in her hand. Frowned. Began to hum again. 'This doesn't make sense.'

'What do you mean?'

'The music. It starts off as "In the Bleak Midwinter", but then it goes – nonsensical. They're not the right notes at all. There's no melody, no music. It's just . . .' She searched for words. 'A discordant jumble of notes. Until you get to near the end and then it's the carol again. Very odd. Listen.' She went over to her piano and began to play. The first notes of 'In the Bleak Midwinter' sounded, haunting and melancholy, and then, as Nell had said, there followed notes that made no sense at all, no melody, nothing.

Beattie retrieved the sheet of music from Nell. 'Thank you. And this?' She passed 'O Little Town of Bethlehem' to Nell.

Nell played with slender fingers. 'There, see? The same as before. It starts off as the right notes, then goes into a jumble.'

'Away in a Manger' and 'Hark! The Herald Angels Sing' followed the same pattern.

'Is that what you expected me to say?' Nell said.

'Honestly? I'm not sure. But now you do say it, I'm not surprised. Thank you so much, Nell. You have no idea how much I appreciate it.'

'Will you tell me what it's all about? Or is it only between you and Patrick?' The hostility was back in her voice.

'Nell,' said Corrigan. 'I have no idea what's going on.'

'Really.' She was disbelieving.

'Truly.' His voice had a desperate edge.

Beattie thought she should perhaps leave them alone. 'Thank you again, Nell. I'll leave you in peace.' She looked at Corrigan. 'I can find my own way home, Corrigan, if you want to—'

'No.' Nell's voice cut across her. 'You go too, Patrick. There's nothing more to say.' Her voice was full of steel, and Beattie admired her for that. 'And besides, I have a classroom full of children to deal with tomorrow.' She showed them to the door.

'Thank you again.' Beattie held out her hand.

Nell took it without smiling. 'I wish I could say it was a pleasure, but . . .'

'I understand, Nell, truly I do.'

Nell nodded. 'Good luck,' she said stiffly.

'Thank you. You really have been helpful.'

The door clicked closed behind them and the silence of the fog closed round them too.

They walked away in silence.

'She isn't going to forgive me easily, is she?' said

Corrigan. 'She wanted me to take that job at her father's firm and now it might be too late.'

'It might not be. Too late, I mean. She loves you, Corrigan. Very much. Perhaps it would be a good thing to get a nice steady job and a family. After all, you suffered in the war and—'

'I know all that, Beattie.' Corrigan cut her off. 'I know I got this in the war.' He jabbed at his eye socket, drew his hand down his scars. 'And I want them to count for something; that's why I decided to do what I do. And yes, I know I haven't exactly saved the world or unmasked a spy, but I do feel that I have helped some people. And though I do love Nell, do I love her enough?'

'Only you can answer that.'

'The job, with her father?' He stared straight ahead.

'A good, steady job by all accounts.'

'In the back room. Somewhere where I wouldn't be seen by the public, by the paying members of society who might be put off by my scars.' His laugh was hollow. 'Nell is accepting of me, but her father is another matter. Still, the job would pay well.'

'But you would always think you weren't good enough, being kept away like that.' Beattie could see his dilemma.

'Just so.'

Their breath was lost in the air.

'Anyway,' he said gruffly, 'are you going to tell me what that was all about? The music, the carol? I think you have worked something out.'

Beattie opened her mouth to reply, to fob him off, but then there came the noise of an engine, a vehicle going fast, and a black car without any lights came out of the darkness and fog, straight towards them.

The headlamps burst on, blinding them. The noise of the engine was deafening.

The car wasn't going to stop.

Beattie stumbled, slipped, threw herself against Corrigan, causing them to fall hard into the railings on the other side of the pavement. They landed in a heap on the ground.

The car continued towards them with a growling roar and she could smell the stink of petrol and oil and exhaust fumes.

Moments before it was going to hit them, the car swerved, narrowly avoiding them, before speeding off into the night, the sound dying in the fog.

The pair of them lay where they were for a moment, Beattie conscious of Corrigan's body under hers. 'Are you all right?' she said.

'I will be once you get off me,' he grunted.

Beattie stood, then held out a hand to help Corrigan up. He flexed his left leg. 'Won't have done that leg much good. Blasted eye. I didn't see it coming. I heard it but couldn't see it.'

Beattie acknowledged the frustration in his voice. She brushed herself down, ignoring the throbbing in one of her wrists. Not broken. A mild sprain, perhaps. Grazes on her palms.

'Are you hurt, Beattie?'

'I'm fine, thank you.'

'Once again you saved my life. Now I am doubly indebted to you and I think we are bound for life; that's what the Irish say.'

'If you save a life, you are responsible for that life. And it's the Chinese who say this; I certainly don't.' She felt a little shaken. 'Do you think—'

'That whoever it was meant to kill us? I don't know. Probably not, just scare us. They certainly weren't offering us a lift.'

She was quiet. What could she say?

They began walking again, Corrigan with more of a limp than normal, Beattie ignoring the pain in her wrist.

'We're a partnership, aren't we?' Corrigan said.

'Are we?' she said.

'I've told you everything I've been doing.'

'I doubt that,' she said.

Corrigan looked affronted. 'I have, so. Anyway . . . ?'

She sighed. She was not going to get rid of him without some sort of explanation, that was obvious. 'I can, but not here. Too public.'

'I'm in sore need of a whiskey,' he said hopefully.

Beattie thought of Corrigan's favourite pub with its noise and its smoke and the singing, Lord, the singing, and she thought of his office with its mean fire and frost and ice on the inside of the windows. Her head was throbbing. Her wrist was aching. 'We'll get a cab to my house.'

Corrigan laughed. 'That invitation was not issued with much joy or happiness, Miss Cavendish.'

'Should it have been?' she retorted.

CHAPTER TWENTY-SEVEN

Her flat was chilly, but she quickly made up the fire and flames were leaping in the grate. Corrigan was making himself comfortable – perhaps too comfortable – on her sofa and looking round the flat with interest.

'This is posh, Beattie Cavendish. Your own bathroom, too, I would imagine.'

Beattie glared at him. He was making fun of her. 'It belongs to my uncle.'

'Your uncle?'

'Yes, while he's in Scotland – oh, never mind.' Beattie was fed up of explaining herself.

'He's a fearsome one, though.' Corrigan pointed to the mask on the wall. 'I wouldn't want to come across him on a dark night.'

'I'm used to him now.' She busied herself making a gin and it for herself and pouring a whiskey for him, trying not to wince at the sudden pain in her wrist, but Corrigan must have seen something in her face.

He jumped up. 'Beattie, are you hurt?'

'It's nothing. My wrist, that's all. Landed heavily.'

'Let me look.' He took her wrist gently in his hand,

pushing up her sleeve very carefully. He felt around her wrist. He had good hands, broad with strong fingers and square, neat nails. His touch was featherlight. She shivered.

He frowned. 'Am I hurting you?'

'No.' His touch was disturbing her.

'Badly bruised, I'd say. I could put a bandage on it if you like?'

'No, it'll be fine. I've coped with worse.' She avoided his gaze.

He pulled her sleeve back down. 'You'll live.'

She tried not to snatch her arm back. 'I expect I shall. Do sit down, Corrigan.'

'Now,' he said, when he was settled again, 'spill the beans. What exactly is going on?' He sat back in the chair and sipped the whiskey. 'Not a bad drop,' he said. 'Considering it's not Irish.'

Beattie had been trying to think what best to say as they were sitting in the cab, but still had not come up with the answer. He deserved some sort of explanation, particularly as he had helped her by getting Nell to talk to her, at some cost to himself. But what could she say? She could hardly talk about spies and codes and dodgy Russians; he would probably laugh her out of court. And it could, it would, give away who she really worked for. She sat down in the armchair opposite him.

'I mean,' Corrigan carried on, 'my seventh son of a seventh son intuition is telling me that there's a lot you're not telling me. For instance.' He swallowed a good big drop of whiskey and held up his forefinger. 'One. Why are you so interested in a piece of music? A carol. That, as I understand it' – another large drop of whiskey went down his throat – 'wasn't a carol at all. Or something.' He held out his glass. Beattie took it and filled it with more amber liquid. 'And where did you find it? Tell me that, darlin'?' His Irish accent was becoming stronger with every sip and gulp of whiskey. 'And has it anything to do with Sofia Huber's death? I assume it must have.'

'It has something to do with Sofia's death as I'm sure everything is connected. I just have to find the connection.'

'Go on.'

'I found the music in the Bowens' house.'

'I see.' Though he clearly didn't by the glazed look in his eyes, most likely due to the whiskey. Beattie was glad. Perhaps he would forget everything about this conversation by the morning. 'Two.' His forefinger pointed at her this time. 'What's with all the warnings off we've been getting from men and women in hats? Why are they always wearing hats?'

Beattie opened her mouth.

'Three,' said Corrigan, before she could speak. 'Why was Kit killed? Murdered. And we shouldn't let his death go without . . . without . . . note,' he finished with a flourish. 'And four.' The forefinger was being waggled at her now, the whiskey almost finished. 'I can't remember four.' His eyelids were drooping. Perhaps he would fall asleep before she had to answer. 'That leopard rug is a damn fine thing.'

'I saw Leo Scott. He's found a witness, someone who saw Kit being thrown over the bridge,' she said, to give him something.

Corrigan's vision cleared and his head snapped up.

Beattie was reminded of when he had appeared to be fast asleep when they were at Polly's but did, in fact, hear everything. He was a suspiciously good actor. She wondered what he'd hoped she would give away if he pretended to be drunk.

'Why hasn't Scott told me?'

'Perhaps he tried. Perhaps you were in the Wagon and Horses when he called.'

Corrigan didn't react to her jibe. 'Is this witness sure it was Kit?'

'As sure as he can be.'

'And will the witness talk?'

'Stanley Dawes is his name and no, not to the police.'

'So,' said Corrigan, thinking, 'if Stanley talks to Leo Scott, he'll be able to write a story about it, as long as his news editor fella doesn't stick his oar in.'

'He could put himself in danger.' Beattie was worried.

Corrigan frowned. 'He's a sensible lad. Shrewd, too. I think he can look after himself. What about Martin?' Another sip of his whiskey. 'Where's he gone?'

'I don't know. He's not answering his telephone, so if I have the chance I'll go to his house tomorrow.'

All at once there was a knocking on the door and a good deal of shuffling of feet. 'Coo-ee, Beattie, Beattie, are you there?' A voice came through the wood. 'She'll be fast asleep, Gerald, I've told you.'

Oh Lord, Ashley. A drunk Ashley.

'Yes, Gerald.' Felicia's voice. Hard and slurred. 'I didn't want to be at this old cow's place at all. Why are we here? Spinster typist.' A loud sniff. 'If she couldn't be bothered to join us at the Heywoods', then bloody good riddance.'

322

'That's my girlfriend you're talking about.' Ashley, defending her.

'Felicia—' Gerald's voice.

'Don't "Felicia" me. We were having a jolly good time until you dragged us away. I want to go to a club.' Beattie imagined her pouting.

'The tiresome threesome,' Corrigan whispered.

'How did they get past the night porter in that state?' Beattie found herself whispering too. 'I was supposed to go to a ghastly party but cried off with a migraine.'

'Because you wanted to talk to Nell.'

'Yes.'

'It was so important that you were happy to miss a party with Ashley?'

She didn't answer him.

'Come on, old girl, open up before these two break the door down.' Gerald's smooth tones.

'We know you're there because I can see a light under the door. Is the migraine better?' Ashley's voice was wheedling. 'Come on, Beattie, please. Gerald said he bet you didn't have a migraine at all and we should come and see you.' More banging on the door. 'Have you got one?'

Beattie had to hope the neighbours were totally deaf.

'Please go away, Ashley.'

'Don't be like that, Beattie.'

'Be like that,' said Felicia. 'Come on, Ashley, I told you, she's not worth it.'

'As I said, I have a migraine.' Beattie was fed up with the three of them.

'Is there someone with you?' Ashley banged aggressively on the door.

'Oh, for pity's sake, what a rabble.' Beattie got up to tell them to go home, certain the neighbours of the flats on either side would be complaining any minute, but as she opened the door Felicia fell into the hall, undoing her coat and letting it drop to the floor. She was wearing a man's suit with an ivory silk blouse, the Peter Pan collar pinned with a diamond brooch. The outrageous effect was slightly spoilt by her patchy lipstick and pale face, mascara smeared beneath her eyes, and Beattie thought she could see a trace of white powder under her nose. Ashley, in grey flannels, was brandishing a champagne bottle and Gerald was as smooth as ever in a velvet jacket, a laconic smile and, when he caught sight of Corrigan, a raised eyebrow.

'And who might you be?' he asked.

'I was just going,' said Corrigan, standing and pulling his coat on. 'So don't let me get in your way. Top of the evenin' to yous.'

Beattie glanced over. What was he doing, exaggerating his accent like that?

'Don't go on account of us, dear boy,' said Gerald, his gaze firmly fixed on Corrigan's facial scars and missing eye.

Corrigan did not flinch. 'I'm not,' he said eventually.

'Who have we here, Beattie?' Ashley swayed on his feet, pointing at Corrigan with the champagne bottle. 'It looks like it was a good job Gerald had us come here.'

'Don't be silly, Ashley. This is Patrick Corrigan, a friend of mine. He was just leaving.'

'What a cosy scene. And entertaining a man after dark without a chaperone. Tut tut, Miss Cavendish.' Felicia

324

gave her a nasty smile. 'And an Irishman. That won't make you very popular with my father. I knew there was something distinctly off about you.'

Beattie had a sudden desire to tell Felicia exactly what she knew about her father and Sofia and the baby who would never be born, but she held her tongue. Now was not the time and she would be doing it for all the wrong reasons. But she wanted the girl and her companions to leave. 'It has absolutely nothing to do with you, Felicia, who my friends are. Nor anything to do with your father,' said Beattie coldly. 'Now pick your coat up and leave my home.'

Felicia stared at her, but Beattie was good at that game and it was Felicia who dropped her eyes first.

'We had a near miss with a car earlier,' said Corrigan. 'We were lucky to escape without being seriously hurt.' He said it casually, as if they hadn't been frightened out of their wits for a few brief seconds. Beattie wondered what the purpose of telling the three visitors this was. 'Could have been a nasty accident. Though I don't reckon it was an accident.'

'Why do you say that?' asked Gerald, his long fingers holding a lighted cigarette. 'You don't mind, do you?' he asked Beattie, belatedly and rudely.

Beattie merely lifted an eyebrow.

Felicia looked as though she'd have been rather pleased if the car had its target.

'It was all very deliberate. But then it turned away at the last moment, so either the driver got cold feet or it was only sent to frighten us,' said Beattie, though she didn't know why she was telling Gerald this.

'I think you are being a bit dramatic, don't you?' Gerald looked at her with a clear gaze that made her trust him even less.

'Perhaps,' she said. 'Though it seemed as though he was intent on injuring us.'

'He?'

'Could have been a she. Does it matter?'

He shrugged.

'I thought you were my girl, Beattie,' said Ashley, interrupting, his mouth turning down at the corners. 'So I don't know what you're doing with a one-eyed Paddy.'

Beattie closed her eyes briefly. He hadn't heard a word about the near-death experience with the car. 'I won't have you talking about my friend, a guest in my house, like that. Please go, Ashley, and I'll talk to you when you're sober.' She pushed him out of the door, fighting back the desire to tell him, forcefully, that she was nobody's 'girl', least of all his. She made herself smile and took his rather clammy hand. 'I will see you tomorrow, darling. Lunch, perhaps?'

'Lunch.' He thrust the champagne bottle at her – empty, she noticed. He moved backwards and forwards on his toes. He nodded. 'Yes. Indeed. Lunch.'

'Good.' She pecked him on his cheek. 'Now, go, and take those two with you.'

They all trooped down the corridor towards the lift, Ashley with his hands in his pockets looking downcast, Felicia defiant and warbling a song Beattie didn't recognise and Gerald smoking with insouciance.

Beattie and Corrigan looked at each other. They both began to laugh. 'Who are those people?' said Corrigan in between breaths. 'Friends of yours?'

'Not bloody likely,' said Beattie.

'But Ashley Bowen is?'

Beattie sobered up, stopped laughing, sorted out her brain. 'Yes. He is. There's something about him that interests me.'

'I would have thought you are too . . .'

'Too what?' She couldn't let this line of conversation continue. 'I like him a lot. You haven't seen the best of him tonight. He can be kind and generous.' Oh dear.

'I would have thought—'

'Your thoughts have absolutely no relevance to me. None whatsoever.'

He smiled. 'I've been told to mind my own business very forcefully.'

'Yes.'

'But you are going to tell me the relevance of the music, aren't you? Now that we're blood brothers and everything.'

'We are not . . .' She stopped as she saw Corrigan smiling. 'You're teasing me.'

'A little. So tell me.'

'Corrigan—'

'Beattie. Someone killed Sofia Huber. Killed Kit. Tried to kill us, or at the very least frighten us badly. Now they might all be different people or they might be the same. I think you owe me an explanation.'

She sighed. 'Edwina Bowen is sending secret messages to, I think, the Russians, on sheet music.'

Corrigan stared at her. His mouth twitched and he burst into laughter. 'Edwina Bowen, the wife of a hopeful Foreign Secretary, is a spy? Is that what you're telling me?'

'Yes. The music on those pieces of paper I showed Nell is code. Not music at all.'

What an irritating man. All he could do was laugh. Maybe it was a good thing that he didn't believe her.

Corrigan stopped laughing. 'In the name of all that's holy, you're serious, aren't you?'

She nodded.

'Beattie.' He took a deep breath. 'Are you really a typist?'

'I teach girls how to type, yes.'

Corrigan shook his head. 'No, you don't. I don't believe you. How would a typist come to that conclusion? But,' he said slowly, 'I do believe you about the music. It sounds – so preposterous that it must be true. And you're a clever woman, Beattie.'

'The Soviets want to make an atomic bomb. I suspect Edwina Bowen has been gathering information from Ralph Bowen about our progress – careless talk, pillow talk, papers left in the open, I don't know – and giving or selling it to the Russians.'

'What do we do?'

'*We* don't do anything, Corrigan. I know people. I'll take it to them.' Even now Beattie was unwilling to take that step and tell Corrigan who she really worked for; after all, she had signed the Official Secrets Act.

Corrigan stared at her in silence for a moment. She could see disappointment in her in his face. 'Very well. But remember, we could still be in danger.'

'I know, Corrigan.'

'Right.' Corrigan stood and stretched, shaking his leg, pain flitting across his face. 'Time to be on my way.' He hesitated. 'Look, if you go to see Martin Huber tomorrow, may I come with you?'

Beattie nodded. It would be good to have his company.

'Shall I meet you outside his house? About ten?'

Beattie shut the door behind Corrigan and leant back against it, exhausted. It had been quite a day. Both her head and wrist were throbbing now, and all she wanted to do was to crawl into bed. Tomorrow she was going to find out what Martin had been up to. She listened out for the *ding* of the lift, for the creak of its door opening and closing. She picked up the whiskey tumblers and took them back to the kitchen.

As she was drying the glasses there was a knock on the door.

She was wrong; Corrigan had not gone away. What did he want to say now? Honestly, he really did have the cheek and blarney of the Irish.

She flung the door open. 'What do you want, Corrigan?'

She stopped. It was not Corrigan but an unsmiling Gerald. She looked behind him, but there was no sign of Ashley or Felicia.

'If you're looking for the other two,' he drawled, 'they've buggered off to find more champagne. I waited down the corridor until the bogtrotter left.'

'Don't talk about Corrigan in that way,' she said stiffly.

'Sweet on him, are you?' he sneered.

She sighed. 'What do you want, Gerald?'

He blinked, like a cat ready to pounce, she thought. Suddenly she was a little afraid of him. He grabbed her wrist. It hurt, but she managed not to cry out – she didn't want to show the man any weakness. His face was close to hers, and she smelt brandy and cigarettes on his breath. His grip was strong, his face set in hard lines, eyes glittering. Briefly she wondered if she had underestimated him.

'Again, what do you want, Gerald?' Her voice was steady.

'A warning.' The wafts of alcohol made her feel queasy, but Gerald was not drunk. 'Be careful; you're meddling in things you don't understand. You are an amateur. Stick to typing, do you hear me? Before you and the bogtrotter get hurt. Badly.' He let go of her wrist and shoved her back inside the house, then turned and walked away as if he had done a perfectly courteous house call.

Beattie watched him, cradling her wrist.

Who the devil was he?

And she was thoroughly fed up of being told what to do by men who thought they could intimidate her.

They were wrong.

CHAPTER TWENTY-EIGHT

Beattie slept badly, tossing and turning until her sheets were a twisted mass around her body. And, however many times she thumped her pillow, she couldn't get comfortable. Eventually she gave in and got out of her bed, put on her silk dressing-gown and padded into the kitchen to make a cup of tea.

Her mind was a jumble of thoughts. Was she right about Edwina Bowen and her spying? Beattie had to admit a grudging admiration for her ingenuity. The White Pearl Club was also involved, and Sofia Huber had worked there for a short while. Was that a coincidence? Was Sofia Huber's murder connected to Edwina Bowen? She curled up on the sofa with a rug around her shoulders and a hot water bottle at her feet. Her tea grew cold on the table beside her as her thoughts raced around her head. One thing she did know was that she had to take her suspicions to Anthony. That was her job. And she needed to do it first thing in the morning.

She must have dozed off, because the next thing she knew there was knocking at her door – loud and furious. Her heart stopped. Not Gerald again, surely? She shivered.

She looked at the clock on the mantelpiece. Six o'clock. In the morning. Not Gerald again; he'd already delivered his warning. So who was calling this early?

Standing up, she yawned. 'Just a minute,' she called, and hurried to her bedroom to throw some clothes on. The knocking stopped, then started up again as if to tell her she was taking too long. 'All right, all right,' she muttered, opening the door cautiously.

'Beattie. Please, it's me. Let me in.'

Standing outside her door, teeth chattering with cold or fear, was a dirty and dishevelled young man. He was wearing a cap but no coat or scarf. His jumper had a hole in the front, and his trousers looked as though they would walk themselves to the washing tub. Martin Huber.

'What are you doing? Come in.' Beattie held the door wide, and Martin rushed in, slamming the door behind him.

'Hold on, Martin. Where's the fire?'

'There is no fire and I am so cold.' Martin looked on the edge of tears and as frightened as a faun. There was a large bruise on his cheek that was yellowing at the edges, and a scratch with crusting dried blood which ran from his ear to the corner of his mouth. His hands were a mass of cuts and grazes.

'Come and sit down.' Beattie wrapped her rug around him. Her hot water bottle still had a vestige of warmth, so she gave him that too. 'I'll make you a hot drink, and then we can talk.'

'Thank you so much, Beattie. Thank you.' He shivered dramatically.

Beattie shook her head. 'No, I'll draw you a bath; it'll warm you up and wash that grime off you.'

An hour later and Martin was washed and dressed in an old shirt and trousers of Beattie's. He was tucking into bacon and egg she had cooked, and was already looking so much better, though the bruises were more livid now the dirt had been washed off.

'What happened to you, Martin? You left Saltergate Island where you were safe. Who were the people you went with? Were they your friends?'

He shook his head miserably. 'No. They said they were. They said they had news of my parents and could help them get to England. They were Polish. They told me not to say anything to your parents or sister because if I did they might not be able to get my parents back.'

Beattie's heart sank. 'And what happened?'

'They drove me to London and threw me into a cellar. Then two more men came and wanted to know where Sofia's diary was. I told them I did not know. But they kept hitting me.' He undid the buttons of the shirt and Beattie gasped when she saw the yellow, green and purple bruises across his stomach and chest. 'I'm sorry,' he said, doing the shirt back up, 'I know it is not proper for a gentleman to open his shirt in front of a lady, but I had to show you in case you did not believe me.'

'I believe you, Martin.' Who wanted Sofia's diary so badly that they would kidnap her brother and beat him up? What had she written?

'They did too, eventually,' he said. 'I thought they were going to kill me, but they blindfolded me and took me to a bombsite somewhere in London. I managed to make my way back here.'

'You did well.'

'And my parents are not coming to England, are they?'

Beattie looked at him with great sympathy. 'No, Martin. I would think not.' She sighed, looking at her hands. She knew she had to tell the young man about his sister. 'Martin, did you know that Sofia was pregnant?'

Martin sat back in his chair. 'No, I did not. Oh.' He shook his head, the corners of his mouth turning down. 'Our parents would have been so disappointed.'

'I know it's a lot to take in, but I think she truly loved the father of her baby.'

'Who was he?' Now his expression had turned stern and he looked older than his years and Beattie could see the disapproval marking his face. Martin may have loved Sofia dearly, but she thought it was pretty clear that her brother might not have been a great support to her in her hour of need.

Beattie bit her lip. He had a right to know; Sofia had been his much-loved sister. But what would his reaction be? She didn't want him to run off and confront Ralph Bowen; there wasn't any point to that – though perhaps there would be for him. Beattie battled with her conscience. She had no problem with telling a lie if it would serve the greater purpose, but she also liked to see fairness. And surely it was only fair that Sofia's brother should know about the father of his sister's baby?

He banged the table with controlled violence. Beattie watched him calmly. 'You must tell me,' he said.

'It was Ralph Bowen. He really loved her, I do believe that.'

Martin's eyes narrowed. 'I see. Her employer. He took advantage of her.'

'No, no. I've spoken to him, and he said they loved each other.'

'But he is an old man.' His fingers were tapping the table.

'He loved her, Martin.'

'So he did not kill her?'

'No.'

'You can't know that.'

She gripped his arm. 'I don't, but I believe it. And you must too.'

Martin stood, pushing the chair away so hard that it fell over. 'Sofia's diary, I am going to look for it.'

'I thought you said it had been stolen?' said Beattie, righting the kitchen chair.

'I said it was gone. It was not in its usual place. I now wonder if Sofia hid it somewhere in the house?'

'If you think it's a good idea, Martin. Look, I am meeting Corrigan – you remember Corrigan? – outside your house today, but I have to see to something first. You could meet him, though, and look for the diary together.'

'You do not think there will be bad people there?'

'If there are, Corrigan will know and he'll keep you safe from harm. Will you tell Corrigan from me that I will see him later?'

Martin inclined his head. 'Of course.'

'You will go straight to the house?' It was so early, she would ring Corrigan and ask him to meet Martin.

'Yes. Thank you so much for the food.'

'If you find Sofia's diary—'

'I will show you.'

'It could be important.'

Martin narrowed his eyes. 'Why?'

Beattie hesitated. 'There might be information in it that is useful for the government.' She could go no further.

'Your government?'

'Yes.'

Martin looked at her, a steely expression on his young face. 'I see. Once again, thank you, Beattie.' He let himself out of the flat.

Beattie shut the door behind him, wondering if she had done the right thing telling him about Sofia's baby and its father, and mentioning the government. There had been a look in his eyes that troubled her.

CHAPTER TWENTY-NINE

Corrigan, too, had slept badly, but his reason was more to do with drink swirling around his system than with thoughts swirling around his brain.

He had arrived back at his home-cum-office full of restrained anger. He couldn't think of a word bad enough to describe Gerald Silver, so he took out his anger and frustration on a bottle of whiskey. Now he groaned as he tried to open his eyes, realising he was clutching the empty bottle to his chest. He tried to sit up. Mistake. His head hurt. A lot. Nausea rose in his throat. At least the drink had kept him warm overnight.

Stupid, stupid, stupid. Why did he let that man get to him with his air of entitlement and superiority? He only didn't land him one out of respect for Beattie, but my God, he would love to wipe that supercilious smirk off his face.

He took a deep breath and swung his legs over the edge of the bed.

After sticking his head under the cold tap, Corrigan felt mildly better. A cigarette and cup of coffee later, he felt better still. Breakfast was not on the menu, though.

He wandered into his office, having a dim recollection of, after stumbling in, picking up an envelope that had been pushed under his door and throwing it onto his desk. At the time he had been pleased with the accuracy of his throw.

There it was. A large envelope with his name written in the middle. He tore it open and saw it was from the journalist, Leo Scott.

Corrigan, he read. *Can you meet me at Bruno's Café on the edge of Clapham Common at half past seven tomorrow morning? Leo Scott.*

He looked at the clock. Just gone seven. Good. He shrugged on his coat and went downstairs.

The fog was even thicker than the day before, and his footsteps echoed on the pavement. A bus loomed out of the gloom, a conductor by its side, walking along the kerb beside the driver's cabin in order to guide the vehicle. There were long queues at the Tube station, too, as Londoners tried to get to work without using cars or buses. He had heard on the wireless that visibility in the Port of London was less than ten yards and the fog was so thick it was impossible to use cranes to unload the cargo. Corrigan could barely see six feet in front of him and thought how easy it would be to become lost. It was very eerie.

Suddenly the lights of Bruno's Café appeared, piercing the dense air, and Corrigan pushed open the door, embracing the warmth and the smell of fresh coffee beans.

As usual, the little café was full, even at the relatively early hour – good coffee had only recently arrived in the capital and was proving popular, especially after the ersatz coffee of the war years – and there was very little room to move; all the wooden tables were occupied. Thankfully, Leo Scott had already arrived, and waved to him from a corner table. Corrigan made his way over, taking off his gloves and unwinding the scarf from around his neck. He took off his hat and coat and laid them on a spare chair before sitting down.

'Bloody hell, that fog,' he said, by way of greeting.

Scott nodded. 'It's quite something, isn't it? The government have got to do something about the pollution otherwise it's only going to get worse, as we keep saying in the paper. Anyway, we're not here to talk about the air in London. Breakfast?'

Corrigan shook his head; his stomach was still rebelling. 'Just a coffee, thank you. Bruno is a specialist.'

Scott called the waitress over and ordered two cups of coffee and toast and marmalade.

'So,' said Corrigan, sipping the cup of coffee that had been set down on the table, 'what did you want to see me about?'

'I came round to your office last night, but you weren't there.'

'Clearly.'

Scott blushed, and Corrigan regretted his sarcastic reply. 'I was having my life saved by Beattie Cavendish.'

Scott's eyes grew wide. 'My God, what happened?'

Corrigan briefly told him about the car driving directly at the pair of them as they were walking back to Beattie's house. He didn't, however, say anything about Beattie's theory regarding Edwina Bowen. It wasn't that he thought it couldn't be plausible, but that he wanted to talk more about it to her, to try and find out what Beattie's role in the whole affair was. And Leo Scott was, after all, a journalist.

'Who might it have been?'

Corrigan shrugged. 'Someone who thought we were getting close to whoever killed Sofia Huber.' Or someone who knew Beattie had made a connection between Edwina Bowen and the White Pearl Club and possible spying. Were they one and the same, or was it possible there were two factions telling them to keep their noses out of their business?

Corrigan took a piece of toast and spread marmalade on it. He bit into it and chewed slowly, thinking, thinking. Then a familiar feeling crept over him, that feeling of foreboding. He closed his eyes, letting it fill him. A gentle buzzing in his head . . .

'Hey, that's my toast, you know.'

Scott's voice brought him back to the café, the smell of coffee and the tang of orange in his mouth. 'Sorry,' he said with a wry smile. 'It seems I was hungry after all. What did you want to speak to me about?'

Scott looked around the café before talking. 'Stanley Dawes. The man who saw Kit being killed.'

'I know who you mean,' said Corrigan impatiently. 'Beattie told me. Please don't tell me he's dead now too.'

Scott smiled briefly. 'No. I had another talk with him; he was a bit more sober this time, so . . .'

'He was drunk when you spoke to him first?' Corrigan's voice was sharp.

'Yes, but I believed him. He was only drunk because he was really scared. Anyway, as I say, I spoke to him again and he put a bit more flesh on the bones. The car was black, looked official, our Stanley said.'

'Police?'

Scott shook his head. 'I'm not sure, but from what Stanley said more like *official* official, if you know what I mean. And it all adds up, doesn't it?'

'Does it?'

'Look.' Scott moved the plate of toast and marmalade out of the way, just as Corrigan was about to take another piece. 'Do you remember me telling you that my news editor had leant on me about my original Sofia Huber story because he had been leant on from above?'

Corrigan nodded.

'And I thought that might have been MI5?'

Corrigan nodded again. His stomach rumbled. He pulled the plate of toast towards him. 'Go on.'

'Stanley Dawes told me the two men who threw Kit over the bridge—Corrigan winced—wore black coats and trilby hats.' He leant back in his chair, a satisfied look on his face.

'Leo, half the gangsters in London wear black coats and trilbies.' He spread another piece of toast with marmalade, ignoring Scott's look of annoyance.

Scott frowned. 'Stanley also said the men didn't talk at all as Kit went over; they peered over the parapet until they heard the splash.'

'Did he see what they looked like?'

'Ordinary, he said.'

'Not foreign-looking? Olive skin, black hair, beards?'

Scott laughed. 'Like the stereotype of a Russian, you mean?' He sobered up as he took in Corrigan's expression.

'You mean it, don't you? My God, is there a Russian connection in all this?' He whispered the last words, while looking around the café again.

Corrigan considered him, wondering how much to say. 'Who knows?' he said eventually. 'But did you bring me here to tell me that because the men who murdered Kit were wearing black coats and trilbies that they were from MI5?' He laughed. 'That's a big leap to make.'

'Well, they wouldn't be police officers, would they?'

'Probably not.'

'And they were obviously professional.' Scott was eager to press his point home.

'Obviously.'

'And no evidence Kit was involved with gangsters. Only the White Pearl Club. And you.'

'Fair enough.' Yet Corrigan was feeling uneasy. He remembered Beattie talking about the Watchers from MI5, and they dressed that way. What if Scott was right? 'Did the men say anything?'

'No, I told you. They were silent as they forced Kit over the bridge.'

'Afterwards. Did they say anything afterwards?'

'Oh, I see. Yes. "Job done." They said "job done".'

'That's all?'

'Could they be MI5?'

'Honestly?' said Corrigan, rolling himself another cigarette. 'I don't know, but . . .'

'But?'

'It seems probable, yes.'

Honey. Buzzing in his head. Newly mown grass. The scrape of cutlery on dishes. Snatches of sentences reaching his brain: '*I said to him, I said . . .*' and '*His mother's coming to stay*' and '*too much paper*'. The sizzle of the grill. There was danger. The sensations weren't as pronounced as those he'd experienced in his office, but they were there. He stood up abruptly. 'Leo, I've got to go. Don't worry, you'll have your story, the full story. But don't poke around.'

'Poking around is what I do.'

'Be careful, then. Very careful. Whoever these people are, they're ruthless. If you get in their way they won't hesitate to kill you and I can't have that on my conscience.'

'You won't. Don't worry. But where are you going?'

'There's someone I've got to see.'

'The enigmatic Beattie Cavendish?'

'Perhaps.'

He rushed out of the café to join the queues at the Clapham Common Tube station. The queue moved so slowly, it seemed as though there were hundreds of people crowding into the entrance hall. Then he heard people talking about two trains colliding near Clapham, causing a short circuit, which then set fire to a power sub-station, cutting off the current. Trains were being delayed. Tube trains too, in all likelihood.

It was taking too long.

He had to get to Martin's house and wait for her there as they'd agreed; that was all he could do. Damn the woman for being so secretive. He had no idea where she worked. Whitehall? A private office somewhere? Could be anywhere. He had respected her wish for keeping herself to herself and now he was paying for it.

Beattie needed him.

CHAPTER THIRTY

It had taken Beattie what felt like hours to reach Mayfair and the office at Chesterfield Street; the crowds in the Tube had been dreadful and everything was taking longer because of the fog. She had never known it so bad; even the Berlin Airlift had been suspended.

She sat down at her desk, worry nibbling at her mind. She tried telephoning Martin at his house once again. Still no answer. She sighed, gathered her thoughts and dialled Anthony Cooper's internal number to ask to see him.

As ever, his head was down and his pen was scratching across paper. He had two manila folders open beside him. His jug of water. A glass. The room was draughty. The clock on the wall ticked ominously. The spider plant drooped.

Scratch, scratch, scratch.

Was she right? Could Edwina Bowen be a Soviet spy? The wife of the Shadow Foreign Secretary? And a Catholic priest was almost certainly involved. Had Sofia Huber found something out about Edwina Bowen, and she'd been killed because of that knowledge? Had she written something incriminating in her diary? Perhaps there had been blackmail. The thoughts chased around her head. Her hands were clammy, her mouth dry.

Anthony Cooper put down his Waterford pen and clasped his hands together on the desk.

'Miss Cavendish. You have brought me some news about Ralph Bowen? Something his son might have said to you, perhaps?'

His son? Ashley. She had scarcely given him a thought.

'Not entirely.'

'Not entirely. I see. To what do I owe this pleasure?'

'I think Edwina Bowen is a Russian spy.' There. She had blurted it out, and it sounded like something from a Dashiell Hammett novel.

Anthony Cooper raised his eyebrow. 'I see.' He poured himself a glass of water. 'And what leads you to this conclusion?'

Beattie told him about the music she had found in Edwina Bowen's study, how she had taken it from the locked drawer, followed her to St Margaret of Antioch – a Roman Catholic church, she explained – had seen the consternation on her face, the priest's face, and a man to whom they both spoke. The man left, angry, and she had followed him to the White Pearl Club, a club owned by Russians. She took a deep breath. 'Where Sofia Huber, the lover of Ralph Bowen and the mother of his unborn baby, had worked.' She also told him about finding someone – she was careful not to name Nell and not to bring Corrigan into the whole affair – who could read music and who said what she had found in Edwina Bowen's study was not musical at all, and definitely not the Christmas carols they purported to be. 'That was when,' she said, 'I knew

Edwina Bowen had to be selling or giving, I don't know which, secrets to the Russians.'

Anthony Cooper carefully capped his pen. 'That is quite some tale, Miss Cavendish.'

'It's not a "tale", Mr Cooper. Look.' She reached inside her handbag and brought out two of the sheets of music. 'This is the music. Have your coding experts look at it. I tried, but the code is tough.'

He took the music out of her hand. 'Thank you.' He sat back in his chair. 'Nothing about Ralph Bowen?'

She shook her head. 'No.'

'Yet the chatter has been about him and not his wife.' He sucked on his teeth. 'What are we to do?' he muttered. 'What are we to do?'

Suddenly Anthony Cooper seemed to realise Beattie was still sitting in front of him. He bared his teeth in a parody of a smile. 'Perhaps we have been looking in the wrong place.' He slapped the manila folders shut. 'Good work, Miss Cavendish. Now leave this with me.'

'What about Sofia Huber's murder? I still think it's connected.'

Anthony Cooper frowned. 'No. I don't think so.'

'Why not?' Beattie had to sit on her hands to keep her temper. She thought she had persuaded him to look into everything with her story.

'Sofia Huber was the victim of a petty thief. But this business with Edwina Bowen, well, that could be important. Thank you for bringing it to my attention.'

'And Kit Pearson?' She heard the angry desperation in her voice.

'Who?'

'I told you about him the other day. He was found dead after wanting to talk to Patrick Corrigan.'

'I know nothing about a Kit Pearson, and, as I said' – his tone hard – 'thank you for bringing this to my attention.'

'What are you going to do with the music?'

Another raised eyebrow. 'I will show it to the right people, don't worry. I will have it analysed. And you can now be relieved of anything more to do with Ashley Bowen. In fact, thank you for your hard work but now, if I were you, I would forget all about this and return to your translations until I have another assignment for you.'

Beattie couldn't move. She wanted to know what was going to happen. She wanted to know that Edwina Bowen would be brought to justice. She wanted to know that someone would be held responsible for Sofia Huber's death. And she wanted to know why she had been summarily dismissed from the job she was doing.

'I said thank you, Miss Cavendish. Now run along.' He sipped his water. Opened the manila folders. Uncapped his fountain pen.

Beattie left, doing all she could not to slam the door shut behind her.

When she arrived back at her desk, Beattie tried to bury herself in her translation work, trying not to think about Edwina Bowen, or any of the Bowens for that matter, nor Sofia or Martin. Martin. She groaned. She was supposed to meet Corrigan at Martin's house. She looked at the clock on the wall. Too late to get there now. She tried to damp down the irritation, quickly turning into anger, that was fizzing along her bones. *Run along*. What a loathsome little man, talking to her like that. And what an idiot she was for taking it. She looked around the room, at the men busy at their desks. She knew that at least two of them had been given assignments that had really meant something, that had achieved something, unlike her, who had been asked to babysit the son of an MP who may or may not be a 'person of interest'. And now, just like that, she had been relieved of that duty. She shook her head. This was ridiculous. All she was doing was sitting here feeling angry with Anthony Cooper and sorry for herself.

It would not do.

She heard a voice outside in the hallway. Anthony Cooper's.

'I'm going out, Miss Laing. I'm not sure when I'll be back.'

'Of course, Mr Cooper. Don't forget you have a meeting with the minister at four o'clock this afternoon.'

'I hadn't forgotten.' His voice was waspish.

'If you could sign these papers for me before you leave, Mr Cooper.'

'Really, now, Miss Laing?'

'It's important, sir. Five minutes, sir.'

There was a huff and a puff and a silence. Beattie imagined him giving Miss Laing one of his tight smiles before reading through the documents and signing them.

All at once she made up her mind, but she had to be quick.

First, she made a quick phone call, dialling the number written on a piece of paper secreted in a hidden pocket of her handbag, imagining a small, functional office in Eastcote. Then she tidied her files into a neat pile. 'I'm going out for a while,' she said, to no one in particular. And no one looked up.

CHAPTER THIRTY-ONE

Corrigan had taken his life in his hands to reach Beattie's flat in Pimlico, having to weave around buses and cars and people on his Royal Enfield. A journey that would normally take less than twenty minutes had taken twice that. There was no way he could ride at speed, not in the fog.

He jumped off the Enfield and raced into Stranger's Square, making his way to Beattie's block. The lift took an age.

'Beattie,' he shouted, as he banged on her door. 'Beattie.' Nothing.

He put his ear to the door, but he could hear nothing.

Leaving Stranger's Square, he jumped back on the motorbike and headed – slowly – for Martin Huber's house. She must be there. They were supposed to be meeting outside the house at ten o'clock. Perhaps she had gone there early. Perhaps she was at work, wherever that was. Somewhere secret. He knew she was special.

'Oi, look where you're going on that bloody thing,' a voice shouted at him as a bus conductress and bus emerged out of the fog. 'You'll get yourself killed at this rate.'

Corrigan waved a gloved hand in apology, and went

even more slowly, thinking only of getting to Martin's house safely.

What would he do if Beattie wasn't there?

He arrived in a foul temper. Another longer than usual journey.

Peering through a ground-floor window, he saw cushions tossed on the floor and papers strewn over the carpet. Broken ornaments. Books thrown aside. If he wasn't mistaken, the peacock and the pigeon had been knocked from their perches.

The sensation of evil was not going away; the buzzing in his ears was becoming stronger.

Corrigan pushed the front door. As before, it was open.

The air quivered. There was definitely someone inside.

He stepped over the overturned elephant's foot umbrella stand, not bothering to be quiet as he knew if there was someone in the small house they would surely know he was there.

'Hello?' he called.

No answer.

He walked down the hallway and pushed open the door to the small kitchen. Every single drawer had been opened and rifled through, the cupboards also. Even the pots and pans had been swept off their stand and thrown on the ground.

He turned around and went back into the sitting room.

Gerald Silver lounged by the fireplace smoking a cigarette and looking perfectly at ease. He was wearing his usual attire of velvet jacket and shirt, complete with ostentatious scarf, and held a gun down by his side. A Walther PPK modified to enable a silencer to be attached to the barrel, if Corrigan wasn't much mistaken. He quite wanted to wipe that supercilious smile off Silver's face.

'Ah, the Irishman,' said Silver, waving the cigarette around. 'I should have expected you.'

'Where's Beattie?' snapped Corrigan.

'La Cavendish? I have no idea.'

'Martin Huber?'

'Again, no idea.'

'What are you doing here, then? Are you responsible for the destruction?' He kept his good eye on the gun.

'Ah.' Gerald bent down and picked up the pigeon, setting it back on the table. 'I'm afraid so. Looking for a diary. Know anything about it, old chap?'

'No, *old chap*, I don't.'

'Hmm. Apparently Sofia Huber kept one, charting her *liaison* with the Shadow Foreign Secretary. I think it could be interesting.'

'I don't care what you think, quite frankly.'

'Look.' Gerald inhaled, and then, clamping the cigarette between his lips, held out his cigarette case. Corrigan hesitated, then took one. Perhaps it would foster good relations. Unlikely. He leant forward to accept a light, wondering if he could snatch the gun.

'Don't even think about it, Corrigan,' said Silver, as if he had guessed his thoughts. 'I'll have that other eye out before you can say "Geronimo". So, once more, Corrigan, the diary? I know you and Beattie have been as thick as thieves over this Sofia Huber killing. I know this diary could have what we might call sensitive information in it, and we wouldn't want it to fall into the wrong hands, would we?'

'All depends on who is right and who is wrong.'

Gerald laughed. 'I am on the side of the angels.'

'Really,' said Corrigan wryly. 'I'd like to see the devil, then. Who are you, Gerald? MI5? KGB? Or just a flat-footed copper?' The buzzing in his head was quieter now, though his nerves were still tingling. Beattie still occupied his mind. What was the time?

Gerald shook his head. 'It doesn't matter. Now, I can't find the diary here. Any ideas where it might be?'

'No,' said Corrigan flatly. 'None. How do you know about it?'

'Dear Felicia, of course. We talk about everything. Correction, *she* talks about everything and she's very angry with her father. She doesn't like Beattie much, either. Thinks she's a gold digger and rather plain. And she thinks I like Miss Cavendish a little too much. Maybe I do, maybe I don't. Who knows?' He smiled. 'And now you want to get hold of the diary too.'

Corrigan ignored Gerald's remarks about Beattie. 'If it will help us find Sofia Huber's killer, then yes.'

'You do know you're meddling in things that don't concern you, don't you?'

Corrigan shook his head. 'I don't know what you mean. All I know is that you're as thick as thieves with the Bowens. But I don't know why.'

'Old friends,' Gerald said. 'You followed Ralph Bowen.' It was not a question.

'So?'

'I imagine Edwina wanted to know how much he knew about her life.'

'Something like that.'

'The diary. Do you know where it is?'

Corrigan laughed. 'Damn diary. No, I don't.' He stubbed out his cigarette in a nearby ashtray.

'I'm inclined to believe you.' Gerald looked at his watch. 'I don't have time to wait for young Martin now.' He sighed. 'I have a job to do and I don't want you interfering.' Keeping the gun trained on Corrigan, he took a pair of handcuffs out of his pocket. He threw them to Corrigan. 'One on your wrist, and now go through to the kitchen. Hurry up, please.'

Corrigan had no choice. He walked out of the sitting room to the kitchen.

'Put the other handcuff round the foot of the oven,' ordered Gerald.

The oven was one of the new, modern gas cookers. Sturdy. A gas pipe coming from it and disappearing into the wall. Corrigan put the handcuff around the leg as instructed. The cooker was heavy, and he also didn't fancy pulling it away from the wall, not with the gas.

Gerald watched. 'I don't want to kill you, Corrigan, I think that would cause too much trouble; you will not be easily dismissed, forgotten about. I don't even want to hurt you. But I have to slow you down. I don't want you interfering.' He nodded with satisfaction at the sight of Corrigan chained to the cooker. 'I'll leave the key in the sitting room.'

'You're all heart, Gerald.' Corrigan sat on the floor, stretching out his legs.

'I'll be seeing you,' he said, giving Corrigan an annoying little salute.

After Gerald left, Corrigan tested the handcuffs, but they were not going to break.

Bugger.

He began to shout, hoping that someone might hear him. The trouble was, there weren't many people out and about in the bloody fog.

No one heard him. His throat hurt, his eye socket throbbed, his scars were aching.

At least he was alive.

Half an hour later, he heard a key in the lock and Corrigan heard a gasp of shock.

'Martin,' he called. 'It's me, Corrigan. I'm in the kitchen handcuffed to the cooker.' It sounded daft.

Martin stood in the doorway, a look of confusion on his face. 'What are you doing here?'

Corrigan bit back a sarcastic retort – now was not the time. 'The key to these handcuffs is in the sitting room; please can you find it?' He spoke evenly and calmly, not want to alarm the young man any more than he was and hoping Gerald hadn't thrown the key into the general mêlée of the room but had put it on a table.

Martin nodded and went straight to the sitting room.

He came back with the key, and soon Corrigan was free. He rubbed his wrists. 'Now I've got to find Beattie, but I've no idea where to start.' Then he saw Martin clutching something in his other hand. It looked like a small book.

'What's that?'

Martin looked at it as if he were seeing it for the first time. 'Oh,' he said. 'It's Sofia's diary. I've just found it hidden inside Olaf.'

The bloody peacock.

CHAPTER THIRTY-TWO

The fog was impossible.

She saw Anthony Cooper turning left at the end of Chesterfield Street onto Curzon Street and hurried after him. Visibility was terrible, yet he was walking quickly, purposefully, untroubled by the fog.

Half Moon Street. She lost him. She had to hope he was heading for Green Park.

She hurried, not seeing anything or anyone. A car horn sounded. Close. She jumped out of the way as the car passed her slowly, its driver hanging out of the window, trying to see the road ahead.

Yes, there he was, disappearing into the park. If she wasn't careful, she could lose him completely.

The trees dripped water, looking like ghostly apparitions. The grass was wet and slippery beneath her feet. Paths appeared and disappeared. Once or twice she stumbled into a bench before she saw it. Occasionally a person would emerge out of the fog like an apparition. It was a nightmarish version of the world.

Still Anthony Cooper walked on, still she followed, still he was unaware of her. She was cold; she pulled her coat further around her, reassured by the solid presence of the Beretta in her pocket.

Then he walked faster, and Beattie lost him again.

The park was silent. She stopped and listened hard. There were no footsteps, but was that the murmur of voices nearby? It was. She crept closer until she could see two figures facing her, sitting on a bench.

Anthony Cooper and Edwina Bowen. Well.

Had they seen her? She crouched behind a tree. She could still see them. The pair were deep in conversation. She watched as Anthony Cooper put his hand inside his coat and took out a piece of paper. No, two pieces of paper. Was it the sheet music she had given him? It looked very much like it. Edwina Bowen took them, her hand over her mouth. She shook her head. She looked concerned. More than concerned, she was agitated. Then she took a deep breath, appearing to centre herself, and looked straight ahead. Anthony sat carefully unwrapping a foil parcel. His lunch? He ignored Edwina Bowen. They could be strangers sharing a bench.

Somehow, she wasn't surprised; there had been something decidedly 'off' about Anthony Cooper from the start. He had obviously not thought much of her, had not realised how tenacious she was, and that was his mistake. She had pushed and worried at the conundrum of who had murdered Sofia Huber and now had ended up with a spy conspiracy. Her suspicion about Edwina Bowen had been spot on and Anthony was her handler. A Russian spy.

They began to talk, and Beattie strained to hear what they were saying, every muscle tense, every sinew stretched. She wished she could get closer. Their voices carried over the thick air.

'So she knows?' she heard Edwina Bowen say.

She? Was that her?

'She came to me this morning with these.' He put the papers back inside his coat.

Yes, it was.

'Only two.' Edwina Bowen smiled, or perhaps it was a grimace.

'There are more?'

'Of course there are more,' she snapped, but quietly. 'Four were taken from my bureau. Four. Detailing important research on the bomb. To put us months ahead. We have been compromised.'

'You went to the club once. That was unwise, of course. And it compromised us.'

'I wanted to see them together, Ralph and that girl. And I did. I knew he went there; I was having him tailed.' Her voice was bitter. 'I can transcribe what I know again, but . . .'

'Your secret has been discovered, though I doubt the Cavendish girl is aware of their importance.'

Beattie smiled grimly to herself.

'I'm tired, Anthony.' Edwina Bowen leant forward, her shoulders hunched. 'Ever since that wretched girl found out what I was doing I have felt on borrowed time.'

Wretched girl? Sofia?

'If the little trollop hadn't had an affair with Ralph . . .'

'That had nothing to do with it. She was your housekeeper, after all; she would have had eyes and ears everywhere. And I understand she studied music as a child.'

'But she might not have threatened to tell Ralph. I would have been able to control her.' She put her hand over her eyes.

'Perhaps. She wanted to marry Ralph, didn't she? Get rid of you. This was ideal. You would have to have gone quietly and most probably Ralph wouldn't have given you away as it would have destroyed him and his career. And then there is the diary. We still haven't found that and it has the potential to blow us all out of the water.' Anthony was all business.

'I don't know how much she really loved my husband. She wanted money. To keep quiet. Wanted to go home to Germany. That doesn't say to me that she wanted to love, honour and obey Ralph.' Edwina Bowen's back was straight, her shoulders stiff, her hands clasped in her lap. 'Her death was . . . unfortunate.'

Beattie held her breath. They were in a play, the actors in their places, lines set to be delivered. She waited. Was Edwina Bowen going to reveal what Beattie had been searching for, the killer of Sofia? Did the Russians kill her?

Edwina Bowen stood. 'I must go now. It takes a while to get home with this wretched weather.'

Anthony Cooper nodded. 'Leave me to deal with the Cavendish girl.'

Edwina Bowen slowly walked away, disappearing into the fog.

Beattie stayed still, watching Anthony Cooper, wondering what he was going to do next. She soon had her answer, as he began to eat a sandwich from the open foil packet. He chewed neatly and methodically. Beattie had to watch him eat all four squares. With crusts. He then stood and walked away from the bench.

She felt something cold jab at the side of her neck. The muzzle of a gun.

Bugger.

'Don't move a muscle,' said a voice in her ear. 'Not until I tell you to.'

She recognised the voice. She turned her head slowly, to look Edwina Bowen in the eye.

Edwina smiled, a cold, piranha-like smile. Gone was the seemingly distressed woman of a few minutes ago; a cold, calculating woman had taken her place. She kept her gun hand steady as she patted the pockets of Beattie's coat and fished out the Beretta.

'That won't do us much good, will it?' she said, putting the little gun in her own coat pocket.

She meant business and Beattie felt a curl of fear in her stomach.

'Now,' said Edwina. 'Move back, slowly and quietly because we don't want to make a fuss, do we?'

'Don't we?' Beattie said. It earnt her a painful jab in the neck from the muzzle of the gun.

'No,' said Edwina. 'And we don't want Anthony seeing us. He might not approve. Do it, or I will use this. Without hesitation. No one will hear. No one will care. Understand?'

Beattie nodded.

'Good. Now, walk backwards. Slowly and quietly.'

Beattie took a step back, then another, and another.

'More,' commanded Edwina.

Beattie moved. Perhaps she should scream now.

An instant death sentence.

Edwina lowered the gun; Beattie breathed and balanced on the balls of her feet, preparing to run.

'Good try, Miss Cavendish.' Edwina poked the gun into Beattie's side and linked arms with her, huddling close to her, the gun pressed hard against her. 'There. Now we look as though we are really good friends. Or perhaps mother and daughter. Smile a little, there's a good girl. We'll have a lovely walk, perhaps sit down on a bench, have a lovely little chat.'

Beattie thought of the brooch she had pinned onto the front of her coat that morning, and how she could whip it out of her lapel and expose the deadly barbed dagger and stab Edwina through her eye before she would even know what was happening. But then she might not find out what game Edwina was playing. 'That would be jolly,' she said, keeping her tone mild.

Edwina gave her a sharp look.

They walked for some minutes, and the fog looked as though it was thinning.

'Quite the inquisitive nose you have, Miss Cavendish,' said Edwina conversationally as they walked.

'I don't know what you mean.'

Edwina laughed. 'Following Anthony Cooper. Suspecting him in the first place. Your boss.'

Beattie pressed her lips together.

'Not going to confirm it? It really doesn't matter. Not now. Though perhaps I should have killed you when I drove my car at you and that pesky Irishman. Still, there's time to take care of him, too.'

Beattie felt she was not going to get out of this situation easily.

'You were far too intelligent for Ashley. And you have more about you than Anthony would acknowledge. He thought we could keep you under control. I had my doubts, and I was right, wasn't I? Felicia didn't like you either, but that's because she thought you were dull and after money. Still, there we are. I think we'll sit here.' She indicated a bench. Beattie sat. There was no one around.

'Know I will keep pointing the gun at your side, Beattie,' she said with a smile. 'And again, I will use it if I must. I don't care, you see. I have a feeling my days are numbered, but I do want to find out how much you know.'

Beattie turned to look at her. 'And if your days are numbered, what will happen?' She was genuinely curious.

'Then I shall be whisked out of the country to a place where I will be welcome.'

'The Soviet Union.'

Another smile from Edwina. 'Indeed. But I have more to do.'

'More to sell, you mean.'

Edwina looked almost hurt. 'Not "sell". I don't do it for money. I do it for the good of the world.'

'Really?' Beattie maintained a mask of politeness. Inside she was calculating the risk of overpowering Edwina; after all, she was younger and fitter.

'Yes, I admire the Soviet Union's attempt to bring communism to Eastern Europe, and, hopefully, beyond. I also fear a world in which this country and the United States hold the balance of nuclear power unchallenged. And naturally I've been getting away with it because ultimately men don't believe women make good spies.

Look at Anthony. He had no idea of your intelligence. Such stupid creatures.'

Beattie tensed. Now. She could do it now, throw herself at—

A mother and two children loomed out of the fog. One of the children, the boy, was holding a lead with a small brown and white dog on the end of it that was wagging its tail with enthusiasm.

'My goodness,' said the woman to Edwina and Beattie. 'This is such foul weather, isn't it?' She shivered dramatically.

'Isn't it?' said Edwina warmly. 'Not really the day for a walk.'

'No indeed, but the little dog needs to get out and quite frankly, so do I with these two scamps.' She laughed. Edwina joined in.

For one awful moment, Beattie thought the woman was going to sit down next to them.

'My dog's name is Ginger.' The little boy addressed Beattie.

'He bites sometimes,' said the little girl.

'That's not good,' said Beattie, finding her voice but willing the little family to leave them, to disappear, to carry on with their day. 'But he looks a lovely little dog.' *Please go*, she pleaded silently. *Go*.

There was an awkward silence.

'Well,' said the woman, 'we must be getting along.'

'Goodbye,' said Edwina, smiling. She waved at the children, who waved back. The dog yapped.

The woman, her children and the dog disappeared back into the fog. Beattie closed her eyes with relief.

'What a charming family. As I was saying,' Edwina continued, settling herself on the bench, 'for the good of the world. Soviet Russia does not want to be left behind. Stalin does not want to be left behind. During the war our Soviet atomic programme was puny compared to America's. But now we have scientists working away and a Soviet bomb is much closer than you in the West realise.' She frowned, as if thinking she had said too much, and she had. Beattie filed that information away, knowing she would impart to the right people. If she got out of this particular fix.

'Anyway, Beattie, you know it all, don't you?'

'The music, the secrets hidden in code, yes. Very clever.'

'It is, isn't it?'

'But,' said Beattie, 'what about Sofia?'

'Sofia? This bench is rather hard, don't you think? Sofia Huber, yes. The little slut. That is one loose end we need your help with. The reason you're still alive.'

'Did you kill her?'

Edwina sighed. 'Oh dear, do we need to discuss this now? But if you insist, yes. Not me personally, but I gave the order. She'd found out about the music, you see. Too much snooping and listening at doors. Doesn't do anyone any good. I'm sorry,' she said, not looking in the least bit sorry and all Beattie wanted to do was lean across and throttle her.

'You let the killer into the house.'

'Not exactly. I gave him a key. Earlier I had told Sofia I needed to see her in my study later that evening. It's a good job you didn't arrive any earlier.'

'I see. I thought as much. The pane of glass your killer

364

broke was a mistake. He broke it from the inside, leaving glass on the path outside.'

'I shall reprimand him. However,' she said briskly, 'enough of that. We do need your help.'

'Help? I'm not giving you any help.'

'Oh, I think you will.' A vicious smile. 'I do know where you live. I followed you and Martin to that charming island off the Essex coast. And what a lovely family you have. You see . . .' Her eyes glittered as she leant towards Beattie. 'Having Sofia killed was a little mistake on my part as I didn't realise she'd written a diary. I was a bit too, shall we say, hasty. Not that she didn't deserve it. Felicia knew, you see, and told me about it, but too late and she didn't know where it was. I should have found out about it before Sofia died.'

'The diary that could give you away.' Beattie nodded.

'There.' Edwina's expression was triumphant. 'I knew you'd understand. We need to find the diary otherwise all could be lost.'

'But it won't matter if you are, as you put it, "whisked out of the country".'

'It matters. Who knows what else the girl saw and heard.'

'Did you set your thugs onto Corrigan?'

'The one-eyed Irishman is very tough, isn't he?' She shrugged. 'Means to an end. Now, if you tell me where the diary is, or where Martin Huber is, then I will let you go and we can all get back to our lives.'

Beattie tensed her jaw muscles. 'And naturally you knew that I'd found out about the diary because of my report to Anthony. Well, I don't know where it is, or where Martin is.' She doubted Edwina would let her live.

Edwina sighed. 'And if you did I expect you wouldn't tell me. Come on.' She stood up, and when Beattie was standing, linked arms again. They began to walk along the path.

'Where are we going?'

'Back to your flat.'

'My flat?' Was she imagining it, or was there the sound of a twig snapping?

'The diary could be there.'

'It isn't, Edwina, I promise you.'

Edwina laughed. 'As if your promise means anything. We really need this diary, and if we don't find it, I will systematically destroy everyone you love before killing you.'

At this, rage coursed along Beattie's bones and in one movement, she whirled away from Edwina, knocking the gun from her hand and drawing the brooch-cum-dagger from her lapel. She lunged towards the older woman, aiming for her eye, but Edwina was too quick, and threw herself to the ground in an attempt to retrieve her gun. Beattie kicked the gun into the undergrowth.

Edwina looked up at her, her expression turning from fury to surprise as a neat bullet hole appeared in her forehead, fraying the skin at the edges.

Beattie crouched down low, looking around, listening, her heart thudding.

A rustling of leaves. The trees *drip drip dripped* water onto the ground.

A figure emerged from the fog.

Gerald Silver.

Beattie was not surprised to see him – after the phone call she'd made, she had expected him.

'Beattie Cavendish,' he said. 'Good morning. I'm glad I'm not too late. Mr Smith told me what you were doing.' He put his gun into his coat pocket and grabbed Edwina's body under the arms. Then, with a few grunts and a lot of effort, he dragged her into some convenient undergrowth. 'The old girl was surprisingly heavy,' he said, brushing leaves and dirt off his trousers.

'You can't leave her there,' said Beattie. 'Someone may find her. Children, dogs.'

Gerald grimaced. 'In this weather? I doubt it. She won't be there for long, don't worry. We don't like to leave loose ends.'

'No,' said Beattie. 'How can you be like this?' She had to breathe slowly, recalibrate, think clearly.

'Like what?'

'So – calm about it all. You've known the Bowens for years. You're friends with Ashley. And yet here you are, calmly shooting his mother in the head.' But as she asked the question, she remembered Luc, how she had loved him and how she had killed him all too easily.

'It's a job, Beattie. That's all. A job for my country. The same as you are doing. I have to say I was surprised to find out that you were GCHQ. We – I – have been keeping an eye on Edwina Bowen,' he said. 'We were curious when you turned up at Ashley's side and wondered if you were KGB too. You seemed a bit too bright for someone as dim as he is.'

'"We" being MI5.' The phone call to Walter Smith, the avuncular head of COS, before she left the office had been most productive.

'I see you are well-informed.'

'Poor Ashley, he doesn't deserve any of this.'

'He'll be fine. He'll never know about his mother and I'm sure his father will be made to resign. Now, tell me about Edwina and Anthony Cooper.'

Beattie put all thoughts about Felicia and Ashley out of her head; there would be time later to come to think about what would happen to them. 'I presume Anthony is her handler?'

Gerald nodded. 'You presume correctly.'

Beattie told Gerald about the music, the carols, the wrong notes, the church and the White Pearl Club. Walter had instructed her to tell it all. However, unlike with Walter, she left out Corrigan and Scott and Martin and Nell. There was no way she was going to implicate them.

Gerald whistled. 'That is quite a tale. And pretty devious. Congratulations. I'm not going to ask you how you worked it out, though I suspect it involved that Irishman of yours. There is the diary,' said Gerald, 'which we believe corroborates all you have said. We would like it. Your Irishman was not co-operative.'

Beattie went cold. 'If you've hurt him—'

Gerald waved dismissively. 'He'll be fine.'

She gritted her teeth. What had he done? 'Neither of us know where the damned diary is and if you have hurt Corrigan I will come and find you and—'

'And what, Beattie Cavendish? I'll tell you what. Nothing. You can't.' Gerald sighed. 'About the diary, I'm beginning to believe you. Even Martin Huber couldn't tell us. I was going to have another go at him but, you know, *tempus fugit*.'

Beattie felt sick as she thought about Martin's poor face

and all his bruises. This was a very dirty business. 'Perhaps we'll never find it.' She tried not to look where Edwina's body was lying in the undergrowth. 'What are you doing now? About Anthony?'

Gerald smiled. 'Anthony was a surprise, I have to say. We will probably make him disappear – after all, he knows too many secrets himself – or we might try and turn him.'

'So that he'll work for you.'

'For us, Beattie, for us.' He looked at his watch. 'I suggest you go and find that bogtrotter of yours now, before he starves to death.'

She damped down her rage. 'One more thing, Gerald.'

He looked at her, a smile on his cruel lips.

'Kit Pearson. Was that down to you?'

'Ah. The queer. I'm afraid he was in the way. Unstable. Knew too much. Somehow knew Edwina was working for the Russians. Probably to do with his frequenting of the White Pearl Club. Sorry. So you see, best not to tell anyone what went on here today because you too could have an unfortunate ending.' He smiled again. 'But then you're COS, so you know the score. Toodle-pip.'

CHAPTER THIRTY-THREE

PROMINENT CONSERVATIVE MP RESIGNES
by Leo Scott of the *Daily Dispatch*

Ralph Bowen, Shadow Foreign Secretary, resigned today after being caught in a raid at the notorious White Pearl Club in Soho. His son, Ashley, who has recently been seen in the company of the Honourable Letitia Wingfield, said his father was full of remorse and apologised for letting down the people in his constituency.

Ralph Bowen had been Shadow Foreign Secretary for three years. He is estranged from his wife of thirty years, who is believed to now reside in the South of France.

The bench was under a cherry tree in the colourful church gardens that would, in the spring, be covered with a thick coat of pink and white blossom. The inscription was simple: *Kit Pearson 1927–1948*. Corrigan was sitting on the bench, his face turned up to the blue sky and the feeble November sun. His eyes were closed and he was frowning. Beattie sat down next to him.

'That was a lovely memorial service, Corrigan. I'm sure Kit would have loved it.' The church had been tranquil, with its chandelier lighting, stained-glass windows and polished wood around the altar. St Paul's Church in Bedford Street, Covent Garden, near to where Kit had rented rooms, was known as the Actors' Church, as it was close to the theatres of the West End and many famous names had a plaque on the wall or a bench dedicated to them. Kit's friends from the White Pearl had turned up, including Marlene who had come in full Marlene costume, wanting to 'add a bit of glamour' to the proceedings. Rose had worn her feathers in her hair, and other friends from the club had come with painted faces and dazzling dresses or tailored dinner suits.

'Hmm. Maybe. I didn't know what to do for the best.' He kept his eyes closed. 'Had to do something with the money. Parents didn't want it.'

'No,' said Beattie sadly, thinking about Kit's parents, who were both small and mousey and harried-looking. Mr and Mrs Pearson took their son's body back for burial in Yorkshire. They had never wanted him to go to London and now they were determined to take him home and forget the 'terrible' life he had led. 'It ruined him,' they said. And they didn't want the money offered to them by a mysterious benefactor for a memorial service. 'He was an ordinary boy, who became mixed up with the wrong sort of people and had a terrible accident.' Beattie understood.

'I didn't know him,' she said now, 'but from what you said, Corrigan, I imagine he preferred the smoke and stink of London to the fresh air of the Dales.'

At this, Corrigan grinned and the grin smoothed his frown lines away. 'Too right.'

'And the Actors' Church. That was inspired.'

'I reckon he liked to be someone else most of the time, acting a part.'

'Did you know George Bernard Shaw set the opening of *Pygmalion* under the portico?'

'No. But I'll be sure to bring that fact up when I'm short of small talk. Beattie, you're always full of fascinating information.'

'Am I?' She stood. 'Come on, Corrigan, everyone has gone to the café now. Time we joined them.'

The frown was back on Corrigan's face. 'Who gave me that money for the memorial, Beattie?'

'I don't know.' Though she had an idea it was one of the secret services. They had Kit's blood on their hands.

'Really? I see. And who was the man in a black suit and a bald head like an egg? He was sitting at the back of the church.'

'Bald head?'

'Don't pretend you don't know him. I saw you deep in conversation.'

'That was Walter Smith, a friend from work. It was kind of him to come,' said Beattie casually.

'Wasn't it? And totally unnecessary.' He finally opened his eyes but still didn't look at her. 'To the café,' he said.

The café was full of people chatting and smiling in the way mourners did after a funeral or memorial service. There were proper cloths on the tables, and it was warm with a haze of steam and cigarette smoke. An urn gurgled away in the corner. Beattie saw Marlene, deep in conversation with the vicar from the church, and Rose talking animatedly to a young man in a beautifully cut suit who occasionally wiped a tear from his eye. A special friend of Kit's, perhaps? Even the Kuznetsov brothers had turned up, glowering in the corner. This had been another of Corrigan's ideas – to hold the wake where he'd shared a meal with Kit after escaping from the coppers outside the club and where Kit had enjoyed coming. ('At least,' Corrigan said to Beattie as they'd made their way down Bedford Street, 'we don't have to climb gates and walls and trespass through gardens to get there.') Flo, her large figure encompassed in a tent-like maroon dress that probably didn't see the light of day often, and with her hair in stiff rolls, had put on a good spread of doorstep sandwiches and bowls of nourishing oxtail soup and strong tea, though Beattie could have done with a stiff drink, and she thought Corrigan would be of the same mind.

They sipped their tea without talking. Corrigan brought out a hip flask from his pocket and poured a nip of what Beattie thought was brandy into each of their mugs.

'Corrigan, why aren't you speaking to me?'

He shrugged, reminding Beattie of a petulant boy. And that made her think of Martin, who'd accepted money from Ralph Bowen and was, at this very moment, travelling to Germany to look for his parents, which she thought could only end in heartbreak. He also seemed to have accepted that his sister had been killed by a petty thief, and that the police were working hard to bring the culprit to justice. Beattie had no doubt that one day some poor down-and-out would be framed for the murder. That was the way it worked. She didn't have to like it.

'Corrigan, what's wrong?'

'Nothing,' he growled.

Beattie folded her hands on her lap. 'Come on, tell me.'

He huffed and puffed. 'Tell you? There's so much you're not telling me.' He wouldn't look at her.

Beattie sighed. Really, men could be so peevish sometimes, particularly when they felt they were not the centre of the universe. 'Corrigan, I—'

He held up his hand to stop her. 'It's all right, Beattie, really. I'm sorry. I'm being an idiot. I know you are not exactly who you say you are, and you can't tell me what you do. That's fine. Though what isn't fine is that Silver has got away with murder, literally murder.'

'I know, Corrigan, I know.' She had told him what Gerald had said about Kit. 'But at least Edwina Bowen has paid.'

His expression was dark. 'Yes. And Silver is secret service, I understand that.' He gave a brief, grim smile. 'He probably gave me the bloody money for the memorial service, I shouldn't wonder. And did the diary even prove useful?'

'Thank you for giving it to me. It underlined what we thought.'

'About Edwina Bowen being a spy?'

Beattie looked around the café, but people were busy talking or eating or drinking their tea to take any notice of them. At least he kept his voice low. 'Yes, but . . .'

He rolled his eyes. 'I know, I mustn't say anything. And Leo Scott didn't get the explosive scoop he was hoping for either. Had a D-notice slapped on him. Well, the paper did anyway and now he's ranting about being gagged by the British government.'

'Oh dear. But he did get the resignation story.'

'And what about Ashley? Are you still seeing him?' The question was asked casually, but Beattie sensed an underlying tension in Corrigan.

'Don't you read the papers? You know I'm not. He wasn't the man for me. He didn't seem too upset.' She wouldn't look at Corrigan, even though she knew it was a game they were both playing.

'Very wise. What about his sister?'

'The ghastly Felicia? No, I shouldn't be mean.'

'But she was ghastly.'

'Yes. I believe she's gone down to Cornwall to join an artists' commune. St Ives, I think.'

'And the priest, what happened to him?'

'Ha. I understand he was also caught in the raid on the White Pearl Club. He will be sent to prison, I fear.' Beattie smiled.

'Good. And I see the old boy with the bald head and pebble glasses has come to the wake. Looks a bit out of place here.' Corrigan looked across at Walter Smith, who with his silver-topped walking stick, well-cut coat and smart fedora in his hand looked like somebody's uncle. Hell, he probably was somebody's uncle.

'It was good of him to come.'

'Strange.'

'What?'

'That he should be here.' Corrigan looked directly into her eyes.

Beattie's gaze didn't waver. 'He's kind like that, offering to accompany me.' She stood. 'And I must go and see him as he'll be leaving soon.'

* * *

Corrigan watched as Beattie went over to Walter. Walter nodded, waved to Corrigan as Beattie escorted him out of the door.

He chewed on a fish-paste sandwich. Not his favourite. Beattie was obviously something to do with the secret service, but not Gerald Silver's outfit. Merely thinking about Silver made him extremely angry about Kit's death and the way no one was being held responsible for it. One day, he thought, one day that bastard would get what he deserved and Corrigan hoped he would be the one to give it to him.

She was a brave one, though, that Beattie. He wished he could break through her carapace, get to know the real Beattie Cavendish, but she was too professional for that. He admired her. He tried hard not to think about that odd moment by the taxi, before she went home that strange night, but the more he tried, the more he thought about it, even though he knew it was pointless. He sighed, trying to flex his leg. It ached from his toes through his thigh and up his side. The thought of getting on the Tube and travelling back to his empty, lonely and cold flat was miserable.

Buck up, man. He'd survived worse.

As Beattie closed the café door behind her and Walter, a black Wolseley drew up by the kerb. Walter stood, with one hand on the roof of the car.

'This was a good thing Corrigan did for Mr Pearson.' His breath was like puffs of smoke in the air.

'He should still be alive,' she said, her anger quick to rise.

'I know,' murmured Walter, 'I know.'

'And to think we had a KGB man in our midst.' She shook her head.

'Hmm.'

Beattie blinked, the truth beginning to dawn. 'Did you know about Anthony Cooper?'

'Well . . .'

'Did you know about him when you recruited me?' Beattie kept her voice very calm.

'He didn't want to take you into COS and I like to think it was because he was afraid of you, of your intellect and brain. I, on the other hand, knew what a great asset you would be. And I was right.'

Beattie kept a grip on her temper. 'Do you mean you used me to flush Anthony out?'

A little laugh. 'No, my dear, not at all. But I knew that putting you into the Bowen family would cause a bit of, shall we say, uncertainty in Anthony's mind?' He opened the door of the sleek limousine. 'He didn't want to use you, argued against it. I believe it was the beginning of the end for him. The trouble is, we're looking for spies everywhere.' He tapped his cane on the ground. 'Have you heard of the Venona Project?'

Beattie frowned. 'No, I don't think so.'

'Jolly good. You shouldn't have because it's top secret. The Venona Project came about after a single blunder, a single mistake by the Soviets and thus the presence of Soviet spies in the British government was revealed. We're hunting them down. One by one.' He slid into the car. 'I like working with you. You're tenacious, you see. Brave. Inquisitive.'

'What happened to Mr Cooper?'

'Ah. He managed to evade us. Happily ensconced in the Soviet Union by now. Good luck to him. Jolly cold this time of year. By the way . . .'

'Yes?'

'Nobody ever did find that diary, did they?'

'No,' said Beattie.

'Hmm.' He smiled. 'We'll speak again.'

Beattie watched as the car drew away down the road. Had she been used to make Anthony Cooper uncertain, to trip him up? Had she been manipulated? Walter's flattery cut no ice. Was she angry? No, not angry now, but sad and disappointed. One day, she thought, Gerald Silver would get his comeuppance. And she knew instinctively she had to hold on to the humanity inside her and not become like Gerald Silver.

And the diary. She allowed herself a small smile. Well, that was her insurance. It was safely hidden in her flat. Thankfully Corrigan had taken it from Martin before he'd had a chance to read it, and truthfully, Martin hadn't been interested in reading it. He said he had no desire to pry into his sister's private life. It was Corrigan's insurance too, even if he didn't know it yet, though she probably would tell him when the time was right. No, she didn't trust anyone, and the diary was her way of ensuring she had evidence of Edwina Bowen's and Anthony Cooper's treachery. She might need that evidence one day.

She turned back to the café, to see Corrigan watching her moodily through the window. Not for the first time she wondered what it was that had happened to him in the days after the war. Something that had affected him deeply, according to Nell. Perhaps she would never find out. Not now.

Their eyes locked. She saw past his scars, his eyepatch, his limp. She remembered the moment just before she got into the taxi that night, after drinking in the Wagon and Horses. He was a good man. He deserved better.

She pushed open the door of the café and went over to the table. 'Corrigan, I took the liberty of ringing Nell earlier. She said she would come here and take you home.'

He scanned her face. 'I don't know what I want, Beattie.'

'Of course you do.' She smiled. 'You're the seventh son of a seventh son.'

ACKNOWLEDGEMENTS

My heartfelt thanks must go to Teresa Chris, who is the most supportive and tenacious agent a writer could have. Also thanks to Susie Dunlop and the expert team at Allison & Busby who have worked so hard and shown such faith in me from the start.

To my brother Patrick T Cullen who inspired me to write about Beattie Cavendish and Patrick T Corrigan as we reminisced about our parents and what their lives must have been like during and after the Second World War.

And Jenny Knight – a wonderful writer – who helped me out when I didn't know which way to go. Your coffee/wine/laughter has been invaluable, thank you.

To Melanie McCarthy, thank you for your unflinching support down the years.

To you, the reader, the bookish people on social media and the fabulous librarians, we writers would not be anywhere without you.

I would like to mention two books that were especially helpful in the writing. *GCHQ: The Uncensored Story of Britain's Most Secret Intelligence Agency* by Richard J Aldrich and *Her Secret Service; The Forgotten Women of*

British Intelligence by Claire Hubbard-Hall. Oh, and any book by Ben Macintyre.

Love and thanks to my children Edward, Peter and Esme (and their partners Emily, Jenni and Nick) who champion my books without fail.

And Kim, without whom I couldn't do any of it.

MARY-JANE RILEY was a BBC journalist, presenting radio programmes and major crime stories over the past twenty years. She has also published four thrillers. She lives in Suffolk.